I0676988

A Holiday Wish

A FIVE DIRECTIONS PRESS BOOK

A Holiday Wish

a *Silver Bells* novel

COURTNEY J. HALL

This is a work of fiction. All names, characters, places, and incidents are products of the author's imagination or are used fictitiously. Any resemblance to current situations or to living persons is purely coincidental.

ISBN-13: 978-0692738528
ISBN-10: 0692738525

Published in the United States of America.

© 2016 Courtney J. Hall. All rights reserved.
Except as permitted by the US Copyright Act of 1976, no part of this publication may be reproduced, transmitted, or distributed in any form or by any means, or stored in a database or retrieval system, without the prior written permission of the author.

A Five Directions Press book

Book and cover design by Five Directions Press
Five Directions Press logo designed by Colleen Kelley

FIVE DIRECTIONS PRESS

CONTENTS

1

WHEN I EMERGE from my apartment building's lobby into the late October morning, I know it's going to be a perfect day.

There are several reasons for this certainty. For one thing, I'm headed to The Daily Grind. Already I can taste the rich flavor of their house blend. The one I've never been able to replicate at home despite buying the very same beans from their retail section, grinding them—as needed, no more—in my ridiculously expensive coffee grinder, and brewing them in the coffee maker I blew almost three hundred bucks on. It just doesn't work. I can't stand to think of how much money I would save if it did. And if I learned to bake my own croissants. Then again, if I knew how to bake croissants like the delicate, flaky rolls of bliss behind the glass counter at The Daily Grind, I would be several hundred—okay, thousand—dollars richer but probably the same amount of pounds overweight. So maybe it's better that I'm as hopeless with butter and flour as I am with expensive coffee.

Second, it's a slow day. I have a few final details to take care of for two upcoming weddings and purposely scheduled only two new appointments. That will occupy my morning, so I can spend the afternoon studying magazines, vendor catalogs, and websites, fantasizing about the perfect wedding. It's outdoors, of course; September in a field at sunset, with fairy lights delicate as gossamer strands wrapped around the chairs and twinkling as the sun goes down. Fishbowl vases filled with water and floating gerbera daisy blooms in violet, tawny, and ivory stud the long, rustic wooden tables. Green grass is gilded by the setting sun, then polished silver by moonlight, while a groom in a classic tuxedo dances with a loose-haired bride. She wears an ivory gown that's strapless and form-fitting to the waist, but flares out over her hips in clouds of sparkling, beaded tulle. It's a wedding vision any of my brides would die for me to bring to life for them, but it's mine. All mine.

Which leads me to the third and biggest reason why I'm so convinced that today is going to be the kind of day high-school me would have recorded in painstaking detail in her diary—

Drew is home.

Finally.

I haven't seen him in nearly ten days. I miss him like crazy when he's away. Especially now, when we should be making plans for our wedding. We've been engaged for a year, and people are asking what the holdup is. We've been together for eight years, after all. Not only that, but I'm thirty, turning thirty-one in January, and he's thirty-two. Neither of us is getting any younger. But today, after we're reunited over cups of steaming coffee and a plate of glistening croissants, after I drink in his curly blond hair and hazel eyes that crinkle to the point of closing even when his mouth just hints at a boyish smile, I'll show him everything I've come up with and we can get started for real.

The crisp autumn air smells clean in a way heavy, humid summer air never can. It bites at my cheeks and ruffles the edges of my burgundy scarf. Through leaves burnished gold and crimson the sun dapples the sidewalk and bounces off the shop windows as I hurry past. It's so nice out this morning that if it weren't for the promise of coffee, croissants, and Drew, I would have been a little disappointed to come to the end of the half-mile walk between my apartment and The Daily Grind, which is on a quaint tree-lined street just a few doors down from my own shop—Silver Bells Wedding Designs. It's a play on my name, Noelle Silver, and the fact that I specialize in Christmas weddings. They're my absolute favorite. Something about the holiday season just lends itself to gorgeous weddings. But Drew's the outdoorsy type and has his heart set on getting married outside. If he wasn't, we would definitely hold the ceremony at Christmas.

The bell on the door jangles a familiar welcome as I step through. I'm immediately enveloped by the best scent in the world—fresh-brewed coffee and things baking. It's a weird time; just nine o'clock, when high-school students are already in class and most working people are at their desks in offices scattered across the town. But there's a college campus just a few blocks away, and some of the tables are occupied by students buried in books, their lattes a permanent accessory like a backpack or pair of earbuds. I spot a two-top by the window and drop onto the chair, setting my canvas tote of wedding stuff on the dark wood floor beside me. I always prefer window seats to those buried in a dark corner. I like to watch life go by.

It also lets me see Drew the second he comes into view. He parks his black Prius halfway down the block, practically in front of my office, and gets out. He's dressed in dark jeans—every day is casual Friday at his office—and a hunter green button-down shirt, a light gray blazer draped over his arm. The golden sunshine bounces off his only slightly darker hair, and even from here I can see how the color of his shirt makes his eyes more green than hazel.

Beautiful. I grin to myself. He's mine.

The bell jangles again as he opens the door and enters the shop. He glances around, looking for me, and even after eight years together my heart gives an erratic little *thump* when his gaze lands on me. I lift my hand in a wave. He hesitates, then smiles as he heads for our table.

I go to get up, to throw my arms around him, but before I can he puts his briefcase on the floor, drapes his blazer over the back of his chair, and leans down to peck me on the cheek.

"The usual?" he asks, and walks to the counter before I can respond.

I sit still, trying to ignore the little buzz of dismay that ripples through me. Seriously? Ten days apart and that's how he greets me? Anyone looking at us might have thought I was his sister, not the woman with whom he planned to spend the rest of his life.

He's probably tired. Jet-lagged. He'd been in Texas and gotten home so late last night he hadn't even wanted me to come and pick him up from the airport. Poor thing.

I watch him chat with the barista, a twenty-something guy with floppy blond hair who looks like he should be carrying a surfboard across a Hawaiian beach instead of serving coffee in a sleepy little suburban-Philadelphia college town. Drew turns around, a cup of coffee in each hand, and starts back toward me. He sets the cups on our table, but he doesn't sit.

"Croissants," he says by way of explanation, and goes back to the counter where he takes a plate from Surfer Boy.

I reach for my cup as the buzz becomes more of a rumble. Tired or not, Drew is never distant. But he's said three words since he arrived and none of them has been about how much he missed me and couldn't wait to get home to me. How jet-lagged could he be? Houston is on central time, only an hour behind us.

Finally he eases into the seat across from me and puts the plate in the middle of the table. I glance at it. Two croissants nestle together like lovers, and I'm hesitant to separate them. Instead I sip my coffee. It's black, the way I like it. No milk, no sweetener to muddle the flavor. It clears my head, sharpens my focus. What am I freaking out about? It's a beautiful day, and Drew is here.

I smile, set my cup down, and reach for Drew's hand just as he lifts his own cup to his lips. He grimaces. "No sugar," he complains, and jumps back up. He goes to the counter beside the pastry display case and grabs a few packets of sugar. Then a few more. He counts what's in his hand and puts a few back. Then he picks up one more, and a wooden stirrer.

What the hell is he doing? Unlike me, Drew requires sugar in his coffee. But just one packet—two if it's an extra large. Certainly not seven to nine, which, from my vantage point, seems to be the number clenched in his fist. Is he that desperate for an energy boost? Why not just dump an entire Red Bull into his cup?

The rumble starts to feel like someone's next to me with a jackhammer on full blast. Something is wrong.

Drew meanders back to our table with a quick pit stop to admire the display of travel mugs before he slides onto his chair. He tears open a packet of Sugar in the Raw and dumps it into his coffee. He stirs vigorously, his eyes trained on the whirlpool he's created inside his sixteen-ounce cup. He doesn't look at me. My heart thumps, a bass drum in my chest.

"I missed you," I blurt out, unable to take the silence a moment longer. I force a smile. "Ice cream in front of *The Tonight Show* doesn't taste half as good without you."

He lets go of the stirrer, and we both watch it swirl around the cup of its own volition until the tiny coffee whirlpool fades and disappears. After a while, he meets my eyes.

"I missed you, too," he says.

Funny. I should feel relieved, right? I don't. He looks strange. Oh, he's still Drew—the broad shoulders of a high-school quarterback despite being only a year away from attending his fifteenth reunion, the smattering of freckles that have yet to fade even though summer's been over for six weeks, the curly blond hair and the innocent grin I so wish he'd flash at me right now. The package still looks like Drew. It's what's inside that's different.

I try another tack. "Did the trade show go well?" I know how high-pressure those things can get—he's told me. They sound a lot like weddings. Maybe something went wrong.

"It went fine." He rolls the empty packet of sugar between his fingers, making what looks like the world's tiniest joint.

Speaking of weddings... "I brought some things I want us to look at." Maybe talking about our own wedding will wake him up. I lift my bag from the floor and withdraw the binder inside, the one I've stuffed full of flower arrangements, menu options, and color schemes.

"What kind of things?" he asks.

I force a grin. "Wedding things."

It looks like he tries to smile, but fails. "Noelle—"

I plow ahead. "I know how you've always wanted to get married outside, and if we're going to do that, it has to be in late September or early to mid-October. Lots of venues will already be booked, and I might be able to pull some strings, but I don't want to if I don't have to."

"Noelle—"

I open the binder to the section labeled *Venues,* find my favorite—an old farmhouse just outside of town—and push it across the table toward him, shoving the plate of untouched croissants out of the way.

"What do you think of this?" My nerves vibrate like too-tight guitar strings. Why do I feel like I'm going to hate what comes out of his mouth once I let him speak?

He barely glances at it. "It's nice." He closes the binder, moves it aside. "Noelle, we have to talk."

And there it is.

He's not tired. Not jet-lagged. Not upset about a catastrophic trade show or how Surfer Boy forgot to put sugar in his coffee. Whatever his problem is, it has to do with me.

I swallow hard, making my throat muscles ache. I feel hot. I'm glad I left my hair down today because I can imagine how red my ears are—that's what happens when I'm nervous. They glow like beacons, announcing my mortification to anyone who looks at me..

"Okay." I don't recognize my own voice. Since when do I squeak?

He sucks in a deep breath. Lets it out. The napkins on the table flutter.

"This isn't easy," he mutters.

Not easy? For him? Does he think it's cake for me, waiting to hear what he wants to say and knowing it's probably going to hurt?

"Noelle, I—we can't get married now."

Everything goes silent except for the roaring in my ears. It sounds like when you're a kid and you press your ear to a conch shell and your mom tells you that's the ocean in there—that, but a hundred times louder. I wish it had started before Drew spoke, so I could act like I hadn't heard him and go on living in my happy little fantasy world.

"What?" My throat is so dry the word barely manages to scrape by.

"I'm so sorry, Noelle. I thought I could, but…" He trails off. "This last week showed me. It's not the right time for me."

"The right time for *you*?" What—eight years together isn't enough? What could he possibly still need to wait for? "What about me? We're supposed to be a team, Drew. Making decisions together and all that stuff. Anyway, it *is* the right time for me." I clench my hands into fists. It's better than emptying my coffee cup on him. Right?

He shakes his head. "I'm sorry," he says again. "I just can't do it."

"Why?" I demand. "What happened in the last week that showed you it's not the right time? For you?" But as the words leave my mouth it becomes crystal clear, and I feel sick.

"You're not just asking me to postpone the wedding, are you?" I whisper.

He bites his lip, shakes his head.

God. He's ending it. I'm on fire. That's the only way I can describe the way I feel. My guts churn. My heart might have stopped beating—I'm not sure.

"Why?" It's all I can manage.

"I—things haven't felt right. For a while." He drops his sugar-packet joint and folds his arms, holding them close to his chest. "I still care about you. I just…"

What. Is. Happening?

"If you still care about me, we can work on it. Whatever it is."

He's shaking his head before I even finish speaking. "I thought I could, Noelle." He hugs himself tighter. Is he trying to comfort himself or shut me out? I can't tell. "I just don't feel it anymore."

Well, that changes things. I stare at a sticky, dried-up coffee drip on the table. It looks like a heart, which is so ironic I almost start to laugh—until the next thought hits me.

I don't want to ask it. But I do anyway.

"Were you even in Houston?"

"Of course I was in Houston! You know about the trade show. I do it every year." But his fair skin pinks, and I know I've hit on something.

"But you weren't alone."

"No, of course not." He shifts in his chair. I've made him uncomfortable. Good. "Pete went, and Tim and Asif…"

"And Heidi?"

He gets redder. "Well, yeah. She's my assistant."

"Your assistant." I nod. "Of course. And what exactly did she assist you with while you were gone?"

Drew looks like he's being strangled. "Noelle, don't do this."

I wonder how long he thought he'd be able to keep it from me. I imagine Heidi—just-out-of-college Heidi, with the long, glossy red hair that matches the glossy red lips and the low-cut shirts that were all obviously made by six-year-olds in Singapore. I'm torn between laughing and gagging.

"God, Drew." I almost feel sorry for him; I really do. "Sleeping with your assistant? Could you be any more of a cliché?" I shake my head. "When did it start?"

He wiggles in his seat again. "Labor Day weekend. While you were doing that wedding in Wildwood."

I might fall over. I really might. *Labor Day weekend. Almost two months ago. I never even realized.*

He has the nerve to look abashed. "I didn't mean for it to happen, Noelle. It's just that you and I never see each other, and—"

"Spare me." My emotions are all over the place. I've gone from scared to sad to amused to angry in the space of about forty-five seconds. I don't know exactly what to do. "Why now, Drew?"

He frowns. "What do you mean?"

"I mean why tell me now? Why not after the first time it happened, or—here's a novel idea—before you cheated on me at all? Why even ask me to marry you? Were you ever sure about us?"

"It was never like that, Noelle." Now he sounds defensive, as if I'm the one who's wronging him. He's got balls, this guy. "I was sure about us when I asked you to marry me. I loved you."

"Loved. Past tense."

He looks at his hands and says nothing.

I don't want to know the answer, but I ask anyway.

"When did that change?"

"I don't know," he replies. "A few months ago, maybe? The beginning of the summer? You were so busy with your weddings, you were hardly ever home. I got lonely. The Friday before Labor Day, you were already gone and after work we all went out for drinks…"

He trails off, as if he wants to leave the rest to my imagination. That's a dick move. I have an active imagination. I have to, in my line of work. And once it gets going, it knows no bounds. Drew is aware of this, and somehow leaving me to fill in the blanks is crueler than telling me the sordid details himself.

I hate him.

"I see," I mumble.

"Noelle, I swear I never meant to hurt you. Not like this."

"Then how?" To my horror, I feel my eyes begin to fill with tears. I have to get out of there. He will *not* see me cry. He doesn't deserve the satisfaction. "Never mind. I have to go. I have appointments. There are people out there who really do love each other, who are faithful, and who aren't lying when they say they want to spend the rest of their lives together."

I stand, bumping the table. Drew never put the lid back on his coffee and some splashes out, splattering his shirt. I'm petty enough to feel happy that he'll have to walk around stained and smelling like stale coffee all day. He glances at the stain before he gets to his feet.

"Noelle, I'm sorry." His hands make a helpless gesture that seems half-assed to me.

"Just don't." I can't even look at him. He disgusts me. No, he doesn't. I love him. I don't want to walk out of here. If I leave, it's over.

I glance out the window, toward Drew's car, and something makes my breath catch in my throat. A flash of orange-red that I could have sworn was a glare from the sun—but the sun doesn't wear knockoff Oakleys and red lipstick.

I whirl back to face him. "You *brought* her here?" I demand.

He shrugs, and it infuriates me.

My hand itches to slap him. I don't know who he is. He's turned into a stranger, right in front of my eyes.

"What, did she want to make sure you went through with it?" I don't let him answer. "Never mind. Don't worry. I'm leaving." I have just enough foresight to grab my purse and tote. My coffee sits abandoned on the table. Will I ever be able to taste The Daily Grind's house blend without reliving this moment? I doubt it. Looks like I'm losing two of my great loves today.

I shove through the door and into the dazzling sunlight, which temporarily blinds me. A breeze teases the ends of my hair. It's not even right for a day to be so gorgeous, not when my heart is breaking.

I hear a thud as Drew rushes to catch the door before it closes on him. "Noelle, wait."

I whirl around with such force that he stops. "I've wasted enough time on you," I say. "It's Heidi's turn now."

I resist the urge to flip off Heidi, waiting patiently and, oh, so confidently in the passenger seat of the Prius, just a few cars down—in front of my office. Skank. They deserve each other.

Instead of giving her the finger, or both fingers, I turn away. Head for home. My stomach rolls. My eyes are swimming in tears. But I refuse to give them any more satisfaction. *I* will be the one who leaves.

So much for my perfect day.

I'm just a few steps from my building when my phone rings.

2

I SKITTER TO a stop in the middle of the walkway as my heart lurches into my throat. For an insane moment I hope with every fiber of my being that it's Drew, that he's realized what he's just thrown away. I drop my tote bag on the ground, scrabble in my purse for my phone before it stops ringing, and read the name on the screen.

Erin.

I'm flooded with disappointment, though I know I shouldn't be. I'm fortunate to be rid of a guy who would string me along for eight years before finally proposing to me, cheating on me, and dumping me. I am! I blink back the tears that have reappeared and tap the *Answer* button.

"Hi," I force myself to say.

"Noelle? Where *are* you? Did you forget that you've got two appointments this morning?" Erin is flustered, which is a pretty normal state for her. "Your first one will be here in half an hour. Are you on your way in?"

Shit. I forgot. If I walked into my office now I'd still be early, for me. Erin, however, considers fifteen minutes early to be ten minutes late. But that doesn't even matter now, does it? How am I supposed to meet with a happy couple, sit down with them, and plan their wedding, when I've just found out I won't be having my own?

"I don't think so," I choke.

"What do you mean, you don't think so?" She pauses. "Are you okay?"

"No." I step out of the way as a young mother I recognize from the third floor emerges from the lobby with her toddler in a stroller. She smiles at me in greeting, and I at least have the self-awareness to be embarrassed when I can't muster a smile back for her. She must think I'm a bitch.

"Are you sick?"

"I—yes," I reply, and I am. Sick at heart. My stomach doesn't feel that great either. "I can't come in today. I'm so sorry. I should have called, but…" But what? But I was too busy having my world ripped away from me?

"Okay." Erin is no longer flustered but concerned, which is nice, but I'm not about to tell her what's really going on. I'm having trouble admitting it to myself, let alone to someone else. "Do you want me to reschedule today's appointments?"

"Yeah. Please. And all of my appointments for the rest of the week. But don't reschedule them. Cancel them."

"I'm sorry?" Now she sounds confused.

"Cancel them. I don't know when I'll be able to meet with them." *Or if I ever will.* Somewhere in the back of my mind I know I'm freaking her out, but at the moment I'm too self-absorbed to care.

"Okay," she says slowly, and I can tell she's wondering if I've lost my mind. "Sure. I'll cancel them. Call me later?"

"Sure," I say, though I know I won't. I don't want to talk to anyone today. Or tomorrow. Or possibly for the rest of my life.

I drop the phone back into my purse and pick up my tote bag, though I could probably just leave it there on the sidewalk. I don't know when I'll need it again. I trudge through the door into the lobby and up the stairs to the second floor. My hand is shaking so badly when I try to unlock my door that I drop my keys, twice, but I finally manage to get inside. My apartment is much as I left it—last night's half-full teacup on the small dining room table, dishes in the kitchen sink, unmade bed and clothes on the floor outside the bathroom. Is that why Drew left me? Because I'm a slob?

I choke on the sob that moves up my throat and dump my things on the floor beside a coffee table strewn with magazines. Once in my bedroom I take off my boots and toss them into the corner. I tug off my skinny jeans; the very pair Drew once said made my "ass look edible." Gross. I should have known then. I replace them with a pair of sweatpants that developed their first hole when I was a senior in college but that I refuse to throw away because, unlike most sweats, the fleece lining inside never balled up and got rough. I unwind the scarf from my neck, lift the long brown hair I spent half an hour that morning artfully tousling, and put it into a kind of topknot I've probably only ever worn to the gym. I contemplate scrubbing off my *is she or isn't she wearing makeup?* makeup, but that takes far too much energy, so it stays. I hate myself for spending so much time on my appearance that morning. If obvious and overdone was what Drew had always wanted, what had he ever seen in me?

I stand in the middle of my bedroom. I'm unsure of the next step. Do I crawl into bed? Dig into what's left of the pint of Phish Food in my freezer? No—that would make me a hypocrite. I'd already blasted Drew for being a cliché and sleeping with his assistant; I don't want to let him win by becoming the pathetic ex who drowns her sorrows in ice cream. It's a little after ten in the morning, and I have no desire to turn on the TV. Daytime television has always annoyed the crap out of me. My stomach still churns, and I'm not hungry at all.

Maybe some tea. I plod toward the kitchen, where my stainless steel kettle waits patiently on the stove like that old friend you might not see for years but when you do, it's always like no time has passed. I go through the motions of filling it with water and lighting the burner, but the normally comforting actions do little to comfort me now. I rinse the cup from the dining room table and go to the cabinet where I keep my tea collection. I'm a bit of a connoisseur. I have teas from all over the world, in all different blends. Black, green, herbal; English, Chinese, Indian. Flavored teas for certain seasons and medicinal teas for sickness. But I don't think I have one for the total annihilation of the future I'd planned with the love of my life, so I choose my old favorite—Lady Grey, blended in-house at a specialty tea shop a few miles away. A tea shop I'd discovered with Drew.

"Ugh!" I cry, and shove the box back into the cabinet. That's how it's going to be from now on, isn't it? The most innocuous thing is going to remind me of him. My favorite tea. Certain foods. TV shows and commercials and songs and scents and pictures and books and even my *clothes*.

I'm going to have to move. Move and burn all of my stuff.

I seize the first tea my fingers come in contact with and open it without looking. The scent drifting from the box tells me it's key lime coconut black tea. One of my favorites in the summer, especially iced, but in late October? Not so much. Whatever—it has no connection to Drew, so I withdraw a teabag, drop it into my cup, and wait for the kettle to whistle. When it does, I pick it up, but my hand is shaking so bad again I have to put it down before I spill boiling water all over myself. I grip the edge of the counter with both hands and try to catch a breath that doesn't want to be caught. My throat is tight. My lungs won't expand. Am I hyperventilating? I squeeze my eyes shut against the telltale burning of tears. But it doesn't do any good. They spill over my cheeks, scalding them, and there's no stopping it. My mouth opens to let out a wail, and I slide to the floor, dropping my face onto my knees and folding my arms over my head. I can't get up. I don't want to get up. I'm perfectly content to spend the rest of my life on my kitchen floor, despite its desperate need for a good sweeping, and cry myself into old age and hopefully senility.

I can't control it. The misery pours out of me in gallons of tears, gross, snotty snuffling noises, and wet hiccups. My entire body heaves. It makes my ribs hurt. I don't know how long I sit there, crying so hard I think I might puke. But at some point, there's a knock on my door.

I lift my head, wipe my eyes with my hands. The kettle is screaming and I know there can't be much water left, so I force myself into a standing position and turn off the burner. The knock comes again. I'm not stupid enough to think it's Drew, not really. But I can't help the tiny fissure of hope that threatens to crack my grief.

I must look disgusting. I can't breathe through my nose, and my eyes feel swollen. I can tell that my hasty topknot's gone lopsided, and there just might be smudges of dust on my butt from sitting on the floor. I won't open the door. It's probably nothing important anyway—one of the neighbors selling fundraiser pizzas for their kid, or the super finally coming to fix the leaky pipe under my bathroom sink. Drew had insisted I let him fix it, as I'd been waiting for the super to do it for months. Maybe I should have. Then the super wouldn't be bothering me now, when all I want to do is curl back into my ball. And die.

A third knock.

"Noelle?" A female voice. "Are you in there?"

Damn Erin and her compassion for other human beings! I should have told her I have diarrhea. Nobody just drops by when you tell them that.

"Noelle?"

I guess she won't go away until I prove to her I'm not dying.

"Give me a sec!" I call, and go to the bathroom where I make the mistake of looking in the mirror. Ugh. Just as I thought, my eyes are a swollen red and smudged-mascara mess, and my cheeks look both shiny and sticky. Gross. I splash cold water on my face, which helps just a little, and give up on my hair, pulling it back into an only slightly less messy ponytail. I still look like I could frighten small children, but older ones would probably be okay, so I go to the front door and open it. Erin stands there, blond hair in a much sleeker ponytail than mine, cheeks pink not from hysterical crying but carefully applied blush and exposure to fresh air, and not a mascara smear to be seen. She holds her purse in one hand and a paper bag in the other. I immediately recognize The Daily Grind's logo and want to throw up.

"Hi." I open the door wider to allow her in. "I'm not dying."

She enters, dropping the bag on my coffee table, and turns to look at me. "Are you sure? You don't look so hot."

"I'm sure." I move past her to the kitchen, where I refill the still-hot kettle. "Tea?"

"Sure. Thanks." I hear rustling and turn my head in time to see her scraping my mess of magazines into a neat pile in the upper left corner of my coffee table. I don't feel much like laughing, but that almost gets a giggle out of me. Poor Erin—

always trying to make me more of a Felix than an Oscar. After three years you'd think she'd give up, but no. Her one consolation is that I'm not dirty. Just sloppy. And you apparently can't tell to look at me, which is a good thing.

"So what's wrong?" Erin asks. "It's early for flu season."

"I don't have the flu." I take another teacup from the cabinet and drop a teabag in it.

"A cold? You sound sort of stuffy, and you look a little swollen in the sinus area."

I half-laugh, half-sob. "Thanks. But no, not a cold."

Her next words come hesitantly. "Stomach stuff?"

"No!" I turn back to her and immediately feel guilty. She looks truly concerned. What will she say when I tell her that my body's fine—it's my heart that's dying?

"I'm sorry," she said. "I shouldn't have come barging in on you if you're sick. I know visitors are the last thing I want when I don't feel well." She picks up her pink purse and slides it over her arm. "I'll let you rest. There're croissants in the bag if you want them."

My stomach does a little flip at the mention of croissants, but not in a good way. Maybe this breakup is a good thing— after all, if I can no longer eat my favorite pastry, I'll save money *and* calories.

"No, no, *I'm* sorry." My hands are steadier now, and I carefully pour steaming water into each cup, watching the teabags come bobbing up to the surface. I carry each cup to the dining room table, and we sit down. I stare into my tea for a minute, studying the liquid as it gets darker, and then tug on the teabag's little string. I wonder how to say it out loud—that I'm not getting married after all, that Drew's dumped me in favor of someone who'd barely been old enough to vote in the last election. Not that her age is what bothers me. Not entirely.

"Noelle?" Erin's voice is tiny, like a little girl whose mother has just sent her to timeout. "You're starting to scare me."

I sigh and shove my teacup away.

"Drew came home last night," I tell her, though she already knows this—she'd had to listen to me all day yesterday practically singing my excitement.

She frowns and nods.

"We met for coffee this morning." Erin's forehead wrinkles. She picks up her spoon to stir sugar into her tea, and I sigh again. She's not usually this dense. She's going to make me say it, isn't she?

The heat of tears stings my eyes again. "He called off the wedding."

I jump at the clatter her spoon makes when she drops it onto my dining table.

"What?" she gasps. "Why?"

I blink furiously, but a tear manages to escape and slide over my cheek. My chest muscles contract, and I hunch over. It hurts. It hurts.

"He doesn't love me anymore," I moan, and the tears start again, full-force.

"Oh my God," I think I hear Erin say through my sobs. Her chair scrapes against the floor, and then her arms are around me. I catch a vague whiff of flowery perfume, which I would hate on myself but which suits her perfectly. My tears soak the pristine sleeve of her sheer watercolor-printed blouse, the one with about forty-two colors that I'd borrow if she didn't have two and a half cup sizes on me. She doesn't even seem to mind that I'm snotting all over it. She hugs me to her, rocking me back and forth like a baby, stroking my hair and crooning nonsense. It's exactly what I need.

It feels like hours have passed by the time I'm finally spent. My cheeks are stiff with dried tears, and a throbbing, aching pressure has taken residence behind my eyes. I sprawl on the couch with the cool wet washcloth Erin's given me draped over my face and listen to the dull hum of the TV's low volume and the rush of water in the kitchen sink as my assistant washes my dishes.

"That's not part of your job description," I call. I sit up and rub the cloth over my face, trying to erase any sign of tears. This is ridiculous. I'm not the first woman to be dumped by her fiancé. I won't be the last. But most of all, it's not permanent. A bit of thinking has convinced me. Drew won't be happy with Heidi of the Drugstore Lipstick. Drew likes intelligence, and the few times I spoke to her did little to convince me that Heidi had anything going for her in that department. He likes ambition and drive—how many times has he told me how amazing he thinks it is that I started my own business? Yet Heidi's idea of ambition seems to be sleeping with the boss. That might give her a temporary boost, but it certainly won't hold his interest. Not the way I held it for eight years.

I feel better than I have all day, or at least since Drew sat down in front of me this morning. I roll off the couch just as Erin shuts the water off and slides the last plate into the overloaded drain board.

"Thank you," I say. "You didn't have to do that." She didn't have to straighten up my living room, either, but it looks like she did. It hasn't been this neat since the day I moved in.

"Well, it didn't look like you were going to." Erin ventures a small smile, as if to gauge my reaction, and seems relieved when I laugh. "You look a little better. How are you feeling?"

"Better." I think I might even feel hungry, but then I catch sight of the abandoned bag of croissants and know I can't do it. Not yet. "Thank you so much for being here today. You have no idea how much it helped."

"Why wouldn't I?" Erin finishes drying her hands and hangs the towel on its hook over the sink. "I know you're my boss, but we're friends, too. Right?"

Warmth suffuses me. We are friends, it seems. Good ones. "Right."

"So…" Erin looks down at her feet, points a booted toe. "What about work?"

"Oh." Right. Work. I'm kind of responsible for her income, aren't I? Suddenly I feel awful for having her cancel my appointments. I've got two weddings on my books for the rest of the year and they've already been paid for, the money allocated for certain things. If I'm not bringing in any more money, how am I supposed to pay her? But I don't know. I don't know if I'm ready. Oh, I know Drew will come crawling back. But the question is when. Do I have what it takes to plan the amazing wedding I promise each of my clients while waiting for my fiancé to remember me?

I race through the math in my head. The business account has more than enough in it to pay Erin's regular salary and an adequate one for me. Erin's cleared the next few days for me, so I have until Monday to get myself together. I can do that. I've already paid the rest of the year's rent on the building, so I don't have to worry about that. And it should only take Drew a few weeks to realize that he's made the biggest mistake of his life. Silver Bells will be fine. A few days off is all I need.

"Okay," I say slowly. "You go in. Answer the phones and all that stuff. I'm going to keep the next few days for myself, though."

"Understandable." Relief relaxes her face. "I can hold down the fort until you're ready to come back. However long it takes."

"Monday," I say with certainty. "If anyone calls, schedule them for after Monday. I'll be fine by then."

"If you're sure." She smiles.

But by the next morning, the denial stage is already over, and I'm not sure at all. Of anything.

3

It's EARLY EVENING on Thursday before I manage to summon the energy to roll out of bed and do anything other than pee or get a glass of water. I do it not because I want to, but because I need a shower in the worst way. I stand under the steaming water until it starts to get cold, using the expensive shampoo and conditioner I save for special occasions—I think I deserve it. I even take the time to comb the knots out of my wet hair. I put on clean sweatpants and a tank top. Then I stand in the middle of my living room, which is strangely uncluttered since I've spent the past two days confined to my bedroom, and wonder what to do next.

Eating might not be a bad idea. I haven't since Monday night, and I'm honestly surprised I don't feel worse. Shouldn't my blood sugar have dropped or something? Shouldn't I have a migraine, or at least tremble a bit? But I feel okay. An emotional wreck, to be sure, but physically just kind of blah. Energy-less. I go to the fridge, open the door. One glance tells me all I need to know—I have nothing with which to make a proper meal, unless I want a ketchup-and-Caesar dressing sandwich with a side of fuzzy strawberries and a glass of expired milk to wash it all down. I'm even out of bottled water.

I wasn't planning on getting back at Drew by starving myself to death. I'm going to have to go to the grocery store.

This sucks.

I'm not ready to face the world.

You have to. You want revenge on Drew? Get it by getting on with your life.

I return to the bathroom and tie my damp hair into a messy bun. My brown eyes are slightly bloodshot and comfortably nestled into some serious dark circles, but a swipe of concealer takes care of it. Mostly. I tie a multicolored scarf around my neck, put on a denim jacket, and slip into a pair of Reeboks so old they've pretty much molded themselves to the shape of my foot. There. I'm presentable. No one's going to run away screaming, but no one's going to hit on me, either. That's okay. Getting hit on is the last thing I want.

The grocery store is pleasantly uncrowded for a Thursday night. My cart and I slip through the aisles unnoticed as I load it with butternut squash and a bag of apples, pasta and yogurt, a value pack of chicken breasts, and a loaf of bread. I'm okay. This is easy. I can do this. I ignore the sting of tears that seems to show up at random as I stroll through the seafood section, contemplating salmon and averting burning eyes from the few couples I see, couples obviously shopping for dinners they will prepare and eat together. I ignore frazzled mothers with small children, children I used to think I'd have until Drew told me it was over. Whatever. Nobody *needs* children. The world is already overpopulated.

I ignore them all. That is, until one of those small children, in an effort to get away from what seems like the world's most annoying older brother, hurls himself blindly into the side of my cart, sending it skidding across the floor and himself into a screaming tantrum.

Seriously? I think as I watch, feeling strangely distanced, as the kid kicks and punches the dingy linoleum floor and cries—either in pain or frustration, I'm not sure. *Your brother's annoying so you're throwing a tantrum on a dirty floor? Wait till you're my age, kid. Wait until things that are actually bad happen to you and you can't fling yourself on the ground in public and scream.* His face is bright red and wet, and mucus drips from his nose in a shiny trail. His screams bring to the scene the seafood manager and a guy with a push cart loaded with bags of frozen shrimp. Big Brother stands there staring, along with half the store, but their mother is apparently nowhere to be found.

Anger bubbles in my veins. What kind of mother just leaves her kids unattended in the middle of a grocery store? Does she not know what kind of havoc they can wreak? The fury burns, a heat that extends from the top of my scalp to the tips of my shaking fingers. It's all I can do not to shriek at Big Brother, who gawks at his sibling stupidly, mouth hanging open, unevenly cut blond hair sticking up and making him resemble a deranged cockatoo.

I have to get out of here before I start screaming at random kids. I'm not usually a confrontational person—but this whole grieving process is doing a number on me. I guess this is the anger stage.

Forgetting the salmon, I go after my cart and retrieve it several yards away, where it rolled to a stop next to a display of crumb cakes. Finally, something is going my way! Because these aren't just any crumb cakes but my favorites—the ones loaded with brown sugar, butter, trans fats, and probably carcinogens. The ones I've been studiously avoiding for months, so I could fit into the wedding dress of my dreams.

But now I don't have to worry about a bulging belly and back fat, do I? Nope. I pick up a cake and toss it into my cart. Then I notice the sign—two for four dollars. Considering one usually costs nearly four dollars itself, it's a sale I know I'll hate myself for passing up. I can always freeze one. I grab another cake. I mull over the possibility of a third, but even though the idea of not caring is appealing right now, I have the presence of mind to know that someday I'll probably want to wear real clothes again and it will help if they fit. I push my cart away before I can give in to temptation. Among the other healthy items I've chosen the cakes look ridiculous.

A redheaded teenager in a green employee's apron greets me with enthusiasm as I roll into her lane.

"Hi! How are you?" she chirps.

I can barely muster the effort to smile at her. I think forty-five minutes in the grocery store was more than I was ready for. I feel a sudden raging need to get away from people. "Fine, thanks." I put two gallon bottles of water on the belt.

"It was beautiful out today, wasn't it?" she says. *I wouldn't know; I spent it inside.* "I love this kind of weather. Not hot, not cold. Fall is my favorite season."

Yogurt. Apples. A head of lettuce and some tomatoes.

"I can't stand summer. I don't handle heat well." Pasta, milk, eggs. "And winter … ugh! Too cold. And I hate snow." Cereal. Chicken. *Is she still talking?* Why do some people just love the sound of their own voices?

"Uh huh," I say. I put the crumb cakes on the belt and push my cart to the end of the lane. I take my debit card from my wallet and run it through the terminal attached to the register.

Crumb cake. $3.89.

"Wait," I say. "Those cakes were supposed to be on sale."

"Really?" She squints and leans toward the screen. "They're not coming up on sale."

Clearly. I force a smile. "They're supposed to be. They had a sign. Two for four dollars."

"Hmm." She taps a button on her keyboard, scans the cake again. *$3.89.* "Hmm."

Isn't there some kind of price override button? "Can you maybe call a manager?" I say.

She shrugs. "If they were on sale, they would be ringing up at the sale price." She hits another button. Scans the cake again. *$3.89.* Now she's charged me for three cakes, at full price.

"They. Are. On. Sale." I grit my teeth and try not to sound as livid as I suddenly am.

She shakes her head. "I don't think so, ma'am."

Ma'am? Okay, that does it. "They're on *sale,*" I growl, leaning toward her. She jerks back. "So either take them off my bill and rering them at the sale price, or I *will* report you to your manager, and you *will* be fired."

Her eyes wide, she taps a few buttons. I watch as my total shrinks. She scans the cakes again, and this time they come up at two dollars apiece. My fury subsides as quickly as it came, and I'm suddenly mortified. Did I really just threaten a teenager and her job over some pastries and make myself the subject of the inevitable social media video? What is *happening* to me?

At least she's stopped talking. She announces my total at a volume I'd need a hearing aid on full blast to hear, but it's okay, I just want to get out of there. I enter my pin number and wait for the terminal to approve it. When it does, she hands me my receipt, pinched between her thumb and forefinger—evidently in an attempt to avoid any chance of touching me. I can't blame her. She must think I'm a maniac. I *am* a maniac.

I stuff the last of my bags into my cart. My face is flaming again, but it's from embarrassment and regret now instead of rage.

"I'm so sorry," I mumble to her, before shoving my cart away and into the parking lot as quickly as I can.

Guess I won't be shopping there for a while.

After I get home and put my groceries away, I force down a cup of yogurt and an apple, and I think about calling Erin. I haven't heard if she's scheduled any appointments for next week, and I wonder what she'll do if I tell her to cancel those, too. I wonder if I should tell her to find another job. Can I honestly go back to planning weddings? Can I look at venues, suggest signature cocktails, design color schemes without completely losing it?

My phone rings, and I'm a little relieved that I won't be able to come up with an immediate answer. My sister Kate's name flashes across the little screen. I swallow hard. Kate has the perfect life, with a husband who adores her and a three-bedroom house with a rambling green lawn and a legitimate picket fence. I haven't told her about Drew. I guess now I have to. She knows me too well—she'll hear it in my voice, no matter what words I'm saying.

"Hey," I say.

"Hey. What are you doing answering? I was going to leave a message. Isn't it date night?"

Oh, crap. She's right. In the haze of the last forty-eight hours I've completely forgotten that Thursday, for the last eight years, has traditionally served as date night unless I had a rehearsal dinner. Whether Drew and I went out or stayed in, we did it together.

Something inside my chest squeezes my heart, and it takes a second to remember how to breathe.

"We, um, couldn't do it tonight," I say. "He had to work late." She'll never believe me. She knows Drew was gone for a while—he wouldn't cancel date night for more work.

"What's wrong?" she immediately demands.

"Nothing."

"Tell me." Her voice has taken on its "I'm the big sister" quality, the one that in thirty years has never failed to get me to do exactly what she wants, whether it's making her bed for her or confessing that my friends and I raided her closet for a night out.

I'm getting uncomfortably warm. I set the phone down and unwind my scarf, take off my jacket. A lump of misery presses on my throat from the inside.

"Noelle?" Her voice is tinny. I pick up the phone and press it to my burning ear.

"We broke up," I choke.

"What?"

"Don't make me say it again, please."

"Oh, my God. Noelle. Why didn't you tell me?"

I remain silent, wiping at the tears that managed to make it past my eyes and snake down my cheeks.

"Are you okay? Of course you're not okay. What can I do?"

"Nothing," I say. "Nobody can do anything. It's over. He doesn't want me. He's with Heidi now."

"Who the hell is Heidi?"

"His *assistant*," I wail, and dissolve into a fresh flood of tears.

"For God's sake—" There's some muffled rustling as I picture Kate covering the phone with her hand and whispering to her husband, Jacob. *"She's totally lost it,"* I imagine her saying. *"I'm afraid to leave her alone. She might hang herself with one of her scarves."*

"I won't, I promise," I say aloud.

"What?"

"I won't kill myself."

"I—I know." Kate sounds a little confused, and I realize I've worried her. "Noe? Do you need me to come for a visit? I can, for as long as you need me."

"No." I mean it. But then something hits me. The answer to my multitude of dilemmas, perhaps?

I don't need her to visit. I can just move back home.

Would that be too much like running away, though? I'm supposed to be an adult, able to face life's ups and downs with maturity and if not ease, at least some dignity.

And where would I live? I have a decent amount of money socked away in a savings account—money I thought would pay for my wedding—but as far as I know, mortgage lenders and landlords alike frown upon a lack of steady employment.

I could live with my mother, but I'm thirty years old. Running away *and* moving back into my old One Direction-papered bedroom? Pathetic.

"Are you sure? Springhollow is such a small town … aren't you afraid of running into Drew?"

Yes. Yes, I am. More afraid of that than of being perceived as a little girl who went scurrying back home to Mommy when life dealt her a crap hand. I think. And of life-sized posters of Harry Styles in his "I just got caught in a wind tunnel" phase.

"I can help out. Run your errands, that kind of stuff. Until you know you'll be okay."

"I'm okay," is all I say. I wipe at my eyes. They're leaking, again. "So what's up? You never call on date night. Must be something important."

"It is…" she trails off. I know my sister well enough to know that whatever it is, she's afraid to say it. What could possibly be worse than what *I* had to tell *her*?

My heart stutters. "You're not getting divorced, are you?"

"What?" She sounds horrified. "No, of course not. The opposite, actually."

"Renewing your vows?" That would be weird. They've been married a few years, but don't people usually wait a decade or something to do that?

"No. Maybe not the opposite, then." She draws a deep breath—I hear it through the phone. "Noelle, I'm pregnant."

I let my own breath out in a *whoosh*. Funny, I hadn't even realized I was holding it.

"Kate! That's amazing! Congratulations!" Do I feel a twinge of envy? Yes, of course. But it's not overwhelming. Despite tonight's episode in the seafood department I want kids too, one day. Losing Drew might mean losing that chance. But for her entire life my sister has wanted nothing more than her own baby. Even when we were children playing house, she was always the mom. Sometimes she was even better at it than our actual mom. "How far along?"

"Four months," she says.

"You waited this long to tell me?" I screech.

"I wanted to wait until the first trimester was over before I told anyone." Her voice is soft. I understand why.

"I get it," I say. "Wow. That's incredible. I'm so happy for you!" I really am. She's wanted this for so long, and after three heartbreaking disappointments … I can't imagine how over the moon she must be.

"It's considered high-risk." She's blunt. "Even though I've made it this far, there's no guarantee I'll carry to term. I'm not on bed rest, yet, but they're keeping an eye on me."

That dampens my enthusiasm. I saw what three miscarriages did to her. She's probably terrified of getting too excited.

"It's promising though, right, that you've made it into the second trimester?"

"Yeah. I didn't make it this far with—the others. So that's a good sign." I hear it in her voice, the refusal to pin all of her hopes on this baby. My heart simultaneously leaps and aches for her.

That does it. I'm going home. Who cares if anyone thinks I went running away from my broken engagement? My sister needs me. But I hate the thought of leaving Erin without a job. Maybe she'll come with me. We could be roommates. Felix and Oscar, together again.

Who am I kidding? Her entire life is in Springhollow. Her family, friends, the caterer she's been crushing on since the day I hired her. She'll have no trouble finding a job. She's qualified for just about anything. Maybe she'll even start her own wedding business. She's learned a lot from me, plus she has the business acumen I sorely lack—the reason I hired her in the first place. My bachelor's degree in English might not get me any farther than a manager's position at Starbucks, but Erin has a business degree. She'd do great in the real world.

But there's nothing left for me.

"I'll help," I tell Kate.

"What? How? You're nearly a hundred miles away."

"I'm moving home. I just decided." Maybe I should check with my mom first, to make sure she's okay harboring her thirty-year-old spinster of a daughter for a time.

"Don't be ridiculous. You have a life there. Your own business. What are you going to do, shut down Silver Bells?"

"That's exactly what I'm going to do." I feel surer of myself than I have in the last few days. "I can't plan other people's weddings when I can't even make mine happen. Who's going to hire me? Like you said, Springhollow's a small town. You know how small towns are. In a few days everyone will know my wedding was called off, if they don't already. They'll probably publish it in the *Springhollow Stalker*." That was Drew's clever name for the town newspaper, the *Springhollow Talker*. "Town's Golden Boy Ditches Fiancée for Busty Airhead in Biggest Cliché in Town History." I make a noise that's half laugh, half sob. "God."

"If you're sure…"

"I'm sure."

"Well, I can't deny I'd love having you back. I miss the crap out of you. And I'd love for my kid to know his or her aunt as more than just a pixelated image on a computer screen or a disembodied voice from a cellphone."

"I want that too." I do. This is a good decision, I feel it.

"Well," Kate says. "This is amazing of you, Noe. I'd like to feel sorrier about what you're going through, but if it means you're coming home, I just can't." She laughs a little, and I try to chime in, but it doesn't really work. It's okay. Once I'm home and busy helping take care of my sister and her baby, I'll feel better. I'll get over it. Being so far away will do me good. "I'm sure you've got a lot think about. Keep me posted though, okay? Let me know when you have a rough idea of when you think you'll be here."

"I will," I promise, already making a mental list of the things I need to do. Tell my landlord I'm leaving and get the security deposit back. Tell Erin she'll need to find a new job. Shut down the business. Pack and, presumably, purge my life of everything Drew.

"I love you," my sister says.

"I love you, too." And I do. She's my best friend. There for me through everything. Now, I get to do it for her. Nothing, and I mean nothing, is going to keep me from going home to her. To my old life.

Even if it makes me a failure.

4

BOTH MONDAY AND I start off stormy. I've only slept two and a half crappy, fitful hours when my phone alarm, which I purposely keep set to the most obnoxious tone I can find, jolts me awake. With the sound comes the memory of how Drew always hated it.

"Does it have to be that one?" he'd complain. "There are dozens to pick from. Why that one?"

"Because the more obnoxious it is, the less likely I am to sleep through it." I thought I was being clever. When it goes off today, I lie still, allowing myself to feel just a little happy that it negatively affected so many of Drew's mornings, and I let it sing its unbearable song for a full three minutes until I hear the guy in the apartment below mine stirring. Then I turn it off before he can take what I can only assume is a baseball bat, or maybe a golf club, to his ceiling. It wouldn't be the first time. Twelve years of ballet classes and near-daily Pilates workouts on my living room floor might help me maintain a ballerina-ish figure, but apparently I do *not* have a ballerina's grace. At least I don't think he'd say so. Screw him. It's just a phone. How loud can it be through his ceiling? *There are worse things in life, buddy.*

I stumble bleary-eyed and clumsy into the bathroom. A quick glance out the window reveals a sky that looks just as cranky as I feel. I shower and dress as quickly as I can, giving as little thought as possible to what I look like. I'm going to close my business down today—no need to look like a supermodel for that. Besides, it'll just be Erin and me. After last week, I can't imagine she'll bat an eye if I show up makeup-free and in mismatched clothes. She'll probably have a hard time looking at me anyway, once I tell her she's unemployed.

Yeah, today will *really* suck.

I dig an old travel coffee mug from one of my cabinets. No way am I going to The Daily Grind today. Or ever again, probably. It'll be hard enough just walking past it. Even the aroma of my own less than adequate home-brewed coffee brings tears springing to my eyes. *Stop. You can't live your life like this, crying whenever you smell coffee!* I wonder if it even bothers Drew, if he'll continue to get his coffee and breakfast sandwich there every morning even though he passes at least two Wawa stores on the way from his apartment to his office. He probably will. It wasn't *his* heart that was broken at that small table by the window. The Daily Grind isn't ruined for *him*. I hurry through shutting my coffeemaker down, smashing the lid onto my cup so I don't have to think about it any longer than necessary.

It's cold and raw outside and it's not even five seconds before fat raindrops are meeting explosive deaths against the sidewalk, my clothes, and my head. I run to my car and dive inside. Getting a remote starter was a good idea. The heat's already on full-blast and within moments it's dried my shirt, is in the process of drying my hair, and I'm really starting to dread what I'm about to do.

But it has to be done. Kate needs me, even if no one else does.

True to form, Erin is already at the front desk. That desk is a study in stereotypical girlyness—it's rosy and ridiculous and very, very neat. The pen with the gigantic fluffy feather that must have been yanked from a very fancy flamingo gives me a perky wave as I approach the door. Erin's been going through a catalog, too. I know this because it's lying next to the phone and isn't in its proper place—a magazine file where catalogs and brochures are grouped by purpose, and then alphabetically. When I push through the door, she's lifting her pink coffee mug, the one that inexplicably says "#1 Grandma," to her lips. All that pink clashes with the black and orange Halloween lights Erin's roped around the reception area.

The cup's ascent halts when she sees me, rakes her gaze over my clothes, seems to note that I don't have my usual work tote with me, and widens her eyes.

Slowly the cup descends. It lands on the desk with barely a sound.

"Hi," she says, and her tone is careful. She knows something's up. She's good like that.

Well, it's not like you're trying to hide it.

But does she expect what I'm going to say? Does she think I'm just going to ask for more time, or does she already have a suspicion that I'm about to take away her livelihood?

"Hi." I take off my coat, hang it on the silver hook next to the door. "Listen, Erin, I need to talk to you."

"Okay," she says. "But first—"

"No," I interrupt. "I need to do it now. Before I lose my nerve."

But of course the phone rings, and Erin dives to answer it. *Sure, Erin, go ahead. Put off the inevitable and make it that much harder on both of us, why don't you?*

I perch on the ivory couch in the reception area and wait for her to get done talking. From the sound of it, it's one of those obnoxious telemarketers who call six or seven times a day wanting to speak to the person in charge of the electric bill. Usually she shrieks, "Get a real job!" and hangs up on them, but today she's chatting like it's her best friend from high school on the other end. Hot, prickly guilt rolls over me. She must know what's coming.

I sip my coffee, lukewarm now. Yuck. Just the flavor of it on my tongue is enough to send waves of nausea rippling over me. I guess it's not just The Daily Grind's house blend but all coffee that's ruined for me now.

I stand with the intent of taking it into the bathroom and dumping it down the drain, but the door behind me opens.

"Hello," says a female voice. "I'm Brooke St. John. I called earlier?"

I glance at Erin, still on the phone, who gives the girl a little wave.

"I'll be right with you," she says, covering the receiver with her hand. "But this is Noelle Silver, the owner." She goes back to the phone, leaving me little choice but to acknowledge Brooke St. John.

The girl's a stunner, for sure. Thick golden hair, smooth ivory skin, enormous blue eyes. Already I picture her as a bride. On a beach somewhere, definitely; maybe in Cape May among the colorful Victorian houses. In a loose ivory crepe sundress with a high-low hem. Barefoot, of course, her hair down and wavy, one side pinned back. Carrying a bouquet of daisies and beach grass. A faceless groom barefoot as well, in khakis and a white shirt. Bridesmaids in dresses similar to hers, but in different blues the same as the varying shades of the ocean. Of course, without speaking to her I have no idea what she has in mind, but this is what I think when I see her.

Not that it matters. It's not like I'll be doing her wedding.

"Hi," she says, giving me a sweet but dazzling smile. "It's nice to meet you." She extends her hand, and I can't help but shake it.

"You, too," I say. "Can I get you anything? Coffee or tea? Water?"

"I'm fine, thanks," she says. She glances at the door, shakes her head. "Everett should be here any minute. I told him nine o'clock."

"Men," I offer. *Hopefully he's not still passed out in his assistant's bed.* Of course I don't say that out loud. Not to this beautiful girl with the dreamy eyes I've seen on so many brides. She doesn't deserve to have her hopes dashed. Then again, neither did I.

Erin hangs up the phone and comes around from behind her desk, a bright smile on her face.

"Hi, Brooke," she says warmly. "It's so nice to meet you! Did Noelle offer you coffee?"

"She did, thank you," Brooke said. "I'm fine. Just waiting for Everett. He's always late, but I thought he'd make an effort for this." She shrugs and laughs. "I should have known."

"Can I take your coat? I know you probably don't want to start chatting with Noelle until Everett's here. Would you like some magazines? Anything to eat? I can go to The Daily Grind and get you something."

I look at Erin. Why is she falling all over this girl? Erin is friendly and enthusiastic, of course; it's one of the main reasons I hired her. She takes up for me when I get lost in the creative process of wedding planning. But she doesn't overstep her bounds. Why, then, does it sound like she wants to invite Brooke to a slumber party at her house?

And why haven't I said anything about how I'm not taking on any more weddings? It's mean of me to waste this girl's time.

"Look—" I say, but I'm interrupted yet again by a blast of raw wind that flutters the feather on Erin's pen as the door swings open and a guy barges through.

"Sorry," he says, bending to kiss Brooke's cheek. "I couldn't find the damn key to my bike, and the Jeep's getting an oil change. I had to walk." He straightens and glances around the room. His eyes land on me, and I am suddenly incredibly conscious of my faded black yoga pants, drapey—okay, stretched out—gray tee, and air-dried, frizzy hair. I say a quick prayer of thanks that I had the presence of mind to throw a purple scarf around my neck and hope that it detracts from the homeless chic thing I have going on. A ridiculous reaction, of course. He's engaged. And I'm no more in the market for a boyfriend than I am for a WaveRunner.

But I'm not dead. And this guy. Is. Gorgeous.

If he's not a cheating jerk as well, Brooke St. John is one lucky girl.

"I would have picked you up! You shouldn't be riding your bike in the rain anyway," she chides him. I hear the love in her voice and it sends a nasty jolt of envy through me, making me cringe. "It's dangerous."

The guy—Everett—just laughs and takes off his leather coat. He tosses it onto the couch behind him. I wait for Erin to run over and pick it up, unable to stand it lying there marring her perfect, neat reception area and getting our magazines all wet, but she doesn't, and when I look at her I see why. She's staring at the guy as if he's a member of her favorite boy band. I can practically see the drool glistening on her chin.

"I'll get that," I offer, sarcastically, and Brooke shoots me an apologetic glance.

"That was rude, Everett," she says. "This isn't your living room."

"It's okay," Erin chirps. "Nobody ever sees the coat hooks."

"I'm sorry." Everett steps from Brooke's side and comes to me, taking the jacket from my hands. His fingers brush mine, and another jolt goes through me—this one pure sizzling energy. I jerk away as if his hands have flames shooting out of them. He gives me a curious glance before turning and very deliberately hanging the jacket on the coat hook by the door, where it promptly begins to drip all over the floor. I barely notice. I'm a whirlwind of confusion.

"My big brother was raised by gorillas," Brooke says with a roll of her eyes.

Brother? Erin trills her laughter. It's just background noise as I observe the two in front of me. They couldn't look more different. She's honey-haired and light-eyed; the hair that peeks from beneath his knit skull cap is dark and wavy, as are his eyes. Dark, that is. Not wavy. She's petite where he's muscular—not in an ex-football player way like Drew, but more like someone whose ability to carry you out of a burning building would be only a little surprising. And he's got at least five years on her. Maybe closer to ten. But on closer inspection I see similarities. The shape of their jaws, for example. Their straight noses. Light, smooth complexions.

And of course, both are romance novel-cover beautiful. I can only imagine what Brooke's real fiancé looks like.

I'm almost disappointed that I'll never find out.

"It's not a problem," I say in response to Brooke's apology. And it's not. Not my problem, anyway. If the carpet gets so wet mold grows underneath it, the next tenants of the building will have to worry about it. Not me. "But listen. I'm sorry, but I can't help you."

In my peripheral vision I see Erin's head jerk toward me. Well, I'm sorry if she's surprised, but she should have let me tell her my plans before Miss Springhollow came waltzing in!

"Is it because my fiancé isn't here?" Brooke asks. "I *am* sorry about that, but he's in Canada right now. His mom has cancer and she's all alone, so he's staying with her while she goes through chemo. I explained it to Erin on the phone, and she said it was all right."

Everett remains silent, the look in his eyes suggesting that he wants to issue some sort of challenge. He wants to dare me to tell Brooke I won't do her wedding. Well. He doesn't scare me.

Though my heart does give a nervous little *thump*.

"No, it's not that." I make my hair into a ponytail with my hands, then let it flop over my shoulders in all its frizzy glory. "It's not uncommon to just meet with the bride at first. Sometimes she brings her mom, sometimes the maid of honor. Although a brother is unusual."

"Maid of honor lives in Arizona," he says. His voice is deep, with just the slightest raspy quality to it. "I'm the best man."

I refuse to be intimidated. "Then I guess that explains it." I take a deep breath. Might as well get it out. "I can't help you because I'm not taking on any more clients. I'm shutting down Silver Bells."

The words land like a skydiver with a busted parachute. All three of them stare at me. For a while. So long, in fact, that I start to sweat a little.

"Noelle?" Erin's voice is strangled.

I glance at her, hoping she can read the apology in my eyes. This isn't how I'd meant to tell her.

"I'm really sorry," I say. "If you like, Brooke, I can give you a list of a few other wedding planners. Ones I really trust. I'd never send you to someone I didn't think would make you happy."

"Noelle?" Through gritted teeth this time. "Can I talk to you for a second? In private?"

"Of course. Excuse me, please." Brooke nods wordlessly. Everett crosses his arms. I feel his gaze on me as I turn and follow Erin into the conference room.

She shuts the door behind me.

"What is going on?" she demands.

"Erin, I'm *so* sorry you had to hear it like that, but I tried to tell you before they showed up!" I try my hardest to keep my voice down. "I just can't do it. I agonized over it all weekend. I'm going to turn over next year's weddings to other planners. I already made a list. And then it's over. I hate to do this, especially to you. But you'll find another job. I'll write you a letter of recommendation. It'll be so good it'll win a Pulitzer. But I just can't do this anymore." Tears scald my eyes. Again. "I can't do weddings for people when I'm not having my own."

Erin touches my arm. "I understand that, Noelle. I really do. I promise. But don't rush to make a decision. Maybe you should do just one more wedding. Just to see. If you get through it, then think it over. I know how much you love this work. Once you're over Drew—don't look at me like that. I know it won't happen overnight. But once you're over him, I think you'll miss it."

"Maybe," I allow. "Maybe you're right. But it's not that easy. I've already made other plans."

Erin frowns. "What other plans?"

"I'm going back home."

"You're leaving town?" Now Erin's eyes look like they might get misty.

"My sister Kate is pregnant." Saying the words aloud sends another tiny twinge of envy through me. "It's high risk, because of her miscarriages. I'm moving back home to help out. I don't know … it just seemed right. The timing."

"It's definite?"

I shrug. "Well, I haven't told my landlord yet, but I did tell my sister. She's expecting me. So yeah. It's pretty much definite."

"Oh." Erin's shoulders sag a little. "When is she due?"

Kate didn't tell me, but even I'm capable of that much math. "Sometime in March."

For some reason this perks Erin right back up. "That's actually perfect," she says.

"Perfect for what?"

"Brooke wants to have her wedding on Christmas Eve. You can still do it and make it home in time to help Kate."

I start to laugh. It's just too ridiculous. "Christmas Eve? Are you kidding me? That's less than two months away."

"I know. She knows. That's one of the reasons why she came to you. Jessica Berman told her you did her wedding within a short time frame."

"Jessica Berman's wedding was planned in five months. Brooke can't even give me two. And it's Christmas Eve. This isn't short. This is practically nonexistent." I laugh again. "Christmas Eve. Good one, Erin."

"Noelle, honestly. I think you'll regret this."

Something about her tone makes me stop laughing. "What do you mean?"

She glances at the door. "Brooke St. John is an *orphaned heiress*," she whispers.

This is too much. "You've been DVRing too much *General Hospital*."

"I'm serious!" Her eyes are so wide I can see white circling the blue. "Her parents were loaded. Her dad was one of the top neurologists on the East Coast. People would come from all over the world to see if he could cure their brain tumors and stuff."

Seriously, this smacks of a soap opera plotline.

"You are off your rocker," I inform her. But my curiosity is piqued, and I can't help asking. "What happened to them?"

"They lived in a mansion on Springhollow Hill. You know the hill you can see from Main Street?" I nod. Of course I know; it's a town landmark. "Fifteen years ago there was a house fire. The parents died. Brooke was nine and home alone with them, but somehow she managed to get out. Anyway, they left Everett and Brooke all their money. Those two out in the lobby are millionaires, Noelle."

Okay, so it's a fascinating and tragic story. But it doesn't change my mind. I grew up without two nickels to rub together. I don't hold millionaires in any higher regard than I do the homeless guy that stands outside the local Wawa wearing one shoe no matter what time of year it is.

"Are you suggesting I ditch my sister to do a spoiled little millionaire heiress's dream wedding?" I ask. Does Erin even realize what it'll be like, planning a wedding for a millionaire? Custom dresses. A menu starting at three hundred dollars a plate. A reception in some swanky hotel or something downtown, with imported flowers and waiters in designer tuxes and champagne from a very specific vineyard in Côte des Blancs. And me making phone calls and sending e-mails twenty-four hours a day trying to make it all happen.

Even if I was at all still interested in planning weddings, this is a job I might hesitate to take. Even if I had two years instead of two months.

Erin's face turns—what else?—a little pink.

"Maybe," she says. "Although I wouldn't call her spoiled. She's actually very unassuming. I don't know her personally, but I know some stuff about her. She doesn't live the way you'd think someone with her money would."

Oh. Well, in that case.

Is she right? Should I do one more wedding to see if my heart is still in it? Or could ever get back in it?

But now I'm thinking about what it involves. What any wedding would involve. Visiting venues, picking out a gown. Choosing flowers and menus and lighting. At Christmas. My favorite time of the year.

No. I can't. I just can't. No matter how unassuming Brooke St. John might be, it's still a wedding.

"I'm sorry," I say. "But no."

Erin sighs, and I swear even her hair looks depressed at my answer.

"Okay," she says. Her tone of voice lets me know that she clearly thinks I'm making some huge mistake.

"I'm so sorry," I repeat. "After they leave, I'll get to work on your letter. And we need to talk about the Fantana and Jameson weddings. I'm going to turn them over to you."

She shrugs and opens the door, heading back out to the lobby. I feel like absolute crap.

"I'm really sorry, Brooke," I say when I reach her. "But I have a personal situation I just can't ignore. Believe me. I'd love to do your wedding." She doesn't have to know I'm lying. "But I can't. If you give me your e-mail address, I'll get a list together of reputable wedding planners I think would be willing to work with you on such short notice."

"I don't want another wedding planner," Brooke says. "I want you."

Everett leans against the wall. I feel his gaze on me. I try to ignore it.

"I—can't," I repeat. I'm not sure why she's so set on me. I know I'm really good at what I do. I've worked hard to build a reputable business. But I'm hardly setting the world on fire, and I'm not the only one around. Springhollow is a suburb of Philadelphia. There are dozens of wedding planners just twenty minutes away who would gladly do a lavish wedding for an *orphaned heiress.*

"Please." Her tone's adopted a cajoling quality. "This is so important to us. Will's mom might not make it to next Christmas. She's going through chemo, but she's stage three. And Christmas Eve is her favorite day of the year. She says that Christmas Day is a letdown, but Christmas Eve is so full of possibility. It's the perfect day for a marriage."

"I—"

"And Christmas weddings are your specialty," she continues. "I've been on your website. Your portfolio is *amazing.* It's exactly what we want. Please. Let us be your last clients."

I'm shaking my head no when Brooke reaches into her oversized purse and withdraws her checkbook.

"How much money will it take?" she asks.

"It's not about that," I protest. "My sister is having a baby, and she's already lost three. She needs my help." Why am I telling these strangers Kate's private business? "I'm already committed to moving back home to be with her."

It's like I haven't even spoken. "How much do you charge?"

Damn. She might be humble, but she sure is stubborn. "I can't really say up front. The total cost depends on the menu, the flowers, all of that stuff. But there's the base fee, which just covers my service. On such short notice it could be pretty expensive."

"I don't care," she says. "I need all the help I can get."

I peek at Erin. She gives me an encouraging nod.

I won't cave. I won't. If I try to plan this girl's wedding, I'll just end up ruining it. I don't have it in me to make her dreams come true when mine are crumbling all around me. "Ten thousand dollars." It's a ridiculous amount, and technically not even true since I've never had to worry about planning a wedding in seven weeks before, but I'm hoping it will push her out the door.

"Okay." She pulls out her checkbook and sits down on the couch. While she scribbles, I shoot Erin a helpless glance. Rich kids. What is it about the word "no" that they don't understand?

"Here." Brooke's back in front of me before I know it, and she holds out a check. "I know what I'm asking you to do isn't easy. I know two months isn't long at all. I'm sorry for that, but there isn't really anything I can do. If the doctors were more confident..." She trails off. "It has to be this year." She gestures with the check. "Take it. Please."

I don't want to. But it's as if my hand has a brain of its own. I reach out and take the check between two fingers.

"Brooke, it's not a matter of the money," I say again.

"Just think about it," she begs. "Please."

"I can't—"

"My phone number is on the check," she informs me. "Give me a call." She shocks me by giving me a hug before she turns and heads for the door. Everett, with a final wordless look at me, grabs his beat-up and dripping leather coat from its hook and follows her out into the rain.

I deflate once they're gone. I don't even have any words.

"Well, I guess I'll call Ron and let him know to put the building up for rent," I say to fill the silence.

Probably not the best thing I could have said. Erin resembles a perky blonde hound dog right now, the way her mouth is turned down. She just shakes her head.

Oh, well. I'll do all I can for her. But really, there isn't anything else I *can* do. My mind's made up.

I head for the conference room and toss the check in the trash can on my way. It misses. I sigh. Even her freaking check won't take no for an answer. I bend down, pick it up, and almost fall over onto my butt when I see what's written on it.

Pay to the order of Silver Bells Wedding Designs, it says. *In the amount of twenty-five thousand dollars.*

5

"Is THIS A joke?" I demand.

"Not at all," says the irritatingly calm voice of the girl on the other end. "I told you I wanted to work with you."

"I quoted you ten thousand dollars."

"I know. And I also know you don't actually charge that much. But I'm still willing to pay more than double it."

"Clearly." I don't understand at all. Even a wedding planner in the heart of the trendiest neighborhoods in Philadelphia couldn't get away with charging ten grand just for the privilege of their service. If they tried charging twenty-five, they'd be laughed right out of business. I don't get it.

I fiddle with the corner of the check, rumpled now from being handled so much.

"I know it's short notice. I know I'm asking a lot. But I want you to do my wedding, Ms. Silver." Her tone is soft and pleading. And she makes me feel old. *Ms.* Silver? She makes me sound like a spinster librarian who only leaves her pile of books to go home and play with her nine cats before eating a bowl of cereal for dinner and falling asleep in front of *Masterpiece Theater*. Is that even still on?

"Is this how you get people to do what you want, then?" I can't help asking. "You throw money at them?"

She goes silent, and I immediately feel terrible. Seriously, why am I such a bitch? It isn't Brooke St. John's fault that my fiancé dumped me. It's not her fault that my sister might have a fourth miscarriage. And it's not her fault that the thought of planning *my* dream wedding for *her* makes me want to curl into a ball and ask someone to set me on fire.

"Not usually," she says at last. "But it got you to call me, didn't it?"

She has me there.

"Look, Ms. Silver—"

"Noelle, please," I interrupt. I can't take it. I'm only thirty. Way too young for *Ms.*

"Noelle. Hear me out. I completely understand that you want to be with your sister. I promise I do. My own brother is my best friend in the world, and I would never in a million years desert him if he needed me. I find it really admirable that you're willing to close down your business so you can help her. But please. Will is his mom's only child, and this would mean so much to both of them. She's waited long enough."

I swear I hear her sniffle.

"If she's that bad, will she even be able to travel? I don't mean to sound insensitive. If I'm going to work with you—and that doesn't mean I am—I need to know about any limitations or problems that might come up."

"We're hoping," she says. "She lives in Toronto. That's not exactly close, but much better than if she was in Vancouver or something. And if she ends up not being able to make the trip, we were hoping to set up some kind of livestream where she could watch it on her computer at home."

Well, she seems to have thought of everything.

"Please, Noelle." She's practically whispering. "With what you just told me about your sister, I know you know where we're coming from."

She's going to make me break. I can feel it.

"I'll pay you more. Thirty thousand. Thirty-five?"

"No!" I emit a nervous little laugh. "God. No. Even twenty-five thousand is way, *way* too much. It's insane."

"I know what I'm asking you to do," she says. And even though I wonder how that's possible, I get the feeling that she really does. "I know this won't be easy for you. Keep the check. Think of it as a retainer. From what I hear, you're worth it." I'm worth twenty-five grand? Who the hell told her that? And why isn't it on my Yelp page? "I promise I'll do everything I can to make this as painless as possible."

I bite my lip so hard it hurts, and I'm shocked I don't taste blood. Twenty-five thousand dollars is a lot of money. Too much. My work is difficult and stressful—especially when crunched into a time frame of less than two months, during the busiest time of the year—but not twenty-five thousand dollars difficult. I can't help feeling like it's a bribe. But why would she bribe *me*? I'm good at what I do. But there are plenty of others out there who do what I do, and do it just as well. Better, in some cases.

Still, that money could come in *really* handy. Even after I pay Erin her share. If I'm careful, it could support me for however long it might take to find a job back home. If I find a job quickly, it could be the down payment on a little house so I don't have to rent anything. In a house I can stomp around as loudly as I want without some popped-collar preppy banging on my floor.

I really don't want to take advantage of Brooke. I know what it's like to be accused of working with someone—or in my case, being with someone—just for the money. I wasn't with Drew for that reason, of course. In fact, the biggest reason I had for starting my own business was so I could be independent in case the need ever arose. I didn't want to end up like my mom, digging for change in the couch to take Kate and me to McDonald's for dinner.

I can make my own money. I don't need anyone else's.

Still ... twenty-five thousand dollars...

This, I guess, is what's known as a quandary.

Kate and her baby. Brooke, Will, and his dying mom. Drew and Heidi. My past. My future. So many reasons why I can't do this, but so many reasons why I should! What do I do?

"Noelle? Are you there?"

"I'm here." I suck in a breath and the words pretty much fall out of my mouth. "Okay. I'll do it."

Erin squeals like a cheerleader when I tell her my decision. "I knew you would. I'm so happy. And not just for me. Well, yeah, I'm happy to still have a job for the time being." Guilt scorches my face. "But I'm happier that you're doing it. This will be good for you. Wait and see."

"I hope you're right." I hold the phone to my ear with one hand and with the other scribble a list. *Venue. Food. Invitations. Wedding dress. Wedding party. Dresses, tuxes.* "I have no idea how I'm going to get this done in less than two months!"

"You will." Erin's confidence in me is a little unnerving. "If anyone can, you can." *Photographer. Videographer. DJ?*

"I'm going to need your help," I warn her. "Lots of it. Did you have plans to go to Florida to see your parents for Thanksgiving?"

Nobody ever accused Erin of not catching on. "I'll cancel them. I can always switch my plane ticket for the New Year."

"Thank you," I say, and hope she has an easier time breaking the news to them than I had with my own mother. As if I hadn't felt awful enough for putting Kate off for two months, my mom couldn't understand why I can't take a three-day weekend to drive the hundred miles to Blackton and have dinner and go Black Friday shopping. It's hard for my mom—she never remarried after my dad walked out, and Kate and I are the only family she has left. At least she felt better when I finally told her I was coming home for good after the holidays.

"So what's first on the agenda?" Erin asked.

"I already e-mailed Brooke a copy of the interview," I said. I tap my pen on my notebook, leaving tiny black dots all over my sloppily scribbled list. "She promised to have it back to me by tonight. She's coming to the office at nine tomorrow. I'm going to call around to a few venues to see if anyone has anything available for Christmas Eve." *That* should be easy.

"Okay," Erin says. "Want me to call a few dress shops to see if anyone can squeeze her in for an appointment?"

"That would be great. Thank you." *Tap tap tap.* "Make sure you let them know that it's Christmas Eve, and that there won't be months to mess around with alterations. They have to have a good selection already in the store. And if it has to be ordered, it needs to fit her when it gets here. I'll go through my binders, too, and try to come up with a few color schemes. Though that will be easier after I get her answers. I don't even know what colors she likes." *Tap.* "I'll spend a few hours going through old issues of *The Knot* looking for ideas. I have a feeling I'll be up late tonight."

"Is Everett coming back with her tomorrow?" Erin asks innocently. Too innocently. I have to laugh. "What?"

"Don't act like you have no idea," I tease her. "I saw you drooling over him this morning. Funny, I didn't think you went for scruffy. Or leather-jacket-wearing."

"I don't," she admits. "You know my type." Of course I do. Erin's been drooling over Brady Cole, a caterer we sometimes work with, since the first time she laid eyes on him. With his neat brown hair, clean-shaven jaw, and wholesome politeness, he is the polar opposite of the stubbly and sullen Everett St. John. Then again, Drew's a clean-cut pretty-boy with a ready smile. Too ready, I know now. Maybe an unkempt bad boy *is* the better option.

For Erin. Not for me. Biker or golden boy, it doesn't matter. I don't want either.

As promised, Brooke's interview, the one I give to all new brides so I can get ideas about their vision, appears in my inbox shortly after I force myself to make and eat a Caesar salad for dinner. It's been six days since Drew, and food still doesn't go down easily. Just something else to hate him for. I love food. If I wasn't a wedding planner, and if I had any innate culinary talent whatsoever, I might have been a chef. But since last Tuesday, everything I put in my mouth— whether I make it or not—tastes like I'm gnawing on a two-by-four.

Well, everything except wine. Chardonnay always tastes good.

I set my glass aside and click to open the attachment. The document fills my screen and I groan—none of the answers are shorter than a paragraph. But on second thought, that will probably help. If Brooke knows exactly what she wants, it'll cut down on a lot of the hemming, hawing, and "I don't know, what do you think?" that's typical of women who don't have a clue what they're doing when it comes to planning a wedding. The biggest problem will be finding everything she wants with practically no time to look for it.

I scan it, looking for answers to the most important questions first. I go weak with relief when I see that she doesn't plan to invite more than seventy people. That should make the daunting task of finding an available venue on Christmas Eve slightly less impossible. I highlight the essay Brooke's written about her dream gown—including the fact that she's aware she'll probably have to buy off-the-rack, and that she's fine with it—copy it and paste it into an e-mail for Erin. It should help her get started with dress shops. Then I print the whole file and slip it into a manila folder. I don't have the energy for the rest of it right now. Oh, I know I said I'd get on it right away. And I'd meant it. But now, faced with the New Testament-length document that is Brooke's description of her perfect wedding, I realize don't have it in me. Not tonight. I'll do it tomorrow.

"I'm sorry, Noelle," Dawn at the Springhollow Country Club says. "None of our rooms are available on Christmas Eve. We already have a wedding in the Diamond Hall, the banquet room is being renovated, and you know the mayor's family has Christmas Eve dinner in the Sapphire Hall every year."

"Yeah, I know." Damn it, the Sapphire Hall would have been the perfect size! "Thanks anyway, Dawn. Have a happy holiday." I end the call and draw a thick black line through *Springhollow Country Club,* then toss my pen down with such force it goes skittering across my dining room table. It rolls off and falls to the floor. I almost expect a warning thump from the floor below, but Mr. Popped Collar must have had an early tee time.

That's it, then. I'd known the country club would be a long shot, but it was my last shot too. I've exhausted every possible venue in a twenty-mile radius. Unless the Heiress to Springhollow wants to get married in a fire hall, that is.

Not that there's anything wrong with that. I've done a few perfectly beautiful weddings in the local fire hall. But somehow I don't think that's what someone like Brooke would have in mind. Still…

It'll be Christmas Eve. She can't get married outside, for God's sake. And I've already Googled both her and Everett to see if their houses are big enough to host a wedding. You'd think at least one of them would have been, considering they're millionaires. But it looks like Erin was right, and the St. Johns *aren't* flashy, because their houses are very much average-sized.

I go back into my files and find the number I'm looking for.

"Springhollow Fire Company!" an enthusiastic voice chirps.

"Hi. This is Noelle Silver from Silver Bells Wedding Designs—"

"Oh hi, Noelle! This is Amy Bunch."

"Hi, Amy!" I remember her. Mid-forties, tiny. "I'm hoping you can help me."

"I'll definitely try."

"I've got a wedding to plan. A small one, no more than seventy people. Is the hall available on Christmas Eve, by any chance?"

"Christmas Eve?" She sounds as incredulous as I felt when Erin told me.

"I know." I laugh a little. "They didn't give me much time."

"I'll say." On the other end I hear pages flipping. "Actually, wow. Yeah. You're in luck. We're free."

I go so weak with relief I almost drop my phone. "Oh my God thank you."

Amy laughs. "I'm guessing we were your last option?"

"I'm not going to lie. You were." We both laugh then. "It's nothing against fire hall weddings. You know that. It's just … she isn't exactly what you picture when you think of a fire hall bride."

"Is she local?"

"She is. Brooke St. John? Do you know her?"

Amy's surprised release of breath makes a harsh noise on the phone. "You've got to be kidding me. Brooke St. John? Getting married *here?*"

"I take it you do know her."

"You can't be Springhollow born and raised and *not* know her. It was a huge story about fifteen years ago. Haven't you heard it?"

"Bits and pieces. Her parents died in a fire." Only then does the horrible irony strike me. *Crap. What have I done? I can't ask her to get married in a fire hall!*

"They did. She was little, eight or nine. She was lucky her brother turned eighteen right afterward. Otherwise she'd have been shipped off somewhere. To relatives out west, if I remember right."

"Everett got custody?" That explains the protective vibe I get from him. He's more father than big brother. And Erin had said she was nine when her parents died. If Everett was almost eighteen, that makes Brooke twenty-three and him thirty-two.

Same as Drew. I wonder if they know each other.

"He did," Amy says. "Passed on college to stay with her."

A feeling I can't identify washes over me. Is it pity? Awe? "My friend told me some of that, but I accused her of watching too many soap operas."

"It's all true. And really sad."

"It is sad." I write *Springhollow Fire Hall* in my notebook, underneath the pile of black lines I already made. "Amy, thank you so much. You're a lifesaver."

"No problem. I'll e-mail over the contract in a few minutes."

"Perfect. Brooke's supposed to be at my office at nine. I'll have her sign it then." I glance at the clock. It's almost twenty to nine, and I need to get going. Erin should be there at any minute and Brooke shortly afterward. I'm not the praying type, but I shoot a quick request out to the universe that Brooke isn't totally horrified at the thought of having her dream wedding in a fire hall. I really wish I'd had the presence of mind to remember how her parents died, but it's too late now. And it's not like I had any other options.

Erin and Brooke are chatting like old buddies when I finally arrive at my office, strategically parking at the other end of the street so I don't have to walk past The Daily Grind and mourn again the loss of my favorite pre-work ritual. Brooke's hair is piled in a complicated-looking topknot, and I make a mental note to ask her how she did it even as I pat my own hair self-consciously, glad I took a few extra minutes with the curling iron and that the weather is cooperating to keep it under control.

"Good morning," I say as I hang my coat on the nearest hook. I took more care with my clothes this morning, too, ditching my stretched-out tee and yoga pants for black skinnies, button-down chambray, and boots. I even put on earrings. Erin looks relieved.

"You've got coffee?" I ask Brooke. She holds up her mug—we don't do Styrofoam at Silver Bells, and she's drinking from a mug shaped and painted like a pumpkin. Erin swaps the mug collection out every season. If I still drank coffee, I'd be sipping from my own ceramic gourd. I don't know where she finds them. But I'd be lying if I said I didn't kind of enjoy the eccentric charm they lend to the place.

"I do," she says.

"Great. I've got some information for you. Should we go back to the meeting room?" I sound short, a little angry. I'm not. Not at her, anyway. But I try to soften my tone. "Thanks for getting the interview back to me so quick. It was a big help."

"It's the least I could do," she says as she follows me to the back of the office. *No, offering me twenty-five thousand dollars is apparently the least you can do.* "I know what I'm asking of you is not going to be easy."

"Well, we've cleared the first hurdle." I gesture for Brooke to sit at the round wooden table. I take the seat across from her and take my notebook out of my tote. "I managed to secure a venue."

"That's great!" she exclaims. "I thought it would be a lot harder." Her cheeks go pink, and she looks so happy I almost can't tell her.

"It would have been. If—" Erin enters the room, distracting me, and slides into the seat next to mine. She opens her notebook and positions her pen over the page. The pink feather flutters like the world's most obnoxious flag.

"If?" Brooke prods.

I sigh. "If not for the Springhollow Fire Hall."

Erin's pen falls from her hand and makes a *thwap* as it lands on the notebook. I feel her eyes on me, but I won't look at her. I'm only watching Brooke and hoping her reaction isn't to flee into the street, sobbing at my lack of consideration for her personal situation. I wouldn't blame her if she did.

She doesn't.

"Great," she says. "I was there for a friend's baby shower not too long ago. It's a nice room."

A sigh of relief I hadn't even known I was holding comes hissing out of me, making Erin's feather pen dance like it's had a few too many Red Bull and vodkas.

"It is," I say. "I've done weddings there before, and when it's decorated, it's beautiful. It *will* be beautiful, I promise. You won't even know where you are. Once we settle on a color scheme, we can start talking about flowers and lights and place settings—"

"Sorry I'm late," a male voice interrupts. All three of us look up to see Everett in the doorway. He's not dressed in Hell's Angel chic today but in black jeans and a black-and-gray striped sweater like a normal, albeit gloomy, early-thirtysomething guy. "Again. You've got to start making these meetings later. I haven't seen 9 A.M. since high school."

"Sorry," Brooke says. "But guess what? Noelle found a venue. The fire hall's free. That's where the wedding will be."

He's halfway to the last empty chair and stops dead. He looks at her, and then at me, like we're crazy.

"Isn't that great?" she prompts him. I could be wrong, but it sounds like she's injected a fair amount of warning into her tone.

Beside me, Erin is doodling frantically in the margins of her notebook. She doesn't look up.

And I feel awful. How could I possibly ask them to do this? I'm a terrible person. I should just hand the check back now.

"Oh, it's great," he finally says before dropping into his chair. "Fantastic. I'm sure it'll be perfect."

I can't look at him. This is horrible. I don't want to hurt them, but I don't have much of a choice. I can't let personal situations get in the way of planning the perfect wedding.

As much as I wish things could be different, I have a job to do.

6

ONE STEP. Then a second. Then a third. That's all. I just have to move my feet. One in front of the other. I can do it—I've been doing it since I was ten months old. I was a pretty young walker. Talker, too. My mom always said that I completely bypassed the baby talk stage, that I was speaking in full sentences before I was a year old. She'd thought I was a genius. That I'd grow up to be a physicist or something. Probably not a wedding planner. And definitely not a wedding planner whose own wedding crashed and burned. She'd never say a word, but I can't help but wonder how disappointed she is at the failure I've turned out to be. Thirty years old and suddenly single, pushed over for someone younger, perhaps slightly prettier, who's probably around all the time.

My breath catches in my throat. There's a roaring sound in my ears. What causes that? I've always wondered. Each booted foot feels like an ornery child has wrapped himself around it and is trying to keep me from getting anywhere. It's damn near impossible to trudge up the sidewalk to the entrance of the fire hall. But I have to, because Brooke and Everett and I are meeting with Amy Bunch today, and trying to figure out how we're going to turn the room where the majority of Springhollow's old ladies play Bingo on Friday nights into a room suitable for Brooke's dream wedding.

A cold wind whips a hunk of hair into my mouth, and I pull my rust-colored peacoat closer. How does it feel like the dead of winter when glorious, sunny autumn was only a few days ago? The air's raw. The sun's gone, and stark black branches claw at the gray-white sky like they're trying to bring it back. Everything's colorless, drawn. Looking around me is like looking in the mirror.

"Noelle!" calls a melodic female voice. I turn from where I've planted myself in the middle of the sidewalk and see Brooke approaching, Everett trailing a few feet behind her. Against the backdrop of gray and darker gray Brooke is almost blinding. Golden hair topped by a pine green beret, a coffee-colored trench over mustard-yellow pants flowing into flowered rain boots. Anyone else would look like a box of crayons in that getup, or a kid whose mother finally gave in and allowed her to pick out her own clothes. Brooke looks like a walking Burberry ad.

Everett's usual monochromatism lets her shine. Although closer inspection reveals that his jeans today are dark blue, not black.

He gives me a curt nod when he sees me looking. Brooke envelops me in a hug, as if we've known each other for years instead of days.

"Are you sure you're okay with this?" I ask her. "I mean, with your parents."

"It's absolutely fine," she says with a small smile. "I knew going in that my options were going to be seriously limited. And I know it's the best you could do, and that once we're inside it won't feel like a—what it is. So yeah. I'm all right with it."

From the looks of it, though, Everett's not. A quick glance reveals that his eyes are narrowed, flicking between his sister, me, and the looming "Springhollow Fire Hall" sign that hangs over the entrance. I may be imagining it, but it looks like a spasm of pain contorts his face for a split second.

I want him to know that I'm sorry, that I didn't have any other choice. If it were up to me, Brooke's wedding would be in the country club's Diamond Hall, with its pendant fan vaulted ceiling that makes it look like some European Gothic church. But Everett doesn't look as if he'd be receptive to an apology. His arms are crossed over his chest, his spine rigid, his mouth closed. So I don't say a word. It's not like I think telling him I'm sorry will make him forget what happened to his parents, so why bother?

"Well," I say when the silence becomes too awkward for any other words. "Let's go in."

Amy waits for us at a round table in the office, a binder open in front of her. She springs to her feet when she sees us. With her short red hair and green sweatshirt plastered with Christmas stocking and snowman appliqués, she looks like an elf on leave from the toy factory.

"Hi!" she gushes as she approaches Brooke with an expression that suggests she wouldn't be half as excited if she were meeting the Virgin Mary herself. "Brooke? I'm Amy Bunch. It's such a pleasure to meet you."

"It's a pleasure to meet you, too," Brooke says. "I'm so sorry that Will couldn't be here. But this is my brother, Everett. He's the best man, and he's standing in."

Amy's face goes a bit dreamy when she looks at him, and there's no doubt that he notices. He probably gets it all the time. He coolly takes the hand Amy offers and shakes it.

"Hello," he says. He's friendly but makes no effort to flirt with her. Her face falls a little. So little I think no one notices but me. I'm trained to pick up on that stuff. All it takes is one unnoticed raised eyebrow to ruin a wedding—that raised eyebrow could signify that the bride is giving serious thought to slipping out a dressing room window. If I don't catch it, I can't fix it.

"Should we get to work?" I suggest. "We've only got seven weeks."

"Oh, of course!" To her credit, Amy doesn't let disappointment stand in the way of business. Maybe I could learn from her.

She leads us back to her table. The four of us fit around it comfortably. At least I *would* be comfortable if I wasn't next to Everett. The hostility is just rolling off him, and I have to wonder what exactly I did to make him hate me. Is it really the fire hall thing? If so, I completely understand, but he *has* to realize that I had no other options. And his sister seems okay with it. Shouldn't that be what matters?

As if you would know anything about what it's like to be in his place. Your parents are still alive. Your father walked out on you, but at least he isn't dead. Let it go. Just do your job.

So I do. At least, I try.

But then it occurs to me that aside from the horrifically ironic fact that his sister has no choice but to get married in a fire hall, he might believe he has a real reason to not like me. I mean, Brooke's paying me twenty-five thousand dollars. I don't know and wouldn't presume to know anything about how much money they have and how it's distributed between them, but that's a pretty big chunk. Does he think I'm taking advantage of her?

It's a sickening thought. And the worst part is that I'm not even sure he's wrong. As uncomfortable as I am with the amount written on that check, I'm already mentally spending the money. If that doesn't mean I'm taking advantage of her…

Well, now I feel like I need a shower.

That's not possible at the moment, so instead I try to forget that the best man hates me and focus on my bride and what she wants. And I have to say that Brooke St. John, despite giving me the shortest time frame I've ever had to work with, is pretty much the easiest bride I can remember helping. So far, anyway. She knows exactly what she wants, oohs and ahhs over the photos Amy shows her of previous weddings, and chooses the color scheme I'd been silently praying she would—blue in shades of sapphire and ice, with white and silver accents. Amy promises round, elegant tables covered in snowy white linens.

"I'm not sure if I want floral centerpieces," Brooke muses. "They're pretty, but sort of predictable."

"We can do this." I take out my own binder and flip to a page I've looked at least a zillion times, since I wanted it for myself.

"See? Instead of flowers, we can do these tall glass vases and fill them with Christmas balls," I offer. "If you want."

She pulls my binder closer and stares at the page. "I love it!" she exclaims. "We could do silver and white on the guests' tables, and maybe blue at the bridal table."

See? Easy.

Except my heart still thumps in a nervous staccato. I can barely keep my eyes off my left hand and the slightly paler stripe of skin where my engagement ring once was. The tips of my ears are on fire, and I'm finding it a little difficult to get in a good breath. My brain knows that I'm here for Brooke, but the rest of me seems unable to believe I'm not here discussing my own wedding. *This should be me and Drew sitting here.* Not Brooke and Everett.

I watch Everett beside me as he leans over my binder with Brooke, listening carefully as she weighs the pros and cons of different flower combinations and possible lighting setups. He points to a picture of an ice sculpture and murmurs something that makes her laugh, but I don't hear what it is because my attention is on his fingers. They're long and slender, but the nails are short and jagged, as if he prefers his teeth to scissors. Drew's hands were square and masculine, the nails even with smooth edges. My emery boards were constantly going missing, and I suspected it was because he stole them.

Whatever Brooke says back makes Everett laugh, too. His laugh is dark and husky. He doesn't have dimples like Drew. In fact, there's nothing little-boyish about him. His face is an oval, with a jaw obscured by dark stubble that probably hasn't seen a razor in oh, four or five days. His hair's a little too long, too. It's almost black, with the type of curls that make it look like he has a hell of a time controlling it. Maybe that's why he keeps it too long. He keeps tucking it behind his ears, only to have it spring free within seconds. I'm half-tempted to offer him the hair tie in my pocket.

Guys in Springhollow don't look like Everett St. John. Drew and all of his friends are clean-cut and sporty. Any one of them could have modeled for J. Crew. Everett looks like he belongs on the cover of *Guitar World*.

"What do you think, Noelle?"

Brooke's voice jolts me back to awareness, and I guiltily realize I have no idea what she's asking me about.

"I think…" I squint to see the page open in front of her. It's an enormous Christmas tree wrapped in white lights. "I think it might be a little big for the room."

Everett folds his arms and sits back. Brooke's gaze, when I force myself to meet it, is full of pity.

Great. She knows. Everyone in town must be talking about how I was dumped.

"I agree," she says as my face flames. "Amy says they'll have their own tree. Smaller than this one. Do you think I should keep it? Or will it take up too much room?"

I sit up straighter. *This is your last wedding. Do it right. Don't let yourself get distracted.*

"I think it'll be fine," I say. "You're only having seventy people, and that's if everyone RSVP's yes. It'll be tucked away in the corner, right, Amy?"

"Right."

"It'll be fine," I repeat. "Keep it."

"Okay." Brooke flips the page. The next one is a list of possible cocktails. I would go with the snowflake martini, if it was my wedding. But it's not.

Everett leans forward again to look at the page with her. He stretches one arm out to point at something electric blue and served in a Collins glass. The arm is wrapped in the sleeve of a charcoal gray sweater. I wonder why he doesn't wear color. Drew likes color. He has button-down shirts in almost every shade sold at Express, except for anything yellow. He hates yellow. So does Everett, it seems. Yellow, and green, and red and orange and white and possibly brown and blue, except when it's jeans.

He senses my attention and possibly even my judgment. He has to. What other explanation is there for the way his gaze suddenly shoots up and meets mine? He isn't smiling anymore. Heat seeps from the tips of my ears to flood my cheeks. He probably thinks I was checking him out. Well, I wasn't. He's gorgeous, but so not my type, even if I was looking. Which I'm not.

In fact, who knows? Drew might be outside waiting for me right now. It's been a week. Maybe he *has* come to his senses. One week of Heidi, undiluted by time spent with me, has to have been enough for him to see reason. He's probably standing on the sidewalk, having called the shop and found out from Erin that I'm here. He's got a bouquet of purple orchids in one hand, because he knows they're my favorite and they've always worked at softening me after a fight, and in his other hand is the engagement ring I just mailed back over the weekend despite both Kate's and Erin's insistence that I sell it.

"I was wrong," he'll say. "You have no idea. She's not what I want. You are, Noe. You always have been."

My heart gives a little thump of anticipation. I can't help it.

Those hopes are dashed, of course, when we leave Amy after about an hour and a half. There are no repentant fiancés on the sidewalk with flowers and jewelry, begging to be forgiven and taken back. And even though I know it's stupid, I feel like my heart's breaking all over again. I saw it so clearly.

"What do you have going on this afternoon?" I ask Brooke, forcing myself to shake off the tragic little reverie I've created for myself. "We should get started talking about invitations."

"I have rehearsal at four, but I'm free until then."

I glance at my watch, the one Drew gave me for my last birthday that makes my heart hurt whenever I check the time but with which I can't seem to part just yet. It's early, just about noon, and I have a few things to go over with Erin in preparation for the Fantana wedding this weekend. It's the first one she'll be doing alone and she's terrified.

"Can you come to the shop around one? I'll buy lunch." I probably won't eat it, but I don't mind treating her.

"Sure," she says. "Oh! I meant to say something earlier, but I forgot. I think you and Everett should have each other's phone numbers. Will is out of touch so often, and I've got rehearsals like crazy coming up. Ev can speak for me. He knows what I want."

I glance at him. His hands are stuffed into his jeans pockets, his shoulders hunched to ward off the cold—or maybe me. He doesn't like me. It's obvious.

"Okay," I say, reluctantly.

He shrugs.

We exchange cellphones and type in each other's contact information. I give him my full name, cell and office numbers, and e-mail address. When I get my phone back, I just drop it into my bag without looking. He probably gave me a fake number, anyway.

E.S.J. 610-555-4617.

He couldn't even be bothered to type his full name.

"Asshole," I mutter, and shove the phone into the pocket of my coat before hanging it on the hook by the office door.

"Who? Me?" Erin asks.

"No. Everett St. John." I bite off the words as sharply and as quickly as I would bite the stems from the broccoli my mother forced me to eat as a kid—swallowing them fast, so the taste couldn't register in my mouth. "He hates me. I have no idea why."

"He may be having a hard time with Brooke getting married," Erin says. "You saw the guest list. They have almost no family. She's all he has."

"It's not my fault," I grumble. "She's the one getting married. I'm just helping."

"He's not going to get mad at her."

"Well, he shouldn't be mad at *me*."

"I'm sure he doesn't hate you. He just doesn't know who else to take it out on. He'll come around. I bet he feels like he's losing her, and you're the easiest target. It can't be easy for him. He must feel like he has no one left."

I imagine the list of guests and attendants Brooke showed me and remember that it took up only a single page. Two columns, but still. Erin's right, again. In addition to her business acumen Erin has a great talent for making me feel about as big as an ant. And not even one of those black carpenter ants that are an inch long. Nope. More like a regular sidewalk ant. The kind you don't even notice when you step on them and squash them.

So I lack empathy. Let's add another fault to the ever-growing list of reasons why Drew left me.

"Are you ready for Saturday?" I ask. Anything to change the subject and to veer my mind from the direction in which it insists on heading.

"No."

"Shut up. You'll do great. Here, look. I made you a minute-by-minute itinerary." And with that, my attention is sufficiently diverted.

By one o'clock Erin is as ready as she'll ever be for her first wedding without me, has left to pick up lunch (under strict instructions *not* to get it from The Daily Grind, although I miss their turkey, apple, and cheddar panini almost as much as I miss their croissants), and Brooke is back. She's changed into black leggings and an oversized sweatshirt, her hair in a ponytail and sneakers on her feet. I remember that she mentioned something about being in rehearsal and realize I have no idea what she meant.

"Are you an actress?" I ask her. The town has its own theater and puts on plays several times a year.

"No," she says. "A dancer. Well, a dance studio owner. You know Art in Motion, on Cambridge? That's mine."

"I drive by there all the time!" I love ballet. I did it as a kid and think about taking it up again even though now, at thirty, there's no way anything will come of it.

"We do *The Nutcracker* every Christmas," Brooke explains. "And I know I'm a crazy person for putting on a ballet *and* getting married at the same time, but when we found out about Will's mom…"

"I understand," I assure her when she trails off. "Don't worry about anything. Concentrate on your show. That's why you have me."

Even though I am *so* not in the right headspace to be planning a wedding. But I can't help the words as they come. Turns out I like Brooke. Even if she wasn't paying me twenty-five grand, I'd want to step up for her.

If I wasn't leaving Springhollow at the end of all this, I might even enroll at her dance studio.

Three o'clock arrives, and we've not only eaten salads that Erin brought back but gone through every page of the catalog I get from the stationer in town. Brooke has chosen the exact design I would have, if I were the one planning a Christmas wedding instead of the one lamenting a broken engagement.

"Okay," I say, after we've gone over the details a dozen times to make sure everything is right. "I'll send the order right away. They'll still take about three weeks, but they'll be beautiful."

"I trust you," Brooke says with an easy smile.

It surprises me, how easy it is to smile back at her.

Until she's gone, and Erin is staring at me with an expression that's a weird mixture of pity and fear. She tucks her hair behind her ears, fiddles with the cuff of her magenta sweater. Classic Erin-is-nervous moves.

"What?" I ask. "Are you still worried about Saturday? Please don't be. You're going to be great."

"It's not that. I wish it was." She sighs. "I debated whether to tell you this. But you're going to find out anyway. And I'd rather you find out from someone who cares about you than from the *Talker*."

My heartbeat stumbles and my ears get hot. Again. They've only just started to cool off!

"What?" But my throat's gone dry, and it sounds more like a puff of air than a word.

"Before I went to get lunch, I stopped at the jeweler, to see if the rings for the Fantana wedding are ready." She swallows hard—I see the muscles in her throat contract. "Drew was there."

"Oh." I instinctively move my left thumb to rub at my ring finger and cringe when it meets bare skin. Will I ever get used to that? "I mailed him my engagement ring. I'm sure he was selling it back." It's sweet of her to be so concerned.

"I don't think so." Erin comes out from behind her desk. "He was talking to a saleslady. He didn't see me."

My heart starts to thump harder while I wait for her to finish her story.

"He might have been trading in the ring."

Trading it in? For what?

"I don't think Heidi will know what to do with a necklace that didn't come off a fixture near the register at Forever 21." A feeble joke.

"He wasn't buying a necklace." She takes a step toward me. "Noelle, I heard him tell the saleslady that he was going to propose to Heidi."

"Oh." My heart's not thumping anymore. I think it stopped. "Really?" My eyes are on fire, and through vision blurred with a sudden onslaught of tears I see that Erin's wrapped her arms around herself. Why is she doing that? Why does she need comfort? I'm the one whose ex-fiancé is buying a new engagement ring barely a week after ending his last engagement. I'm the one who should be hugging myself. Or at least making it look like I'm hugging myself while I try to keep everything—my heart, my guts—from spilling out of the huge hole that's been torn in me.

Drew is proposing to Heidi.

He's really not coming back.

I hiccup, and with that tiny movement of diaphragm into lungs, the agony pours out.

7

IT'S FRESH, RAW—like it was the first day. Like the entire past week didn't happen. But this time, instead of collapsing to the floor, I run to the bathroom in the back of the office and pull the door shut behind me. Erin tries to follow, but I lock myself in. After a few minutes her knocks subside and she stops calling for me. I grip the sink with both hands and force myself to look in the mirror.

I'm hideous. There's no denying that. Red, swollen eyes. Puffy cheeks. I'm in desperate need of some lip balm. My chest simultaneously aches and feels hollow, and my legs are spaghetti-ish, like I just ran a 10K without all the insane prep work that usually goes into it. Drew and I are really over. I know that now, and it somehow makes this bout of grief feel even more painful than the first. But there's something else buried in there, too. Beneath it. Some kind of weird, hidden … I don't know what to call it. Strength? Not that I feel strong. No, I feel like if I wasn't clutching this sink for dear life I'd slither right to the floor. Maybe determination is the better word. Determination to keep Drew from discovering what a mess he's made of me, of my life and my future. Determination to keep him from knowing exactly how deeply he hurt me. And what better way to do that than to fully commit to throwing Brooke St. John the wedding of the century?

It takes some time but the tears slow to a trickle before stopping altogether. I splash my face with cold water and, when that doesn't work, wet a paper towel and press it to my cheeks and forehead. I dig an old Chapstick from my pocket and slide it over my lips. Strings of hair cling to my damp face, so I pull it back. I straighten my sweater over my jeans and allow myself just a moment to be grateful that I'd purchased the rich plum color rather than my usual black or brown. It really is a flattering color when my face doesn't resemble a half-ripe tomato.

I take a deep, shaky breath, turn, and open the bathroom door. I half-expect Erin to be standing there wringing her hands. She's not. I find her back at her desk, phone receiver in hand, fingers poised over the keypad as if she's about to dial someone.

She must hear me, because she puts the receiver back in its cradle and turns to me.

"Are you okay?" I can tell she means to sound comforting, but doubt permeates her tone. I don't blame her.

"No," I tell her. "Would you be?"

"No," she admits.

"But I appreciate what you did. Thank you. You were right. I would much rather have heard it from you." I try to smile. It must look terrifying. "If I had to hear it at all." I gesture to the phone. "Who were you calling?"

"I was going to call Brooke," Erin stammers. "To tell her that she might be dealing with me more than you. I didn't know if you'd be up to handling the rest of the planning. I'm sorry if I overstepped." Her face is hot pink.

"It's okay." At least she wasn't calling Brooke to tell her that Silver Bells couldn't do her wedding at all. "But I'm fine. It's fine. I can do it."

"Are you sure? I really don't mind. I mean, I know I've only ever assisted you, but if I do well at the Fantana wedding—"

"You'll do great at the Fantana wedding," I assure her. "But I need to do this. Mostly for myself, but also for Drew. I don't want him to have the satisfaction of knowing how much power I gave him over me." Not yet, anyway. He'll figure it out soon enough, once I'm gone.

"Okay." She smiles at me. It's tentative, and I can see she doesn't really believe me, but at least she's willing to humor me.

I'll prove her wrong, though.

I hope.

🔔

"So how are you feeling?"

"Good! I'm good," my sister says, and I imagine her on the other side of the phone, standing in her sunny little kitchen with her hand resting on the slight curve of her belly. "I had a doctor's appointment yesterday, and she said everything looks normal. Perfect, even."

"That's great," I say, and mean it. "Did you find out what it is? A boy or a girl?"

"Nope."

"Are you serious?" I screech. "How can you stand the suspense? I'd have to know immediately. There's a lot of planning that goes into a nursery, you know."

"I do know," Kate replies. Crap. Of course she does—she's done it three times, only to be left with an empty crib.

"Kate, I'm sorry."

"Don't be. Sometimes I forget, too. Well, no. Forget isn't really the right word. They're always in the back of my mind. I guess I've just learned how to compartmentalize. You know? Each one has their own little place, and if I don't focus on it, it's easier to make it through the day. I guess it helps that I never actually got to know them or see their faces." She pauses. "Does that make me sound horrible?"

"No." And I'm not lying to make her feel better. "It makes you sound strong."

"Well, I don't know about that." She laughs a little. "We all have to figure out ways to get through the day. Speaking of that, how are you?"

I debate telling her about Drew and his big purchase. Can I stomach any more sympathy, no matter how well-meaning? Then again, this is my sister. We never had the sibling rivalry thing that a lot of kids do. We fought on occasion, usually over things like whose turn it was to play with the Barbie whose foot had been gnawed to oblivion by our dog, Waffles. But when the going got tough, we were there for each other.

"Noe? You there?"

Barely. I sigh. "I'm here. Drew is, um, apparently proposing to Heidi." The words sneak past the lump that suddenly materializes in my throat. I close my eyes to ward off the inevitable tears.

"What?" Now it's Kate's turn to screech.

"Yeah. Erin saw him in a jewelry store. Trading in the ring he gave me for something for *her*." Something gaudy and cheap-looking, I have to assume.

"You should have kept your ring. He ended the engagement, not you. You weren't obligated to return it."

"Well, I didn't want to keep it!" I glance at my hand. Yup, the pale stripe is still there. Why couldn't Drew have dumped me in July, so I could hurry up and tan the bare spot away? "What would I have done with it?"

"Sold it! I'm sure it was worth a lot. You could have gotten enough money for it that you could come home now, rather than hanging around to do the Poor Little Rich Girl's wedding."

"I'm actually glad I decided to do Brooke's wedding," I tell her. "She's great. If I wasn't leaving town, we might stay friends after the whole thing's over. And she's practically a celebrity here. I figure there's no better way to stick it to Drew than to show him I can plan a wedding for a famous person."

"Hmm."

"What?"

"Well, if you really wanted to stick it to him, wouldn't you stay in Springhollow? You know, to show him that he can't chase you away?"

She has a point. Staying in town would probably confuse him more than me doing an awesome wedding just before running away, never to be seen again. But can I stay? Especially now that I know that he's proposing to Heidi? Drew is one of Springhollow's Golden Boys. His wedding will make almost as much news as Brooke's. I should know—he'd warned me, back when I was going to be the bride.

"Maybe," I say. "I guess I'm kind of hoping that the guilt of running me out of town eats away at him until he's a decrepit old man on his deathbed wondering how he got stuck with a wife whose boobs are bigger than her brain when he could have had me. And my B-cups."

Kate laughs. "B-cup chest, triple-D brain."

"I don't know. Maybe you're right. I just don't know if I can stick around here. Springhollow's a small town. I'm bound to run into them. A lot."

"I get it," Kate says. "Don't get me wrong. I can't wait for you to come back home. And Mom's already planning your homecoming party. But I want you to be sure that you're doing the right thing for you. I don't want you coming home if there's a shred of doubt in your mind. You have a life there. I don't want you to end up regretting the decision to leave it behind."

"I have a business here," I counter. "That's all. Businesses close every day, and the earth keeps spinning. Drew was my life here." Pathetic, huh? "Without him I have no reason to stick around. Anyway, I'm not *really* running away from him. I'm coming home to help you. Remember?"

"Okay." She won't argue with me. "At least you'll be home next Christmas."

"And I'll have a niece or nephew I can spoil." Despite everything I can't help smiling. My life is actually pretty good, considering. I may have crappy taste in fiancés, but at least I'll always have my family.

Saturday afternoon I drive to meet Brooke at Blush, the trendy bridal shop at the end of Main Street opposite my office. It's only November fifth, but already the Victorian-style lampposts lining the sidewalk are dressed in wreaths and twinkling light-up snowflakes. It's a windy, gray day, and if Drew hadn't completely destroyed Christmas for me, I'd be excited. But I'm not. Instead, I'm sort of pissed. I'm just not sure who I'm pissed *at*. Drew for ruining my favorite time of the year? Or the town planners and TV stations for decorating and airing Christmas commercials, respectively, without taking into account the fact that this will be my worst Christmas ever?

"Stop trying to one-up Thanksgiving!" I reproach the red-bowed wreath that hangs over my parking space. A little kid in a puffy coat and knit hat turns from his mom, who's stuffing envelopes—probably Christmas cards—into the mailbox and stares at me.

Great. Now I'm yelling at inanimate objects. Which stage of grief is that again?

I turn into the wind and hurry toward the shop, away from the judgmental eyes of first-graders.

Blush is blissfully warm and softly lit. Under any other circumstances I'd be enchanted by all the ruffles and bows, georgette and lace, rhinestones and pearls. Instead my throat gets tight. My hands tremble on the end of my noodly arms. My legs feel a little weak and—yup, there go my ears, burning like Yule logs. The sound system plays a delicate string-quartet version of "Let it Snow."

I can't breathe. The edges of my vision darkens.

Am I having a panic attack? A heart attack?

I want, more than anything, to turn and run right out of there. Before I faceplant onto the lush ivory carpet.

"Hello," says a voice. "May I help you?"

No. Not unless you're a licensed therapist with the ability to prescribe medication. Strong medication.

I turn to face the register, where an impeccably dressed, dark-haired woman about my mother's age wears an expectant smile. She must be new. I've been here at least a dozen times, and we clearly don't recognize each other. I swallow hard, testing the muscles of my throat to see if they're too paralyzed to let me speak.

"I'm Noelle Silver," I manage to say. "My client, Brooke St. John, has a three o'clock appointment?"

"Oh, yes. Miss St. John is already here. Follow me, please."

I force a smile. "I know the way. Thanks."

I hobble on legs that feel like water balloons to the rear of the store, where Brooke stands at a rack of dresses, her back to me. She traces a dreamy finger down the lacy bodice of a full-skirted ball gown.

"Hi," I say. "Sorry I'm late."

She turns to me. "You're not! I was early. Rehearsal went well, so I came here right from the studio. Darcy went to grab a few more dresses. I showed her some pictures of gowns I like. I hope you don't mind?"

"Of course not. You should have exactly what you want. I'm only here to make recommendations. And make sure you don't get ripped off." I drop my bag on the overstuffed couch against the wall. I should go over to her, look at dresses with her, but I honestly don't think I can. So I press my back to the wall, trying to avert my eyes from the clouds of white and ivory in front of me.

No easy task, in a shop that sells nothing but wedding dresses.

Darcy arrives in a sea of tulle and lace. I've worked with her before, and she's good—I don't doubt that she already has Brooke's dream dress in her arms. That bodes well for me, too. It means I'll be out of here sooner, back home in flannel pajamas with a cup of tea and anything but a Christmas movie on the television.

"Hello, Noelle!" she sings as she hangs the gowns on a rack. "How are you?"

"Doing well, thanks, Darcy," I respond even as I wonder if she knows. We'd spoken a few times about me getting in there to browse the dress selection for myself. Clearly, that's not going to happen now.

"Really? Even with a mere seven weeks to plan the wedding of the decade?" Darcy gives Brooke a conspiratorial wink, and Brooke laughs.

"She's handling it like the pro she is," Brooke says. I manage a weak smile.

"I wouldn't expect anything less." Darcy hangs the last gown, and Brooke moves to the rack.

"These are all beautiful." She sighs.

From the safety of my vantage point against the wall, I can already tell that she's right. I might have imagined Brooke as a summery, casual beach bride the first time I saw her, but there's no doubt in my mind that she'll be equally able to pull off the sleek elegance required of a holiday wedding.

"Why don't we start with these?" Darcy suggests. She removes three gowns from the rack and takes them into the dressing room. "Just holler if you need help."

"I will!" Brooke disappears behind the glossy white door, and I'm left alone with Darcy.

I'm wincing before she can even open her mouth, which she does almost immediately.

"Noelle, honey, I'm sorry," she says. "I saw Drew's mother at the bank, and she told me. What a slime."

I shrug. I don't want to do this now. "It wasn't meant to be, I guess." My throat aches. It seems the lump has decided to take up permanent residence.

"You're better off. And honey, it's so brave of you to be doing this for Brooke. I don't know if I could. I think I'd just want to crawl into a hole and never come out again. I can't believe how strong you are. I really admire you."

Strong? I'd laugh if I wasn't so close to tears. Obviously she can't see that I'm practically gasping for air, that the pristine white wall behind me is solely responsible for the fact that I'm even upright. I must be a better actress than I thought.

"Thank you," I mumble.

Darcy gives me one of those smiles that are usually reserved for consoling people who have just buried a loved one.

I'm starting to feel a bit nauseated when Brooke emerges from her dressing room, a vision in layers of satin and lace. Not exactly the distraction I need, but it'll have to do.

"What do you think?" she asks, and I hear the nerves in her voice.

"Sweetie, you're breathtaking," Darcy says. "Come on over and step up here." She gestures to the stool that's perched in the middle of the triple-mirror setup. Brooke complies, lifting the full skirt, and stares at herself.

"I look like a bride," she whispers.

She really does. I close my eyes, take a deep breath, count to five.

"It's beautiful." And I mean it. "But I don't know if it's you."

"What do you mean?" Brooke twists in the mirror, hindering Darcy's ability to fasten the seed pearl buttons that go up the back.

"It's a little too common." Darcy straightens up, mouth full of pins, and raises an eyebrow at me over her tortoiseshell-rimmed glasses. "Sorry, Darcy. I didn't mean that as an insult. It's absolutely gorgeous. But it looks like something you'd see on any bride, anywhere at any time. There's nothing really special about it."

"Yeah, you might be right," Brooke says. "I don't know if I'm feeling the princess skirt." She lifts a handful of the skirt, then lets it drop.

"I'm not feeling it," I say. "I know I've only met you a few times, but I've taken note of your style. It's part of my job. I think you'd be happier in something a little more unexpected."

"So no ball gowns?" Darcy asks.

"I don't think so. But it's up to Brooke." I glance at her, and she shakes her head.

"I agree with Noelle. No ball gowns."

"Okay." Darcy goes to the rack and separates a good portion of full-skirted dresses from the rest of the bunch, leaving a collection of sleeker, more fitted gowns. "Let's get you into some of these."

The fashion show continues. Brooke's a knockout in each of them, yet we both manage to find something not quite right. The color isn't white enough; the buttons are spaced too far apart. The neckline is too high or too low; the skirt is too full or too binding and makes it hard to walk. Someone with Brooke's money could easily find a dress she liked and have it altered into something that's exactly what she wants, but with the time crunch, she says she'd rather not do that. Too much room for something to go wrong at the last minute.

I can tell she's starting to panic, though. The rack Darcy filled with gowns is getting dangerously empty.

"Don't worry," I tell her softly as I button up the back of one of the last dresses. "There are other shops around."

I fasten the last button and give her a little push toward the mirrors. As she situates herself on the stool I pull out my phone and start to tap out a note to call Happily Ever After, the bridal shop in the next town over. A few seconds later I realize I haven't heard a sound. I look up and see Brooke's stunned reflection in the mirror in front of her.

"Wow," she says softly. Darcy's grinning. And despite the little thrill of envy that vibrates through me, I have to admit it. The dress is absolutely perfect.

It's fitted but not too tight, hugging her through the hips where it falls into a skirt that skims her legs and flares into a soft bell at the knees. The scalloped boatneck collar emphasizes her delicate collarbone, and a band of white and silver circles her narrow waist. Its long sleeves skim her arms to the wrist where, like the skirt, they flare out and cover her hands to the first knuckle. The entire thing is made of elaborate white lace over a lining of sheer fabric. It's gorgeous. I can't believe we wasted so much time when the perfect dress was hanging there all along.

"That's it," I tell her. The grin on her face, reflected in the mirror, tells me she agrees.

The three of us are so entranced by the vision in front of us, the one that looks like a magazine page come to life, that I almost don't notice that someone's joined us.

Almost.

8

BROOKE'S EYES LIGHT up, and she whirls around. "Everett!"

He's silent, his eyes on his sister. Not in a creepy way, but in a way that suggests he can't really believe what he's seeing. His gaze rakes over her, from her messy bun to the plum-painted toenails just barely visible beneath the hem of the gown.

In the mirror I watch him. His jaw flexes just a bit, and I doubt anyone notices. His Adam's apple slides up and back down as he swallows. My muscles coil in defense before he can even say anything. If he dares to ruin this for her—well, he's going to hear about it, at least. It's not like I think I could take him in a fistfight.

"You look beautiful," he says. He clears his throat. "You look like Mom."

The tension flows out of me, leaving me feeling weak. Brooke blinks fast. The telltale glisten of tears sparkles in her eyes. Darcy must feel like she's intruding on some tender family moment because she busies herself by gathering and taking the rejected gowns back to whatever rack she found them on. I wish I could go with her.

"Thank you," Brooke says. She clears her own throat, gestures to the large bag in Everett's hand, the one I hadn't noticed until now. "You brought it?"

"Yeah." He walks over and hands it to her. "It took me a while to find it, but it's in perfect condition."

As carefully as if she was dealing with an original copy of the Bible, Brooke reaches into the bag and withdraws a white cloud of something. She takes one end carefully between her fingers, lifts her arm over her head, and lets the other end unroll into a blanket of delicate netting.

It's a veil.

"It was my mom's," she explains. "It's from the eighties, but I don't think it's too dated. Do you?"

"Let's see." I take the veil gingerly between my fingers, acutely conscious of Everett's gaze on me. The last thing I want to do is damage something that belonged to their dead mom. I inspect the netting for holes, discoloration, or any other signs of wear or age and don't find any. The top, the part that would fasten the veil to Brooke's head, is a simple circlet of leaves wrought in silver and rhinestones. It's actually really pretty.

"No, I think it'll be fine," I say. "We'll put it on you and see how it works with the dress." And I pray it does. I'm getting the feeling that the veil is nonnegotiable, and if it clashes with the gown, the search will have to start all over again.

But it doesn't. Even with Brooke's hair looking like something Cinderella would wear to the gym, the veil is perfect. The silver leaves echo the pattern of the dress's lace, while the veil itself is simple enough that it lets the dress speak for itself. Considering we're working with something from the era of blue eyeshadow and Aqua Net, that's a feat.

"It definitely works," I tell her. "You think?"

"I do." She turns in a circle, twisting to try and see herself from every possible angle. "Wow. I thought it would be harder than this."

Everett coughs. Brooke stops her twirling to look at him.

"I meant picking out the dress," she says softly, as if placating him. "That part was easier than I thought."

"I know," he replies, and smiles at her.

It's a shame he's so miserable most of the time. He's as blessed as Brooke in the looks department, and that smile could make any girl want to throw herself at him. Well, any girl who wasn't hung up on a fiancé who'd dumped her.

Darcy reappears. "So we've made the final decision?" she asks.

"Seems like it," I reply. "I don't even think we'll need to do much in the way of alterations. It's a little long. But unless Brooke goes on one of those wedding-day crash diets, I think it'll be fine."

"Wonderful. Brooke, honey, you go take the dress off and hang it up. You can leave it in the dressing room because we'll be keeping it here for your next fitting. Actually, before you take it off, let me get a few measurements now while I have you. Follow me." Darcy leads Brooke to the back room where the in-store seamstresses do their work. They disappear, and I'm alone with Everett.

Well, this is awkward. I'll be the first to admit that I'm not the most outgoing person, unless it's strictly business-related. I guess you could say that this is, but given the impression Everett's given me—that he wants nothing more than for me *not* to do business with his sister—I'm unsure of what to say. So rather than try to come up with something that will inevitably make me sound like a total idiot, I go back to my phone, pretending to check my e-mail.

"Hey, Noelle?"

Thud. The phone slips out of my fingers. Thank God the floor is carpeted.

Everett picks up my phone and hands it to me almost before I can register that I've dropped it.

"Thank you." I stuff it into my purse.

"Sure." He folds his arms over his chest. "Listen. I want to apologize."

"Apologize? For what?" Not what I was expecting, given his self-defensive position.

"For being kind of a jerk. This whole thing...well, it hasn't been easy on me. Brooke's all I have left, and I feel pretty protective of her. I kind of feel like I'm losing her. As dumb as that sounds."

Exactly as Erin said. "I understand that."

"But I think when I saw her in the wedding dress, it hit me that she's not a little kid anymore. And that it doesn't matter how much I want to take care of her. It's time to let Will do that." He gives a tiny shrug that makes me think of a boy who doesn't want to let on that he's upset about getting yelled at. It's kind of endearing.

"I get it," I say. "I have a sister too. I know how it feels to want to protect her."

He nods. "Anyway. I just wanted you to know that I'm not going to be an asshole anymore." His smile is slow to come, but it eventually makes it. "I'm going to be a real best man. Brooke's maid of honor is her best friend from college, but she lives in Arizona. She won't be here until the weekend before the wedding. So if there's anything that needs to be done, you can ask me. I'm more than willing to help out. And I work at night, so my days are free."

Well, look at that. Everett St. John *does* have a personality, and it's not a terrible one.

"Thank you." I hope he means it. "That helps a lot. I may take you up on it, so if you're just saying that, now's the time to tell me."

"No. I mean it."

"Okay." I don't know what to say. If he's decided I'm not Public Enemy Number One, this is all going to go a lot more smoothly.

"And I know this can't be easy for you either," he continues.

"What do you mean?" The words come out a little more sharply than I intended.

"I know Drew Emmons," he says. "We graduated from high school together."

"Ah." Yeah, I should stop him, but I don't have the energy. I should just assume that every single resident of Springhollow knows I was dumped. If I get into the habit of shutting down everyone who decides to mention it, I'll have to turn Brooke's wedding over to Erin just to have the time to acknowledge them all.

"He was a shithead then," Everett continues. "Apparently nothing's changed."

A snort of unexpected laughter escapes me. I thought I was the only one to think of Drew as a shithead, and worse. Surely no one else in town thought he was anything less than the perfect son, friend, and fiancé.

Shows what they know. They're all morons.

"You can do better."

Wait. Did those words really come out of Everett St. John's mouth? The same mouth that's done pretty much nothing else but scowl at me since the moment we met?

"Thanks," I say. It's awkward, but no other words come to mind.

Brooke comes back then and it's all I can do not to run over and hug her in gratitude. I've never been good with words when put on the spot and for some reason Everett makes me feel like a gawky teenager all over again. I should hate him for that. Adolescence was bad enough when I lived it. I have no desire to go through it again at thirty years old.

A few lone flurries are falling from the sky when I pull my car into its parking spot. It makes me angry all over again. It's too damn early! Since when does it snow before Thanksgiving? We're in suburban Philadelphia—not Siberia!

My intent is to hurry through the lobby and up the stairs to my apartment, pour a glass of wine (screw the tea), and sit in a bubble bath until I'm cold and pruny. But the mailman's been by and through the teeny, tiny window of my mailbox I can see that it's stuffed, so I take a minute to empty it out. I shove the mail into my bag without sorting it. It's never anything good anyway. Just bills and junk.

My apartment is still eerily clean. It's weird. Like someone else has been living here. In a way someone else has, though, right? I'm definitely not the same person I was a week and a half ago. I haven't been leaving dishes on the table or throwing my clothes on the floor. I don't even remember making the conscious decision to stop being a slob. Some part of me must think that if Drew finds out I put my clothes into a hamper now, he'll come running back.

"Ha," I burst out before I can stop myself. *Heidi's* getting a ring. I bet she picks up her clothes. You can't be too careful with poly-spandex blends.

I can still hardly believe it's only been a week and a half since my world fell apart.

I head for the bathroom, where I'm comforted by the fact that there's a sloppy dribble of shampoo dried to the shower wall. *See, Drew? You haven't completely ruined me.* I turn on the water, wait for it to get hot, and dump in a capful of lavender vanilla bubble bath. My tub is deep, and it'll be a little while before it's full enough to get in, so I go back into the living room and pull the mail out of my bag.

A credit card offer, a Clipper magazine, and a menu for the new Chinese place around the corner go into the junk pile. The electric bill stays, unfortunately. So does my December issue of *Cosmo*—that'll go into the tub with me. I toss an ad for a home security company into the trash and a coupon for a massage into the maybe-I'll-want-that-someday pile. A few more pieces of junk, another bill, and at the very bottom of the pile, a card.

A card? Who sent me a card? My birthday's not until January. And it's barely past Halloween, way too early for Christmas.

But if it *is* a Christmas card, I'm setting it on fire.

The envelope is white, and I don't recognize the handwriting. There's a return address—someplace in Indiana—but no name. Who do I know in Indiana? No one. I slide my thumbnail under the flap and curse when the paper slices into the pad of my thumb.

I stick the thumb into my mouth and manage to use the other hand to tear the envelope open the rest of the way. I slide the card out. Flip it over.

A cartoonish bride and groom grin up at me. My heart lurches in my chest.

"CONGRATULATIONS!" the card shrieks.

I should throw it out. I shouldn't read it. I don't even know anyone in Indiana. It's a mistake. Never mind that my name and address are clearly printed on the front of the envelope. It can't be for me. I'm not getting married.

I open the card.

"Best wishes on your engagement!" chirp words printed in Comic Sans. And that should be enough to make me vomit, right? Normally it would be. Except there's a handwritten message underneath those hideous words, and the message is signed *Love, Dad.*

My mother is silent on the other end of the phone. I can't tell if the silence is because she's upset, or because she's guilty.

"Mom?" I prompt her. She needs to say something. Anything.

"Sweetheart, I didn't tell him," she finally says. "I didn't even know he was in Indiana. I have no idea how he found out."

I let my breath slide out in a relieved rush of air. I guess I'd known that all along. And it's not like my mom would lie. No, lying had been my dad's forte.

"Okay." But now my only suspect has been found innocent and I have no other persons of interest. Kate already swore on the life of her unborn child that she hadn't been the one to tell my dad about my engagement. "I just don't get it."

"I don't either." I can almost hear the thoughts swirling in my mom's head. "Maybe one of your cousins told him?"

I'm doubtful. I only have two cousins, both of them on my dad's side. Sarah and Jess. They're my dad's brother's daughters, a little younger than me and living in Florida. I can't remember the last time I saw either of them. We don't even really talk, except on social media once in a while.

Then it hits me, and I can't believe I've been so dense.

"Facebook," I whisper.

"What?"

The pieces are falling together now.

"I'm friends with Sarah and Jess on Facebook." It's the only thing that makes sense. I don't log on often and only changed my relationship status to *Engaged* within the last month or so. And after it all fell apart, I got so busy with Brooke's wedding—and, okay, avoiding as much of the outside world as possible—that I hadn't logged in to my profile to change it back to *Single*. One of my cousins must have seen it and told their dad who told my dad, who for some reason thought I'd welcome a congratulatory note from him.

He was wrong.

"That's probably it, then," my mom agrees.

"Ugh." Now I'm going to have to fix it. But at least I won't have to get in touch with my dad to tell him the wedding's off. I'll just switch my status back to *Single* and let Sarah or Jess do the rest.

My mom does her best to distract me by telling me all of the things we're going to do together once I'm home. She's talked to one of her friends who manages a Victoria's Secret and might be able to get me a job as a keyholder. I try not to laugh. It's all too depressing. My mom means well. I know that. But I have a degree from a school that tends to get lumped in with the Ivy Leagues. I may not be doing anything with it, but I know I didn't rack up two hundred grand in student loan debt to spend my days arranging bras.

"Sounds great." I hope she can't tell that I'm lying through my teeth.

After we hang up, I grab my laptop and power it on. I pour a glass of wine—my third of the night—while I wait for the loading screen to disappear. When it does, I immediately pull up my Internet browser and log into Facebook. It's been so long I almost don't remember my password, and then when I do, I almost want to puke because it's *Drew0315*. Our anniversary. Guess I should change that. But to what? *Dumped1024?*

When my news feed loads, I've got dozens of notifications to go through. The first five turn out to be more "Congratulations on your engagement!" messages from people I haven't spoken to since college graduation and yes—there's one from my cousin Sarah.

There's at least thirty more, but I don't read them—just click on them to get them out of the way. I have a few friend requests that I completely ignore. Maybe one's from my dad—who knows? Only when the notifications are cleared do I take a few seconds to skim the updates of the people whose lives I actually do care about. There's the usual political rants, cat photos, and a video of someone falling down with dozens of likes and comments. An old high-school classmate apparently gave birth at some point and has plastered my feed with pictures of her baby sleeping, smeared with baby food (at least I hope that's what it is), flopped over in a carseat, and grinning toothlessly. But even the envy I feel doesn't stop me from scrolling through.

No, it takes a huge photo of Drew with his arms wrapped around Heidi to do that.

My finger stills over the mouse like my entire hand's gone dead. I can't tear my eyes away. They're at some kind of party, obviously. Drew's in a black button-down shirt, his face split into a kind of grin I can't ever remember seeing on him. Heidi's heavily lined eyes are half-closed, and her glossy pink lips are forced into something that makes her look like a slutty mallard. They look happy.

Did Drew ever look that happy in photos with me?

I inhale. It's deep, shaky.

Why didn't he unfriend me? Did he *want* me to see this?

Screw changing my relationship status. I'm going completely off the grid.

It takes a few minutes, but I finally figure out how to disable my profile. It prompts me several times to make sure that I'm *sure,* even showing me a list of friends who will apparently curl up in a ball and die if I leave. I don't care, not about any of it. I don't care about how the country is apparently going down the tubes because someone's idea of the wrong candidate won the election. I don't care whose baby is eating solid food and whose cat tries to fight its own shadow. I don't care what people are eating for dinner or where, and I really, *really* don't care that Drew and Heidi are happy.

Okay, maybe that last one isn't completely true.

It won't always be like this, will it?

9

"So how did it go?" I ask Erin over breakfast Monday morning. "I figure I would have heard from you if anything went really wrong." She's brought me a huge pumpkin muffin from the bakery down the street from her place. I appreciate the gesture, but I don't have the heart to tell her that my taste buds seem to have gone AWOL. It doesn't matter what I eat. Salad, steak, cereal. Everything tastes and feels like a mouthful of wood chips.

I wash down a dry bite of muffin with a sip of tea. Lady Grey, thankfully *not* purchased from the tea shop I'd discovered with Drew. I threw that one out. Along with about ten other flavors—a lemony one he made for me once when I had strep throat, a few others I'd bought on the rare occasion we'd grocery shopped together. And his favorite. He was always more a coffee guy than a tea guy, but he fell in love with a spicy, gingerbready flavor I found in a craft supply store, of all places. I only saw it that once, and he was insane about not drinking too much too often. He wanted to make it last as long as possible. He even made me keep it in the freezer so it wouldn't go weak. He probably misses that stupid tea more than he misses me. I hope it tasted like freezer when he drank it.

I took a *lot* of pleasure from dumping that one out and watching the tiny leaves flutter into the growling garbage disposal.

"It went really well, actually," Erin says. "The photography ran a little over time, but nobody complained. Brady put out a few extra hors d'oeuvres and everyone was happy."

Including her. I can tell by the way her cheeks flame at the mention of his name. Something clenches in the general area of my heart. That sensation's getting a little old. I know it's only been two weeks, but come on. Does *everything* have to remind me that I'm alone?

"I knew you'd be great." I pop another small chunk of muffin into my mouth and wince. Cardboard, I say.

"How about the dress fitting?" Erin asks.

"Perfect. She found her dress, thankfully. It's beautiful. Wait till you see her in it."

"What's it look like?" she asks. "Did you take pictures?" And only then does it occur to me then that I'd normally have taken a few cellphone photos right there in the shop. The fact that I didn't think to take a single one speaks volumes about my state of mind. Getting out of the wedding business can't happen a moment too soon. At least with bra fittings I won't be expected to take photos.

"Um." I gulp some tea." No."

"Oh." Erin's face starts to morph into the pitying expression I've seen on her way too many times in the last ten days. "Noelle, are you sure you're all right with this?"

"I'm fine." I flick a crumb of muffin across the table.

"Because I feel guilty about forcing you to take this job. I've been thinking about it, and I'm really sorry for pushing you. I thought it would help you to have something to take your mind off Drew." She laughs a little, then sighs. "I probably shouldn't have picked a wedding."

"What else would you have picked?" That's it. I can't eat any more. I roll the remains of the muffin in the paper bag it came in and toss the whole thing into the trash can.

"I don't know."

My cell rings then, saving us both. I pounce on it.

It's Brooke.

"Hey," I say.

"Hi," she replies. "I'm glad I got you. How soon does Amy need to have the preliminary guest list?"

"Six to eight weeks before the date. So, last week."

"Crap. I thought so." I hear noises, like she's knocking things over.

"Is everything all right?"

"Well." *Thump.* "I don't know."

Instinctively I sit up straight. My shoulders tense. "What's wrong?"

"Nothing, really. I mean, nothing that can't be fixed. I just—I can't find the guest list."

"Oh!" I relax. "Just the guest list?" This isn't horrible. The guest list is short. She's right; it can be fixed. But it'll have to be done as soon as possible. Even without the RSVPs coming in yet, Amy needs a rough number so she can tell the caterer.

"I just misplaced it."

"When did you see it last?"

"I had it Saturday. I'd been working on it, and it was on the table next to my bed. After I got home from Blush, I went into my room to put the veil in my closet. Then Everett and I ordered dinner. He was here for maybe two hours. After he left, I talked to Will on the phone for a while, then I watched a movie and went to sleep."

"Was it there when you went to sleep?"

"I don't remember." Her voice quivers, and I hope she doesn't start to cry.

"Okay." I pitch my voice so it sounds calming. There are plenty of worse things that could happen. This is practically nothing. "Don't worry about it. It'd be a different story if you were having two hundred and fifty guests. But you've got what, seventy? Tops? It'll be easy. We'll get together and just come up with it again."

"Okay." She sniffles. "Sorry. You're right. It's not a big deal. I got some bad news last night, that's all."

"Oh no. What's wrong?"

"Nothing wedding-related. Not really. It's Will's mom. The doctors told him the chemo doesn't seem to be working as well as they hoped."

"Oh, Brooke. I'm so sorry."

"We knew there was a chance. But she's been feeling so good lately, we just hoped. She's still stage three, but she's three-B now. Anyway, he's going to be staying with her a little longer than he thought. He won't be here until about two weeks before the wedding." She sniffles again.

Should this make me immediately suspicious? Because it does, and I can't help it.

Did anyone besides Will himself say that he's actually *in* Canada? How do we even know he's with his mom? For all any of us know he could have some Canadian side piece feeding him poutine in nothing but a hockey jersey while Brooke patiently waits for him to come home and marry her.

I close my eyes and count. To five, and then ten. Just because *my* fiancé cheated on me doesn't mean they all do. I hate myself for immediately jumping to that conclusion when poor Will is watching his mom die in front of his eyes.

I hate Drew for turning me into the kind of person who *would* jump to that conclusion.

"I'm sure he hates it," I try to assure her.

"He said he does. He hates being away from me and wishes he could help out with the planning. He feels terrible."

"Would it help if I called him? I might be able to think of a few things he can do even from there. That might make him feel more involved. Not to mention give him a few distractions. I'm sure he could use them."

"Really? You'd do that?"

"Of course! It's not the first time I've had to. A lot of guys travel for work and aren't able to be as involved in planning as they want. It's the same thing, really." And a lot of guys say they're traveling when they're actually cheating. *Shut up, Noelle.*

"I think he'd really like that," Brooke says. The change in her voice is already marked, and I feel a little pang of guilt. That guy had better hope to whatever god he believes in that he is *not* cheating on her. Because if he is I will murder him. "It would give him something to focus on."

"I'm on it," I say.

"Will Hurley." The voice that comes through my cell is a rich baritone. I can almost *hear* how gorgeous he is. But what else did I expect?

"Will? Hi, this is Noelle Silver. Your wedding planner?"

"Yes! Hi! How are you?"

Hmm. He sounds genuinely happy to hear from me.

"I'm great," I say. He's a stranger. I can lie to him. "Listen, I talked to Brooke earlier, and she told me about how your mom's not doing well. I'm so sorry to hear that."

"Thanks," he says. "It's been rough. Was Brooke really upset?"

"Well, she wasn't happy. But of course she understands."

"Damn." Some muffled noise. Is he shooing his mistress to the next room? "I hate hurting her like that. The doctors said my mom would be done with her chemo the week before Thanksgiving. I was going to come right back and help with as much of the wedding planning as I could. But the doctors say…" He trails off. "Well, I'm sure you know. It isn't good. I'm glad Brooke has you. She's so happy with what you've been doing. I know the wedding will be perfect."

So we have a flatterer on our hands. Great. Drew is a flatterer. He never has a bad thing to say to anyone. Which, come to think of it, is probably why I had zero idea he was even the least bit unhappy with me.

"That's the idea," I say. "Anyway, I'm sorry to bother you, but Brooke seemed to think it might help you feel better if there were things you could do to help with the planning."

"Oh, that'd be great," he says. "I'm not doing much besides some stuff around the house and driving my mom to appointments. I'm glad to be with her, but I'm going a little stir crazy. So tell me anything I can do. Please. I'm happy to."

"Really?" I'd expected him to say that he couldn't, for whatever reason. Weird schedule, no Wi-Fi, the desire to let Brooke have the wedding of her dreams without any intrusion from him. My BS detector starts to go off. He might be too good to be true.

"Of course."

"Okay." Crap. Now I'm going to have to give him some jobs. Even though I'd told Brooke otherwise, there really isn't much he can do from another country. "Do you have e-mail access there?"

"I do." He tells me the address, and I scribble it down, then read it back to him to confirm. "That's it."

"Okay. Great. I'll make a list and send it over to you."

"Thanks so much," Will says. "This means a lot. And I really look forward to meeting you when I'm finally home."

"Same here," I say. "I hope your mom starts to feel better." We exchange goodbyes and hang up.

But my phone rings again before I can even call Erin over to help me come up with something, anything, for Will to do from Canada.

It's Brooke again.

"Everything's fine," she assures me. "I still haven't found the list, but I'm working on coming up with it again. I just remembered that I wanted to ask you something."

"What's that?"

"Well, we tried to get our usual group together for Thanksgiving, but it's just not happening. Some have to work, some of them are going home, and my friend's boyfriend wants to surprise her with a trip to Jamaica, where he plans to propose. I guess we're at that age where grown-up stuff starts to take precedence over tradition." She laughs a little, but it's sad, and I feel so bad for her and her brother. How the holidays must suck when you have no family. "Now with Will not coming here, it'll just be Everett and me. Kind of lonely. So I was wondering, if you don't have any other plans, if you and Erin could join us for dinner."

Huh. Not what I was expecting.

Truth be told, I hadn't even thought about Thanksgiving. Usually Drew and I would head to Blackton for dinner with my mom, Kate, and Jacob. Obviously this year that isn't going to happen, and I guess that's why, aside from the few minutes it took to tell my mom I wasn't going to be coming home, I hadn't thought about it at all. Not to mention the whole dead taste bud thing. A huge dinner doesn't sound particularly appealing.

I go over the options in my head. I can stay home, have a turkey sandwich that tastes like something you'd find on the bottom of a hamster cage, and be depressed that I'm alone. I can go out to eat, waste money on food I don't want, and again, be alone. Or I can throw some Stove Top into a casserole dish and have dinner with other people who will hopefully cause enough of a distraction that I won't remember that I'm alone.

"I—well, I'll have to talk to Erin," I say. "Her parents spend the winter in Florida, and I know she's staying here but not whether she's made other plans. But actually, yeah, I'd love to come. Thank you."

"Oh, good!" she exclaims. "We'll be eating at Everett's. I'll text you the address."

"What can I bring?" Hopefully one day my appetite will come back, because I love cooking. Wait, scratch that—I love the *idea* of cooking. I hoard cookbooks and read them like novels. Unfortunately, I'm one of those rare people who can burn water. I silently beg any higher power that might be listening that Brooke doesn't ask me to do anything more complicated than opening a can of yams and dumping it into a saucepan where, hopefully, the syrup doesn't end up permanently scorched onto the bottom.

Is that why Drew left? Because I couldn't cook? Because I'm sure I could learn. The college offers courses. I just never had time to take one.

"You don't have to bring anything! Everett is a frustrated chef and pretty controlling about the whole thing." She laughs. "I could barely get him to agree to let me bring a bottle of wine. But I'm not a great cook. He got all the culinary talent in the family."

"Please, let me bring something." I can't show up empty-handed. Dinner with millionaires, and all that.

"Well…" She trails off. "Maybe a salad? Ev likes to show off a little and everything's always really delicious, but heavy. I wouldn't mind having something light to cut through all of his bread and cream sauces."

Salad. Perfect. I make those for myself all the time and only rarely screw them up.

"Salad it is. Should I tell Erin to bring anything, if she can come?"

"Oh, she really doesn't have to. But if she insists—how about an appetizer? My brother's always so focused on the meal that he doesn't realize that people don't want to wait around three hours without something to snack on."

Erin will like that. She makes a killer cheese plate, with grape leaves and everything.

"I'm sure that'll be fine."

"Great! I'm so glad. This will be fun."

Fun. Yup. That's it.

Thanksgiving. Typically a family affair, right? Mom and dad, siblings, grandparents, aunts, uncles, cousins, all seated around the table laughing as they pass the cranberry sauce. At least that's how it is on those cheesy TV specials. But they never seem to take into account those of us who don't have a mom or dad, because one parent decided to split and take off halfway across the country without a word to anyone until a random congratulatory card shows up in the mail twenty years later.

Am I bitter? No, not at all. Why do you ask?

The first few Thanksgivings after my dad left were rough. I would watch my mom put on a brave face, cook a perfect turkey, and set her table to look like something out of a Williams Sonoma catalog. Linen napkins and everything. She was an only child, so we had no aunts or uncles or cousins, but her parents would come. Even as a ten-year-old I could tell my grandfather felt a little uncomfortable as the only one in the house with even a passing interest in watching whatever football game was on during dinner. My grandmother would fuss over my mom, pretending like she was helping to cook but really just hovering in case my mom collapsed under the strain of it all, an oven-hot ceramic dish landing on top of her and green bean casserole flying everywhere. I picked up on this stuff even as a kid, and it made me not only sad but furious at my dad—even more than I usually was. Where was he? What had we done to chase him away? Why weren't we good enough for him?

When I was thirteen, Grandma died of cancer. Two years later Grandpa had a heart attack. After they were gone, my mom stopped trying. Thanksgiving became just another day. A depressing day, to be sure. But not much different than any other. It got better once Kate met Jacob, and once I met Drew. My mom started cooking again and putting a little effort into it. Last Thanksgiving, I was newly engaged and reveling in the fact that I had an actual family again.

Guess the joke was on me.

But it could have been even worse. Kate and I could have been Everett and Brooke—orphaned without a relative in the world to step up for us. We had our grandparents, our mom. They had no one. My dad might have chosen another life over us, but at least he was out there somewhere. Everett and Brooke's parents loved them but died. Which of us had it worse?

The Monday before Thanksgiving I hit the grocery store, armed with a list to attempt a very fancy salad as my contribution to the St. John Thanksgiving. If Everett is serving a gourmet feast, the least I can do is show up with something a little more interesting than a bowl of iceberg lettuce and some croutons.

I'm lost as soon as I walk in. I drove two towns over to avoid my usual grocery store, the one I haven't been to since threatening the cashier over two crumb cakes I threw in the trash as soon as I got them home. I have to wander around a bit before I start to get my bearings. I need mesclun mix and pears, dried cranberries and pecans. I'm going to attempt to candy them myself. I pick up two bags just in case. Nobody likes scorched nuts. I peruse the shelves of salad dressing, wondering if I should pick out a bottle to be safe or try and mix up my own with some olive oil and white wine vinegar. Screw it—it's Thanksgiving. I'm going all out. Homemade vinaigrette it is.

The recipe doesn't call for it, but years of Saturday mornings drinking coffee in front of cooking shows makes me think that a little goat cheese might take my salad over the top. I head to the dairy aisle, which, in my usual store, is where it would be. But it's not. I find mozzarella and cheddar, Monterey jack and blocks of Swiss, but no goat. I turn in an awkward circle. Ricotta, cream and cottage. No goat. The deli, maybe?

The basket, heavy from the bag of pears and, okay, the half-gallon of pumpkin ice cream I hope to enjoy once my taste buds reanimate, is starting to cut painfully into my fingers as I approach the refrigerated kiosk thing by the prepared foods. Luck, for once, is on my side. I find logs of goat cheese immediately. But now I'm faced with a new decision. Do I want plain, or cheese mixed with herbs? Chèvre with honey or rolled in black pepper?

Most of the ingredients in the salad are sweet, so the honey's out. The vinaigrette will have herbs in it so I don't need more. I feel like a real chef when I pluck the black pepper chèvre from its nest beside cubes of artisan cheddar and marinated mozzarella.

This will be a salad that could get me my own Food Network show.

I'm absurdly pleased with myself when I turn from the kiosk to head for the registers. I'm almost halfway to the self-checkout when I remember I'd meant to grab a few gallons of water.

I know exactly where it is in my usual grocery store. In this one, I have to search. I pass the aisles with my eyes on the signs dangling from the ceiling, telling me where to get cereal, spices, and light bulbs. Where the hell do they keep bottled water in this place? I keep walking, staring at the signs—*Lunchbox, Pet Food, International*—only stopping when I walk into a half-full cart left abandoned by an end cap of Chips Ahoy.

Pain explodes in my big toe and rockets up my shin almost to my knee. It hurts so bad I don't even stop to get embarrassed about the possibility of anyone seeing me. In a store this crowded an audience is inevitable. I put my basket on the ground, grip the handle of the cart with one hand, and reach down with the other to massage my toe through layers of boot and sock. I blink back tears. It hurts. I wonder if the toenail is still connected and gag at the thought of what I might find when I get home and take everything off.

A hand appears beside mine.

"Are you okay?" says a voice. A male voice. A disturbingly familiar male voice.

I look up from my administrations into the dark brown eyes of Everett St. John.

10

OF COURSE.

He frowns. "Noelle?"

"Yup." Or at least what's left of me. Cripes. First my heart, now my toe. What's going to be next to break?

"What are you doing?"

I touch my foot to the ground and put tentative pressure on it. Ouch. "Well, I was trying to walk. This isn't my usual store, though, and I didn't realize that here people leave their carts in the middle of the floor instead of taking them down the aisle."

His mouth quirks. I think he's trying not to laugh at me.

"Well, you could have looked in front of you," he says mildly. Of course he's mild. He hasn't just destroyed one of his extremities.

"I shouldn't have to."

"Okay." He holds the cart steady while I attempt to put equal weight on both feet. "Can you walk now?"

"I don't know." I hear the petulance in my own voice and get embarrassed all over again. I sound like a four-year-old. "Yes."

"Good." He gestures to my basket. "Making a salad?"

"Yeah. For Thanksgiving dinner. I hope you like goat cheese." And if he says he doesn't, he's getting extra.

"Love it. I didn't know you cooked."

"I don't, really. But I try."

"Oh."

There's an awkward pause then. I sense that he longs for escape as much as I do. "Thanks," I say to fill the silence. "For the dinner invitation."

"It was Brooke's idea," he replies.

Annoyance creeps over me, prickling under my skin and turning just the tips of my ears into fiery little torches. What is wrong with this guy? Can't he just say *you're welcome* and act like he wants me there?

"But I'm glad you're coming," he continues. "With just the two of us it would have been sort of depressing."

Now was that so hard? Even if it's a lie?

"I hear that," I say before I can stop myself, and feel mortified all over again. He knows Drew, knows that we were engaged, and somehow found out that it ended. They may talk again at some point. I can't seem vulnerable—it's the last thing I want Drew to think.

"I should go," I say before I humiliate myself any further.

"Okay." He glances down at the cart, at my hand that still clings to it. "You sure you can walk?"

I release the handle like it's turned into some kind of weird lizard that might crawl up my arm and grab my basket instead. The pain in my foot is easing, and I should be able to get away without limping too obviously.

"I can walk. Thanks."

"Okay. Well. See you Thursday?"

"See you Thursday," I confirm. He gives me a nod before dramatically pushing his cart into the next aisle. I'm not sure if I should laugh or shake my head. So I do both.

Early in the afternoon on Thanksgiving Day, the GPS in my phone delivers me to a modest-sized house at the very edge of town. Just like Google Earth told me a month ago, the house isn't huge. It's well-kept, with a manicured lawn and neat hedges, a driveway clean of even a speck of WD-40, and white-framed windows set in a neat façade of irregular stone the color of ground cardamom. But it in no way screams *look at me! I have money!* the way it could have. Might have, if it were my house.

What can I say? I like displays. I'd be a crappy wedding planner if I didn't.

I put the car into park and shut the engine off but don't get out. I feel a little shaky. My legs and arms tremble, and my heart thumps like the bass that comes from the rebuilt Corvette that shows up on the street outside my apartment at three o'clock almost every morning. Nearly five years living in that building and I still don't know who or what they're there for.

I won't lie. I'm nervous. Nervous about getting through my first holiday in eight years without Drew. Nervous about trying to do it with a group of people too small to effectively distract me, two of whom I don't know that well and one of whom makes me uncomfortable. Nervous that my salad will taste like lawn clippings even though one-third of the pecans came out flawlessly candied and my vinaigrette is a surprisingly perfect balance of tangy and sweet. Nervous that this will be my new normal—spending holidays with people I can barely call friends just so I'm not alone.

I get out of the car.

Force myself, step by step, up the walkway to the front door.

Lift my hand. And knock.

Then wonder if I have enough time to run back to my car and drive away without anyone seeing me.

It's a hope that's dashed almost as soon as it materializes. The door opens to reveal Brooke, and she looks happy to see me.

"Hi!" she exclaims. "Happy Thanksgiving!" She steps aside to let me in.

"Happy Thanksgiving." I'm unable to match her level of enthusiasm, but when she hugs me, I give her a one-armed hug back, my other arm weighed down by the gargantuan salad bowl.

"I like your dress," I tell her. It sounds like the kind of small talk people make when they don't know what else to say, and it kind of is, except that I *do* like her dress. It's long-sleeved but short, in a purple, magenta, and gold ikat print with a flared skirt. Hmm. I wonder if she'd let me borrow it.

"Thanks! I like your outfit, too." I glance down at my own clothes, the ones I'd chosen after trying on a good eighty-five percent of my closet. I didn't want to look like I was trying too hard, but I also didn't want to look like a slob. I wanted to be comfortable but not enough to fall asleep on the couch after dinner. I finally settled on black jeans, camel-colored ankle boots and a drapey white top, with gold earrings and a chunky gold watch Kate and Jacob gave me for my birthday. I kept my makeup minimal and left my hair down because as it turns out, I'm having a pretty good hair day.

Brooke takes the salad from my hands and leads me through the foyer into the living room, where I'm immediately whacked in the face by the most delicious scents. It smells like Thanksgiving, but on steroids. There's the familiar fragrance of a roasting turkey, gravy, and mashed potatoes. But there are other notes in there, too, and I want to try and place them. Sage, maybe. Black pepper. Something sweet, like brown sugar. Something creamy and almost vanilla. Something even a little pungent. Soy sauce? Whatever it is, it smells amazing.

Is it my imagination, or do I sense my taste buds finally waking up from their month-long coma?

"Thank you so much for bringing a salad. Everett is up to his elbows in butter and heavy cream, and I can feel myself expanding just standing in the kitchen with him," Brooke says. She lifts the edge of the plastic wrap—the very plastic wrap I fought with so hard I almost ended up with a black eye—to peek inside the bowl. "It looks delicious!"

"Thanks. I hope it is." Her enthusiasm is contagious. I could be jumping the gun, but it's possible that I might end up happy I came.

"Glass of wine?" she asks. Yes. Please.

"That'd be great."

"Red or white?"

"White, please." I can't even look at a glass of red wine without getting a migraine that feels like my brain is being slowly picked apart with a salad fork.

She disappears with my bowl and I take the opportunity to explore the living room of Everett's house. It's neat—way neater than any bachelor pad has the right to be, and I wonder if he's got someone that comes in and cleans for him. I almost feel wrong being here, as if my messy tendencies could permeate the air and infect him. The theme is minimalistic. There's not much in the way of decoration. In that way, it's very much a guy's room. The furniture is sleek and black, with one long couch running the width of the room, perpendicular to matching chairs and aimed at the large flat-screen TV perched on the wall over a white-bricked fireplace. There's some art on the walls—abstract splats of black, gray, and blue on a sea of white. The floors are immaculate, shiny blond hardwood, the only covering a cloud-gray area rug beneath the black coffee table.

It's nothing like Drew's place. Drew's apartment was neat too, but it had personality. The furniture was high quality but none of it matched. He had tables in practically every kind of wood there was. The living room walls were covered in photos of family and frat brothers, the walls in his bedroom hung with posters of his favorite band. Okay, so that part was weird. Sleeping there made me feel like I was doing something illegal, or like I had to worry about his mom busting in and catching me there. I'd had big plans for our bedroom once we lived together, and they did not involve the Foo Fighters. Maybe that's why he'd never broached the subject of us living together.

Sure, Noelle. That's why. It had nothing to do with the fact that he didn't love you.

My pitiful attempt at enthusiasm ebbs and disappears, and I'm back to feeling awkward.

"Here you go!" Brooke returns with my wine and hands it to me. "Everett says he's sorry he hasn't come out to say hello yet, but he's in the middle of basting and cannot be interrupted." She rolls her eyes.

I sip the Chardonnay in my glass and close my eyes as the familiar (but, of course, better, since this is St. John wine and probably costs two hundred bucks a bottle) buttery, woodsy notes hit the back of my tongue.

I can do this. As long as there's wine, I can hang on.

The doorbell rings then, something that sounds vaguely like part of the Rachmaninoff concertos my dad used to listen to. It's a weird memory, one I haven't had in longer than

I can remember. Even weirder is the fact that it makes me feel sort of homesick.

I think about the card I somehow couldn't bring myself to throw away and instead stuffed into the back of my sock drawer.

"Hi!" Erin exclaims, entering the living room in a cloud of perfume and pink, her arms weighed down with a massive wooden board piled high with a variety of cheese and crackers, apple slices and dark purple grapes, and small bowls of nuts.

My stomach grumbles and I look down at it, amazed. Really amazed. It seems like I'm *hungry*. It's an alien sensation.

Okay. Is Everett's house some kind of vortex that took me from my old pathetic life into a parallel universe where I'm *not* mourning the fact that I'll probably be alone forever?

Brooke sets Erin's cheese plate down on the coffee table and goes to get her a glass of wine as well. Erin asks for pink moscato—what else? Before Brooke can come back, Erin's next to me, murmuring in my ear.

"Can I just say that this is one place I never thought I would spend Thanksgiving?" she hisses. "I mean, I grew up in this town. The St. Johns are like celebrities."

"So you've said." I take another sip. "It *is* weird."

"It's a shame you're leaving town," Erin continues. "This is a tradition I think I'd be okay with starting. I can always go to Florida for Christmas."

Brooke comes back before I can answer, and that's okay, because I really don't have any idea what to say in return. *Is* it a shame I'm leaving? I talked to both Kate and my mom this morning while emulsifying olive oil and white wine vinegar and they sounded like they had everything under control. Even Kate, who's not on bed rest but under strict instructions to "take it easy," seemed to have no problem tackling the vast majority of the side dishes while my mom handled the turkey. They said they would miss me, of course, and I know they meant it, but honestly, what difference would my presence have made? I would have just burned my contribution to the dinner and made everyone depressed by moping around and bemoaning my failed engagement.

I tip the rest of the wine into my mouth and swallow. I will *not* ruin this holiday for everyone else because I can't seem to put an end to my own pity party.

"Hello," says a voice. I lower my empty wine glass. Everett has emerged from the kitchen and comes toward us, wiping his hands on a dish towel. He's immaculate in dark jeans and a fitted black shirt. Seriously. There's neither a splash of gravy nor a smear of olive oil anywhere to be found. If it were me cooking, I'd have already changed clothes three times by now and would still have globs of potatoes clinging to me like buttery barnacles.

"Happy Thanksgiving." He greets Erin first, giving her a hug that's friendlier than I've ever seen him. I frown. Does he like her or something? Her pink-clad arms go around his neck in what appears to be a kind of stranglehold, but he doesn't look like he's being strangled. He looks like he's enjoying it.

When he turns to me, I immediately go all awkward adolescent. Will he hug me too? Do I hug him back?

Why am I worried? He's just a guy.

A guy who may or may not think I'm out to rob his sister blind. But just a guy.

"Happy Thanksgiving," I mumble. His arms do go around me in a sort of hug, one arm over my shoulder and another loosely at my waist, but there's no commitment to it. Barely any contact. So I respond in turn. I can be standoffish too. His hand gives my shoulder an awkward pat before stepping back. As he backs away, his chin grazes my cheek.

"Thanks for coming," he says.

"Thank you for having us." I pass my empty glass from my right hand to my left, for lack of anything better to do.

"I'll refill your glass," Brooke says, and plucks it from between my fingers before I can ask for a glass of water instead. "Be right back! Erin, you okay?"

"I'm good!" Erin lifts her still-full glass.

"How's your foot?" Everett asks.

Heat floods my face and my toe, though it's pretty much back to normal, gives a sympathetic throb of mild pain.

"It's fine." I shrug and laugh a little. "Turns out they didn't need to amputate."

"What?" Erin asks. "What happened to your foot?"

"I very thoughtlessly left my shopping cart at the end of the aisle in the middle of the floor," Everett says before I can say pretty much the same thing. "Noelle just happened to stumble into it."

"Plow into it is more like it." Brooke brings back my glass and a dark bottle of beer, which she hands to her brother. "My big toe took the brunt of the impact."

"That's the worst!" Brooke exclaims.

"Tell me about it."

"It was my fault," Everett says.

"More mine," I argue. Now that I'm not in agonizing pain from a possibly detached toenail and no longer mortified about the fact that I tripped over a three-foot-tall, four-cubic-foot metal cage on wheels, I can see that I probably should have looked where I was going. "You were right. I could have looked straight ahead, rather than up."

"Well." Everett lifts the bottle to his lips and drinks. "It could have happened to anyone."

"Right," I agree. And the four of us fall into uncomfortable silence. I can literally hear the ticking of a clock as the seconds pass without someone saying something. I glance around. I don't even see a clock.

"I should get back to the kitchen," Everett finally says.

"It smells great." Erin is basically batting her eyelashes at him. If we were at the table, this is right about when I would kick her. But Everett responds with a grin.

"Thanks. I hope it tastes as good. I'm trying out a new marinade. Probably should have given it a test drive before Thanksgiving, but it just came to me this morning. I have high hopes. Hey, Brooke. Put on some music, will you?"

"Sure." Everett disappears into the kitchen as Brooke makes her way to the wall, where an impressive audio setup sits on a shelf above one of the black chairs. "Any requests?"

"No Christmas music," I say quickly.

"No, don't worry. Aside from the *Nutcracker Suite*, for obvious reasons, I don't let myself listen to Christmas music until tomorrow." She presses some buttons.

"I'm easy, then. Erin?"

"Anything but death metal."

"How about this?" Brooke presses another button, and the soft twang of an acoustic guitar fills the room.

"Good choice!" Everett yells from the kitchen.

We sit on the couch, the music surrounding us, making small talk and picking at Erin's cheese plate. I play it safe, sticking mostly to the fruit and crackers, but I'm completely shocked when I take a tentative bite of sharp cheddar and it doesn't make me want to puke. Even Erin notices. She doesn't say anything, but she gives me an encouraging smile. I imagine that on Monday morning, she might have two muffins waiting for me.

We sit down to dinner at around five o'clock. Everett's made enough food for about twenty people and I'm not sure the four of us will be able to fit our plates among all of the serving bowls and dishes. It all looks amazing, but even though it looks like traditional Thanksgiving food, everything seems to have some gourmet twist.

"Roasted rutabaga in brown butter and sage," he says, pointing to what I'd assumed were Yukon gold potatoes. "Parmesan butternut squash gratin. Pan-roasted Brussels sprouts with cranberries and pancetta, cinnamon maple glazed baby carrots, and pumpkin cornbread stuffing with figs and chorizo. And of course, Noelle's salad."

Is he *mocking* me?

I choose to ignore him. "*Pumpkin* cornbread stuffing?" I say instead. With sausage and fruit? I can't decide if it sounds gross or amazing.

I hope it's gross.

"It's *so* good," Brooke says. "He made the cornbread Monday, let it get a little stale, and then used it in the stuffing. Keep it on your side of the table, Ev. Otherwise I'll eat the whole bowl. Noelle, you've got to try it."

"Okay." It might not be the smartest thing I've ever done considering I've only just gotten my appetite back, but I'll give it a whirl.

We pass the side dishes around as Everett lifts a terrifying-looking knife and slices into the turkey. Of course it's perfectly cooked and juicy. I take two slices and lay them on my plate beside the rutabaga—which I've never tasted, but which looks inoffensive enough—a pile of carrots, the Brussels sprouts, and a small scoop of stuffing. *Figs and chorizo.* I consider my palate sort of sophisticated, but I really don't know about this.

"What's the tradition?" Erin asks. "Do we say grace or something?"

"We usually just do the go around the table and say what we're thankful for," Everett says. "But we don't have to."

"Yes, we do!" Brooke says. "This year especially. There's so much more to be thankful for."

"Is there?" From his tone I gather Everett doesn't think there's nearly as much to be thankful for as his sister does.

"Of course!" Brooke's face is glowing with happiness and once again I'm struck by the difference between them. She's so happy, so easygoing and cheerful I'd probably hate her if she wasn't so genuine. He's sullen, sort of rude, and obviously always wants to be somewhere else—at least when I'm around. Is it just the way he is? Or does he dislike me that much?

I turn my head away from him and focus on Brooke.

"I like that idea," I say. "You can go first."

"We all have to hold hands," she says.

"We do?" Erin's cheeks flame again. Of course they do—look where she's sitting! I bet that at this exact moment she's thinking about how perfectly her right hand will fit into Everett's left.

"No, we don't," he says.

"Yes, we do. We always did." She gives an apologetic shrug. "We used to do this with our parents. We have a really small family, and most of our relatives live on the West Coast and we'd go out there for Christmas, so Thanksgiving was always just the four of us. And this is what we did." She takes my right hand with her left.

I sneak another glance at Everett. His gaze is firmly locked on the butternut squash gratin. Everything is falling into place, and now I feel like a complete ass for being so judgy.

It might have a little to do with me, and the fact that his sister's paying me twenty-five grand to do something that should only cost her five. But more than that—he must miss his parents like crazy. No wonder he's miserable.

Sympathy wells up and washes over me.

Under the table, I stretch out my left hand. My knuckles clumsily graze his denim-clad knee, and he jumps a little but continues to stare at the table like he half-hopes his mom and dad will materialize in the middle of the glazed carrots.

I don't retract my hand. After a few seconds that feel like days, his fingertips bump mine and slide against my palm. They're warm. A quick movement on both our parts, and we're holding hands, our fingers intertwined. He presses his fingertips against my knuckles, and I can almost feel the pain coming from him. On top of my own misery, even though so far I've managed to keep it at bay, it's almost too much.

11

"I'm THANKFUL FOR a lot of things," Brooke says. "My dance studio is successful, I have a roof over my head and food on my plate—" *Of course you do, you're loaded,* I can't help thinking, but I actually find it charming that she doesn't take it for granted—"good friends, an amazing fiancé, and the best brother in the world." She grins at him. "It doesn't get much better than that. But this year I'm also thankful for Noelle and Erin and everything they're doing to make sure that Will and I can have the wedding of our dreams and the ability to start our lives together." She smiles around the table. "Who wants to go next?"

"Erin," I blurt out. I'm still thinking.

"Oh. Okay. Um." Erin tilts her head like she does when she's thinking hard. "I'm thankful for my family, of course, even though I don't get to see them as much as I'd like. I'm thankful for my friends. My home and my job."

Guilt stabs at me. She means the job I'm taking away from her.

I wish I could think of something to do for her besides writing a stupid reference letter.

"And I'm thankful to all of you for your willingness to let me be a part of your holiday," Erin finishes.

"Noelle?" Brooke prompts.

It's my turn? I thought we were going around the table.

"I'm thankful for…" I trail off. What *am* I thankful for? A fiancé who cheated on me and life plans that evaporated like a puddle in summer? The fact that he's running me out of town, away from my home, my business, and people who may or may not become friends?

Bitter, party of one, your table is ready.

"I'm thankful for my mom and sister, my brother-in-law, and my new niece or nephew," I say slowly. Maybe if I drag it out I'll make them think I said more than I did. "For the best assistant ever, and amazing clients." Brooke beams at me. "And I'm thankful too for you guys and your invitation to dinner today."

I feel like I should say more, but that's all I can think of. Maybe they should ask me again once I'm home in Blackton. I'm sure I'll find a lot more to be thankful for there.

"That's it." My voice sounds feeble even to my ears.

"Your turn, Ev," Brooke says.

He takes a deep breath, and I feel his fingers tense. I wonder if Erin feels the same thing on her side. She must— she's watching him, pity in her eyes.

"I'm thankful for my stereo system. My bike and my guitar."

Brooke rolls her eyes. "Ev. Come on."

"I'm not done." He clears his throat. "My friends. My home. My job, which I enjoy even though I don't need it." Lucky him. "And my sister, the only real family I have left. I'm most thankful for you."

"That's sweet," Erin says.

Brooke's eyes are bright with tears. "Love you, bro."

"Love you too." His voice is low. He clears his throat again. "Let's eat."

My appetite could not have returned at a better time. Every bite of food I take is freaking amazing—yeah, even the pumpkin cornbread stuffing. In fact, that might be my favorite part. Even the turkey, which isn't usually too exciting, tastes different somehow.

"How did you do this?" I ask Everett.

"Oh, I just brined it," he said.

"Really? Soaking it in salt water made it taste like this?" I'm absurdly jealous of all the sandwiches these two are going to be able to make out of the leftovers.

"Not only salt water. Some thyme, crushed red pepper, celery seed, and a whole bottle of tamari."

"Wow." Not anything I would have ever figured would taste good together. But it does.

"I'm glad you like it." His smile is tentative, crooked. "Your salad is good too."

It is, in fact. I'm sort of proud of it. "I candied the pecans myself. Didn't burn more than two-thirds of them."

His smile becomes a grin.

Dinner is nice. That's really the best word for it. It's calm and starts off sort of quiet, but I can sense the four of us getting comfortable with each other. We chat about movies and music, TV shows, and even sports, which it turns out none of us pay any attention to. Inevitably, the main topic turns to Brooke's wedding.

"I can't believe it's only four weeks away!" she says.

"You and me both." We laugh. "No, really. It's coming together. In fact, on Monday I'll be picking up your invitations."

Everett listens, but he doesn't join in. I guess he's still absorbing the fact that he has to let his sister go. His devotion to her is sort of sweet.

Halfway into dessert, which is some sort of pumpkin tart with a shortbread crust (no boring pumpkin pie for this crew), a cellphone rings. It's not mine or Erin's. I recognize our ringtones. But Everett gets up from the dining table and retrieves his phone from the kitchen. He has it pressed to his ear when he comes back.

"Are you serious?" he says. He closes his eyes, and his annoyance is undeniable. "But I've got my sister and her friends over for dinner. Can't someone else do it? I know Brett didn't have any plans today." A pause. "Of course he's not answering. I'm the only idiot who would do that. Okay. Fine. I'll be there as soon as I can." He disconnects the call and looks so pissed off that for a minute I swear he's going to hurl the phone across the room. I even duck a little, just in case.

"Be where?" Brooke asks.

"Work."

"No!" she wails.

"Sorry. Rob called out and they're expecting a crowd. Thanksgiving night is always busy. For some reason." He shakes his head. "Don't rush. You can all stay here for as long as you want and help yourself to leftovers. I have to brush my teeth." He disappears down the hall.

"Well, this sucks," Brooke says.

"Where does he work?" Erin asks.

"The Library."

"Really? I haven't been there in years," I say. "I always liked going on acoustic open-mic night."

"They still have it," Brooke says. "Actually, I think it's on Thursday." She drinks the rest of the water in her glass and sets it down. "What do you think? Should we go with him?"

The Library is in Newbury, the next town over. Springhollow has no bars—it's been a dry town since its inception sometime in the eighteenth century, despite the huge college campus right smack in the middle. So when we were in college, we would pile into the car of whoever was unfortunate enough to be designated driver, ride the ten blocks across town into Newbury, and drink. Some nights we'd just play pool. Other nights we'd do karaoke. There would have to be a *lot* of beer involved for me to get into that. But mostly we went for acoustic night. I've always been a sucker for live music. Even more of a sucker for a guy with a guitar. Which, of course, doesn't explain how I ended up with Drew, who looks like the quarterback of the football team that he was all eight years of high school and college.

Everett's a bartender. I didn't know that. We drive separately, him on his bike and the rest of us in Brooke's Range Rover. He gets there first and is already behind the bar when we arrive.

Nothing's changed. The walls are still exposed, faded red brick covered in band posters and dartboards. The pool table still sits near the bathrooms. So near, actually, that if anyone is playing, it's easier to go outside to pee than squeeze past them to get to the toilets. There's a corner with a small stage that a real band would never fit on, and too many tables for any kind of dance floor. And the floor, which was covered in jute carpet probably decades before I was born, is still tacky on my shoes and a weird grayish-brown color that I have to guess it originally wasn't. It's dim and smells of cigarette smoke even though Pennsylvania banned smoking indoors years ago. It feels strangely like home.

And it's crowded. Maybe it wouldn't be for a regular Thursday night, but considering it's Thanksgiving and everyone should be home on their couches in various stages of tryptophan-induced lethargy, it's busier than I'd thought it would be.

"What'll you have?" Everett asks when the three of us take seats on tattered barstools in front of him.

"I'll have a cosmo," Erin says. Everett pulls a bottle of vodka from underneath the bar.

"You know what I want," Brooke says. He plops a bottle of Budweiser in front of her. It's the last thing I would have pictured her drinking. Brooke looks like the kind of girl who would be totally at home with an apple martini or something garnished with a hibiscus. But a bottle of beer usually reserved for football tailgaters with hairy painted chests and bulging guts? I never would have guessed.

"I'll have the same." I don't know why I say it. Maybe it's because I know all too well what a wine headache feels like, and I know I don't want one. Maybe it's because this isn't the kind of place for frou-frou girly drinks. Most likely, it's because I feel like drinking a beer at the Library will take me back in time eight years, when things were simple and I was happy and in love.

"You got it." Everett uses a bottle opener to flip the cap off another bottle of Budweiser and puts it down in front of me.

Brooke grins. "Cheers," she says, and clinks the neck of her bottle against mine.

I lift the bottle to my lips and take a long, deep drink. The carbonation smacks the back of my throat, followed by an explosion of bitterness I should have expected but didn't since it's been so long since I've had an actual beer. I swallow before I can cough it back up and all over Erin, who daintily sips her cosmopolitan. Tears prick my eyes. The back of my throat feels a little scorched. *Blech.*

I'm thirty, not nineteen. What the hell was I thinking?

I'll finish it, but then I'm switching to liquor.

More people stream in as the night progresses. A few people bring their acoustic guitars to the makeshift stage and play a couple of songs. I give up beer in favor of Southern Comfort and Diet Coke, and the night starts to take on a warm, pleasant haze. Sitting at the bar with Brooke, Erin, and Everett, I'm shocked to discover that I'm enjoying myself. I've been so wrapped up in work, and then in my grief, that I don't remember the last time I had real fun.

Which is probably why Drew had to go searching for it away from me.

"Another one?" Everett asks when I put my drained glass on the bar in front of him.

Should I? No, I should probably stop. I had wine with dinner, and since I got here I've had the beer, two Southern Comfort and Cokes, and I'm comfortably buzzed—enough to enjoy what's going on around me but not so bad I can't hold a conversation.

"No, I'm good," I say. It's good timing, too, because I'm starting to get the feeling that my bladder's at full capacity.

"I'll be back," I tell Erin and Brooke. "Watch my purse." I slide off the bar stool and snake between the tables, glad that nobody seems interested in pool tonight and I'll be able to get to the restroom without having to wrestle with anyone.

While I'm drying my hands, I check my reflection in the mirror. My eyes are bright and sparkly—most likely a temporary effect of Southern Comfort, but sort of pretty if I do say so myself. My hair's gone only a little frizzy, and most of it is tamed by a quick combing with my fingers. And I was definitely smart picking out this top. I'm not overly stuffed from dinner but Diet Coke bloat is a real thing. I pull the top down and straighten the hem over my jeans, wrap my arms around myself and lean closer to the mirror. I'm not ugly. I'm not a vain person, but I can see that much. Before I can stop it, the thought invades my head.

Does Everett think I'm pretty?

"Don't even go there," I warn my reflection. "Moron." I use my paper towel to grip the grimy bathroom door handle and pull it open, then toss the towel behind me into the trash. I think it makes it. I don't stop to look.

Because when I emerge from the bathroom, I see dark blond curls and bright red hair. A neat button-down and an obscenely tight sweater. Heads bent together. Fingers entwined.

Drew and Heidi.

It's all I can do not to turn around and run right back into the bathroom because I feel like I'm going to throw up, and the last place I want to do it is on the floor practically at their feet. I might splash them.

On second thought...

Pull yourself together. You're in public!

I don't know where to go. I can't just stand there, they'll see me. But to get back to my spot at the bar I'd have to walk right by them. How long have they been there? Did they see me go into the bathroom? Screw that. I take the long way back, past the stage, practically having to walk behind the guy that warbles a terrible cover of a Psychedelic Furs song. It's loud. Everything is too loud and too bright.

I get back to the bar and thump into my stool. I'm so riled up my balance is off.

"Want some water or something?" Everett asks.

"Another SoCo and Coke."

"I thought you were done?"

"I changed my mind." He shrugs and fills another cup for me. I lift it to my lips to drink. The ice in the cup smacks wetly against my upper lip, and I have to swipe my hand across my mouth when I put the cup down.

"Noelle?" Erin sounds concerned. "You okay?"

"Fine." I drain the cup and try not to cough. Southern Comfort is not something that should be chugged, especially not when mixed with bubbly soda. "Another one."

"Maybe you should slow down," Everett suggests. "How about just a Coke this time?"

"Nope." I run my fingers through my hair and lean on the bar. "I want to have fun. It's been way too long since I've had fun."

"If you say so." He gives me another drink. I down that one too.

"Another."

"Noelle, come on." It's Erin, I think. I can't tell. How come I never realized how similar she and Brooke sound? Maybe it's Brooke.

"I'm fine," I say. My heart thuds against my ribcage. The dim lights swirl. It looks pretty. "I'm great. Best Thanksgiving ever." I give Everett my biggest smile. "Thank you for inviting me." I take a gulp from the glass he sets in front of me.

Erin and Brooke are talking to each other. I can't hear them over the music. Erin is making crazy gestures with her hands. Brooke waves, and Everett leans over the bar. She whispers something in his ear.

I take another gulp. I think they're talking about me. "Are you talking about me?"

"Nope." Everett picks up my empty cup. "How about another?"

"Yep." What a great guy.

He fills the cup and hands it back to me. "Enjoy."

I drink. I can barely even taste the alcohol now.

Brooke sits next to me, a bottle of water in front of her. Everett is on the other side of the bar serving people. Erin has disappeared. No, wait—she's next to me too. Not with Brooke. On the other side. Where's Drew? He should be here too. No, wait. He's with Heidi. Over by the bathrooms. Holding her hand.

Anger flares inside me. He shouldn't be with Heidi. He should be here, sitting on a barstool next to me. He's *my* fiancé, after all. What's he doing with her? He's such a jerk.

"I'll be right back," I tell my friends. "I'm going to tell Drew he's a jerk."

"No!" Erin puts a hand on my arm. "Don't do that."

"Why not? He is."

"I know he is. He's a huge jerk. Probably the biggest one I know. But you don't want to tell him that. Not here."

"Why not?"

"Because it's too loud," Brooke says. "He won't hear you."

"Oh." She's right. It is loud. "Maybe I should write him a note instead."

"That's a great idea," Erin says.

"You want to do it now?" Brooke asks. "There's paper and pens back at Everett's house."

I consider that. Yes, that's a good idea. I've always been better with writing my thoughts than saying them out loud.

"Yeah, let's do it now."

"Okay." Brooke waves again, and Everett comes back to our side of the bar. "We're taking Noelle home," she says.

His lips move, and I can't really make out what he's saying, but I could swear it's something like "Good idea."

"It is a good idea, isn't it?" I ask. "Because in a note I can say exactly what I think without getting all messed up."

He glances at Brooke. She nods.

"Right," Everett confirms.

I put one foot on the ledge that runs around the perimeter of the bar and hoist myself up. I fling my arms around him. His curly hair is soft on my cheek.

"Thank you for all the drinks," I say. "And for dinner."

"You're welcome."

I give him a kiss, aiming for his cheek but landing somewhere between his jaw and his chin, holding on for just a second longer than is necessary before I pull away.

"Don't worry," I whisper. "That was only in case Drew was looking."

"No worries," he says. "Good luck with your note."

"Thanks!"

The three of us go outside to Brooke's car. Erin helps me into the front seat.

"Thank you," I tell her as she buckles my seat belt. "I love you."

In the dark parking lot her teeth shine white as she laughs. "I love you too." She gets into the backseat. "Let's go."

Brooke starts the car and pulls out of the parking lot. I lean my head against the headrest and stare out the window. I think about what I'm going to put into my letter to Drew. I'm furious with him for showing up with Heidi and ruining my night. If not for him, I might have actually had a nice Thanksgiving. Asshole. He ruins everything. Lives *and* holidays.

When I wake up the next morning, I'm pretty much in agony. My head throbs in time with the beat of my heart. My tongue feels like someone's cut it out and replaced it with a jumbo cotton ball. My stomach writhes and threatens to rebel. I can't even think about the horrible taste in my mouth.

"Ohhh," I moan. This will be the hangover to end all hangovers. Black Friday, indeed.

I feel like death.

But that's not even the worst part.

The worst part is that I don't have a freaking clue where I am.

12

I'M IN A bed, at least, so I'm not really scared. Not like I would be if I was in a parking lot next to a dumpster. But I don't recognize this bed. It's definitely not mine.

I force myself into a sitting position and wince in agony when my head whirls. I clutch the comforter and take a deep breath, waiting for the pain and the nausea to recede. Then I survey my surroundings. Carefully, because whoever this room belongs to, I'm sure they won't be happy if I vomit all over it.

The walls around me are painted gray and unadorned. There are two windows with white curtains vertically striped with black and blinds that are closed, so I can't look outside for any familiar landmarks. The ceiling is white, the floor some kind of blond hardwood. The furniture is wood, painted black. The comforter clenched between my fingers is a slightly darker gray than the walls and covers black sheets. A really masculine room, but whose?

How drunk did I *get* last night? Did I actually go home with someone?

"Oh, God." I drop my head into my hands. *Ouch*. Not smart.

But wait. The bed I'm in is no bigger than a full. Two pillows, but only one dented. A quick glance at the table next to me reveals a glass of water, a bottle of Pepto-Bismol, and a little pile of aspirin.

And a note.

First things first. I put every last aspirin into my mouth and swallow them down with a gulp of water, which I then chase with a swig of Pepto. The chalky liquid on my tongue makes my stomach flip over again, but I manage to keep it down. I take another swallow of water to rinse the taste out. I've always loathed Pepto-Bismol.

I rub my eyes. Mascara flakes off and sprinkles like tiny Goth snowflakes onto the comforter. I'm glad there's no mirror in the room. I can't possibly look any better than I feel, and I feel pretty terrible. The thought of looking at my own face is horrifying.

I stretch out a hand and pick up the sheet of paper on the bedside table. The handwriting is small and masculine, and when I squint to focus on it my head hurts even worse. Thankfully, it's only a few short lines.

Noelle—hope you're feeling okay. Here's some aspirin and Pepto. You'll probably need it. If you want the bathroom, it's down the hall to your left. I went out to grab breakfast. Be back soon.—E.

E. Everett?

Oh, crap.

Please tell me I didn't pass out in Everett's house. In his bed!

How the hell did I even get here? The last thing I remember is asking him for another drink, telling him that it had been too long since I had fun. And I told him that … why?

The memory, when it comes, hurts almost worse than the pain in my head.

Because Drew was there. With Heidi. Snuggling in a booth.

And then after I consumed my weight in a liquor no one under the age of seventy should drink at all, let alone in the quantities I had—I kissed Everett to make Drew jealous.

I have *got* to get out of here. Preferably before E. comes back.

I push back the comforter and cautiously swing my legs off the bed so that my feet touch the floor. I wince—it's cold. I push myself into a standing position but have to close my eyes and sit back down when the motion makes it feel like someone's set off a bunch of dynamite inside my skull. I take a deep breath, count to five. Then I try again. This time I stay standing. I lurch around the room, finding my clothes neatly folded and lying on top of the glossy black dresser. My boots sit beside the closed door. For the first time I realize that I'm swimming in a t-shirt and sweatpants that are most definitely not mine.

Yup. I appear to be wearing Everett's clothes. Kill me now.

I stumble down the hall—to the left—and find the bathroom. My reflection is as bad as I thought. The circles and mascara smudges beneath my eyes would make a panda envious. My skin is splotchy and dry. My hair is a mess, matted and flattened to my skull on one side with way, *way* too much volume on the other. I wonder at the chances of Everett having some kind of ponytail holder. Maybe I'm lucky enough that Brooke or one of his girlfriends left one lying around.

Lucky. Ha.

However, someone's been kind enough to leave a toothbrush still in its packaging on the side of the sink, next to a tube of toothpaste. I guess a bartender of all people would know what someone suffering a hangover would consider most important. I turn on the water, wet the brush, and squeeze about half a pound of blue toothpaste onto the bristles. I brush for a good minute past the American Dental Association-recommended one hundred and twenty seconds, spit, and wonder if anything has ever felt as good as a clean mouth.

I'm not a nosy person, but I search the medicine cabinet in hopes of coming up with something that will make my hair look more like something naturally growing from my head and less like something one might see blowing across a road in the middle of the desert. The best I can do is a fine-toothed comb. I stare at it while gathering the courage to actually use it. This will *not* be fun.

Five minutes later the comb is missing a few teeth and the pain in my head has started to radiate down my neck, but my hair is lying flat. Well, flat-ish. It'll do. I might have a clip or something in my purse. If I could remember where I *put* my purse.

I splash cold water on my face and pat it dry with the towel hanging on the hook on the wall. Then I hobble back to the bedroom in which I'd spent the night, shut the door, shed the oversized sweats, and put my own clothes back on. I find my purse on the floor next to the dresser.

As humiliated as I am to even be here, I have to admit it was really nice of Everett to leave me medicine and a note. I should write my own and thank him. I think there's a pen in my purse. *Ohmygod—he left a note.* Does that mean he was in the room while I slept? Of course it does. He can't send paper through walls. He was in here. Looking at me as I slept—most likely with my mouth hanging open and a trail of drool snaking down my chin. And snoring.

On a scale of one to ten, my level of mortification is at about a two hundred and thirty-one.

I'm out of here.

And right as that thought materializes in my head, I hear the front door open. And shut.

He's back.

My stomach turns but for a different reason this time. How am I supposed to walk out there and act like I didn't make a complete jackass out of myself? I mean, I'm almost thirty years old. My days of getting drunk for fun or to chase the bad feelings away are long over, and have been for a while—clearly, since I most likely would have been able to handle twice as much liquor ten years ago. How many drinks did I have? And while I'm pretty sure I can account for everything I said and did, what if I'm wrong? What if I did something besides kiss his cheek?

Only one way to find out, I guess.

Climbing out the window isn't really an option in my present state.

I suck in a deep breath, let it out, and open the door.

He sits at the table in the dining room, two takeout cups of coffee and a bagel or something in front of him. His back is to me and there's a newspaper spread out at his elbow.

A newspaper?

I didn't know people still read actual newspapers. Even the *Stalker* has gone mostly online. I find it sort of charming that he hasn't succumbed to pervasive technology. As I stand there watching, gathering the nerve to make my presence known, he turns the page.

I take one step forward. The floor creaks under my foot, announcing me, and I smother a curse.

Everett twists in his chair. He looks annoyingly well-rested.

"Good morning," he says.

"Good morning." I hesitate, not sure where to begin. Thank him for giving me a safe place to stay, medicine, and a toothbrush? Or should I get right down to it and ask if I did anything that should make me contemplate driving my car off the bridge into the Springhollow Creek on my way home?

"You hungry? I got coffee and bagels. I can toast one up for you. I have butter and cream cheese too."

Am I hungry? My stomach has calmed down some, and I don't feel like I'm on the verge of throwing up anymore. And as far as I can recall, gorging myself on carbohydrates the morning after drinking always helped.

"Okay," I say. "No butter or anything, though. Just plain. Thank you."

"No problem." He gets up from the table and heads into the kitchen. I hear him push down the lever on the toaster. "Coffee?"

"No, thanks," I say. "I don't drink coffee." I eye the cup on the table in front of me. It's from Wawa, not The Daily Grind, but I'm not taking any chances. "I'm sorry if you bought me one."

"Not a problem. I can drink both. I *do* drink coffee. Is there anything you'd like? Juice? Tea?"

Ooh. "Tea would be good." Just the thought of some Earl Grey has me feeling measurably better.

"You got it." He gestures to the table. "Sit down. I'll bring it to you."

I obey, lowering myself into the same chair at which I sat during dinner last night. Thoughts race through my head. He's being nice, and doesn't seem in a hurry to get me out of his house, so maybe I wasn't so awful last night. Do I dare ask?

"Hey, Everett?"

"Yeah?"

Here goes nothing.

"What, um—" I swallow hard. "What did I do? Last night?"

I hear him chuckle. "You drank a lot of Southern Comfort."

"I know that." My head throbs in agreement. "I mean, what did I do because of it?"

He comes back into the dining room and hands me a mug full of tea, whorls of steam fluttering above the rim. I hold it in both hands, lower my face and inhale. It's not Earl Grey—smells more like your everyday orange pekoe—but I don't care. It's tea. It smells good.

I take a sip, burning my tongue. It tastes good too.

I hear my bagel pop up, and Everett goes back into the kitchen, returning a few seconds later with a plate. He hands it to me, then sits back down. He turns the page of his newspaper, gulps from his coffee.

Doesn't speak.

"That bad, huh?" I finally say with an awkward little laugh.

He shakes his head. "Nah," he says, and with that one little word I feel myself relax. "I've seen way worse." He takes another drink. "And it's not like you didn't have a reason. I can't say I wouldn't have done the same if I was in your place."

My gut twists. "Did he, um." I pick a chunk from my bagel. "Did he see anything?"

"You mean did he see you kiss me?" I wince and force myself to nod. "I don't think so. But even if he did, I wouldn't worry. It's not like we were making out in the middle of the floor." Oh, God. No, we weren't. But still.

"Okay. Good." I chew the bagel chunk and swallow it before making myself meet his eyes. "I'm not worried, though."

"Don't be. He doesn't deserve your concern." The animosity in his voice shocks me. I didn't know he cared. It's kind of sweet.

"Thank you. For watching out for me."

"Brooke and Erin did the hard part," he said with a crooked smile. "They got you out of your clothes and into bed." Well, it's definitely a relief knowing *he* didn't undress me. "All I did was let you sleep it off."

My ears are on fire. I rip off another piece of my bagel.

"And I switched you to straight Diet Coke about three drinks before they decided to take you home. You didn't even notice," he continues. He's still grinning. "So you can thank me for the fact that you're just mildly hung over, rather than hurling all over the place."

Mildly hung over? He thinks this is mild? He'd change his mind pretty quick if *he* felt like someone had dropped an anvil on his head, Looney-Tunes style.

"Thanks," I say dryly.

I eat the rest of my bagel in a silence punctuated only by the turn of newspaper pages. I squint to see if I can read anything, but I can only see enough to realize that it's the *New York Times*. Arts section. Book reviews, I think.

I wonder what kinds of books he reads. Drew wasn't big on books. Unless they were comic books. He also read *Maxim* pretty religiously.

Something tells me that no matter how hard I look, I won't find an issue of *Maxim* anywhere here. Not that I'm going to look. I don't really care. It's refreshing, that's all.

My plate is empty, and my tea is cool enough that I can drink it down without blistering my esophagus. So I do. I set the mug down, twist my hair into a knot, and let it fall back down.

"I guess I should go," I say. He looks up from his paper.

"Okay," he says.

"So, thanks." What's that, the third time I've said that? "For last night. And for dinner, too. It was amazing."

"I'm glad you enjoyed it. Do you want any leftovers?"

I can't help laughing. "I think I've taken sufficient advantage of your kindness already. But thanks." For the fourth time.

"You're welcome." He pushes his chair back and stands up. He walks me to the door. I have to wait while he fiddles with a few locks, then pulls it open. "Take it easy today, okay? Get some rest. You're probably pretty dehydrated."

"I wish I could. I have a lot of work to do for the wedding. I promised Will last week that I'd get him a list of stuff he can do from his mom's, and I still haven't done it yet."

"Right. Will. Well, we don't want Will to feel left out, do we? After all, this is the wedding of the century." He still looks friendly enough, but something in his tone has changed. Like I just reminded him that his sister is about to blow twenty-five grand on me. Twenty-five grand that he probably thinks I don't deserve.

Well, I don't. It's an outrageous amount of money. This is why the check still sits in my desk drawer instead of collecting interest in my savings account.

"No," I say, for lack of anything better. "It's always good to get the groom involved in any way possible."

"Don't let me keep you, then." He reaches over me and opens the storm door, pushing it out and holding it. "See you later. Drive safe."

"I will," I mumble.

I feel thoroughly flattened. I step outside into the cold November sunshine and trudge down the walk to the street, where my car has been sitting since yesterday afternoon. I get in, put on my seatbelt, put the key in the ignition, and turn it. I turn on the heat and wait for it to stop blowing cold and warm me up.

Before I drive away, I take one more look at Everett's front door.

It's closed.

🔔

Well, it's a pathetic list, but it's a list. *Come up with a bunch of songs you want the band or DJ to play. Decide if you want white, silver, or sapphire blue cummerbunds. Pick 4 hors d'oeuvres from this list of 8.* Honestly, Brooke and I have everything else under control. If the wedding was any bigger, I might be able to tack one or two more things on the list, but it's so small we've really got it covered between the two of us.

Speaking of Brooke. I should call her and apologize for being the freak I was last night. She's a client. She shouldn't have seen that.

"It's okay, Noelle," she says.

"It's not," I protest. "I acted like a complete idiot. I shouldn't even have done that with *Erin* there. So completely unprofessional."

"But I understand," she insists. "This is a small town, and people talk. I knew you were engaged to Drew Emmons, and I knew the story behind your breakup. I just can't believe he showed up there with her."

"Well, he didn't know I'd be there," I say, deciding not to wonder how Brooke knew all of that. "Last night was the first time I'd gone to the Library since I was about twenty-five. I realized that the time I might have spent sucking down mind erasers would be better spent building my business. And I didn't want to risk clients seeing me out. Doing exactly what you saw me do last night." Shame burns in my cheeks. Again.

"Really, Noelle. Please. Don't worry about it. I don't think any less of you. In fact, if I'd seen Will there with another girl, if we were engaged or not he'd still be picking my fingernails out of his eyeballs."

We laugh together but my heart isn't in it. How does she know Will isn't doing exactly the same thing Drew did last night—only in the safety of a bar eight hundred miles away?

"Thank you," I tell her. "I don't feel any less embarrassed, but I appreciate the understanding."

"Anytime. Hey, while I have you, I wanted to ask. Are you at all interested in coming to see my studio perform *The Nutcracker*? I don't know if you're into it, or ballet at all, but I think it's going to be really good this year and I'd like to give you tickets. You know, as a thank you for doing all of this for us."

Paying me twenty-five thousand dollars isn't enough—now she wants to give me ballet tickets?

"Actually, I love ballet." Although it might hurt a bit, since every year I'd dragged Drew into the city to see the Pennsylvania Ballet do *The Nutcracker* there. He'd pretended to hate it.

Or did he?

Maybe he did hate it and only went to make me happy when I selfishly insisted he drop everything and give up a Saturday night to watch people flounce around on a stage in tights.

Slob. Insensitive. Selfish and demanding. If I come up with any more reasons Drew must have had for falling out of love with me, I'll lock myself in the bedroom for the rest of my life rather than inflict my awful self on other people.

How did I miss it all?

"I'd love to go. Thank you."

"Oh, good! Opening night is December eighth. Next Friday. Are you free?"

I scrabble in my desk drawer for the wirebound planner I still use even though everyone else relies on their smart phones. I flip to next week. The rehearsal for the Jameson wedding is that night, but since Erin is handling it for me, I *am* free.

"I'm good for that night."

"Perfect. I'll leave your tickets at will-call. How many will you need?"

I bite my lip. Hard. I don't want to say it. "Just one."

I spend the rest of the weekend talking to the florist about the kinds of flowers Brooke wants for the bridal party (pure white roses, one in full bloom for Will, buds for Everett and Will's two other groomsmen and the single long-stemmed variety for her and her three attendants), calling Blush to check on the status of Brooke's gown, and setting up a menu tasting with Brady Cole on Tuesday afternoon. Will returns my e-mail, and I call Blush again to order black tuxes with sapphire cummerbunds, call Brady again and give him Will's choices of hors d'oeuvres, call the hair salon to confirm Brooke's trial hair and makeup appointment, and talk to Cheryl at Life Made Lovely to make sure the invitations will be ready to pick up on Monday. She promises they will be.

For any other client, I'd probably be pulling my hair out. Lucky for me—for us—the name Brooke St. John carries some weight, and that weight seems to make people want to make her happy.

Late in the afternoon I make myself a peanut butter sandwich and wash it down with a few more aspirin. My work for today is done.

Four weeks ago I wouldn't have said it, but this is turning out to be a lot easier than I'd expected.

13

On Monday afternoon, I put on the news in an attempt to avoid any and all mentions of Christmas. This is a stupid idea, because now that Thanksgiving's over, they seem to have forgotten how to talk about anything else except long lines at the mall and sales figures and the Toy of the Year and coat drives. All stuff I really don't want to think about. Well, I guess the last one's okay, but hearing about kids who need coats is a different kind of depressing.

After I finish dressing and before I leave for the stationer to get Brooke's invitations, I take a few minutes to empty my drain board, pull my shower curtain closed, dry the puddles of water on my bathroom sink, and scoop up the dirty clothes on the floor and dump them in the hamper. I've made a New Year's resolution to stop being such a slob, and I figure there's no harm in starting early. Besides, it might be nice to walk into my apartment without getting my feet tangled in last night's pajamas and almost falling over and breaking my neck. And I'll probably enjoy putting dinner on a plate I don't have to rewash because I left it sitting too long the first time and my pancake syrup didn't come all the way off.

Yes, I'm a new woman.

I'm picking my tea cup off the coffee table when the weatherman says the word *snow*.

"We had thought this system was going to track east and head out to sea," he says as he points to a spinning violet mass on his map. "But now it looks like it'll be pulled onshore instead. It won't be a major storm, but it'll be enough to snarl traffic and make rush hour dangerous. It might not be a bad idea to leave work early if you can."

I glance at my watch, the one Drew gave me. The one I should pawn. It's one o'clock. I've got plenty of time.

Life Made Lovely isn't far from Silver Bells, so I park in front of my own shop and walk the two blocks. The air bites, stinging my cheeks and whipping the end of my scarf into my lip gloss, where it sticks and leaves tiny threads behind. Shouldn't have worn the angora, I guess. I try my damndest to ignore the lampposts with their stupid wreaths and lit-up snowflakes. If I get caught yelling at them again, I'll probably be taken away.

As I approach the town square, men mill around setting up the enormous Christmas tree that will be lit sometime this week with a fair amount of festivity. The tree lighting and the Holiday Village have been my favorite things about Springhollow ever since I moved here for school. Drew and I would go to see the lighting every year, Christmas music piped in from speakers mounted discreetly under eaves and food vendors selling hot chocolate, eggnog, cookies, and even roasted chestnuts. It's seriously like something out of a cheesy made-for-TV Christmas movie. I loved every second of it.

Now, just the thought makes me want to throw up.

I pull open the door and enter the relative safety of the stationery shop. It smells of paper, ink, and a vague whiff of spicy perfume that I guess comes from the woman behind the long white marble counter.

"Hi, Noelle!"

"Hi, Cheryl. How are you?"

"Busy," she laughs. "But it sure beats the alternative. How about you?"

"Sort of slow, actually," I reply before I can censor myself.

"What? You of all people, at Christmas? No way. You're the most in-demand wedding planner I work with!"

Well, since the cat's head and front paws are already peeking out of the bag, I might as well open it completely and let the poor thing run free.

"I'm shutting down," I say.

Cheryl's eyes widen. "You are?"

"Yeah. I'm, um, leaving town. Going back home."

"Oh, no! Why?"

Could she really not know? Everyone else does. The beauty of living in a small town—everyone is aware of every single aspect of your life.

"My sister's having a baby," I tell her. "She's going to need my help." It's not the first time I've said it. It is, however, the first time I realize just how feeble it sounds.

"But you have such a thriving business here!"

Ahh, okay. She only cares about the business I bring her. Well, I guess I can understand that. It's not like Cheryl and I regularly get together to watch *Sex and the City* reruns and give each other pedicures.

"I won't say it hasn't been fun," I say. "I've learned a lot and I've really enjoyed myself. But it's time for a change."

"Well, we'll miss you. You're here for the St. John invitations?"

"I am."

153

"Okay. Be right back." And she is, in less than thirty seconds, returning to the counter with a silver box in her hands. "They turned out gorgeous."

"They always do." I lift the lid to reveal the silver and white creation Brooke chose. The envelopes are white, the silver tissue overlay delicate as gossamer. The paper is thick and snowy, with letters the color of a December night sky pressed into its softness. "Wow, Cheryl. You outdid yourself this time."

"Thank you!" She beams. "It's a real honor to do these. Brooke's mother was a childhood friend of mine."

"I'm sure she'd be very pleased." I turn the box, eyeing them from a different angle. "Thank you so much for getting them done so quickly."

"Oh, it wasn't a problem. Not for Brooke."

I trace my finger over the depressed letters. *"The pleasure of your company is requested at the marriage of Brooke Amelia St. John to William Scott Hurley,"* it says. *"Friday, December the twenty-second—"*

Wait. What?

"Cheryl?" I ask, panic rising in my throat. "There's a problem."

She frowns. "A problem?"

"A big one." So big my hands are shaking. With quivering fingers I pull an invitation from its nest in the box and lay it down on the counter. "The date is wrong."

"You can't be—" Cheryl turns the invitation around and stares at it. Then she glances at the calendar on the wall beside her. "No, it's fine," she says. "The twenty-second *is* Friday."

"I know that," I say. "But the wedding is on Christmas Eve."

"That's not possible," Cheryl insists. "Hang on. Let me get the order."

She disappears to the back again. I drum my fingers on the countertop, more out of horror than impatience. What could have *happened*? Why is the date wrong?

"Here it is." She's got a folder in her neatly manicured fingers. She puts it down on the counter and opens it. "Here's the order you e-mailed me."

I take the offered sheet of paper and scan it. It's definitely from me—noelle@silverbellsweddings.com—to her, cheryl@lifemadelovelypaperco.com.

"Hi Cheryl," it reads. *"Here's the final order for the St. John wedding. 70 of the Star Bright letterpress invitations on white paper in Sapphire, with Silver Sparkle tissue overlay."* And underneath that is the wording. Exactly as it shows on the invitation, except my message distinctly says *"Sunday, December the twenty-fourth, at four o'clock in the afternoon."*

"There. You see?" I stab at it with my index fingernail. "Christmas Eve." My panic is making me short-tempered; I can feel it. That's not the kind of wedding planner I am. I pride myself on staying cool. But this goes a bit beyond the wrong flowers showing up or the photographer getting there late.

"Right," she says. "But then there's this." She hands me a small square sheet, torn from a message pad.

"What is this?" I ask.

"A phone message. I didn't take it, Mark did. But the groom called and changed the date."

"What?" Everything is spinning. Why would Will change the date? How did Will even know where the invitations were coming from? "I'm so confused."

"Me too," Cheryl admits. She turns toward the back. "Mark?" she calls. "Can you come out here for a minute?"

He emerges after a minute, glasses sliding down his nose, ink stains peppering his fingers. He smiles. "Hi, Noelle."

I wish I could smile back. I've always liked Mark. "Hi."

"There seems to have been a bit of a mix-up," Cheryl says, and I want to scream. A bit of a mix-up? Try a catastrophe! The wedding is in less than *four weeks*. Invitations should have gone out a month ago. This is definitely bigger than a bit of a mix-up.

"You took the phone message here, right?" She shows it to him. He glances at it and nods.

"I did," he said. "Why?"

"Who did the caller say he was?" I ask.

"The groom. Will Hurley." Mark points to the spot on the message where he wrote that exact information.

I still don't get it. "Did he give you a reason why the date had to be changed?"

"He said that his mother is sick, and they were pushing the wedding up two days." Mark's eyes, behind his glasses, are wide and blinking fast.

I'm shaking my head before he even completes his sentence. "It's not true. Everything has already been booked. Brooke would have told me if anything like that was going on."

Mark shrugs helplessly. "I just took the message. I'm really sorry, Noelle."

"It's all right, Mark," Cheryl says. No, it's not! What am I going to do with seventy letter-pressed invitations that have the wrong date on them? We can't send them. And I highly doubt Brooke will be into the idea of crossing out the wrong date and hand-writing in the correct one.

Mark escapes to the safety of his production area, and Cheryl turns to me.

"I do apologize for the mix-up, Noelle," she says, and I want to yell at her to stop calling it that. "I'm happy to redo them. Of course, if the error was ours we'd do them for free, but since it wasn't, we'll have to charge for them."

"You should have called me," I point out. "If the information didn't come from me, you should have called to check with me."

"But—"

"I'm sorry. But no." I struggle to keep the fury from my voice. "All changes either come from me or are approved by me. That's how it's always been. This mistake is yours. You should have verified it before printing."

Cheryl purses her lips. "If that's what you want." Something tells me she's not going to miss me as much as she wanted me to think she was.

"It is. And I'm going to need them no later than Wednesday."

"Of course," Cheryl coos.

"Can I take the envelopes?" Thank goodness I recruited a calligrapher to address them rather than having Life Made Lovely print them, except now I'm going to have to give the calligrapher another copy of the address list to make sure they go to the right people and not huts in some native village on an island in the Indian Ocean.

I'm still completely baffled. What the hell *happened?* I'm going to have to call Will.

"Certainly." Cheryl holds the paper with the phone message in her hands. "All of the information is in your initial e-mail, correct? Can I safely destroy this?"

"Please do," I beg. "The wedding is most definitely on Christmas Eve." How am I supposed to tell Brooke what happened?

"I'll call you when they're ready," Cheryl says.

"Thank you." Gripping the box of envelopes in my hands as if they might dissolve and float away, I push out of the shop and back onto the street.

The cold air smacks my cheeks, but it feels good, cooling them down and letting some of my anger and panic subside. I'm still shaking, though. I can't believe someone would try to ruin the most important day of someone else's life, and for no particular reason. No obvious one, either.

The two-block walk back helps. It lets me burn off anxious energy and adrenaline, and by the time I'm back at my car I'm able to think about the whole thing if not calmly, then at least from a place where I can attempt to think about it rationally. I'm still angry, but not out of control. I can funnel that anger toward getting things done. It's good. I'm good.

That is, until my car won't start.

"What?" I say aloud. The only response is silence—silence and the muffled yell of one of the workmen struggling to tether the enormous Christmas tree to the ground in the square.

I turn the key. Nothing. Turn it again. Still nothing. Not a groan, not a whirr, not a click.

Nothing.

And then I see why. I left my headlights on. I don't usually put them on in the middle of the day, but it's so cloudy I'd flicked them on and apparently forgot that quick. My battery must be dead.

Dead, and I'm stranded.

A burning mix of anger and frustration and confusion stings my eyes. I yank my key from the ignition so hard I probably break some delicate computer chip inside, thrust open the door, and go to the door of my office. I pull on the handle before I can register that it's dim inside and the door is locked. I forgot—Erin is doing a final menu tasting with the Jamesons. Normally one of us would be at the shop at all times, but since I'm not taking any new clients, we haven't been as diligent about making sure someone is always available to answer the phone or greet potential brides.

I dig through my keys until I find the one for the shop door. Fortunately, *that* key works. I drop my purse and the box of envelopes onto Erin's desk and sink into the chair. I need my car! I have no time to sit here and wait for my mechanic to bring a new battery. What should I do? Who should I call? I let my AAA membership expire over the summer, and even though I kept meaning to renew it, I haven't yet. So I can't call them. I'd normally call Drew for a jump, but that's obviously not an option. Erin is with the caterer and can't be bothered with my drama.

Who else is there?

I scroll through the contacts in my phone and find mostly former clients, vendors, and family members that live a hundred miles away. There are some others in there, but they're friends I made through Drew, girls who haven't bothered to contact me once since we broke up. And I realize that I've got nobody here. Not a single real friend aside from Erin, and look what I'm doing to her. Abandoning her and leaving her unemployed. If that's the way I treat my friends, no wonder I barely have any.

A sob escapes me. It's quick, though, and I'm grateful when it doesn't give way to a crying jag. There have been *way* too many of them lately. Now is not the time. I have to get my car running, I have to get the envelopes to the calligrapher, and I have to get home.

I could call Brooke, I guess, but she might be having rehearsals. Opening night is next week. And I don't know if I'm ready to tell her about her invitations.

That leaves me with one option.

Everett.

Oh, man. I *really* don't want to call Everett. The memory of his sarcastic, shuttered face as he practically shoved me out of his house on Friday still stings.

But there's no one else. He might have jumper cables—not to mention a vehicle with which my battery could be jumped. I vaguely remember him mentioning a Jeep at some point.

My finger hovers over his phone number. All I have to do is touch it, and my phone will call him. I take a deep breath, close my eyes, and press. What if he doesn't answer? What if he's at work, or doesn't want to talk to me?

"Hello?"

"Everett?" My voice cracks with relief. I cough.

"Yeah. Hey, Noelle."

"Hi. Listen, I hate to do this, but I didn't have anyone else to call. My car is dead. Well, the battery's dead. I think."

"Okay." Silence. "What do you need?"

"I need a jump, or a ride home so I can call my mechanic and see if he can send one of his guys out to put in a new battery, or fix it or something. I don't know." My voice is verging on hysteria. I inhale hard and force myself to calm down. "Sorry. I didn't mean to freak out. It's been a stressful few hours. And I still have things to do, which will be difficult without a car."

"Okay," he says again. He pauses. "Where are you?"

"At my shop."

"Okay. I'll be there in about fifteen minutes."

The call disconnects. I slump down in Erin's chair, not sure whether to feel relieved or that much more anxious.

While I wait for my knight in slightly tarnished, dented armor, I put a call in to my mechanic. I was right not to rely on him first. They can send someone out, he says, but they're swamped. It might not be until tomorrow or even Wednesday. I take a moment to send up a prayer thanking whoever might hear it that Springhollow doesn't have parking meters and is a relatively safe area where I can pretty much be sure that my car will still have windows when I get back to it.

Almost exactly fifteen minutes later, the door to Silver Bells opens, bringing with it a blast of freezing air and Everett, in jeans and a leather jacket. He's got a helmet in his hands.

"What is that?"

"What's what? Hello, by the way."

Is he seriously calling me out for being rude when he pretty much pushed me out his front door just three days ago?

"Hello. What is that? In your hand?"

"This?" He lifts it, looks at it. "It's a bike helmet."

"I know. Why do you have it?"

"Because I'd rather not see my brains splattered all over the street." He shrugs. "It's not unreasonable."

I can't believe him. It's almost December. They're calling for snow. And he expects to take me home *on a motorcycle*.

I grit my teeth. Count to five. He's my only option right now, and it was extremely nice of him to come and help me. Even though it's too damn cold out to even entertain the thought of walking home, it's not snowing yet and I have to assume he knows how to ride. I can suck it up.

"You're right. It's not," I say. I stand up and pick up my bag. "I'm sorry. I just—I thought you'd be bringing jumper cables or something."

"I don't have any."

What kind of guy doesn't keep jumper cables? Then again, Drew only had them because he borrowed mine and never gave them back.

"Thank you for coming to get me. I appreciate it. A lot."

He shrugs. "It's nothing." He heads outside, me following behind. I flick off the light before stepping onto the sidewalk and turning to lock the door. When I turn back, he's holding the helmet out.

"What?" I say. "You can't—you don't expect me to—"

"Yes, I do. I don't want your brains splattered all over the street, either. It's bad enough that I'm letting you ride in that wool coat, but I don't have an extra jacket for you."

I sigh, kissing my good hair day goodbye. Then again, smashing my skull on the pavement would probably make it look even worse.

I take the stupid helmet and put it on. It sits awkwardly, as if a stiff wind would blow it right off.

"Here." Everett pulls off his leather gloves and hands them to me, then reaches out to fasten the strap under my chin. "Better?"

"Yeah."

"Good." He grabs the back of the helmet, pulling it up then down, obscuring my face and, I swear, trying to yank it off my head as painfully as possible.

"What the hell are you doing?" I yelp.

"The roll-off test." He puts the helmet back into place. "It passed. You won't die of massive head injuries if we crash." He takes his gloves back.

"Thanks." I rub my chin, scowling.

"Anytime." He sits on his bike and plants both feet on the ground. He puts his gloves back on, slides forward, and looks at me expectantly.

I hesitate on the sidewalk. How to do this gracefully?

"You've never been on a bike before, have you?" he asks.

I shake my head. The helmet must look ridiculous—I probably look like a Tootsie Roll pop.

"Nope."

"It's okay. I'll hold it steady. Just swing your leg up and over." He watches carefully as I do it, shifting to keep the weight evenly distributed as I settle myself.

"Okay. I'm ready."

He laughs. "No, you're not. Move up closer, and put your arms around me."

I feel a tiny flutter in my chest. I'm having a heart attack, probably. "What?"

"You can't just sit there," he says. "You need to hold on. Pull yourself up so you're secure against my back, and put your arms around my waist."

Oh, hell. I should have walked.

Too late now.

14

I INCH FORWARD. I'd like to keep as much space between us as possible, but he's right—I need to be up against his back. With my arms around him? Why? I've seen plenty of people riding as passengers on bikes with their hands behind them, holding onto the seat. I could try that.

"Arms around *me*," Everett commands. "If you've never done this before, you're not going to want to get fancy. I'd tell you that even if you were a guy."

"Okay," I grumble. I lift my arms and tentatively slide them around his waist.

Ugh. He's right. This does feel safer.

"Good girl," he says, as if I'm a puppy who just peed on a newspaper instead of the carpet. "You ready?"

No. "Yeah."

"Okay. Hold on." With that, he kicks and the bike roars to life, rumbling like an angry metallic bear. He waits for a black Prius (which I fervently hope is Drew until I see the driver is an older woman who couldn't care less that I'm on a bike clinging to a cute, leather-clad guy) to pass before pulling out into the street and starting the journey to my apartment.

"Where do you live?" Everett asks, his voice almost getting lost in the rush of wind that surrounds us.

"Dartmouth Square Apartments," I shout back. He nods, and one of his curls almost goes up my nose.

The bike glides through the streets with more grace than I would have expected, given the fact that it feels like I'm straddling a rocket ship. It really is cold. Too cold to be riding a bike. Even beneath my jeans, sweater, coat, and scarf my flesh erupts into painful goosebumps. I should have worn gloves.

I squish myself closer to Everett and wrap my arms a little tighter. There's warmth coming off him that helps. My chin is against his shoulder, and I have no choice but to inhale the scent of him. It's leather and soap, fresh air and salt. Nothing like Drew, who splashed on a very particular amount of cologne before leaving the house every morning—cologne that had the tendency to give me a headache if I got too close and stayed there too long, even after he'd worn it through a ten-hour workday. And although it had given me a headache I'd thought it smelled clean, good, projecting the very essence of Drew-ness. But it wasn't. It was fake, a facade. Another mask that he wore..

The bike is fast, and within minutes Everett's pulling into my empty spot in front of Building Three. The hum of the engine cuts off. Beneath me, the bike goes still.

"Okay," he says. "Do exactly what you did when you were getting on, except the opposite. You can hang on to me if you need to."

I don't want to need to. Finding myself comparing his smell to that of the guy I was going to marry—and finding said ex-fiancé coming up short—has me a little freaked out. It's a bit too soon to be sniffing other guys, isn't it? But my muscles are weak from being tightly clenched for the last mile, and I wobble when I try to put my right foot down on the curb. I have no choice but to cling to his shoulder as I slide down one side of the bike and swing my other leg over so both feet are firmly planted on sidewalk.

"You're a natural," he says as he does the same.

"Thanks." I feel awkward. Why'd he get off his bike? Does he think I'm going to invite him in? Does he *want* me to invite him in?

"Do you mind if I use your bathroom?" he asks. More mind-reading. "I'll be quick."

"Yeah. No, sure. That's fine," I stammer. "Come on up." I lead him into the lobby of my building. The mom from the third floor is just getting off the elevator. I make it a point to smile at her, to make up for last time when I was so distraught by my world collapsing around me that I couldn't be bothered to return hers. I even throw in a little wave. Normally I might coo at her little girl, too, but I just can't muster the energy for that at the moment.

"Hi," she says. "It's not snowing yet, is it?"

"No, not yet."

"Actually, it just started." Everett points through the door. Sure enough, tiny snowflakes dance on their way from the sky to the cold gray sidewalk. "It's light, though."

"Hopefully storytime at the library isn't canceled. Guess we'll find out!" She smiles at us, at Everett especially, as he's moved from his place behind me to the door, where he holds it open wide enough that her stroller can fit through. "Thanks. Have a good one."

"You, too," I say. She rolls down the walk, makes a right, and disappears.

"Friend of yours?" Everett asks.

"Not really," I say as I head for the stairs. I don't have any friends here, remember? "I just know her from the building."

Everett follows me up the stairs and to the door of my apartment. I turn the key, and when I walk in I'm immediately grateful that I took the time to clean up this morning. There are no embarrassing piles of dishes, no balled-up socks, no water puddles at the bathroom sink, and even the trash can is empty but for the tea bag I used this morning.

"Bathroom's that way," I say, pointing down the hall.

"Thanks." He disappears. I hear the click of the door shutting..

It's then that I remember I left the envelopes for Brooke's invitations on the desk at Silver Bells. Oh, well—it's not like I can do anything with them anyway, not without a car. I pull out my phone, tap out a quick text message to Erin. *Big issue at LML—invitations are wrong,* I type. *Then my car broke down. I'm home now, but when you get back to the office, can you take the envelopes to the calligrapher? They're on your desk. Thanks!* I even give her a smiley face, hoping she won't be annoyed that I've given her another job to do.

I'm getting a headache. I fill my kettle with water and turn on the stove. In the bathroom, the toilet flushes. I hear water run. A few seconds later Everett emerges to find me standing in front of my open cabinet, rubbing my temple with one hand while I root around for cinnamon tea with the other. I swear by cinnamon for headaches. Not even so much the drinking, although it tastes good—it's the smell of it.

"You okay?" he asks.

"Yeah, I'm fine. Just getting a headache. I kind of need my car. And there was an issue at the stationery shop," I say before I can stop myself.

Crap. I guess Brooke's finding out after all.

"What kind of issue?"

I guess I have to tell him now.

"They had the wrong date on Brooke's invitations," I say. I find the cinnamon tea, remove a bag, and drop it into a clean mug.

"Oh, no," he says. "Did you tell Brooke?"

"No." I drizzle some honey into the mug. "I had just gotten back from the shop when I called you. I figured she was in rehearsals." And that she might not need to know, since it would only upset her. "It's under control. They're printing new ones, and they're putting a rush on it. I should have them by Wednesday, which is the day we were supposed to mail them anyway. And Erin's going to take the envelopes to the calligrapher, so they should be ready around the same time. We might lose a day, but that's it." The kettle begins to whistle. I lift it from the stove and start to pour. "It'll work out. It's just stress I didn't need."

"That really sucks."

"You're telling me." I replace the kettle and take a spoon from the drain board. "Do you want some tea? I think I heated enough water."

"No, thanks. I'm good." He shakes his head. "Who told them to change the date? Do they know?"

"Yeah. They said it was Wi—" *Wait a minute.* I drop my spoon and it clatters to the counter, off which it promptly bounces and falls to the floor.

I don't even brace myself for the inevitable golf club to the ceiling. I whirl around to face him.

"How did you know someone told them to change the date?" I demand.

His liquid brown eyes are wide and innocent as a toddler's. "You said they did."

"No," I say slowly, not wanting to give attention to the alarm bell blasting in my head. "No, I didn't say someone told them to change the date. I only said they got the date wrong."

He blinks at me. Doesn't say anything. The alarm screeches louder. This is not happening.

He's busted, and he knows it.

"It was you," I say.

He stands still for a few seconds, then nods. He's not even going to try and deny it.

"Yeah. It was me."

I step away from the counter, away from the mug of water that was boiling hot only a few seconds ago. The temptation might be too much, and I don't want to end up in jail.

"Why?"

He crosses his arms over his chest. "I don't want her to marry that guy."

"That's not your choice!"

"She can't be trusted to make her own choice!" His voice matches mine in both volume and tone. "You don't know her. She's sweet, but so trusting and completely naïve. Will doesn't love her. He's after her money, that's all."

"How do you know?" My heart's thumping. This is insane. Nope. Can't be happening.

"Come on, Noelle." He shakes his head. "How do you *not* know? You haven't even met the guy. He says he's in Canada, but how do you know that's where he really is, or that he's actually nursing his mom through chemo?"

I *don't* know. Didn't I admit that to myself already? But of course, I'm only suspicious because of my own history. The small part of me that's still rational knows there isn't any reason to believe Will isn't doing exactly what he says he's doing. What kind of psycho would lie about a sick mom?

"He's good, though. So good even the PI I hired couldn't find anything on him." He shakes his head. "I wonder how much he offered that woman to shave her head and walk around tied to an oxygen tank."

"You hired a *private investigator?*"

He shrugs. "Why not?"

"Because—"

"She doesn't know him," he interrupts. "Not really."

Deep breaths. In and out. "I don't think Brooke would have accepted a proposal from someone she barely knew."

"But she did. Do you know anything about them as a couple?"

It suddenly occurs to me that I don't. "No." My temple gives a warning throb.

"Well, let me tell you their little love story. They met in April. Not even eight months ago. Every year she hires a photographer to come out and take pictures of her dancers in their costumes. The company she hired sent Will."

"Okay." So what? Love at first sight isn't common, but it's not unheard of.

"He told her he's a photojournalist."

"So? How much money do you think a photojournalist makes? He probably does studio photography on the side." And there I go, pretty much justifying Everett's suspicions.

"Exactly." Blood stains his face. His dark eyes are bright. "A photojournalist *doesn't* make much money. Forty grand a year, on average, and that's with steady work. Will's a freelancer. He has to find his own work. So he shows up and finds Brooke, who, as I'm sure you know, is sort of the town sweetheart. Poor little rich girl with the tragic past." I stifle my gasp. That's the first time he's mentioned it. "What guy wouldn't want that kind of financial security? And she's so young—he's so much older than her—"

"How old is he?" I interrupt. I hadn't realized that part. I'd assumed they were close in age.

"Forty-five." *Whoa. More than twenty years' difference.*

"So?" I say again. But my argument sounds weaker now, even to my ears. "You've never heard of a May-December romance?"

"Sure I have. Doesn't mean I want one for my sister."

"But it's not your *choice*," I repeat.

"It's my choice to make sure nobody takes advantage of my sister."

"It—"

"Look, Noelle. I know you're not from Springhollow. You didn't grow up here, and you weren't bombarded with news articles and TV reports when my parents died. I get that. But there are things you don't know. My parents and I—we were close. Really close. I had them to myself for nine years before Brook was born, and when she came along…things got even better, as weird as that sounds. She was and still is my best friend. And I promised my parents that I'd always be there for her. And when they died—since it was my—" He breaks off and I might be imagining things, but I swear he was about to say their deaths were his fault. "When they died, I promised I'd do whatever it took to protect her, for as long as I could. I'm going to keep that promise, whatever it takes."

"By ruining her wedding? Breaking her heart?"

"Better than letting Will do it."

"Everett—"

"I know how it sounds. I don't *want* to hurt her. And she won't thank me at first. It might be a long time before she realizes I've done the right thing. I've made my peace with that. But she will eventually. Will Hurley's nothing more than your run-of-the-mill scam artist. And I'm going to do everything in my power to make sure he doesn't get his hands on a single dime of her inheritance."

My head is swimming. I feel like I'm on one of those terrifying narrow roads that are carved into mountainsides. I've seen them in movies. I don't know if they actually exist. But whether they do or not, I think this is pretty much how it feels to be riding on one. On a unicycle. In the snow. Going up.

"What about a prenup?" I say. "Did you mention that to her?"

"Of course I did. She won't do it. She says she doesn't want to insult him."

"Why not offer to pay him to go away?"

"I thought about it. But then he'd win. All the money with no commitment."

Well, I'm out of ideas.

"So you're going to do what? Mess a few things up so she decides to call off the whole thing? I'm not sure if you've ever been in love, but it doesn't really work like that. Changing the date on her invitations is an annoying inconvenience, but hardly something to cancel the wedding over."

"You haven't known her long enough," he says with a short laugh. "Brooke's big into signs. From God, from the universe, whatever. If enough goes wrong, she'll start to look at things differently. She'll think some higher power is trying to tell her something. And then calling it off will be her choice."

"Is that why you offered to help me if I needed it?" I ask. "You were hoping I'd give you a few chores so you could screw them up?"

"I won't lie and say it didn't cross my mind."

He's *diabolical*. That he would do something so horrible to his own sister—I can't wrap my head around it.

"You can't ruin her wedding" is all I can say.

"Noelle, I know the wedding is the only part that means anything to you. And don't worry. I know Brooke's already given you a huge check, so you'll still get paid." The venom in his voice makes me jerk backward, almost as if he's physically coming at me.

And it confirms my suspicions—he looks at *me* like a gold digger, too.

"That's not—"

"But I will not allow my sister to ruin her life over a guy. I just won't. It's as simple as that." His expression dares me to argue. "I'm not going to do anything drastic. I'm not going to physically hurt anyone. But I've given this so much thought. Something about that guy just doesn't sit right with me. And I don't know what else to do."

I feel completely helpless. I rack my brain for something, anything, to say to him that might make him change his mind. But if a clean report from a private investigator didn't convince him, I'm not sure if there's anything I can say that will.

"So, what's next? Are you going to tell her?"

Scenarios flash like movie trailers through my head. I could tell her and make her hate her brother, the only family she has left, who, in his own twisted, deranged way is just trying to protect her. I could not tell her, let Everett do whatever he has planned, and have her lose her fiancé and watch her life plans go up in smoke the way her parents did.

Or I could just keep doing my thing, armed now with the knowledge that Everett will be trying to thwart me at every turn like the evil villain he's turned out to be, try to keep a step ahead of him and make sure that Brooke's wedding to the man of her dreams is as perfect as can be.

I don't even have to think about it. I already know the answer. I have my own broken heart, my own shattered dreams. I'd never wish that kind of agony on anyone else.

And while revenge on Drew may have been my initial reason for doing this, it's more than that now. I'm emotionally invested. I like Brooke, and I want her happy.

"No. I won't tell her."

Everett blinks at me, as if he'd expected me to wave a gun at him to get him out of my house before jumping on the phone to tell Brooke everything. "She doesn't deserve to have her heart broken. Especially not by the brother who claims to love her and want to protect her." His eyes spark at that and he opens his mouth, but I don't let him speak. "Just know that if you're that intent on ruining her life, I will be right beside you every step of the way doing everything I can to keep you from hurting her."

"I know," Everett says. "But Noelle, I've been thinking about this for months. Since they first started seeing each other. I know people like Will, and I know what I have to do. Believe me, it's not like I'm going to enjoy it. I'm not a sadist."

I try one last tack. "Did it occur to you that maybe you could just talk to her? Tell her what you're worried about? Maybe you could just spend some time with Will. Get to know him."

He laughs. It's bitter. "You think I haven't tried? She's a kid in love. She thinks he's what she wants. And as for getting to know Will, forget it. He's never even around. Just a few weeks after they met, he took off for Mexico, supposedly to take pictures for an article on the drug cartels. He came back for a week and then he was off to Cuba. Now his mom *has cancer.* For all I know he has a wife and kids hidden so well even my PI couldn't find them, and he's just pretending to be a guy who never knew love until he met Brooke and decided to milk her for every penny she's got."

I want to scream at him that he's crazy. Except that it would make me crazy, too, since almost the exact same thoughts went through my head as soon as I heard he wasn't coming home as planned.

"Why do you think I'm the best man?" he continues. "Why not a friend of his? Why not a frat brother, or a co-worker, or a cousin or something? And he's only got two other groomsmen. Guys I've never met. Guys he probably hired to pretend to be his friends with the promise of paying them off once he's got Brooke's money."

"Well, I haven't met Brooke's maid-of-honor," I argue. "How do I know she exists?" It's a weak argument. But I don't have much else.

"You don't have to know. I do. I've met her at least a dozen times. But I've never met any of Will's friends. And you know what else? *Neither has Brooke.* She hasn't met any of his friends or family. When they found out his mom was sick, she offered to fly back and forth between here and Toronto to help out. He just kept feeding her excuses about why she shouldn't. She was too busy with *The Nutcracker.* His mom was too sick for visitors. Etcetera, etcetera."

I don't know what to say to that. It *does* sound weird. I can admit that. But still—it's Brooke's life. If what she's about to do is the biggest mistake she'll ever make, isn't it up to her to figure it out?

Then again, I'm the one who's shutting down her business and running home to help her own sister with a new baby. Who's to say I wouldn't do the same thing Everett's doing if I thought Kate might be about to make a decision that would ruin *her* life?

My headache's worse.

"I'm not going to let it happen," I finally say. "You can do whatever you have planned. But don't for a second think it'll work. Because it won't. Brooke hired me to make sure she has the perfect wedding. So that's what I'm going to do. I have to."

"Okay. I figured that." Everett nods. "So I guess we're both going to do what we have to do."

I hear what he's saying.

This means war.

15

"THANK GOD THAT'S over," Brooke says as she swipes a moistener stick over the flap of the last envelope and seals it shut. "I didn't think we'd ever get to the end."

"And your wedding's tiny." I take the invitation from her, press a stamp into the upper right corner and slip it into the box with the other sixty-nine. "Imagine if you had two hundred and fifty guests."

"I can't!" She laughs. "Do you have any idea how many paper cuts I'd have with that many guests?" She holds up her manicured fingers and inspects the tips. "I must have about fifty as it is. And they *hurt.*"

"I never understood why paper cuts hurt so bad." I slide the lid on the box. "Sometimes I think I'd rather be stabbed."

"True story." Brooke takes a sip of her latte and as she puts the cup down, the rich, nutty fragrance of espresso and milk wafts up and into my nostrils. I stifle a sigh. It smells *good.* If only The Daily Grind's logo wasn't blazoned on the side of the cup—I might be able to fool myself into thinking I'm ready to go back to coffee. But since the sight of the brown letters makes my stomach dip, I can pretty much be sure that no, I'm not ready. "So what now?"

"We take them to the post office," I say. "We *could* just dump them into the mailbox at the end of the street, but I don't trust it. I'd much rather hand over the entire box at once and make sure they get back there. Especially since we're crunched for time. We can't take any chances on any of them getting lost."

"Sounds good to me."

"And I can take them. The post office is around the corner from my apartment." There is *no* chance I'll risk giving them to Everett to mail. They'd probably end up in the Delaware River.

"Great. Thank you." Brooke glances at the clock. "I've got to get to my trial at the salon. Anything else we need to do?"

"Nope. Not right now."

"Okay then." She gets out of her chair and heads to the front. I pick up the box of invitations and follow her.

She takes her coat from the hook and starts putting it on.

"Hey Brooke?"

"Yeah?"

It's been three days since Everett's big revelation and I haven't been able to think about much else. I've done so much flipping and flopping between telling her and not telling her that it's amazing I'm not walking around with permanent motion sickness. Today I'm leaning toward telling her. *Your brother's crazy; he thinks Will is after your money, and he's going to send you signs that you'll think are the universe telling you not to get married.* I can already hear her laughing.

"Are you sure you don't want a bridal shower?" I say instead.

She shakes her head. "Nah," she says. "I don't need one. I've lived by myself so long that I pretty much have everything I need, and whatever I don't have I can buy for myself. I don't need anyone to buy anything for me. And it's not like I have a big group of girlfriends. I've always been the quality over quantity type." She shrugs but flashes me a grin. "I'm just glad the girlfriends I *do* have are going to be at the bachelorette party. Which, of course, you and Erin are invited to, in case I haven't already mentioned it."

She hasn't. And I should decline. Erin and I are almost always invited to our brides' bachelorette parties, but we don't go because we're usually booked with another wedding. Even if we're not, we don't really consider it professional. I have no desire for a paying client to see me tipsy, wearing plastic male genitalia as a necklace, or having a scantily clad "policeman" making me wear his hat while he sits in my lap.

But hell. Brooke's already seen me well past tipsy. There's no law that says I actually *have* to wear a penis necklace all night. And Brooke's my last bride. Maybe I should go. It can be Silver Bells' last hurrah.

"Sure," I say. "I'll have to see if Erin's free that night, but yeah. It'll be fun."

"Awesome." She pulls a knit beanie down over her hair, which she recently had highlighted so that gleaming strands of icy blond frame her face. It'll go well with the bright white of her gown. "Well, wish me luck that I don't come out of the salon looking like a blonde Amy Winehouse."

"It'll be perfect," I promise. "I wouldn't have sent you to Lynn if I didn't have one-hundred percent faith that you'd love her."

"You haven't steered me wrong yet," Brooke agrees, and I feel a flash of guilt. If only she knew.

I'm a terrible person. Right?

I don't know anymore.

"Good luck," I tell her.

"Thanks!"

She pushes through the door, and I'm left hoping that Everett didn't somehow manage to break into the salon and replace Lynn's hairspray with insulating foam. I'm going to need twenty pairs of eyes to keep one on him all the time.

I follow Brooke out, turning off the light and locking the door behind me. It's Thursday at four o'clock, and I need to get these invitations to the post office before they close, which I'm pretty sure is at four-thirty. The post office is all the way on the other side of town. Then I have to get back by five to bring Brooke's selected cake design to the bakery before *they* close. The two inches of snow we got Monday afternoon have already pretty much melted, and I do have my car back with a bright, shiny new battery, but I'm not looking forward to making the trips at rush hour during Christmas shopping season. In fact, it's a pretty safe assumption that someone might, at best, get the finger—at worst, die.

But it goes better than planned. The invitations are deposited at the post office fifteen minutes before closing and I get promises from the girl at the counter that she will personally see to it that they go out immediately. Then, although it takes me nearly half an hour of stopping and going among a sea of red car lights to make the three-quarter mile drive to the bakery, I manage to get there fifteen minutes before closing and Sam, the owner, happily takes Brooke's completed order form while assuring me he'll have the cake at the Springhollow Fire Hall two hours before the start of the reception.

Whew.

So that's my Thursday night. Busy, but unfortunately not busy enough to keep from being smacked with the reminder that it's date night, and for the sixth time in a row, I have to come to terms with the fact that I have no date.

Seven o'clock is normally the time our pizza or Chinese food would show up. I'd dish it out while Drew flipped through either my ancient DVD collection (and ridiculed it) or the offerings of Netflix, the only streaming service to which I subscribe, asking for the umpteenth time why I had no interest in watching any of the *Star Wars* movies. By seven o'clock tonight, though, I'm on my couch, buried beneath a leopard-print Snuggie I got in a Yankee swap with Drew's family a few Christmases ago. I hold a half-hearted attempt at dinner in my hands, which are free thanks to the awesomeness that is the design of the Snuggie.

I've only gotten three spoonfuls of cereal into my mouth when my cellphone rings.

Brooke.

Crap—I forgot to let her know that the bakery confirmed her order. It's a good thing I'm shutting down my business. My head is just not in the game anymore.

"Hey," I say when I answer. "Sorry. Cuthbert's confirmed the order and said everything's good to go, and they'll have it to the hall in plenty of time."

"No," she says, and her voice is breathy and weird. I sense trouble. I sit up straight, pause the horror movie I've chosen in lieu of the dozens upon dozens of feel-good Christmas movies I can't bring myself to watch, and set my cereal bowl on the coffee table.

"What's wrong?"

"My veil," she says, and now I know why she sounds weird. She's crying.

"What about your veil?" I measure my voice carefully so not to make her panic, but something tells me it's already kind of late for that.

"It's gone!" she wails.

You have got to be kidding me.

"What do you mean it's gone?"

"It's just gone." She hiccups. "I had it in the back of my car, to take in to the trial so Lynn could see how it would look with my hair. I forgot to bring it in, and she just did my hair without it when I told her what it looked like. Then when she was done, I went out to the car to get it, and it wasn't there!"

"Okay. It'll be okay." I take a deep breath. "Are you sure you had it with you? Did you maybe think you brought it, but you actually left it at home?"

"I'm home now." She sniffles. "It's not here. It's not anywhere."

I doubt that. In fact, I have a very good idea of where it is. On the other side of town, maybe buried in the closet of a spare bedroom with black and white striped curtains, dark bedding, and blond hardwood floors.

"It's got to be somewhere." How to get it back without ratting out Everett? Why does he even deserve my silence? That veil belonged to their mother, for God's sake. He knows how much it means to her. How could he take it, knowing how the thought of it being lost would devastate her?

He has no qualms whatsoever about breaking up her engagement. What's a length of thirty-five-year-old netting?

I could kill him. I could honestly kill him.

The third time I bang on the door, I put all of my weight behind it. It isn't much, given the fact that out of the past thirty-seven days I've only eaten regularly for the last seven, but it manages to bring Everett to the door. Finally.

"Hello," he says. "I'm sorry, I don't like Thin Mints."

"I'm not selling cookies," I growl.

"Oh. Well, I've already found Jesus."

"You better hope so. You're going to need him." My fury propels me through his open front door. He actually jumps back as I storm through the foyer.

"What the hell are you doing?"

"Where is it?" I make a big show of lifting those manly black couch cushions and flinging them to the floor, even though I don't really think he has his dead mom's veil stuck underneath one.

"Where's what? And why are you destroying my house?"

"You know what. And why." I go to the closet and yank the door open. There are two jackets—his leather one and a dark gray wool peacoat, which is actually pretty nice and would probably make him look really hot, if he wasn't completely evil—but no veil.

Well, okay. There are more closets. And I have all night to search them.

I start to march down the hall toward my room—I mean, the spare room—but he stops me by planting himself in the archway that separates the living room from the hall. He crosses his arms over his chest. His brown eyes are stony.

"You don't scare me," I say, but it's starting to dawn on me that what I'm doing might be considered trespassing.

"I don't want to scare you. I want you to tell me what the hell you think you're doing."

"Where's Brooke's veil?"

I feel a tiny surge of victory when the expression on his face shifts from a pitiful attempt at ignorance to understanding. He tries to smooth it over, but I saw it.

"What do you mean?"

He must not realize that wedding planners are good at reading facial cues. He knows what I'm talking about, he knows where the veil is, but he doesn't know I know he knows.

"Brooke's veil. What did you do with it?"

He laughs. Shakes his head. "You're nuts, you know that? I didn't do a thing with the veil. It was my mom's veil. I wouldn't destroy it."

"I didn't say you destroyed it. And flattery will get you nowhere." *I'm* nuts? Is he serious? I pop my hands onto my hips. I can assume intimidating poses too. "Did you take it out of her car? Where did you hide it?"

He acts bored. "I have no idea what you're talking about."

Frustration and anger tinge the edges of my vision red. "You know exactly what I'm talking about. Your sister called me twenty minutes ago in hysterics because she can't find her veil. You know, the one her mom wore? Her dead mom?" He jerks a little, and I would feel awful for using that fact as a weapon if I wasn't so furious with him. "The one that is so important to her she cried when she first put it on? Yeah. That veil. You don't honestly think that stealing her *veil* is going to make her not want to marry Will, do you?"

He's silent for a minute.

"She was in hysterics?" he finally asks. The bored act has vanished.

If that's all he got from my little tirade, I'll take it. "She was. Does that make you feel bad? How bad do you think you're going to feel if you actually succeed in this psychotic little scheme, and you manage to separate her from the love of her life? You'll *wish* she was only in hysterics if that happens. Having your entire future ripped away from you does a real number on the psyche." Speaking from experience. "So if you feel bad now, maybe you should revisit your whole plan to *save her* before you completely destroy her."

His eyes meet mine, and there's so much pain in them I almost forget why I'm there and why I'm so furious. In fact, I suddenly want to hug him. He's going about this the entirely wrong way, but maybe I could be a little more sympathetic. They lost their *parents*. He practically raised her. There's a bond there that I can't fully grasp.

I can only hope that it's strong enough to make him see reason, and soon.

"It was under the passenger seat." Brooke laughs, and I swear I've never heard a more beautiful sound than that laughter. *He gave it back.* I don't know how he did it—if he had a key to her car or broke into it or what—and I don't care. I only care that he gave it back. I can't forget the look on his face. He was horrified at the thought of upsetting her. He must have decided it wasn't worth it.

That was easier than I thought.

I'm glad. And not just for the obvious reason, the one where I let my business go out with a bang. I'm glad that he came to his senses and realized what an awful thing he was doing. I know his heart was in the right place. I still don't think he's really a bad guy. Just way too overprotective. Maybe now he'll calm down, realize it's Brooke's life.

"Didn't you check there?"

"I thought I did. I guess not. I slept like crap last night, trying to figure out what could have happened to it. First thing this morning I figured I'd check the car one more time. I pulled the passenger seat up as far as it would go, and there it was. I had to slam on my brakes a few times in the traffic last night. It must have slid under the seat and got stuck."

"I guess." I shake my head, glad she can't see me.

"Between wedding planning, getting the show together, and missing Will, my brain must be somewhere else."

"Well, don't worry. That's why you have me." Not that my head's on any straighter. Between the two of us, we *might* be able to pull this off with only minor hitches. "And you only have a few more weeks until all three of those things are over."

"I can't *wait*."

"So all of the veil drama aside, how did the trial go?"

I sit back as she launches into an enthusiastic description of the updo Lynn created for her and the vampy dark lipstick Brooke at first protested but ended up loving.

"You were right. She knew exactly what to do."

"I told you." My call-waiting beeps. I don't recognize the number, but I should answer it. I get calls every now and then asking if I want to be featured in bridal publications and on websites. If that's what this is, I'm going to have to tell them I'm no longer in business. I don't want to still be getting calls five years from now, when I'm at Victoria's Secret earning my living by putting thongs on mannequins. "That's my call-waiting. I have to go. I'm glad you found your veil."

"Me too!"

We hang up, and I click over to the other line. "Hello?"

"Hello? Is this Noelle Silver?" It's a man's voice. Vaguely familiar, or at least familiar-ish. I don't know who it is.

"Speaking."

"Hi, Noelle. This—well, it's Dad."

I almost drop the phone. It must be a prank call.

A prank? Who would pretend to be your dad in a prank call?

My heart gallops in my chest. I should hang up. I haven't talked to him since I was a child, and I don't have anything to say to him now. But something won't let me put down the phone.

"Hello." My own voice, when it comes, is so icy it even gives me chills.

"Hi, honey."

Honey? Oh, no. This is the man who walked out on me, his other daughter, and his wife. Without a reason. Without a forwarding address. Without a freaking *word*. This guy does *not* get to call me "honey."

"How did you get this number?" It couldn't have been my cousins. I never had my phone number listed on my Facebook profile.

And Kate wouldn't do this to me. Would she?

"I—well, I looked it up." *Damn it.* I never should have added my cellphone number to my business listing. I'd just wanted to be sure clients could get hold of me. I never in a million years thought my father would look me up.

"I see." My blood rushes hotly in the veins beneath my skin. My cheeks and ears burn. What could he possibly want?

"Did you get my card?" He has the nerve to sound hopeful.

"I did." I won't tell him what I did with it (threw it in the trash) or that it expressed a pointless sentiment, since I wasn't getting married.

"Oh, good. Listen, Noelle. I know this is probably a surprise." His voice has taken on a sort of Midwestern flavor. He still sounds like himself, but by way of Chicago rather than Philadelphia, where he was born and raised. I wonder how long he's been in Indiana, to make his voice take on that nasally tone.

No, you don't. You don't care.

"That's putting it mildly." Why don't I just hang up?

"But I wanted to tell you that I'm sorry," he says.

"Sorry? You're sorry?" The word opens an emotional dam I've spent twenty years building, and the words erupt from me before I can stop them. "Sorry for what? For ditching Kate and me? For ditching Mom and forcing her to raise us without any kind of help? Financial *or* emotional? For letting birthdays and holidays and milestones go by without a word? Kate's married, you know. She's had three miscarriages, and she's pregnant again. She might lose this one too." Oops. *Sorry, Kate.* "Or are you sorry for never calling or writing or giving us a single reason why you left us? For making us think we weren't good enough? What exactly are you sorry for, *Dad*?" And there they are. Twenty years of daddy issues, all out in the open. Swirling around like flies on a rotting carcass.

"For all of it," he whispers, and he sounds so pathetic I almost feel sick.

It won't change a thing. No way. There's too much anger, built up and suppressed for too long, for it to go away. Maybe if I'd seen a therapist at some point, I could have handled this better. But I didn't. I was too busy with school and my business and building my life. A life my dad wanted no part of until, inexplicably, now.

"Why now, Dad?" I have to ask.

"Because I've made a lot of mistakes. I want to try to fix them."

I laugh. It's short and bitter.

"You have every right to be angry with me."

"You bet I do."

"And I know I'll never be able to get back the time we missed or erase the hurt I caused." That's true, too. "But I want to try."

I inhale. Let it out. Inhale again. I'm kind of dizzy.

"That's nice of you, Dad," I say. "But if you don't mind, I can kind of only handle one or two life-altering events at a time. Since my fiancé confessed five weeks ago that he'd been cheating for months with his assistant and I was forced to cancel my wedding, I decided to close down my business and move back home. So you see, I'm kind of emotionally booked up right now. Maybe try me again in a few years. If you want."

"Oh, Noelle—"

"Thanks for calling, Dad. But I can't do this now. Goodbye."

With a shaking index finger I stab at the red *End Call* button on my phone's touch screen. It goes black, and my father disappears. Again.

16

On Tuesday I text Brooke to remind her that the florist needs her order by the end of the day tomorrow.

I'm on it, she sends back. *Today.*

Are you sure? I can take it if you're tied up with rehearsals.

Nope, it's good. I gave it to Everett and he's taking it on his way to work at 5.

She gave it to Everett. This is a good thing, right? A way to prove that he really did abandon his efforts to make his sister think the universe or whatever didn't want her to marry Will. But for some reason adrenaline surges through me, making my fingers shake so hard that my first attempt at a reply looks like I've written it in Polish. I backspace until the screen clears and try again.

Okay. Great.

I glance at the clock. It's twenty after four. When she said five, did she mean he started work at five, or he was leaving at five?

And what the hell do I think I'm going to do anyway? Follow him and make sure he drops off the order? That would be psychotic.

Thirty seconds later I'm wrapped in a coat and scarf and sprinting for my car. Okay, so I guess I'm a psycho. I'll let them commit me once the wedding's over.

When I get to his street, I squeeze into a spot at the corner, hoping with every fiber of my being that I'm far enough away that he doesn't realize it's me parked here. His house is on my left, the Jeep still in the driveway, and unless he was crazy enough to ride his bike to work in subfreezing temperatures, which he actually might be, he hasn't left yet. I crank up the heat, turn the radio to a low hum, and wait.

At about four-forty the front door opens, and he comes out. I slide down in my seat and watch as he locks his door and hurries across the lawn to the driveway. It doesn't look like he has any papers in his hands. Maybe the order form's in his pocket. He's wearing some sort of military-looking jacket with about seventeen of them. It's got to be in one.

He starts the Jeep and lets it warm up for a few minutes before backing out of the driveway onto the street. I wait until he's at the stop sign before pulling out of my spot and slowly, slowly going after him. If he sees me and realizes I'm following him, it could get ugly.

And embarrassing.

I make sure to keep at least a full block between us as he winds in and out of the streets. On second thought, this is actually kind of exciting. I feel a little bit like James Bond.

Just a few minutes later we're at the very end of Main Street, where it crosses into Newbury and becomes Front Street. It's here that the best florist in the county keeps her shop, in a little brick building with a cheerful sign suspended over a gigantic bay window that's usually decorated to reflect the season. Right now the window gives a glimpse into a Christmas wonderland, with cheerful red and white poinsettias, holly branches, and pine boughs all covered with a dusting of artificial snow. It would be beautiful if I could manage to focus on it. Instead I let Everett park. I keep going, scrunching down as I pass him, and in my rearview mirror see him sprint across the street and into the shop.

I immediately yank my car to the side of the street. There's no parking allowed on that side, so I flick on my hazard lights, hoping that anyone who sees me might think I'm just waiting on someone to come out of one of the houses. I pull the rearview mirror into the perfect angle to continue my little stalking mission. Less than thirty seconds later Everett emerges from the shop, crosses the street, and gets back into his Jeep. I slide down again, this time pulling my scarf up and over the bottom half of my face so if he just happens to look as he drives by, he won't be able to tell it's me. Hopefully.

The Jeep rolls past, and I stare straight ahead. The last thing I want to do is make eye contact. Forty-five seconds later it's out of sight. I circle the block, park in the spot he just left, and go into the shop.

"Hi, Noelle!"

"Hi, Liz." The owner of the shop has a folder out on the counter. "Sorry to bother you, but do you have a minute? I need to check something on the order for the St. John wedding."

"You're in luck. Everett St. John just dropped it off. I haven't even put it away yet."

"Really?" I hear the fakeness in my own voice and cringe. An actress I am not.

"Sure did. You probably passed him on the street." She lifts a sheet of paper from the open folder and hands it to me.

My eyes scan the form. *Roses. Baby's breath. Camellia. White, white, white.* All looks good. So do the amounts. The paper trembles in my hand as relief floods me. Not only did he bring it, he brought it completely unaltered. Until seeing the proof I didn't realize how anxious I was that we might walk into a reception decorated with black roses and dandelions. And while my little James Bond moment was fun while it lasted, now I just feel completely stupid. I *followed* him. I'm such an idiot.

Clearly the whole episode with the veil was an eye opener. He's definitely changed his mind. I don't have to worry about him. I can go back to focusing on making Brooke's wedding my best ever, which should be easier without worrying about someone fighting me every step of the way.

"Thanks, Liz." I hand the paper back to her.

"Everything okay?"

"Perfect. Sorry about that. I just had a moment. You know how it is."

"The wedding's in less than three weeks. You're entitled to a moment every now and then."

If only she knew.

I get back in my car and drive home, vowing to keep this little episode a secret from everyone.

🔔

It's a perfect winter night. The sky is a velvety sapphire blue, studded with silvery stars. It's cold enough to see your breath but not uncomfortably frigid—exactly the way I like it. The houses are wrapped in Christmas lights that form a streaky kaleidoscope of color in my peripheral vision as I drive to the Springhollow Theater in the heart of town to see Brooke's dance studio perform *The Nutcracker*.

I wish I was headed anywhere else.

If it were last year, I'd be excited. More than excited. I'd be wrapped in my silver scarf that sort of looks like tinsel, the one I only wear between December first and December twenty-fourth. I'd have my own copy of *The Nutcracker Suite* in my car's CD player, and my feet, rather than pressing the gas and the brake pedals, would be itching to battement and fouetté along with it. I'd have the window cracked, letting in a big enough sliver of winter air to remind myself that Christmas is just around the corner. And Drew would be beside me, complaining bitterly of the cold and the music and the fact that I was probably going to kill us both with my driver's seat choreography.

But it's not last year. I'm not wearing that stupid scarf, which is actually pretty itchy and uncomfortable. I'm listening to a local hard rock station, because it's going to be difficult enough to listen to the music in the theater without dwelling on all of the reasons why this Christmas will suck, and I don't want to make it doubly hard. The window's rolled up, heat on full blast—too hot, in fact, since tiny beads of sweat have blossomed along my hairline. Great, now my hair will be frizzy. I reach over and turn it down. And there is no one beside me in the passenger seat, whining that he's cold or asking me to put on "real music" or dramatically grabbing his heart in terror when I should be hitting the brake but I fake a grand jeté instead.

It's not last year. It's this year, and I'm alone.

I park in the huge lot beside the theater and turn off my car's engine. But instead of getting out right away, I pause with my fingers on the door handle. Why am I here? Why'd I say I would come? I'm insane. Three hours locked in an auditorium watching one of my favorite holiday traditions will be sheer torture. I can't do this. It'll *hurt.*

But what *hasn't* hurt since I last sipped coffee at my favorite table at The Daily Grind? Not much. Sometimes I wake up and I can't believe it's only been a month and a half since my world fell apart. It feels like eons.

"You *can* do this," I tell myself.

I squeeze the handle, and the door releases. I touch my booted left foot to the asphalt, and cold air infiltrates my black pants. My skin erupts in goosebumps. I get out of the car, lock it, and hurtle through the lot to the theater.

The entrance is swathed in pine garland and twinkling white lights. An enormous wreath hangs on each of the heavy red doors that lead into the lobby. I pull one of the doors open and go in, where I'm enveloped in blessed warmth and tinny instrumental holiday music.

"Hello," I say to the woman at the will-call desk. "I'm Noelle Silver. I think you're holding a ticket for me?"

"Noelle Silver..." She trails a finger up and down the sheet of paper in front of her. "Oh! Yes. Here you are." She takes a single, sad ticket from her drawer and tears off the end, handing me what remains. "Enjoy the show!"

"Thank you."

The lobby is mostly empty, since it's only minutes to showtime. I'd meant to get here earlier but had some trouble talking myself into it. The doors to the auditorium are open, but the lights inside already flicker, meaning that the show's about to start. I peek at my ticket to see where I'm sitting—row G, seat 20—and sprint to the doors just as the usher starts to close them.

"Sorry!" I whisper when he frowns. Luckily I know the theater well, and even though the lights are permanently down now, I don't need him to help me find my seat. Seven rows from the front, middle section, left aisle seat. Easy.

Except someone's in it.

It's late. Any second now the music will start. I should just slip into an empty seat—any empty seat—and wait until intermission to sort it out. But there aren't any empty seats, except for the one immediately next to the one that's supposed to be mine. It's a packed house. Awesome for Brooke. Not so much for me.

"Excuse me," I whisper. "I think that's my seat."

The person turns slowly to look up at me, revealing his face bit by bit. Angled jaw. Stubbly cheek, made ghostly pale by the lack of light. Brown eyes, curly dark hair. Stony expression.

Everett.

Why? Why now? Why *me*?

"Is it?"

"According to my ticket, yeah."

"Does it matter?" He gestures to the empty seat beside him. "Sit here."

"But—"

The first chords of the overture start then, and a hush falls over the room. Aside from the ushers at the doors making sure no one comes in during the performance, I'm the only one standing.

Sure enough, someone's already annoyed. "Sit down!" he or she hisses.

My, we're just full of the holiday spirit, aren't we? My ears are getting warm.

"Come on," I beg. "Just move over."

He does, but only his legs. He swings them to the side so I can move past him and get in the empty seat next to him.

Ugh. He is a *child*.

Fine. I'll do it. But only because I don't want to be left standing there in the aisle like an idiot, arguing with someone who undoubtedly *is* an idiot.

I climb past him, almost tripping over him in the process and very likely annoying even more people behind us. "Sorry," I mumble. I collapse into the seat and sink down. Everett calmly pulls his legs back into position and stares at the stage as the curtains open and children in Victorian costume begin to twirl around a Christmas tree.

Forget him. It's dark. For all you know he's not even there.

Except he is, and I'm reminded of it when I inadvertently lay my left elbow on the armrest and find his arm already there. He jerks it away.

"Sorry," I whisper again. I pull my own arm back and fold it around my waist.

"It's okay. You can have it."

"I don't need it."

"Really, go ahead."

"I don't need it. Honest."

"*Shhhh!*"

I hug myself tighter as Everett shrugs and puts his arm back on the armrest. I feel bad for the guy on my other side, forced to spend his evening next to the two of us. What's next—a catfight, complete with nail-gouging and hair-pulling?

I sigh, press myself into my seat, and lift my eyes to the stage.

Despite it all I'm quickly enchanted. Have I mentioned that I love *The Nutcracker*? Because I do. I love the story. I love the campy dance-acting. I love the scenery, the costumes, and of course the music. And even though I'm in an emotional place where all of this stuff should be crushing me rather than entertaining me, I find myself drawn into it.

It helps that Brooke's ballerinas are fantastic dancers. Her Clara is adorable. Although I never understood, even as a kid, why all of the girls wanted to be Clara. She has only a few minutes of dancing—most of her time on stage is spent sitting down, watching others perform for her. But I never aspired to be the Sugar Plum Fairy, either. More than anything, given the chance to perform in *The Nutcracker*—which I wasn't, since my mom couldn't afford classes after my dad left—I'd wanted to be a snowflake. I'd wanted an ethereal white costume with a flowy knee-length skirt, crystals on the bodice, and fake snow drifting around me as I flitted around a stage. I wasn't starved for attention—I could share the stage with other girls. I'd always just thought that the snowflakes were the prettiest part of the entire ballet.

They're also the end of the first half, and when Brooke's snowflakes melt away, the curtains close and the lights come up. The spell's broken.

Before I can even stand up and stretch, Everett's out of his seat like a rocket and heading for the lobby. Good. I can take my own seat back and maybe make him climb over *me*.

"Excuse me," says a voice to my right. I turn toward it. It's the guy in the seat next to me.

"Yes?" He must want to ream me out for the little pre-show performance Everett and I put on. "Hey, I'm sorry about all the commotion at the beginning. I hope it wasn't too annoying. That guy—he kind of has an attitude problem."

The guy smiles, and his eyes crinkle endearingly. Nice eyes. Wow, are they ever blue.

"I know," he says. "You're Noelle, right?"

He knows me? How?

"I am," I say. "Do I know you?"

"We've spoken on the phone." He grins now. Dimples explode on his cheeks. "I'm Will."

"Will?" I ask. "*Brooke's* Will?"

"The very same."

"But I thought you weren't going to be back until the middle of the week!" I'm in disbelief—first, because Will is actually here and, second, because he's been sitting next to me for an hour and Everett didn't feel the need to just give me a quick nudge and say "hey, that's Will."

I guess that's why I had to fight for my seat. He might finally be willing to let his sister marry the guy but couldn't make himself sit next to him.

Well, it's better than him waiting until the Harlequin and Columbine dolls busted out of their boxes to jump up and accuse one of us of being after Brooke's money.

"That was the plan," Will says. "But my mom's doing better. I got in this morning."

"Does Brooke know?"

"She was the first place I went." His striking eyes go sort of dreamy, and I can't help the slight melting feeling I get. Everett's wrong. This guy loves Brooke.

Either that, or he's a hell of an actor.

"Well, it's great to meet you." Normally I'd offer my hand, but I hug him instead. I'm determined to make up for every bit of jerkishness Everett has thrown his way. Something tells me this guy will be getting lots of hugs.

"You, too," he says. "Brooke has done nothing but gush about you. She's so happy with the way everything's been going."

"She's made it easy," I say. "She doesn't have a bit of Bridezilla in her. I wish all my brides were as easygoing."

"She is something, isn't she?" He smiles, and it hits me again. Will's handsome. Like, *really* handsome. If he's forty-five like Everett said, he definitely doesn't look it. I'd put him at around thirty-five. He's got black hair, thick and stylishly tousled but not in an "I'm desperately trying to cling to my youth" kind of way. The color makes his eyes look icy blue.

His skin's fair. He seems fit, and he's dressed nice, in dark jeans and a black sweater over a white collared shirt.

Suffice it to say—Will is yummy. Good job, Brooke.

Didn't I call it?

"So your mom's doing better? I'm glad to hear that."

"A little," he says, and his eyes cloud over. "She's not cured, of course. That…won't happen at this point. But her energy's up, and the treatment seems to have paused the spread of the cancer cells. I don't expect a miracle. It's just a matter of time. I know that." He pauses and swallows hard—I see the muscles in his throat contract. "Sorry. I'm just glad that it seems like she'll be holding on long enough to see me get married. At last."

I touch his arm. "I'm so sorry. I can't imagine."

"It's not the easiest thing I've ever been through," he says. "But meeting Brooke has made it a little easier. She's been great. So supportive. I can't wait for them to meet in person."

"You think your mom will be strong enough to make the trip?"

"She thinks so. Anything I think doesn't matter." He laughs a little.

We spend the rest of intermission talking about the wedding and Brooke. He tells me his own version of how they met. We don't talk about Everett. I guess for all the time Will spends away, he's not oblivious to his future brother-in-law's reservations about him.

The lights flicker again, signaling the beginning of the second half of the show, and we settle back into our seats. I stay in mine. I like Will. I don't mind rescuing him from Everett, who, like me an hour earlier, slides into his seat just as the curtain lifts to reveal Clara and her prince, all set to reenact the first act for the Sugar Plum Fairy.

The second act is as captivating as the first. I let the familiar music wash over me and realize that I'm enjoying myself. How is that happening? I'm supposed to be sitting here in a stupor of depression. Not clapping along to the Russian dancers as they twirl with their candy cane-striped hula hoops or laughing at the poor guy—some kid's dad, most likely—that got roped into the Mother Ginger role, with a full face of garish makeup and a huge pink skirt from which little girls come scrambling. But I am. I'm having fun, with nary a Southern Comfort and Coke to be seen.

The Dance of the Sugar Plum Fairy is long over, and Clara, seated in an ornate wooden sleigh, is pulled offstage, waving. The curtain closes. But the music continues and just a moment later, the curtain slides open again to reveal the original scene—Clara's family's living room, everything back to normal, and Clara asleep on a red velvet settee with her Nutcracker in her arms. Which is the only part of the whole thing I don't get. Why a nutcracker? Those things are terrifying. What little girl would want to cuddle up to a wooden soldier with a monstrous hinged jaw meant to pulverize walnut shells?

A maid in a nightgown and cap flits onstage and over to Clara, gently shaking her shoulders. The little girl sits up and stretches. She allows the maid to escort her offstage, the lights go down, and the auditorium erupts into applause.

It lasts until the curtains open again to reveal the cast. The boys bow and the girls curtsy, and then Brooke comes onstage in a long-sleeved black dress, black tights, and black boots. The only part of her that isn't black is her skin and her hair, which is Dutch-braided into a band that goes around her head. Seriously. I need hairstyling tips from her.

"Thank you," she says into the microphone in her hand. "I hope you enjoyed the show." The applause continues until the curtain closes over them a final time, and the house lights finally come back on.

The audience begins to file out, and I find myself squished between Everett, poised like a rabbit ready to run at the sight of a fox, and Will, who can't seem to wipe the proud grin off his face. People stream up the aisle and keep us blocked in. Every time Everett tries to make his escape, someone cuts in front of him. He's making me anxious. I start to feel claustrophobic. But he eventually slithers into a space not immediately filled by a departing audience member and bolts up the aisle, leaving me behind with Will.

"So what did you think?" I ask.

"Amazing. Everything she does is amazing," he says.

I smile.

Eventually we're able to escape our row and head up the aisle into the lobby, where people are milling around and the dancers, still in costume and full makeup, carry bouquets of flowers and pose for pictures. It's reminiscent of my last dance recital, when my dad gave me a bunch of pink carnations and had me pose against a white-painted cinderblock wall with Kate, who was always a jock instead of a dancer and in her jeans and t-shirt totally clashed with my sparkly yellow tutu. That picture sat on my mom's nightstand for years. It may still be there.

Everett's nowhere to be found. Will and I stand together next to a utility closet and watch as Brooke emerges from the auditorium. She spots us almost immediately and gives us an excited wave, but so many people—parents and students—stop her that she can't come over. Even from across the lobby I can tell what's going on. The audience members praise her with wide smiles and hand gestures. The kids hug her knees or her waist, depending on how tall they are. She talks to all of them, smiling, laughing, and returning hugs.

If I ever wondered why she was considered Springhollow's Sweetheart, I wouldn't after watching this. She's got a lot of love in her.

The voices in the lobby die down as the crowd thins, and Brooke finally makes it over to us. She launches herself at Will, flings her arms around his waist, and presses against him. He wraps his arms around her shoulders and rests his chin on her head. Her smile's dazzling; his eyes are closed. They look so completely, blissfully in love that it makes my heart hurt.

"What did you think?" she asks.

"It was great," I tell her. "The Mariinsky Ballet better watch out."

She beams. "Thank you!"

"Although you might have told me who I'd be sitting next to!"

"Surprise." She couldn't grin harder if she tried.

"It really was."

"Where's Everett? He was here, wasn't he?" Brooke eases her grip on Will's waist so she can stand on black-booted tiptoes and look for him.

"Oh, he was here." I can't help rolling my eyes. Then I hear what I swear is a chuckle, but when I look at Will, his expression gives nothing away.

I stifle my own giggle.

Fortunately, before Will and I can lose it completely and have to explain to Brooke what we find so hysterically funny, Everett reappears. He stands next to me. I guess between myself and Will, I'm the lesser of two evils.

Poor Will.

"Hey," he says. His hands are jammed in his jacket pockets and his shoulders are hunched. He must have been outside—I can practically feel December coming off him. "Great show."

"Thanks," Brooke says again. "Thirteen more to go! I'll be a zombie on my wedding day." She laughs into Will's face, but he just pulls her tighter, if that's even possible.

"It's still early," Will says. "Why don't we go out and grab something to eat?"

I'm not hungry. But I'd like to get to know Will. And, of course, keep an eye on Everett around him. I'd really rather not hear tomorrow that Everett managed to poison Will's coffee or something.

"Sure," I say. "I'm in."

"I have a better idea," Brooke says. "The Holiday Village is open. Why don't we go there?"

My stomach does a little flip. The town square's Holiday Village had been one of my favorite things to do with Drew since the very first Christmas I spent with his family, eight years ago. Can I face it at all, let alone accompanied by one of the happiest couples I've ever known and the guy who might or might not have made it his life purpose to split them up?

I guess I'm about to find out.

17

THE TOWN SQUARE is so mobbed it's kind of uncomfortable, but really, what did we expect on the first Friday night of the display? It *is* a town tradition, after all. We drove over in Brooke's Range Rover, but we had to park so far away we might as well have walked from the theater. But I can't help but marvel over how the square is transformed. Just a few days ago it was a street, with store fronts, a mailbox, and even an ancient phone booth that I can pretty much guarantee no one has touched since Y2K. Now it's a veritable winter wonderland sparkling in the moonlight, scented with hot chocolate and roasting nuts while "Carol of the Bells" is piped in through invisible speakers and everything is supervised by a massive Douglas fir that looms above the square like some benevolent, piney overlord.

People mill around—families with shrieking children, groups of high school kids with rainbow-colored hair and not enough clothes for the cold, couples on dates. Of course. What's more romantic than this? If it was snowing, it'd be a scene right out of a made-for-TV movie. People probably think the four of us are on some kind of double date. They'd be half-right. It's obvious from the way Brooke is velcroed to Will's side that they are most definitely an item. Everett and I are another story. We've drifted together because Brooke and Will are in their own little lovey-dovey world, but there's still a good foot of space between our shoulders. Maybe people assume we're on a first date. A blind date, even. We're clearly not a couple.

I wonder if the same thoughts are running through his head, and if they cause the same rush of anxiety for him as they do for me. Probably not. He doesn't seem fazed by much. Except his sister's fiancé. His gaze burns a hole into the back of Will's perfectly cut, charcoal-gray wool trench coat. The suspicion is still there, clearly. It must be difficult watching his sister do something he thinks will ruin her life, yet wanting to stick to his decision to let her do it anyway.

I sidle a little closer. Not close enough to bump shoulders with him, of course, but close enough that he can hear me speak.

"Thank you," I say.

He tears his gaze from Will's shoulder blades and looks at me. "For what?"

"For deciding to let Brooke live her own life." I keep my voice low. The last thing I want is for either her or Will to hear me. "It's obvious how you feel about Will. I'm sure they both know it." Will does, anyway. "That has to be hard enough for her. I'm glad you realized that trying to break them up is the wrong thing to do."

He raises an eyebrow but doesn't say anything.

We keep walking. I pull my own coat closer. It's really cold.

"You're a good brother," I add when the silence becomes uncomfortable.

He smiles. He actually smiles. And I know it's real because the corners of his eyes crinkle. He's smiling! *Wow. I forgot that he's insanely hot.* It's easier to see it now that I'm not fighting him.

"I try to be. Thank you," he says.

"You're welcome."

I'm clutching my coat to my chest so hard the tips of my fingers are tingling. I glance at Brooke and Will, strolling in front of us, blissfully unaware.

"And thank you for not screwing with the flower order," I say, meaning it as a joke, but as soon as the words leave my mouth, I want a hole to open in the street and swallow me. *So much for keeping the whole stalking thing a secret.*

"How do you know I had anything to do with the florist getting the order?"

"I, um—I called Liz. To make sure she got it on time."

"Noelle, I saw you following me. Do yourself a favor. When the whole wedding planner thing is done, don't set your sights on a career as a private investigator. You'd be terrible."

My face is so hot I fully expect flames to come shooting out of my pores.

I sigh. "Well, what did you expect? You hid the veil. It was obvious then that you felt awful about upsetting her, but I guess a little part of me still had no idea if there was something else you might do. When Brooke said she gave you the order, I panicked."

"Just borrow someone else's car next time. I know what you drive." He nudges my shoulder with his.

I stuff my hands into my coat pockets. It's either that or punch him. Which I can't do, because as the one who was following him, I'm sort of the one in the wrong.

I focus my attention on Brooke and Will, walking together just a few feet ahead of me, gloved fingers intertwined.

"Hey," I call to them. They turn around at the exact same time. They're like mirror images, except one is tall and dark and gorgeous and the other is petite and blonde and gorgeous.

"What's up?" Brooke asks.

"I'm going to grab some hot chocolate. Do you want anything?" I need a little space.

"Ooh, hot chocolate sounds good. Yeah, I want one," Brooke says. "Will?"

"Sure," He reaches into the pocket of his coat and pulls out his wallet. I wave him away.

"I got it." Beside me Everett coughs. Well, what did he want me to do? Take their money after I'm the one who asked? "Three hot chocolates? Everett? Anything for you?"

"No, thanks."

"*Great.* You guys stay here. I'll be back in a minute." I turn and hurry toward the concession area, which is set up at the northwest corner of the square and flanked by a group of dancing reindeer.

I'll be longer than a minute. The line's pretty long and doesn't seem to be moving too fast. That's okay. It gives me time to breathe, and isn't that why I ran over here to begin with?

I shiver and shift from one foot to the other in an attempt to get some blood flowing to my extremities. The couple ahead of me—of course, it's a couple; Everett and I must be the only single people here—steps forward. As they do, the woman in front of me drops something. Her cellphone. It clatters to the street, landing right by my foot. I bend to pick it up.

"Here you go." I stretch it toward her. "Doesn't look like it's broken."

"Thanks!" She reaches for it. Despite the cold she's not wearing gloves, and the enormous diamond on her left hand sparkles in the glow cast by the white string lights encircling the square. I swallow the sudden rush of envy and sorrow that creeps up my throat and force a smile as I lift my gaze away from the princess-cut monstrosity on her hand and up to her face.

"You're wel—" The word gets stuck. *No*. Oh, please, no.

It's Heidi. *Heidi*. With Drew. Wearing an engagement ring.

"Oh," she says.

My heart stutters in my chest before starting up again, racing at at least three times the speed it should. *Heidi*. And Drew, who's turning around and locking eyes with me.

No. No, I can't do this.

"Hey, Noelle," he says after an awkward pause.

Hey, Noelle? That's it? That's all he has to say, when he has to be aware that I've just seen an engagement ring on the woman he dumped me for less than two months ago?

Drew clears his throat. "Um. You remember Heidi, right?"

Is he for real?

Of course I remember Heidi. She's the reason my life fell apart. She's not easy to forget.

The world's spinning too fast. I'd like to get off, please.

Heidi, to her credit—at least the little, tiny, minuscule bit I'm grudgingly willing to give her—looks kind of embarrassed. Well, she should be. I would be if I were in her place. Then again, I'd never *be* in her place.

I open my mouth and hope that whatever comes out doesn't make me sound stupid. Or petty. Or the least bit upset that Drew is here, doing something that *we* used to do with another girl who's already wearing an engagement ring.

Before I can say anything, someone's next to me. An arm slides around my waist, a warm body presses itself against my left side. What the hell—

Lips. On my temple. Someone just *kissed* me.

Before I can look to find out who my attacker is, I see Drew's face. I know that face, know it almost better than I know my own. I recognize the tilt in his lifted eyebrows, the pink flush in his cheeks that's evident even under moonlight. The barely noticeable flex of the muscle in his jaw. He's annoyed. Maybe even angry. But at who?

"Everett," he says with a nod of acknowledgment that's way more curt than friendly.

Everett? I turn my head, crane my neck.

Sure enough, it's him. Everett. Everett just kissed me.

What. The. Hell?

The only explanation that makes sense is that somehow, between the middle of the square and the concession stand, I tripped and fell into a vortex that dropped me into some parallel universe. A universe where Everett and I are apparently a couple and Drew is not happy about it.

"Hey, Drew." His voice comes easy, but the arm around me is all tense muscle. He dips his head in Heidi's general direction. "Hello."

"Hello," she says, dumbly, her heavily lined eyes flicking from me to Everett to Drew and back again.

"I'm sorry," Everett says to me. "I know you've been looking forward to tonight all week. But Brooke's not feeling that great, and she wants to go home. Since she drove us, I think we should let her." His arm tightens around my waist. What is he *doing*?

"Oh. Okay. Um, sure." I'm more than a little confused. I've been looking forward to this all week? News to me. And Brooke's sick? She was okay three minutes ago. Then again, this is evidently a different universe than the one in which I woke up today. In this universe, maybe I *have* been looking forward to tonight, and maybe Brooke *is* sick. I look past Everett, searching the crowd for Brooke's bright mane of blonde hair. I find it easily, with Will, right where I left them. She doesn't look sick. She looks fine.

Then it hits me, and I can't believe I was so dense. Maybe because considering the person standing here with his arm around my waist, his lips dangerously close to my ear, is *Everett*, it's almost unbelievable.

There was no vortex. I didn't fall into a parallel universe.

Everett is *saving* me.

"See you around," he says to Drew and Heidi.

"You, too." Anyone who doesn't know Drew as well as I do might assume him to be completely unaffected, but I see the ropy outlines of the tendons in his neck.

What is he so upset about? He dumped *me*! "Take care, Noe."

"You, too," I manage to say before the arm around me tugs me toward Brooke and Will. I almost stumble as Everett turns me around and starts to walk me back.

"Act normal," he hisses. His arm stays in place around my waist. "I'll let go when we're out of sight."

I want to act normal, but this is completely weird. And I can't help going for one more look. I turn my head back to the concession stand, where Drew and Heidi still stand. Their backs are to us so I can't see their faces, but Heidi's got herself wrapped around Drew's right arm, the hand of which is jammed into his pocket—the pocket of the coat *I* bought for him last Christmas, in the exact dark green that brings out his eyes. She's leaning into him, and it looks like she's talking, but it doesn't seem to be a two-way conversation. In fact, his back is stiff and his shoulders are lifted. More Drew body language, this time screaming his fury.

I don't get it. He's engaged to Heidi now. He can't possibly be upset that I've found someone else.

You haven't, though, the little voice in my head reminds me. *He was pretending, to help you.*

Which is weird in itself. Why would Everett help me? Did Brooke send him? She could just have as easily asked Will to fake being my boyfriend for two minutes. Drew wouldn't have known. I can't imagine it being Everett's idea. He doesn't exactly like me.

And to make matters even worse, I can't help realizing that it's been a long time since I've felt anything as good as that arm around my waist.

"You okay?" Brooke asks when we get to her. "I could hardly believe it when I saw them turn around. I almost had a heart attack."

"Me too." My throat's dry, and the words barely scrape past. I wish I'd somehow managed to get that hot chocolate, if only for some lubrication. "I wasn't expecting that."

"Brooke told me that was your ex and his new girlfriend," Will says, and the sympathy in his voice almost makes me burst into tears.

"Yeah." I swallow hard. It doesn't help. "His new fiancée, though."

"What?" Brooke says it so loud that a few people turn to stare at us. "You have got to be kidding me."

"Erin told me a few weeks ago she saw him shopping for a ring," I say. "And she's wearing one. On that finger. I just assumed."

Brooke utters a word that would have been completely expected if she were a two-hundred-forty-pound, bearded, flannel-wearing truck driver. From a five-foot-six, hundred-

and-ten-pound ballerina, it's so ludicrous I can't help the snort of laughter that escapes me. It's desperate laughter, and it doesn't guarantee that once I'm alone I won't curl into a ball and dissolve into tears. But it breaks the tension and lifts the blanket of pity that threatens to smother me even here, now, outside where the air is cold and the sky is clear and my ex-fiancé is buying hot chocolate with a new fiancée that isn't me.

"Thank you," I say when I regain control. "For sending Everett to save me."

"Don't thank me," Brooke says. "That was all Everett's idea. He was heading for you before I even realized what was going on."

The arm holding me steady falls away, but it's not like I need it anymore. Shock has frozen me in place.

"Should we go?" Everett says. "We told Drew you were sick."

"Sure, sure." Brooke's eyes are sympathetic, but I barely notice. *It was Everett's idea.* "Come on."

Our little group starts moving toward Brooke's car, three streets away. I shuffle along like a zombie. I hardly notice the crowd. Why did he do it? What does it matter to him if I'm humiliated and heartbroken in front of hundreds of people, most of whom are probably aware that Drew already broke my heart once? It doesn't make any sense.

I slide into the backseat of Brooke's Range Rover. Everett gets in on the other side. He's careful to maintain a space between us that three of the aforementioned truck drivers could fit into. But as Brooke twists the key and the engine turns over, my peripheral vision catches the movement of his head as it turns toward me.

I look back. I can't help it. He's a complete mystery, and I can't decide if there's more wisdom in trying to solve him or just letting it go.

"Why?" I ask. Okay—guess I'm trying to solve him, then. I keep my voice soft, although I'd be surprised if Brooke or Will can hear me in the front seat over the Christmas music she put on.

"Because I'm actually not a bad guy," he replies, his voice just as soft. "I know you think I am, and I know you think you have good reason to think I am. But I'm not. I hate seeing people hurt."

"And you don't like Drew."

"What makes you say that?"

"At Blush. You called him a shithead. And told me I could do better." And speaking of blush, I do. Thank the gods for dark backseats.

"Oh. You're right." His mouth quirks into a half-smile. "Well, he is. And you can."

I don't smile back. He's so confusing. And stubborn. And angry and sometimes rude and I'm still not a hundred percent convinced he *hasn't* made it his sole mission to destroy any chance I might have at making my last wedding perfect. I should hate him.

So why can't I?

18

"I'M DOING GREAT," my sister says when I call her on Sunday night. She sounds almost guilty, like she hates telling me how happy she is when I've just poured out the story of seeing Drew with his new fiancée. But I'm dying for a change of subject, and of course I don't mind. "I saw the doctor Friday, and she said everything looks perfect. Ten fingers, ten toes, strong heartbeat, amniotic sac is nice and full…"

I make a gagging sound, and Kate laughs. It's the best sound ever.

"So everything should be okay?" I ask.

"Nobody seems to see any reason why it shouldn't be. Of course they're keeping an eye on me. I see the doctor twice as much as a normal person would. But we're in the home stretch now. So far, so good." I hear the joy in my sister's voice, and it makes me feel warm all over, as cheesy as that sounds. But if family can't make you cheesy, who can?

"And you're sticking to the whole keeping-the-gender-a-secret thing?"

"Yup. So far, it seems to be helping."

"Well, if keeping it a secret keeps the baby healthy, who am I to bitch about it? I can still get it presents. They make gender-neutral onesies." Fluffy dresses and headbands, not so much, but in the event Kate has a boy, I'm sure I can hold on to the things I've already bought until someone I know has a daughter. Maybe Will and Brooke will.

"They do," Kate agrees. "So. How are things with you? When do you think you'll be here?"

"Um. I'm not sure."

"Well, what did you tell your landlord?"

"I didn't yet." I glance at the corner of my dining area, where one lonely box half-full of tank tops and sundresses languishes, nearly forgotten. I keep telling myself it's because I've been busy with Brooke's wedding, which is true, but I'd be lying to myself if I didn't admit that for the last few days my mind's been wandering—of its own volition—to a certain place. A place where I don't leave Springhollow after all, but stay. Not as a wedding planner. No, Brooke's is still the last wedding I'm going to do. Seeing Heidi's engagement ring made that clear. But I could be something else. What, I don't yet know. This is just a fantasy. But I'm armed with a fancy degree that put me in way too much debt to waste it. There are lots of things I can do with an English degree. I could write. Go into communications—maybe radio. I like music. I could go into PR. I could get a teaching certificate and teach bored high school kids how to interpret the symbolism in *Lord of the Flies.* That sounds rewarding and not at all thankless. See, the possibilities are endless!

"Really? You should, if you want him for a future reference," Kate says, and I crash-land back in the Real World. "I'm guessing he won't appreciate it if you tell him that you're moving out in two weeks. You'll probably have to make it February now."

"Yeah, you're right." She is. I can't stay here. If I stayed in Springhollow, I'd still have to see Drew. And read about his wedding in the *Stalker*. And I'd miss seeing my niece or nephew grow up.

Oh, well. It was just a thought. A daydream. I'm going home. There's still nothing left for me here.

On Monday morning I'm wrapping my scarf around my neck when my phone rings.

Drew is calling, it informs me.

My fingers go noodly. What? Why? Why is he calling? Should I pick it up? What do I say?

Somehow I manage to grasp the phone, press *Answer,* and lift it to my ear.

"Hello?"

Chalk up one mini-triumph for me. My shock makes me sound like I don't recognize the number. Hopefully he'll think I deleted him from my contacts.

"Noelle?" He sounds uncertain. "It's Drew."

"Hello." Two points scored. I sound completely uninterested.

"Hi. I hope I'm not bothering you. Do you have a minute?"

I glance at the time on my cable box. It's a little after nine. I have to get to the shop.

But Drew is calling, for the first time in seven weeks.

"I have one minute," I inform him.

"Okay. I just—I need to talk to you about the other night."

"What about it?" I ask. "If you have some big news about how you're engaged to Heidi, you can spare yourself the trouble. I saw her ring. But I already knew you were going to propose to her. Erin saw you in the jewelry store picking it out a few weeks ago." I'm trembling. Can he tell? Can he hear it in my voice?

"I'm sorry," he says.

"For what? You broke up with me, remember? You don't owe me anything."

"I'm sorry you had to find out that way."

"Well, it's not like I expected a save-the-date."

"Right." He goes quiet.

"So if that's everything, thanks, but you wasted your time. And now I have to go. Brooke St. John is getting married in less than two weeks, and there are still a lot of details to take care of."

"That's actually why I'm calling," he says. "Are you dating Everett St. John?"

I'd love nothing more than to take a fortifying deep breath right now, but I don't want him to hear me. How do I answer that question? By saying yes? It'd be a lie, and I don't like lying. Then again, he lied to me for months, so maybe he deserves it. Do I say no? Then he'd know Everett's performance on Friday night was just a show for his benefit, which would give him all of the power. I don't want that, either. It's my turn to have the power.

"What's it to you if I am?" I say at last. This, quite possibly, could be the worst response of all. What do I do if he says it means *nothing* to him?

But in that case, why did he call?

"Because, Noelle, despite everything, I still care about you."

I snort. It's a good idea—the force pushes back the tears that threaten to swarm my eyes. "Sure you do."

"I do," he insists. "Believe me. I know it doesn't look like it. And yeah, the way I care about you has changed." Well.

Ouch. "But you can't spend eight years of your life with someone and just stop caring overnight. I can't, anyway."

"Says the guy who's on his second engagement, not even two months after ending his first. I was the first, wasn't I?"

"I didn't call you to fight," he says.

"Then why did you? It's none of your business who I date."

"Oh, I know it isn't." Ouch, again. "But I thought I should warn you. As someone who grew up here, who went to school with him. I know you, Noelle, and the fact that you're seeing him, or whatever you're doing, proves you don't really know anything about him. I'm just looking out for you."

I hate that I'm curious, that I want to know exactly what Drew knows, or thinks he knows, about Everett. I shouldn't ask him to explain. Right?

"Why?"

"Well." Drew pauses. "Everett St. John probably isn't the best choice for a rebound."

"Okay." I'm suddenly furious. "I'm hanging up now."

"Hear me out," he begs. Again? Why am I always the one listening to *him*? "There's a history there. He has some problems. I don't know if he ever got psychiatric help after what happened to his parents, but he should have. He's bad news, Noelle. I'm worried about how safe you are with him."

I want to laugh at Drew and accuse him of being jealous. Except he's made it clear he's not. And as much as I don't want him to be right, there's a piece of me that thinks maybe he is. Not the safety part. Everett's never exhibited any signs of being violent or anything even close to it, and anyway, we're not actually dating, so it's not like I'll be spending a lot of time with him. No, I'm not worried about my physical safety at all.

But the other part rings more true than I want it to.

Because who but a guy with serious emotional problems would even think about doing what Everett planned to do? Even if he *has* decided to let it go, just the fact that he came up with the idea in the first place is troubling.

Maybe Drew is right. Maybe Everett *is* bad news. Maybe I should stay away.

"I appreciate your concern," I say. My tone is stiff. Am I angry with Drew? Or with myself? "But you don't need to worry about me."

"Are you sure?"

"I'm positive." I want him off the phone. I need to get to my shop. I need to forget everything I've just heard.

"Stay away from him. Promise me."

I laugh. "Promise you? Good one. What difference would it make if I did? Promises don't mean anything between us, remember?"

He sighs.

"Are you all right, Noelle?"

How dare he ask me that? Am I all right? Of course I'm not all right. My future went up in flames, and now I have to rebuild my entire life, and it's all because of him.

But will I give him the satisfaction of knowing that?

Not if I can help it.

"I'm great," I say. "I'm about to throw the biggest wedding of my career. It should really boost business once word gets out. And I'm going to have a niece or nephew in the spring." Damn it. Why did I tell him that? It's something the old Drew would have cared about. Not this stranger who's engaged to his assistant. I guess I forgot myself for a second. Forgot him.

"Kate's pregnant again? That's great. I'm happy for her."

"Yeah. She is. She's due in March." I glance at my wrist, forgetting that I'd finally managed to stuff Drew's watch into the depths of my sock drawer where I'm unlikely to ever find it again. My hand is shaking a little. I'm glad he's on the phone and can't see it. "Look, I really need to get going."

"Okay," he says. "But think about what I said, okay? I wouldn't have interfered if I didn't think I had a good reason."

I could ask him to elaborate on his reason, but I just want to get off the phone. I have a job to do. A wedding to plan. Details to finalize.

"Sure." I'm actually planning to do the opposite—to not spend a single second thinking about anything he said today. He's not a part of my life anymore. My decisions are mine alone.

When I finally get myself together and head outside, the tiniest flurries I've ever seen are drifting from an iron-gray sky. It's still cold, too. Really cold. Arctic cold. Polar bears would be comfy cold. Why did this used to be my favorite time of year again? Now I'm counting the seconds until the fourth of July.

By the fourth of July, I'll be gone. Far away from exes who have the audacity to interfere with my life even after telling me they don't want to be a part of it.

Parking's become something of a nightmare since so much of downtown Springhollow is roped off for the Holiday Village, but I'm lucky to find a spot around the corner from my shop. I only have to suffer the subzero wind chill for about ninety seconds before I push through the door and into the blessed warmth of the reception area—draped, by Erin, in tastefully realistic fake pine boughs, strings of twinkling white lights, and clusters of red, pink, and silver Christmas balls. A candle burns on her desk, and its only-slightly-synthetic sugar-cookie fragrance makes the place feel warm and cozy. It's a festive sight, and even the Scrooge I've become can't help but be a little excited by it, and the tinkle of the bells—silver, of course—that she's hung on the doorknob.

I want to tell her about Drew, but she's on the phone. Apparently word hasn't reached everyone that Silver Bells is shutting down at the New Year, and we still get calls from brides wanting my services. What *is* surprising is the way Erin looks. She's frowning so hard I'm half tempted to warn her about wrinkles, and her blonde hair, which is normally impeccably styled even in the worst humidity a Springhollow summer has to offer—and that is some *bad* humidity, trust me—looks ruffled, as if she's been running her hands through it. That's not an Erin move. She gets flustered a lot, but she's more of a hand-wringer.

The tiniest bit of worry flutters in my stomach.

She looks up as I head over to the hook to hang up my coat, and I give her a little wave, to which she responds with a small shake of her head and even more forceful frown. That's not good. The worry blossoms into full-blown fear.

"Okay," she finally says. "That's really, really weird. We'll get to the bottom of it, though. I'll call you as soon as I know something." Her fluffy-feathered pen, pinched between her thumb and her forefinger, *tap-tap-taps* against her desk. "Thanks, Brady."

"Ooh, *Brady*," I venture as she replaces the receiver.

Her cheeks flush, which is a good sign—she's still aware enough to be embarrassed by my teasing—but they don't flame red like they usually do, which is concerning.

"I have some not-so-good news."

"I figured. Let's have it." Might as well keep it coming. I guess it's going to be that kind of day.

"It's so bizarre." Erin shakes her head again. "Apparently Brooke hasn't paid her deposit on the fire hall."

"What?" That can't be right. It was due the Saturday after Thanksgiving—four weeks before the wedding, with the remainder due this coming Saturday. Most brides wouldn't have been able to get away with cutting it so close, but Brooke isn't just any bride. They made special arrangements for her, which is why I'm a little annoyed to find out that she spaced on it. "I'll call her."

I pull my phone from my bag and scroll through my contacts until I find her number. This isn't the worst possible thing that could happen, but it isn't good. I have my doubts that Amy Bunch will tell Brooke she can't have her wedding at the fire hall even if her deposit is two weeks late, but it reflects badly on me and my business, and it's not fair to the people who have already given up Christmas Eve with their families to work for Brooke.

The phone rings and rings, and I'm about to hang up when she finally answers.

"Hi!" She sounds breathless. "Sorry, I almost missed you!"

"It's okay. Do you have a minute? I just had a quick question for you."

"Sure. What's up?"

"Well, I'm sure it's some kind of mistake, but Erin just got off the phone with Brady from Cole Brothers Catering. They're the ones who work with the fire hall."

"Okay. Right."

"And, well, according to Brady, they haven't received your check for the deposit yet."

"What?" Brooke's voice is distant, and there's lots of background noise.

"Your deposit. They don't have it. You mailed it, right?"

"Of course." There's a noise that sounds like a gust of wind blowing directly into her phone's speaker. "Hang on." A few seconds pass, and I hear a car door shut, followed by a much clearer version of Brooke's voice. "Okay, I'm in my car now. Sorry. I was at Charmed picking up the gifts for my bridesmaids. What are you saying? They never got my check?"

"That's what Brady told Erin."

"But I mailed it. The Monday before Thanksgiving, just like we talked about." I hear different noises now, like she's raking through the contents of her purse and maybe checking the glove compartment of her car.

"You're sure?"

"Of course. That's not something I'd forget. I mean, I've been busy with *The Nutcracker*, but having a place to get married is sort of important, right?"

"Sort of." I rub my temples and glance at Erin. She's still tapping her pen. "Maybe it's some kind of accounting mistake on their end. Has it cleared in your checking account?"

"I haven't looked at my checking account in months." She says this in the same tone I might say "I haven't been to the gym in months." I guess I wouldn't scrutinize my checking account either, though, if I had more money than God. Can't really blame her.

"Well, do you remember when you mailed it? What mailbox you went to, what time of day?"

"I didn't actually mail it myself," Brooke says. "I gave it to Everett."

No. No no no no no *no*.

"You gave it to Everett?" I demand, and my voice sounds strangled despite my best attempts to keep it normal. If he did what I'm thinking...

"Well, he offered. He stopped by, and I had a pile of mail on the coffee table that I was going to take with me when I left for rehearsal. He said he was going past the post office and he'd take it for me." A pause. "I know he did, because there was a credit card payment in there, and I've already gotten my next bill. It shows the payment."

I'm going to kill him. Slowly. And painfully. Twice. First for doing it in the first place, and second for making a fool out of me. There I was going on and on about how glad I was he'd decided to stop interfering, and the whole time he knew he hadn't sent the check and he didn't say a word. I can't believe I felt gratitude toward him for daring to kiss me in front of Drew just so I could save face.

"Okay," I say. "I'm going to call Brady at the caterer's and let him know that it looks like it got lost in the mail. Call your bank and put a stop payment on the check, just in case it doesn't turn up."

"Okay." Her voice quivers. "You don't think they'll tell me I can't have the wedding there now, do you?"

"No." At least, I don't think so. "It'll be fine. Where are you now? Do you have your checkbook on you?"

"Yeah. I was on my way to the studio. I teach an adult ballet class at eleven, and after that I go to yoga."

I glance at the clock on the wall. It's quarter after ten.

"Perfect. Write out another check, and I'll meet you there and pick it up. I'll deliver it myself."

"Thank you." Brooke sounds like she's trying not to get weepy. I can't say I blame her. A missing veil of incredible sentimental value, and now a check that's supposed to ensure she even has a place to get married disappears into thin air. I'd be more than halfway to weepy too.

"Do me a favor," I say to Erin. "Call Brady and let him know the check got lost. Tell him I'm on my way to meet Brooke. She's going to give me another check, and then I'll bring it directly to him." I pull my coat from the hook, where it's been for less time than it takes for the coffee in the coffeemaker to brew a full carafe, and yank it back on. Erin, red-faced again, is already chattering into the receiver as I head back out into the frigid morning.

My engine's still warm so I don't have to let the car run. I pull out of the spot so fast my tires squeal. I have twelve and a half more days to make sure this whole thing goes off without a hitch.

Which is easier said than done, with Everett waiting in the wings for his next opportunity to ruin everything.

I've been past Brooke's dance studio in the past, even before I knew it was hers, but I've never been inside. It looks like an old Tudor-revival cottage—and presumably was at one point, before zoning laws made it possible for Brooke to use it to churn out ballerinas—and it's beautiful. Exactly the kind of house I always pictured myself living in. The kind of house I imagine dots the English countryside, perched atop rolling green hills speckled with fluffy white sheep. Drew and I had talked about the possibility of a trip to Europe for our honeymoon, starting in England, where I've always wanted to go. Imagine the tea I could bring home?

I guess Heidi gets that trip now. Or maybe she'll want to go to Taiwan so she can buy her clothes direct.

Let it go, orders a voice in my head. *Let her have him. You are way too good for a guy who wouldn't even wait two months before proposing to the woman he cheated on his first fiancée with.*

The words are a variation on a mantra I've been repeating to myself since October twenty-fourth. But this is the first time I feel like I could actually one day believe it.

It's a strange feeling.

I find a parking spot about half a block down. There's only street parking; leftover, I assume, from when the house was a house. It's still really cold, and I'm very thankful for the soft and cushy plaid blanket scarf Kate gave me for Christmas last year. At first I'd felt like I was wearing an afghan around my neck, but today it is most definitely coming in handy. It's so huge it nearly covers my mouth and nose.

I push open the heavy wooden door and find myself in a cheerful reception area that has that familiar dancer smell— sweat and old shoes, only tinged with the vague fragrance of pine, which I assume comes from the plug-in air freshener I spot on the wall opposite me. A large wooden desk topped with a computer and strewn with papers inhabits the far right corner, and a fake Christmas tree is propped up beside it, twinkling merrily. White plastic chairs draped with coats and dance bags line the paneled wall, and faint piano music tinkles from behind a closed door to my left.

The room's empty.

I have two choices. I can wander down the long hall that stretches in front of me, or I can poke my head into this room and see if Brooke's started class early.

The lure of the piano music is too much to ignore. I walk over to it, put my hand on the knob, and turn.

The door pushes open to reveal a room painted a creamy off-white, with dark wood beams crisscrossing the ceiling and giving it the look of an old Lutheran church—or it would, if one wall wasn't lined with mirrors and the other two long barres. The floor is ivory linoleum, and a complicated-looking stereo system, from which the piano music emanates, stands in a corner. A few older women (older than me, at least) are on the floor in a small group, stretching. They look up when I stick my head in.

"Um. Hi," I say. "Is Brooke around?"

"I'm here!" says a voice from behind me.

I give the women a little wave, wishing I was in there stretching with them, and back out of the doorway.

"Sorry," Brooke says. "Toilet was clogged. Again. Someone, and I'm pretty sure I know who, needs to teach their kid that it is not necessary to use three-quarters of a roll of toilet paper when she's only peeing."

"Ew."

"Yeah. It's become a weekly occurrence." Brooke rolls her eyes. "Anyway, thanks for coming. I am *so* sorry about all this. I called Everett and he doesn't think it fell down between the seats of his car or anything, but he's going to check. Not that it matters now. I already stopped payment, and my bank told me it hasn't cleared anyway." She heads for the desk, and I follow.

That's because your brother has it. Her brother, her infuriating and confusing brother, who vows to ruin her life one minute and saves mine the next. But it's not like I can tell her that.

She pulls open a drawer and retrieves an envelope. "Here you go. I wrote an apology note to go with it. I feel terrible. I feel like things keep going wrong. Look—I'm even wearing tourmaline." She holds out her arm and shows me a bracelet of round black stones speckled with white. She laughs a little. "I need all the luck I can get. I can't help thinking the universe is trying to tell me not to marry Will."

A chill ripples through me. I can't meet her eyes. *He knows her well.*

"It's just the nature of wedding planning," I say instead. "Especially under a time crunch. There's so much to think about. Things are bound to slip between the cracks. That's why you have me."

"And you have been an absolute lifesaver." Brooke grins. "Seriously. If you weren't putting out all of these fires, I probably would have given up by now."

"I wouldn't let that happen," I say. "It's my job to make sure you make it to your wedding day with as little stress as possible. You hired me to make sure you have the perfect wedding. So that's what I'm going to do."

I won't let my guard down again.

19

"I'M SORRY," Erin says into the phone. Another potential bride who hasn't gotten the memo. "We're not taking on any new clients. Silver Bells is going out of business after the New Year." A pause while the familiar, tiny pain slices through me. I hate those words. "I do have a list of other wedding planners in the area that might be willing to work with you. If you give me your e-mail address, I can send it over to you right away."

I busy myself by taking my notebook, the one with *St. John/Hurley* scrawled across the cover in black Sharpie, from my tote and opening it, then removing three highlighters— green for *done*, yellow for *pending*, and pink for *holy crap we forgot about that*. With just ten days before the wedding we need to do our final walk-through. It's always the last thing we do before the actual wedding, and we always do it a week and a half in advance to make sure we've got plenty of time to take care of last-minute and forgotten details.

Erin hangs up the phone, then taps out a few clicks on her computer.

"Sorry," she says at last. "I don't think she believed me. Are you ready?"

I swallow hard. "Ready." It's difficult to believe this is the last time we'll do this. I poise the pen at the top of the page. "Time for the ceremony is confirmed?"

"Four o'clock on Sunday, December twenty-fourth."

"Location?"

"The ceremony room in the fire hall."

"Perfect." I slide my green highlighter over the information. "Flowers?"

"They'll be delivered at two-thirty. There will be two silver urns on either side of the wedding arch in the ceremony room with baby's breath, white roses and camellias, and silver holly leaves."

"What about the snowflakes?" Neither Brooke nor Will have little girls in their families, so in lieu of someone walking down the aisle throwing rose petals, we decided to preemptively scatter iridescent acrylic snowflake confetti in varying sizes from the door to the altar. They have glitter on them, too. I feel sort of bad about that—glitter is a bitch to clean up. Amy Bunch might not be so quick to welcome one of my brides next time. If I was going to have any more brides, that is.

"Shipped yesterday, with a delivery date of next Monday."

I still only have one half-full box sitting in my dining room.

I shake my head. "The officiant's confirmed?"

"Judge McLean. And his daughter's string band will be there to play the ceremony music."

"Excellent," I mutter, drawing more green lines. "Okay, onto the reception. Centerpieces?"

"Coming with the flowers, at two-thirty. Nine thirteen-inch glass cylinder vases with five Christmas balls stacked inside. White, then silver, then blue, then silver, then white.

And one infinity bowl with snowflake-shaped floating candles."

"Okay. Linens?"

"Ten round white tablecloths. Eight for the guests, one for the bridal party, and one for the sweetheart table. Silver cloth napkins, napkin rings, and holly leaves. And white berries."

See, this is why Erin is the perfect assistant. I may have thought this stuff up, but she's the one that's responsible for it happening. The vision is mine. But the flawless execution? That's all her.

A lump rises in my throat. I'm really going to miss her. Miss this.

You don't have to go.

I ignore the tiny and persistent voice, and strike through *Linens* with my green highlighter.

"Deejay?" I sound hoarse.

"Booked and confirmed, but he's waiting on a final list of music," Erin says. "He doesn't have a song yet for the first dance."

I draw a yellow line over *music.* "I'll call them. Menu?"

"Bacon-wrapped scallops, spring rolls, shrimp lejon, and chicken satay with peanut sauce for cocktail hour. Salmon or filet mignon with baby rainbow carrots and broccolini for dinner."

Green line through *menu.* "Cake?" I'd tried to talk her into getting it from Tiers of Joy, the bakery I usually work with, but Brooke had insisted on ordering from Cuthbert's Confections. It's a really cute mom-and-pop place just a block away from my apartment that's apparently been there for a hundred years but hasn't been doing much business since Tiers of Joy moved into town. I actually worried that they might not last long enough to deliver a cake on

Christmas Eve. But Brooke's parents got their cake there, so that's what she wanted.

"Three-tiered vanilla pound cake with Meyer lemon filling and vanilla buttercream, decorated with silver snowflakes made out of sugar. It'll be delivered at three and kept in the refrigerator until the reception."

We go through the rest of the list, checking off things like *rehearsal dinner, photographer, lighting, bridal party attire,* and *rings.* By the time we're done, there's less than a half dozen yellow lines and no pink at all.

"Not bad for a seven-week time frame," I say, proudly showing Erin the list.

She grins. "That's why you're the best."

"You're insane if you think I could have done all of this on my own." But her words send a little fissure of warmth through me. I really am good at this. And I love it. If there was a way, any way, to keep doing it without ripping my own heart open with every bride that walks through my door...

And that thought is all it takes for me to realize that my heart doesn't feel that ripped anymore. Sure, it's still bruised and tender. It will be for a long time, maybe forever. It's too soon to think about it. But the pain isn't raw anymore. It's a dull ache, rather than the sharp, clawing agony it was in the beginning. It's kind of like my heart's been sewn up, and if the separate halves get tugged on too hard, the stitches might be torn out. But left alone, the stitches might get stronger, until they end up able to hold my heart together permanently. Maybe even painlessly.

Huh. I didn't see that coming.

"Erin...," I say, haltingly, unsure even as I start talking what I'm going to say. Am I going to tell her I want to stay?

That I want to keep the business open after all? Am I about to verbalize a decision I may not be ready to make, a decision I might end up regretting?

It's a good thing my phone rings before I blurt out that first incoherent thought.

"More car trouble?" Everett asks when he answers my call.

"You wish you were that lucky." I grind the words out through clenched teeth. I can't take this anymore. "Where is it?"

"Where's what?"

I close my eyes. Probably not smart while I'm driving, but I'm on my way to his house and I need to be much calmer than I feel right now if I'm going to leave him alive to be the best man. Although at this point I'm tempted to tell Brooke that it's too bad Osama bin Laden is dead because he would have been a better choice.

"Will and Brooke's marriage license," I growl.

A pause.

"Is it missing?" He sounds as innocent as a toddler standing next to a mess he made while trying to convince his mom he had nothing to do with it.

"You know it's missing."

"That's weird. Well, I don't have it. Maybe it ended up in the same place as the deposit check."

Maybe it did. Both items could be in his glove compartment. In his house. In the landfill in King of Prussia where almost all commercial trash in the Delaware Valley eventually ends up. The only thing that matters is that the marriage license has disappeared, and without it, Will and Brooke are pretty much screwed.

Frustrated tears bite at my eyes. I will *not* cry.

"Somehow I'm going to figure out how to steal your key to Brooke's house," I say instead. "Or convince her to change her locks."

"You could." He sounds infuriatingly agreeable. "But then you'd have to come up with a reason, and she'd just give me a new key anyway. I'm her brother. But I thought you said you weren't going to tell her what was going on?"

"Which was a stupid decision on my part." I turn onto his street. "I let my own compassion get in the way of practicality. She should have known from day one that you've been behind everything that's gone wrong. Or at least that you were behind the invitations. Once she knew that, your cover would have been blown and you wouldn't have been able to try anything else." I take a deep breath. "Maybe it's time I do tell her."

"Maybe it is."

I pull up in front of his house. "I'm outside. You can either bring the marriage license out to me and I won't say a word, or I can come in and get it and then Brooke and Will find out everything."

He doesn't say anything, but as I watch the front of his house, the door—a simple pine wreath hanging on it and staring at me like a judgmental, pupil-less eyeball—swings open.

So he's going to call my bluff. Fine.

I get out of the car and stomp up the front walk and into the house. My boots make satisfyingly loud thumps on the shiny wood floor. The living room is empty.

Suddenly my bravado flees. What the hell am I doing here? And how exactly did I think I was going to get the marriage license back from him? A wrestling match? A game of rock, paper, scissors? He knows I won't tell them anything. He knows there's time to have the county courthouse issue them another license. Not much time, but enough. A replacement won't be subject to the three-day waiting period. So what is even the point of me being here?

"Oh, hi," he says, emerging from the kitchen with a steaming mug in his hand. The five o'clock shadow that darkens his jaw actually looks more like nine or ten o'clock. He's barefoot, in blue and gray plaid flannel pants, a fitted white t-shirt and a thick-knit olive green cardigan. Any other guy would look like a grandpa who wandered away from the assisted-living facility in that outfit, but somehow he manages to come across like a rock star on his day off.

I should say something. I'm angry. But my mouth's gone dry. So I don't say anything. I just stand there looking, presumably, like the idiot I am.

"Want some coffee?" He lifts his mug and takes a sip.

I shake my head. "No. I don't drink coffee." I cross my arms over my chest, mostly because I suddenly feel really vulnerable, but hoping it'll make me look intimidating and mad. "I want the marriage license back."

"Oh, that. I don't have it." He takes another sip. "You sure you don't want any? It's pretty good. The grocery store was out of my usual brand, so I got something else. I think I like it better."

"What do you mean you don't have it?" His nonchalance is so irritating I almost forget I'm experiencing my first opposite-sex-related positive physical reaction in months.

Almost.

"I don't have it. I told you that on the phone." He leaves the dining area and moves past me into the living room, where the TV is on a music channel set to low volume, and for the first time I notice the photo album open on the coffee table.

I have no choice but to follow him. I position myself behind the couch, though, so his back is to me and I'm at the perfect vantage point to stare at the cowlick on the crown of his head.

"Then where is it?"

He sets his mug down on a coaster and lifts a page of the album, studying it, before turning to the next page.

"Have you ever seen my parents?" he asks.

Not the reply I was expecting, although I have no idea what I *was* expecting. I do know it wasn't a pop quiz about his dead mom and dad.

"No." I'm careful to keep my voice patient, in case he's experiencing some kind of emotional breakdown. "I didn't live here—then."

"I know that." He studies another page. "I didn't know if Brooke had shown you any pictures, though. Don't weddings usually have some kind of slide show with baby pictures of the bride and groom?"

"Some. Not all." And it's usually at the rehearsal dinner, not the wedding, but I'm sure the difference to him is little enough that he doesn't care. "There hasn't been enough time to plan much more than the pertinent details. Especially," I say, suddenly remembering why I'm there, "with me having to run around putting out the fires you keep starting."

Oh, man. Crap. I'm going to need a crowbar to get my big stupid foot out of my mouth.

"Everett, I'm so sorry."

"Don't be." His tone is cool. "Like you said, you didn't live here. Then."

"But I know," I protest. "I should have been more sensitive."

"Why?" He closes the photo album and, standing, turns to face me. "I wouldn't expect you to. You're not from

237

Springhollow, and you barely know me. What you do know you have no reason to like." He takes a sip from his mug. "Do you know how it feels to lose a parent?"

Before I can assure him that yes, I know very well how it feels to lose a parent, he goes on. "It's the absolute worst pain you can imagine. Especially when you know you could have done something to stop it, but because of your own stupidity, your own arrogance, you didn't. So the only thing that keeps you going is the fact that you made a promise to them, and then you do whatever it takes to make sure that promise is kept."

"I know what promise you're talking about." It's not like I'm likely to forget. "You told me when I found out it was you who messed up the invitations. But Everett, you made that promise when Brooke was a kid. When *you* were a kid. And you've done an amazing job. Brooke is such a great person. Wherever your parents are, I'm sure they're proud of how well you've kept that promise."

He looks at me then, and his eyes glitter with what I'm horrified to realize are tears.

"I shouldn't have had to make that promise," he says. "The whole thing was my fault. If I hadn't—"

He breaks off. *Ugh.* That's the second time! What was his fault? What did he *do*?

I want to know, but I won't force him to tell me. Whatever it was, it's broken him. And it's awful enough to see a grown man on the verge of tears like this.

The fight goes out of me. He was right all along—he's not a bad guy. He's just a guy who's cracked under the pressure, most of which it seems like he put on himself. I'm not even pissed at him anymore. I just want to put my arms around him.

It won't be weird. I held onto him for dear life when I was on the back of his motorcycle. A hug's not much different.

And it's not like we haven't already kissed each other. Sort of. Chastely, and on separate occasions.

I move from my position behind the couch to stand next to him, wincing when I smack my knee into the coffee table. "Ow."

"What are—"

"Shut up. I'm hugging you." I lift my arms and drape them over his old man cardigan-clad shoulders, pulling him to me. I want to comfort him. If it hurts *me* seeing him in that much pain, I can't imagine how he feels.

He must be confused, because at first he doesn't move. Or at least he spends a few seconds trying to figure out how to get away from me without being insulting. But after a few seconds his muscles, beneath my arms, relax. His own arms lift and settle around my waist, which makes me jump a little, because even though it was my goal here, it's been a long time since I've been hugged by anyone but Erin or Brooke. His cheek, slightly roughened by regrowth, brushes against mine. It's warm. He's not that much taller than me and it's not much of an issue for him to rest his chin in the space between my neck and shoulder. He smells like soap.

I want him to know that even if I don't know what he blames himself for, I understand. I know what it's like to feel like you're responsible for the loss of a parent. And seeing his pain, I wonder if maybe I haven't been unnecessarily harsh to my dad and his attempts to reconcile. Maybe I should give him another shot, since I'm lucky enough to still have him.

Everett takes a deep breath and pulls me even closer. The weird thing is that this is starting to feel like less of a comforting, friendly embrace and more of a … I don't know what. An affectionate one? A *romantic* one? That can't be right. Everett has no interest in me. But *something's* happening. One of our hearts—we're smushed so close together now I can't tell which one; maybe it's both—is apparently trying to recreate one of Alex Van Halen's drum solos. I think it's the one from "Hot for Teacher." Is it my heart? Or his?

The answer might lie in the sudden trembling of my legs, or the instinctive way my head pulls slightly back just as his does the same. My eyes drift closed. His breath flutters against my cheek. His forehead bumps against mine; we graze noses as he angles his face slightly to the right. His right. My left. One of his hands leaves my waist and comes up to my face, his palm resting warm against my jaw while his fingers slide into the hair I'm suddenly glad I decided to leave down.

I think he's going to kiss me.

For real this time.

I hold my breath and wait for it, the brush of his lips to mine and whatever comes after.

No. I'm not ready for this!

Even though every fiber of my being begs me to stay exactly where I am and let whatever's going to happen, happen, I unlock my arms and slide out of his embrace. His own arms drop to his sides.

"Sorry," I gasp, unable to stand the furrowed brow and the frown that tells me exactly how confused he is. "I just remembered. I—" My gaze swings around the room wildly, looking for any excuse to get out of there, and they land on his coffee mug. "I think I left my coffee maker on."

"Your coffee maker?" His voice is strangely calm.

"Yeah."

He scratches his arm. "I thought you didn't drink coffee."

Crap.

"I don't." My mind scrabbles for a reason. "I was, um, descaling it. With vinegar. The light came on this morning—" *Stupid, stupid, why would the Descale light come on if you weren't using the coffee maker?* "—and I had to run out before it was finished."

"Okay." He doesn't believe me. Why should he? He's not an idiot. No, that's me. I've confused him. I've confused myself. And he might be mad. I've just rejected him and used the dumbest excuse ever for doing it.

Not that I think he likes me or anything crazy like that. We were both caught up in the moment. Emotions running high and all of that. Stranger things have happened. "So, I have to go. But, um, thanks." My cheeks, ears, nose, chin— everything's on fire. What the hell am I *thanking* him for? I didn't even get what I came for.

Or did I?

"Anytime." He picks up his mug with one hand and folds his other arm over his stomach. You don't need to be a body-language expert to read those clues.

"Well, see you." I turn for the door. I can't get out of there fast enough.

I'm outside on the front step, about to pull the door shut behind me, when he calls out. "Hey, Noelle?"

I turn back. "Yeah?"

He takes a long sip of coffee before answering.

"Tell Brooke to check inside the September issue of *Cosmopolitan* in her bedroom," he says.

20

ONCE I'VE ESCAPED and I'm safely locked into my car, the temptation to sit and hyperventilate is pretty damn strong. The last thing I want, however, is to risk Everett looking out his window in a few minutes and seeing me still sitting there with my hands over my face, gasping for breath. It's a struggle, but I gather my sanity—the little bit I've managed to hang on to, anyway—start the engine, and drive.

What happened back there?

The obvious answer is that I almost let Everett kiss me. Well, more than that, actually. I almost kissed him back. And that is what has me really freaked out. I'm not even two months out of the relationship I thought I'd be in for the rest of my life. That in itself is a really good reason not to go around making out with my clients' brothers. But combined with the fact that I don't even particularly like him, and despite random acts of heroic behavior on his part he doesn't seem to like me much either, it forms a situation that makes even less sense to me than the fact that *Keeping up with the Kardashians* continues to be renewed season after season.

And the worst part?

A piece of me—a rather big piece—is disappointed that I ran away before I could let it happen.

What is wrong *with me?*

Am I lonely? Looking for a rebound? Frustrated … in *that* way? The last one's doubtful. Sure it's been a while, but not so long that I can't stop myself from running around town putting my lips on everyone I see. I don't quite think I'm looking for a rebound, either. Granted, I've had a total of three boyfriends in my entire life, but I never struck myself as the rebound type.

That leaves lonely. That must be it.

"You *what?*"

I wince.

"Sorry," Erin says. "I should have screamed that from the other side of the room. But you *what?*"

"I didn't *do* anything, technically."

"That's such crap." Erin holds a dangling rose gold and rhinestone earring to her ear and observes her reflection. "Definitely this pair. Noelle, you just told me that you and Everett almost made out."

"Not *made out.*" I turn my face from her and stare into the full-length mirror in front of us, trying not to let her see how flustered I'm getting. I wish she'd stop. I'm already in a panic because in about half an hour I'm going to see Everett for the first time since … well, since. It's only been two days. "That phrase implies things that didn't happen or even come close to happening. Like the exchanging of copious amounts of saliva. And frantic groping. None of that happened at all."

Erin rolls her eyes.

"But the intent was there," she says as she puts one of the earrings on.

"Not intent. Not really. *Possibility* might be a better word. If I hadn't pulled away."

"Just stop." Erin slides the back onto her other earring and fluffs her hair, which she's finally managed to style not in the china-doll curls she always has when she attempts to use her curling iron but the beachy waves she says she's actually always after. "I watched a few YouTube videos," she'd told me proudly when I got to her apartment. Back when she'd been able to focus on something other than what Everett and I hadn't done.

"Stop what?"

"Stop being in denial. Stop lying to yourself. Stop lying to me!" Her eyes meet mine in the mirror, and they're as bright and excited as if she'd been the one almost making out with Everett St. John.

Not making out!

"What are you talking about?"

"Good lord, Noelle. How can you be so oblivious to your own mind? You like him." She says the last three words distinctly and pointedly, as if I were a three-year-old whose mother was trying to extol the virtues of naptime.

I scoff. "I do not."

"Are you kidding? Look at how you're dressed! And you're only going to see him for about five minutes!"

"What's wrong with the way I'm dressed? I'm going to a party!" I stare at my reflection in the mirror. It's true I haven't dressed up in a while and it does feel a little weird, but it doesn't *look* weird. Does it?

I'm wearing a three-quarter-sleeved, black fit and flare dress dotted with teeny-tiny rhinestones. I bought it almost a year ago with hopes of wearing it to my own bachelorette party, and when I put it on tonight, I'd had to cut the tags off. It hits about four inches above my knee. Instead of the tights and heels I'd originally planned to wear, I put on snug, tall black boots. As a result, I'm showing off about six inches of leg.

Okay. I think I see what she means.

"Do I look like a hooker?" I ask, horrified.

"No, no," Erin says. I think she's lying. "Well, maybe not if we were going downtown. Which is where we *should* be going," she grumbles. Not for the first time, either. "But we're going to the Library. You look amazing, Noelle. Really. It's just … that outfit might be a little intense for a college bar in Newbury."

She's right. She's right! What was I thinking?

"What should I do?" I ask. It's too late to go home and change. "Help me!"

"Let me think." I observe Erin's own outfit as she opens the door to her closet. She's wearing black jeans, black suede pumps, and a drapey, cranberry-red sweater with a hi-low hem. Rose-gold jewelry glitters at her ears and on her wrist. She looks perfect for the low-key setting of the Library.

"You've got boots…" Her voice, coming from inside the closet, is muffled. "How do you feel about leggings? I'm a little curvier than you, but you're much taller. These should fit. If they're too short your boots will hide it." Without waiting for my answer she tosses a wad of black fabric over her shoulder. It lands on her bed.

"Depends on what I'm wearing on top," I say. Leggings might help with the streetwalker factor, hiding the expanse of skin between the hem of my skirt and the top of my boots, but it won't keep me from feeling like a disco ball. I need out of this stupid dress.

"What about this?" She pulls something hot pink from the closet and brings it to me. "It's supposed to be a dress, but I'm sure you could get away with wearing it as a tunic."

I take it from her and hold it up. Even without taking into account the fact that I am three-dimensional I can see that it's long enough. It's a soft velvety fabric with blouson sleeves and a high, rounded neckline.

"It's perfect."

"It's yours, then."

I take off my boots and shed the dress, pull on the leggings—they end in an awkward place between the middle of my shin and my ankle but Erin was right, the boots will hide it—and yank the dress over my head. Like my own dress, it falls into place about four inches above my knees, but with the leggings it's definitely okay.

"Much better," I say with a sigh of relief.

Erin squints at me. "It's missing something." She opens her jewelry box and sorts through necklaces, finally holding one out to me. It's a long silver chain with links the size of the tip of my pinky nail. She slides it over my head, somehow managing to avoid getting it snagged in the Dutch braid headband Brooke taught me, and steps back to observe her handiwork.

"*Now* you're perfect," she says.

After a glance in her mirror, I have to agree.

"Thank you," I say. "This is much better." Impulsively I hug her, careful not to mess up the beachy waves she worked so hard on.

She hugs me back.

"I'm going to miss you," she says.

I'm going to miss you too, I want to say. But somehow I can't make myself form the words.

"Should we go?" I ask instead. "Get it over with?"

"Aw, Noelle. I'm an idiot. I didn't even think about how hard this is going to be for you."

"What do you mean?" Is she talking about seeing Everett? Because that'll only be for a few minutes. I might be nervous, but it won't ruin my night. Not if I get it over with as soon as possible.

"The bachelorette party. Won't it remind you of Drew? Your own party?"

"Oh." Yeah, I guess it should. But I've been so preoccupied with the thought of seeing Everett that it hadn't even occurred to me.

Oh, no.

Is it possible? Is Erin right? *Do* I like him?

No, it's not possible. I'm just embarrassed about the way I left the other day. Not to mention the fact that the bachelor party is happening tonight too, and who knows what kind of torture he has planned for poor Will? I almost feel like disguising myself as a guy and going with *them*, just to make sure nothing goes wrong.

"I'll be okay." I smile at her but catch a glimpse of myself in the mirror, and my smile is pitifully weak.

🔔

"We're the first ones here," I whimper when Erin parks her car in front of Brooke's house. Everett's Jeep is in the driveway, but aside from it and Brooke's Range Rover, the only other car is the one we're sitting in.

"Nah," Erin says. "I bet Will's here too."

That cheers me up a little. I've spoken to Will in passing on the phone and through e-mail, but I haven't seen him since the night of *The Nutcracker*. He's been spending weekends in Toronto with his mom. She's holding on.

"I don't see his car," I say.

"I'm sure he'll be here any minute, then."

"Maybe." My heart thrums. "Okay. Let's go in."

"You sure?"

"Yeah. No. Wait." I pull down the visor and inspect my makeup in the tiny mirror. "Do you have a tissue?"

"Napkins. In the glove compartment."

I take out a napkin that smells suspiciously like McDonald's French fries and proceed to scrub from my lips the bright magenta lipstick I'd chosen so carefully when I was going for the monochromatic thing. In a hot pink top, though, it looks kind of garish. Once I've managed to remove all but a lingering fuchsia stain I take a nude gloss from my purse and apply it.

There. Much better.

"Good choice," Erin says approvingly. "And look, you killed enough time that someone else is here now."

A glance in my side mirror tells me she's right—some kind of silver sedan has parked behind us, and two girls are climbing out. They're bundled up in coats and scarves so I can't really tell what they're wearing but it looks like even the out-of-towners knew not to tart it up for tonight.

The tips of my ears tingle in embarrassment.

"Let's go," Erin says encouragingly.

"Okay." I suck in a deep breath and let it out. What am I so scared of? He's just a guy. A guy I have no interest in, because I'm still mourning my broken engagement. Any attraction I might feel toward him is a result of being lonely and him being around.

We get out of the car. The cold snap hasn't broken yet, and inhaling hurts my nose. The first two guests are already to the door, which is opening, illuminating them in the warm golden light that comes from the entrance to Brooke's house. I've never been in Brooke's house. I wish my head was on straighter tonight, because there are few things I enjoy more than exploring people's homes. You can tell a lot about a person by the way the rooms are decorated.

Like the cold, impersonal style Everett has going for him. It pretty much screams *keep out!*

Stop! my brain chides me.

I'm trying, I retort.

"Hi!" Brooke exclaims when we walk in. Her eyes are bright, her cheeks pink. She's in a wine-colored sweater dress and textured black tights, her hair flat-ironed into a shimmering beige curtain that falls halfway down her back. It looks so perfect I almost jump back when she hugs me—I'm that afraid of contaminating her with my own inherent frizziness.

"I'm so happy you came!" She moves to Erin and hugs her next, and I take advantage of her diverted attention to scan the living room. So far, so good—it's just us girls. The only man I see is framed and hanging on the wall, sitting cross-legged and naked but for a line of rainbow-colored dots running from the top of his head to his—well, a place you don't usually want to see a bright red circle.

"Jenna, Cassie, this is Noelle and Erin. They're the wedding planners, but they're friends too and they're both so great I had to invite them tonight. You'll love them. That's Jenna." Jenna is a short girl with a heart-shaped face and an edgy dark pixie cut. "And that's Cassie," she finishes, pointing to the honey-blonde who, weirdly enough, sort of resembles Erin. "Cassie's my maid of honor."

There's a chorus of *hi* and *nice to meet you*, then the four of us stand there kind of awkwardly while Brooke flits around the room like a butterfly on ecstasy. She checks her phone, looks in the mirror over the couch and fusses with her hair, pulls the curtain aside and looks out the front window, then checks her phone again.

"What's up?" Jenna finally asks. I note the bite of New England in her voice.

"Just excited, I guess." Brooke gives a little laugh. "Actually I think I'm anxious to see if we can get through the night without anything going wrong."

"What do you mean?" Cassie asks.

"Noelle? Care to explain?"

"The entire time we've been planning this wedding it's been the absolute epitome of Murphy's Law," I say. "When you're planning a wedding, things always go wrong, but it's been about once a week." I wonder where Everett is, if he can hear me, and if he's gloating at all the trouble he's caused.

"I keep misplacing things," Brooke says.

"You?" Jenna sounds incredulous. "You're the most organized person I've ever met!"

"Usually." Brooke shrugs. "I guess I just took on too much, what with *The Nutcracker* and everything. That's why I hired Noelle. Without her, I can't start to think about the stuff that might have gone wrong!" She laughs. "I even sat down at one point, just after I found out that the catering company hadn't gotten the check I mailed to secure the hall, and wondered if so much bad stuff happening wasn't a sign that I shouldn't marry Will after all."

The four girls laugh, and I'm about to force myself to chime in when my peripheral vision catches movement across the room.

It's Everett, of course. And he obviously heard what Brooke said.

I try to remember that I'm angry at him for hiding the marriage license, but it's hard to feel angry when every drop of blood in your body has decided that it's a better idea to gather in your face than to stay put where it belongs. My cheeks get so hot I worry that the makeup I so carefully applied is about to melt into puddles on the floor. Beads of sweat pop out on my scalp. My legs and arms go full-on overcooked fettuccine as adrenaline surges and then recedes. All of this happens in the space of a few seconds, and then I can't even worry about it because I'm too busy remembering what it felt like when his cheek brushed mine, when our foreheads were pressed together for that split second before he slid his fingers over my jaw, into my hair, and started to pull me toward him.

"Hi, Everett!" Erin trills, breaking my ill-advised memory. She shoots me a look that tells me she knows exactly what I'm thinking about.

"Hey," he says. His gaze sweeps over the four of us. Is it my imagination, or does it linger a few seconds longer on me?

It doesn't matter, because Jenna and Cassie have turned into blobs of batting eyelashes and twirling hair as they gush over how *good* it is to see him again and isn't it a shame that the bachelor and bachelorette parties are held separately, because all of us would have *such a good time* together? I watch them fall all over him, and any possibility there might have been of me making friends with these two tonight goes soaring right out the window.

"I was hoping we'd be gone before they saw him," Brooke murmurs to me. "They're my best friends, but sometimes I wonder if they only keep in touch with me because they hope one day he'll decide he wants to bang one of them."

"He hasn't?" Why is my voice so high and weird?

"God, no. At least, not that I know of. And if he has, I don't *want* to know. Yuck."

"How come he doesn't have a girlfriend?" Erin pipes up, and I simultaneously want to run out of the room screaming and stick around for the answer. Since the first option would look pretty strange, I guess I have to stand right here and listen to what Brooke has to say on the subject.

"He dated a girl for a while." Brooke glances down at her phone again. "Amanda. She was an interior designer. They went out for about two years. I thought he'd marry her. But then they broke up, about six months ago now."

"Why?" I can't help asking.

"Don't know. He never told me. One day she was there, the next day she was gone. He's here!"

I'm confused for a second until the front door swings open and Will comes in, followed by two guys that look close to him in age but aren't nearly as handsome.

"Hi, beautiful," Will says, grinning down into Brooke's face.

"Hi." She grins back. Their happiness makes my heart hurt. What kind of jerk—let alone a sibling—would want to take that away?

Will says hello to me, and Brooke introduces everyone— Erin, Jenna, and Cassie to Will and Will's groomsmen Stephen, Phil, and Dave to the rest of us.

"So what's the plan tonight?" Cassie asks.

"Apparently a strip club," Brooke replies.

"Don't look at me," Everett says when we all groan. "I know I'm the best man and the bachelor party is my responsibility, but I was outvoted. There's a comedy show in the city I thought we could go see. But Dave and Phil have apparently heard good things about Philly's exotic dancers. Will didn't want to disappoint them."

"Anyway, it's not *just* a strip club," Will adds. "Apparently they have an amazing buffet."

"Just make sure the food from the buffet is the only thing you put in your face," Brooke says.

We all laugh, but a tiny shiver goes through me.

Call it a premonition.

21

ABOUT TEN MINUTES after the guys get there, Brooke's living room is full and buzzing with the voices of close to thirty people who are waiting for the limos to show up and drive us to our respective destinations—mostly girls there for Brooke, including the third and fourth bridesmaids, Emily and Hannah, who I met a month ago when we were hunting for bridesmaids' dresses—but some more guys have shown up too. Apparently Everett was wrong, and Will does have friends. They all seem as warm and friendly as he is, and I have to wonder why Will chose his future brother-in-law as the best man when he had clearly better options to pick from.

Despite my best attempts to ignore him, I keep catching myself watching Everett as he mingles with the guests. Mostly the girls. They *do* seem to like him. And he doesn't seem to hate the attention, either. He's generous with himself, letting one girl lock him into conversation for a full five minutes before moving on to open a beer or refill a wine glass for another. He works the room like a pro, and I'm reminded of Brooke with her ballet students and their parents. I don't think I've ever seen him so approachable.

No sooner does that thought cross my mind than he looks up from his current adoring fan and, as if he can feel my gaze on him, looks directly at me.

Busted.

I stare into my wine glass as though I dropped something into it. *Don't come over here. Don't come over here.* I will the words to leave my brain and carry the message to him, but apparently telepathy is not one of my many talents because suddenly he's standing next to me, close enough that I can smell the soap on his skin again.

"Hey, Noelle."

"Hi." Ugh. I sound like a sullen teenager.

I try again. "How are you?" Brighter this time. Too bright. I sound chirpy. I'm not someone who can pull off chirpy.

"I'm okay." He lifts his beer bottle and gestures to the crowd in Brooke's living room. "Having fun yet?"

Does he really care if I'm having fun, or is he just trying to make conversation?

"Sure. It's a bachelorette party! Of course I'm having fun."

He looks at me while he sips his beer, and I can tell he doesn't believe me. He shouldn't. I've always been a terrible liar. I'm not having a *bad* time, per se. It's just that I can think of at least thirteen other places I'd rather be right now.

"Before I make you any more uncomfortable," he says, "I want to apologize for the other day."

My heart plummets from its comfy spot beneath my rib cage to a point at or around my belly button.

"What about it?" I manage.

"For all of it. But especially for freaking you out the way I did. It was an emotional moment. But I shouldn't have let it happen. Or almost happen. I don't know what I was thinking."

Well, he obviously hadn't been thinking that I was nice or cute, or that kissing me was a good idea. But it's okay. He's right. It would have been a terrible idea. And obviously I'm not that nice or that cute. My fiancé cheated on me, after all, and this guy clearly wants nothing to do with me. Not that it would even work if he did. It's too soon, for one thing, and we both seem to be at high risk of emotional breakdowns. And of course, I'm leaving.

"It's okay," I say. "You didn't freak me out. Not as much as I freaked myself out." That much is true, actually. "I'm not, um…" *Not what, Noelle? Come on, make it believable.* "I'm not really in a place where I should be thinking about that kind of thing. Not yet, anyway."

"I understand. It takes a while to get over something like what Drew did to you." And the way he says it makes me think he knows exactly how it feels.

"It does." I'm practically whispering now.

"There's one other thing I wanted to tell you." Someone bumps into him, forcing him a few steps closer to me. So close I can feel the warmth coming off him. A quick glance around the room shows me that Jenna and Cassie are both giving me a look that can't really be called a death stare but doesn't exactly scream "Let's be best friends!" either.

"What's that?"

"You're right. You've been right this whole time."

"Right about what?"

"About everything. It was terrible. *Me.* I was terrible." He shakes his head. "I see it now. I can't believe I put my sister through that."

I have to say something, but I struggle for words. It doesn't matter. He's talking again.

"I think I realized it the other day, but tonight, when I heard her say that she thought the universe was trying to tell her not to marry him … it hit me. Hard. It's what I'd been hoping she'd say for months now, but when I actually heard her say it, I realized how horrible I've been. Literally the worst brother ever." He laughs a little, but he's obviously not amused with himself. As the half-smile fades, his sadness is evident. "My parents would have been so disappointed. And I hate that you of all people know what I'm capable of."

I'm not sure what to say. What does he mean by me, of all people?

He shakes his head again. "But everything worked out. All thanks to you. If you hadn't been such an irritating bulldog about the whole thing, this might have been over months ago. And it would have been all my fault."

"Yeah, it would have." If I wasn't so thrilled about his crisis of conscience, I might be insulted. A bulldog? Really?

He gives me a crooked grin that almost makes me lose my train of thought. Almost.

"So you don't think he's just after her money anymore? Or that he's hired these guys to act like his groomsmen?"

"I didn't say that."

I must make a face because he laughs.

"Easy," he says. "Don't worry. I might not be totally convinced, but I'm not making it my problem anymore. You're right. Brooke's a big girl. And just in case I am wrong about Will, I plan to start making it up to him. Tonight. That guy's going to have the best damn bachelor party ever. He's going to wonder what made him wait so long."

It all *sounds* good…

"Anyway." He clears his throat. "I'm so sorry for everything I put you through. I know it wasn't just Brooke that was suffering. And I'm glad I got to tell you before you left town. When are you leaving?"

Before I can answer, someone shouts. "The limos are here!"

In the ensuing melee of both groups trying to get to their respective cars, I never do get to tell Everett when I'm heading home. Or ask him why he cares.

In my entire life, I've only been to two bachelorette parties— my college roommate's and Kate's. Gretchen, my roommate, had wanted the typical party, with body shots, a male stripper or two, a sash that said "Bride-to-Be" and ended up stained with spilled redheaded sluts and pictures that probably would have gotten us all rejected for future jobs had she not made them private on her social media profile. Kate's was at the complete opposite end of the spectrum—a wine tasting at Spring Gate Vineyard in Harrisburg, followed by dinner at Char's and a nightcap at some hole-in-the-wall bar Kate's fiancé Jacob pointed us to, where we ended the night singing Britney Spears songs into the karaoke machine.

So I'm not quite sure what to expect from Brooke, who, as far as I've seen, isn't really into the whole *Girls Gone Wild* thing. I actually witness Jenna trying to pin a light-up penis to her sweater, only to see Brooke swat it away and shake her head. She doesn't seem to go for the bachelorette checklist Cassie tries to give her—"I'm getting married in a week; I'm not kissing a bartender! Especially not one of my brother's friends!"—nor does she want to do the scavenger hunt Hannah and Emily come up with. She seems content to hang out at the bar and drink some beer, dance with her friends, and have a good time. Which is fine by me—easily the oldest one there. Okay, so thirty isn't exactly over the hill, but I know I'm too old for a reenactment of Gretchen's party.

Sometimes it's hard to remember that Brooke is only twenty-three. When I was twenty-three ... well, suffice it to say I was nothing like her. I'd have been wearing the illuminated phallus, for sure.

The party actually ends up being a great time. For the first time in weeks I let go of everything and concentrate on fun, which is something I haven't had much of lately. I don't think about Kate and her baby, I don't think about my dad. I don't think about leaving Springhollow, closing down Silver Bells, or ditching my life here. I don't even think about how this could have been *my* bachelorette party if my fiancé hadn't cheated on me, and I don't think—much—about Everett. When he does cross my mind, it's only because I'm wondering if the guys are having as much fun as we are. Mostly.

We stay until the bar closes at two, then shuffle outside into the cold to climb into the limo, which has been patiently waiting for us all night. And a limo in the parking lot of the Library looks absolutely hilarious. The ride home is louder than the ride there, but the words are a lot more slurred. Some of these girls can really drink. But Brooke is mostly sober, and as she sits across from me in the plush velvet-covered seat, she looks happier than I've seen her in the two months we've known each other. The night's gone off without a hitch. As the limo slides into the spot in front of Brooke's house, I realize how much I'd been gearing up for a phone call from the guys that could have sent the entire night careening into disaster.

But it hasn't happened. When Brooke hugs Erin and me goodbye and thanks us for coming, I feel good. Really good. Better than I have since taking on this whole thing. And when I'm finally home, out of Erin's clothes and comfortable in my own pajamas, I send a quick thank you out to the universe that everything seems to be coming together at last.

But the universe has one last trick up its sleeve.

My phone rings at seven-thirty. *Seven-freaking-thirty*. I hear bedsprings below and scrabble for the phone so I can turn the ringer off before Mr. Polo Shirt underneath me takes his nine iron to his poor, undeserving ceiling.

"Hello?" Do I sound half dead? I feel half dead. Seven. Thirty.

"Noelle?"

"Yeah. Hi, Brooke." My muscles go rigid, forcing me to sit up. My throat tightens. This can't be good.

It isn't.

"The wedding is off," she says, and bursts into tears.

🔔

It takes a while to get the story out of her, and when I do, I see red. Bright, slasher-film red. I should have known. I shouldn't have let myself get talked into letting my guard down again. Although what could I have done, at this point? If I wasn't so stupid—so sentimental—I could have stopped this. Stopped it the second I knew about it. Who cares if it would have torn a family apart? I'm a wedding planner. The party is my end game, not the sibling relationship.

Everett got me good, though. I'll give him that. I believed him.

I'm on the phone with Brooke for close to an hour, listening to her as she chokes out the story in a whisper, because most of the girls stayed over last night and she doesn't want any of them to hear her. I finally manage to calm her down to the point where she's willing to stay where she is and not make any further moves, including telling her bridal party. I might be able to help. The only problem is that she's already told Will. Fixing that will take some effort. And before I can even start with Will, I have to get to the root of the problem.

I have to find out exactly how Everett got Will to cheat on Brooke with a stripper.

"Yeah, he's working tonight," Erin says. "He starts at five. What time do you want to go?"

She still sounds a little incredulous, like she can't believe Everett St. John, the rich orphan of Springhollow with the face of a god, would purposely set out to break up his sister's relationship. But when I explain to her that he's been behind everything—the wrong date on the invitations, the missing veil, the lost deposit check, the misplaced marriage license and probably even the guest list that disappeared—and that he confessed everything to me on that snowy day after Thanksgiving, she admits that she doesn't have much reason not to believe me.

"I don't actually know him," she says. "All I know is that he's rich, his parents died in a fire, and he's kind of the hottest thing I've ever seen. None of that necessarily makes him a good person."

"You're right. It doesn't." Don't I know from experience that rich plus hot does *not* equal a decent human?

When was the last time I was this furious? Oh, yeah—about two months ago. When I found out my own fiancé was cheating on *me*.

"I'm sorry, Noelle."

"For what?"

"Well, you were starting to like him. I was hoping he'd help you get over Drew. I'm sorry he turned out to be just another jerk."

For some reason her words bring tears to my eyes. Angry tears, of course. I'm not sad. I'm *pissed*.

"I wasn't starting to like him."

"Oh. Okay." She doesn't believe me. I'm too mad to care.

"I think four is a good time to get there. I'm not sure how early he shows up, and I don't want to miss him."

"Sounds good."

"Are you sure you want to come?" I ask. "I don't want to drag you into the middle. This has been between him and me since the beginning. And I think Brooke should have at least one person on her side who hasn't been keeping things from her."

The guilt I feel is agonizing. I cannot for the life of me remember now exactly what made me think keeping her in the dark was a good idea. I'm as bad as Everett.

"I don't mind," she says. "It's up to you, though."

I think about it as I drop onto my couch. As much as I appreciate her support, I wonder exactly what the point of Erin coming would be other than being my getaway driver if it turns out I need one. Not that I think Everett will do anything to hurt me. He may be a massive jerk, but he's still never given me a reason to think he's violent. I'm sure I'd get away just fine.

"No," I say at that point. "I appreciate it more than you know, but I think that since this started between Everett and me, it should end that way too. I don't want you getting mixed up in it. But thank you."

"No problem." She sighs. "This really sucks, Noelle."

"I know." My temples throb. I'm not hungover, not in the slightest, so it must be stress. "It always sucks when you find out someone isn't who you think they are."

She pauses, then says, "Well, yeah, that. But I meant the wedding. If it's off, so much for your last hurrah."

Funny how that hasn't even occurred to me. Sure I want to patch things up, but not so I can cash the twenty-five-thousand-dollar check that's been in my desk drawer for two months. I haven't even thought about that check in weeks.

No. I want to fix things because they need to be fixed. Brooke and Will are the kind of couple you don't see every day—and I say this as a wedding planner who has worked with more couples than I can count. In the little bit of time I've spent with them I can see that. It's why my own misgivings fled almost the second I met Will and saw them together. The way they look at each other makes my heart hurt. They belong together even if they sneak off to the county courthouse and make it official there without vases full of Christmas balls, twinkling lights, and plastic snowflakes. They don't need me to get married.

They just need me to stay together.

At quarter to four I lock my apartment door and head for the elevator. After about thirty seconds it dings, and the door slides open to reveal the young mom from upstairs, with her kid packed into the stroller.

"Oh, it's okay," I say when she tries to pull it aside to make room for me. "I can take the stairs. It's only two floors." And probably would have been quicker, now that I think about it.

"No, there's room! Come on in." Her smile is friendly. In her brown puffy coat with the fur-lined hood pulled over her head, she looks way too young to have a child. She can't be more than twenty-five, and even that's pushing it. Maybe she's the nanny. I never have seen a dad.

"Thanks." I step into the elevator. There is room, but not much. I squeeze myself against the wall. She's already selected the ground floor button so we just wait for the doors to close again and the descent to continue.

"You're Noelle, right? Two-B?"

"I am, yeah. I'm sorry, but I don't know your name."

"I'm Lindsey," she says. "Telford. Three-E."

"Nice to meet you." I nod toward the little girl, who sits quietly in her stroller clutching a grubby stuffed unicorn. "She's really cute."

"Thanks," she says, her smile widening to a grin. For the first time I notice how pretty she is. She has ivory skin and big green eyes, framed by bold, dark brows. Her lips are full, her bone structure fine, like the silhouette on one of those cameos my great-grandmother wore in photographs. I see Lindsey in ecru lace—something vintage. With seed pearls. "Her name's Charlotte. Don't let her fool you. She's actually a monster."

"Oh, she looks it," I say, as Charlotte turns to me and gives me a dimpled, pearly-toothed grin. I can't help but grin back at her. "How old is she?"

"Three in February."

"Want a reindeer cookie," Charlotte informs us.

"Soon," Lindsey says to her. "First you're going to Grammy and Grampy's. They're going to watch you today." She brushes her hair away from her face and for the first time I notice her eyes look a little wild. "I don't know if you heard about it but there's a baking contest going on through December. Today is the third round."

I hadn't heard, but I've been a little preoccupied. That explains the stress I can feel rolling off her.

"That's so cool!" I say, meaning it. I'm about as good a baker as I am a chef, and well… "You've made it all this way?"

"Well, not by myself. I'm working with Sam from Cuthbert's Confections."

"I know them. They're doing a wedding cake for me."

"The St. John wedding?"

"That's the one. I'm the planner."

"You have no idea how thrilled Sam was to get that order."

"You work there?"

"No," she says, shaking her head. "We're just…partners. Until the competition is over."

Her cheeks are turning red. Interesting. There's obviously more to it and I wish I had time to draw it out of her.

"Well, I hope you guys win. I know business has been a little slow, and they've been around forever. I'd hate to see them close."

"Me, too," Lindsey says, but her voice sounds faraway. There *has* to be a story here. Is she in love with him? Sam's really sweet, and definitely cute—not necessarily my type, but I can see how easily he could be someone else's. "Sam told me you're shutting down, though," she says. "I'm sorry to hear that. He says you're great."

"I—"

The elevator dings again, and the doors slide open, revealing the lobby on the ground floor. The mailman is there stuffing envelopes into one of the boxes.

"I can take that," I say when the mailman tries to shove a bunch of mail into my own box. "I'm Two-B. Noelle Silver."

"Here you go," he says, and hands me the pile.

I barely look at it before stuffing it into my bag. Talk of my business reminded me of what I'm about to do.

"Thanks," I say, and sprint forward to help Lindsey with the heavy glass door. "I got it."

"Thank you," she says. "Well, it was nice to meet you finally! We'll see you around."

For a few more weeks, anyway. Guess I'll never find out the deal between her and Sam.

"It was nice to meet you too!" I say instead. "Good luck with the contest! Bye, Charlotte."

Charlotte waves her toy at me as Lindsey pushes off toward an elderly-looking car with a car seat visible in the back. I slide into my own car and only let it warm up for thirty seconds before I shift into Drive and head for the Library.

It's about ten after four when I pull into the lot. There are a few cars, but I don't see Everett's. Not his bike either. I park at the farthest corner of the lot, under the cover of some trees. Except it's December, and it's not exactly like they provide a big leafy hiding spot. He'll see me, no problem.

I leave the car running so I don't freeze to death, slump down in the car so he has to look hard if he's going to recognize me, and sit back to wait.

I don't have to wait long. Five minutes later a Jeep turns into the lot. It pulls into a spot not far from the back of the bar, maybe thirty-five feet from me, and the door opens. Everett gets out.

I put my hand on the door handle and prepare to let myself out. But something about the sight of him stops me. I thought he'd be strutting like a peacock, so full of himself for finally achieving his goal of breaking up his sister's engagement. But he's not. Far from it. He's wearing a black coat and dark jeans, a black knit hat pulled down over his head so only a few dark curls peek out at the nape of his neck. He clearly doesn't notice me parked there watching him, because he's hunched over like he's in pain.

How dare he act like something's hurting *him*? Shouldn't he be thrilled?

As he shuffles toward the bar's back entrance like an old man after knee replacement surgery, it's evident that he's not. He's upset.

Maybe he didn't have anything to do with it after all.

Crap.

I don't know what's going on, but confronting him here isn't going to help. That much is obvious.

I watch the door swallow him up. I shift back into Drive and pull out of the lot.

I think I know what to do.

22

THE PHONE RINGS. And rings. And rings. I start to lose hope that he's going to answer, and in my head I start crafting the message I'm going to leave on his voicemail.

"Hi, Noelle."

His voice is dull—such a change from what I've become used to that it sends a ripple of pain through me. He shouldn't sound like that.

"Hi, Will."

He coughs. "I guess you heard."

"Yeah, I did."

"Noelle, I swear I never—"

"I know," I interrupt. "Believe me. I know. That's actually why I'm calling."

"Have you talked to her?" The hope that's come into his voice is barely perceptible, but it's there. I pray that my plan works.

"I have," I say. It's not a lie. But what I say next is. "She wants to meet with you. She thinks she might have jumped the gun."

"She does?" Will pauses. "Why didn't she call me herself?"

"Well, she's still angry," I tell him, weaving my tangled web a bit tighter. "She asked me to mediate. It's not uncommon. I've had to do it before when it looked like—I mean, when there was a possibility a wedding might get called off." Another lie. I've never had a wedding get canceled. Except my own, of course. "Can you meet her tomorrow morning at the Sunrise Diner?"

"Tomorrow? I can meet with her right this second."

"Tomorrow." I have to be firm or this will never work. "She said it has to be tomorrow. She's got a few things to take care of tonight. She's not sending the bridesmaids home or anything. Don't worry. I told her not to make any sudden moves. But she said tomorrow, at nine." I hope that's not too early—but the longer I wait, the lower the chances of me being able to fix this.

"Okay." He sighs. "Noelle, I don't know what happened."

"Don't worry." *I do.* "We'll get this straightened out. You two will get married on Christmas Eve if I have to drag you both down the aisle by your hair."

I have to be a little more creative with my next call.

"Library," says a hurried voice when someone picks up.

"Hi," I say. "I'm really sorry, but it's an emergency. May I please speak to Everett St. John?"

"Hang on." There's a clunking noise that sounds like whoever answered dropped the phone on the floor. The voices I hear are muffled.

"Be quick," says one. "We're slammed."

"I will." A fumbling noise, and then a clearer voice. "Hello? Brooke?"

"Nope."

"Noelle. You're calling me at work. She told you?"

"Of course she told me," I say. "I'm her wedding planner. It's kind of important that I know if the wedding is happening or not."

"I didn't do anything," he says immediately.

"I believe you." I try to sound reassuring, although in all honesty I still have no idea if I believe him or not. He hasn't exactly gone out of his way to make me think it's *not* something he'd do, but the Everett I know would have been proud of himself. Not shuffling along like the zombie he was an hour ago. And I have a hard time believing he was putting on a show. I was the only one there, and he didn't even see me.

"Good." The relief in his voice is thick.

"But if this is going to be fixed, I'll need your help."

"Anything. I'll do anything."

Would a guy who told his sister that her fiancé cheated on her really want to help them get back together that bad? I think I'm going to end this phone call more confused than I already was.

"I assume you're working all night tonight?"

"Yeah. I'll probably be home around three. Why?"

"Can you meet me tomorrow morning at the Sunrise Diner? I have an idea, but it's going to need you if it's going to work."

"The Sunrise Diner? Isn't The Daily Grind closer?"

Of course it's closer. But nobody's ever broken my heart in the Sunrise Diner. If I'm going to pull this off, I can't be distracted.

"It is. But the diner's a little more private."

"If you say so. Yeah, of course I'll meet you there. What time?"

"Eight forty-five. Sorry if that's too early, but I've got a full day ahead of me tomorrow. Plus the diner gets mobbed on Sunday mornings."

"No problem," he says immediately.

Perfect.

"Okay," I say. "See you tomorrow, then."

"See you tomorrow." He pauses. "Thanks, Noelle."

"I'll do my best. But don't thank me yet."

At eight-thirty the next morning I open the door to the Sunrise Diner. I'm there at a good time—it's early enough that the Springhollow Presbyterian churchgoers are still listening to their services, so most of the booths are empty. A waitress with frizzy hair scraped back in a banana clip, which I've heard are making a resurgence, and deep circles under her eyes greets me with a smile that's a lot friendlier than I expected, given how tired she looks.

"Just one?" she asks.

I almost laugh. For the rest of my life, probably. But not this morning.

"I'm early," I say. "I'm meeting two people here. So it'll be three." I have no idea if anyone's even going to want to eat once they figure out what I've done, but it can't hurt.

"Do you mind if I have the corner booth?" I ask when she tries to lead me to one a little too close to the front of the diner for my purposes.

"Sure," she says.

"Thanks." I slide into the booth, making sure I'm in a good spot to see the door.

"Coffee?" she asks.

For a second I almost consider it. I really do. But then I remember that in order for this morning to go as planned, I can't be wallowing in memories of my own lost fiancé. I can only deal with one broken engagement at a time.

"Some black tea would be great, if you have it."

"Yup. Anything else while you're waiting?"

I give a moment's thought to ordering three glasses of water but immediately decide it would be better not to have any kind of heavy projectiles on the table.

"Not yet, thanks."

"Be right back with your tea."

She is, and I add sugar, stir, and sip mindlessly as I keep my gaze locked firmly on the door. I hope I timed this right. I remember now the first time Brooke came into my shop, complaining about how Everett is always late. If they see each other, this could go downhill fast.

But he shows up at eight forty-five on the dot. He's a black blob thanks to the milky December sun shining through the diner's front door, but I can tell it's him immediately. I lift my hand in a wave. It takes him a second to see me, but when he does, he heads right for me.

"Hi," I say.

"Hey." He takes off his coat and slides into the booth. "Why are you way back here? I barely saw you."

"I wanted to be away from everyone. Less distractions."

"Okay." He picks up a menu and scans it before tossing it back down to the table. "Like I can eat. Did you order?"

I shake my head. "I'm not hungry."

"Okay." The waitress comes over and he asks for coffee and an orange juice, which she brings almost immediately. She's touched up her lipstick, too.

"Anything else?" she asks.

"No, thank you." He gives her a polite smile. She lingers for a minute, but when we don't ask for anything else, she gives up and walks away. "So what's your idea?"

I glance at my new watch. It's not even nine. How can I kill ten minutes without making him suspect that I really don't have any idea what I'm doing?

Luckily I don't have to worry. The door opens again and Will comes in.

"Hold that thought," I tell Everett, and slide out of the booth.

"—meeting her here," Will is saying to another waitress at the front of the diner when I reach him. He doesn't notice me. I touch the sleeve of his jacket, and he jumps.

"Noelle," he says. He looks awful. He looks his age for the first time since I've met him. He must have been up for the last thirty-six hours trying to figure out how to get Brooke back.

"Hi. I—"

"She changed her mind. She didn't come," he interrupts.

"She was never coming," I say. His face falls even further, if that's possible. "Wait. That sounds terrible. She was never coming, but it's only because she never planned to. She doesn't know we're here."

He frowns. "I'm confused."

"I don't blame you." Well, this is off to a lovely start. "I'll explain. Follow me."

I lead him back to the booth. Everett has his back to us as he stirs creamer into his coffee.

When Will sees him, he stops short.

"What's he doing here?" he demands.

At the sound of Will's voice, Everett turns around.

"Will," he says. "Noelle, what's going on?"

"I'd like to know the answer to that, too." Will's glaring at me.

I swallow so hard the muscles of my throat ache.

"I thought the two of you should talk," I say. I sit and slide toward the wall. "Sit down, Will."

Will remains standing. "I have nothing to say to him."

Everett stares at me. "Noelle, what are you doing?"

"I'm trying to fix this!" I pat the empty space next to me. "Will. Sit."

He remains standing for a few seconds before sighing and sliding into the booth. He keeps a good amount of space between us, though.

"I want to know what's going on," he says.

"So do I." I fix Everett with what I hope is a steely and intimidating gaze. "Everett, I think it's probably a good time to tell Will everything. Including why you said he cheated on Brooke with a stripper."

Beside me, Will goes rigid.

Everett wraps his hands around the glass of juice and stares into it. "Because I thought he did."

"I did *not*!" Will explodes. An elderly couple a few booths away turns to stare at us. The waitress, who had been approaching our table, turns on her white-sneakered heel and disappears into the kitchen.

"It's okay, Will." I pat his hand even though his outburst has me shaking a little. I didn't know he had it in him. "We'll get this straightened out. Do you have any idea why Everett would think that?"

"Because he's the one that paid for the private lap dance!"

My heart drops like a stone.

"Did you really?" I'm not sure if I even want to know the answer. It might be better for everyone if I just get up and leave and let them sort it out. Or kill each other.

Everett sighs.

"I know how it looks." He rubs his hand over his forehead. "But don't you remember what I said?"

"Of course I do." I pause. He said he was done trying to stop the wedding, done trying to break them up. But I'm guessing Will doesn't know that Everett was behind everything that went wrong. Should I say it?

I don't even have a chance to decide.

"I said I was going to give Will the best bachelor party ever. Remember that?"

Oh. Yeah, he said that too.

"Of course." I shove my empty mug to the other end of the table so I'm not tempted to throw it at him. "But seriously. A lap dance? What the hell made you think that was a good idea?"

Will snorts.

"He didn't," he says. "He knew it was a terrible idea. And that's why he did it."

Everett lifts his gaze from the depths of his orange juice and fixes it on Will.

"That's not true," he says.

"Come on," Will retorts. "As if you haven't been going out of your way to break up Brooke and I since the day we met."

I go so cold goosebumps ripple over my skin despite the fact that I'm wearing one of my fluffiest sweaters topped off with the blanket scarf monstrosity.

Will *knew*? Of course he was aware that Everett wasn't his biggest fan. He made that clear at *The Nutcracker*. But he knew Everett was trying to ruin the relationship? That's news to me.

Everett's gone the color of an heirloom tomato—sort of purple, sort of red..

"I don't know what you're talking about," he says.

"Come on, Everett," Will says. "I'm not stupid. And neither is your sister. She would have seen through you eventually. She's just too blinded by love for you to admit that you might do anything to hurt her."

Everett flinches.

"I never wanted to hurt her," he murmurs. "I was trying to protect her." His finger traces a line in the condensation on the side of his glass. He looks completely miserable. And as much as I try to shove it down, sympathy bubbles up inside me. We're not so different, Everett and me. Both of us willing to sacrifiece our own needs for our sisters. He took it in a slightly different direction than I ever would have, but still.

"What did I ever do to make you think she needed protection from me?"

I close my eyes. Poor Will. He's not going to like what he's about to hear.

"Oh, come on," Everett says, and the fire is back in his voice, in his eyes. "You show up out of nowhere, with no other family besides your mom, who is conveniently eight hundred miles away on her deathbed. The one you won't even let Brooke fly up and meet." Will's hands in his lap clench into fists, but he says nothing. "No friends that we know of and a job that takes you out of town for months at a time. Not even a week goes by and the two of you are inseparable. You're all she can talk about. Six months later you're engaged. You're back in Canada to drive your mom to chemo, but you somehow figure out that you can make it back down in time for a Christmas wedding before taking off again for God knows how long. What the hell was I supposed to think, Will?"

"What *did* you think?" Will's voice has gone so quiet I feel a sizzle of danger in the air. Almost without thinking

I inch closer to the wall. "Not that I don't already know. I just want to hear you say it."

Everett remains silent and I wonder what will happen if he refuses to admit it.

Tell him, I plead telepathically. *Just tell him. Get it out and get it over with.*

It didn't work the other night. I don't know why I think it'll work now. But somehow, strangely, it does.

"I thought you were after the money," Everett says. The words land like rocks in the middle of the Formica tabletop.

Will sits back and folds his arms.

"I know," he says.

Everett pushes his glass away. "Why didn't you tell her? Why didn't you try to stop me?"

"We're more alike than either one of us wants to admit."

"What do you mean?"

Will sighs. "I didn't want to hurt her either. I couldn't stand the thought of driving a wedge between you. You two are so close. I'm an only child, so I have no concept whatsoever of what a sibling relationship is supposed to be like. But I could feel how much you two loved each other. That's why I asked you to be my best man." He gives a short snort of laughter. "It's not because I don't have friends. The guys who came out with us last night weren't actors. It's because I wanted you to like me. I wanted you to be my brother, too."

Okay. Am I the only one ready to burst into tears here?

"I never thought you'd accept, though." Will shakes his head. "Why did you?"

"She was so excited when you asked me." Everett shrugs. "I couldn't say no. Then I realized it would be a great way to … well. You know."

"I do. And may I say job well done?" The bitterness in Will's voice is thick.

"I'm sorry, Will. For everything."

"It doesn't matter now, does it." It's not a question.

"Everett, *why?*" I cannot make sense of his reasoning. "You said you were done. That you were going to let it happen. I don't understand."

"I swear, I meant it. Nothing was supposed to go wrong last night." He shakes his head. "I thought it was what best men did. What I was supposed to do. I know how stupid that sounds." He looks at me. "When he came out he looked like a mess. His shirt was hanging half out and he had glitter all over him." I swallow the mad urge to laugh. Now is definitely not the time. "And his hair..." Everett looks up again and glances at Will. "Sorry, Will, but you look like you spend more time on your hair than a girl. I've never seen it as messed up as it was when you came out of that room."

"She was ... enthusiastic."

"I guess I was looking for a reason." He chews his bottom lip. "Will, I'm so sorry. I'll tell Brooke I was wrong."

"Do you think it will help?" I ask. "So much has already gone wrong. At this point she's probably convinced that the universe is having a huge laugh at her expense."

"I'll tell her everything. She deserves to know." His Adam's apple moves up and down as he swallows hard. "I'll go right to her place when I leave here. I'll fix this, Will. I promise."

"I hope so. She'd be my whole world even if she didn't have a dime. The money means nothing. I even asked her if she wanted me to sign a prenup. She said she wouldn't insult me that way."

I glance at Everett. He's shaking his head again.

"And I've waited a long time for her," Will continues. "She's perfect. I don't want someone else." He looks at the waitress, who's approaching us with the timidity of someone approaching a dog that's already bitten her. "I love her. And I'm not giving her up that easy."

"Where is your family, Will?" I ask. "I'm not suspicious. Not at all. Just curious."

"It's just me and my mom," he says. "She'll be here in a few days. My dad died when I was too young to remember him."

Everett and I, both of us with our own versions of daddy issues, murmur variations on sympathetic apologies.

"And my mom really is dying," he says. "I wouldn't lie about that. I don't believe in putting that kind of energy out there." Well, if anything had me doubting his and Brooke's compatibility, that comment would've convinced me otherwise. "It's one of the things that drew us together. She has no parents, and soon I won't either. That's why I didn't have her come to Toronto. I was afraid she'd get attached, and she'd lose someone else she loved. It was dumb. I know that now. I should have given more thought to what *they* wanted. But they have met. They've chatted over video calls, several times. And talked on the phone."

"I feel like shit." Everett sighs.

"You should," I say.

"As for friends. They're mostly from Toronto. There are fewer here. I've only been back in Philly for a year and a half, and most of that time I've been traveling for work."

Everett twists a napkin to shreds between his fingers.

"Coffee?" the waitress asks. She's keeping a few feet of distance between us.

"No, thanks," Will says. "I have to get going." He pushes himself out of the booth, and the waitress moves over to the elderly couple we scared. I think they're talking about us.

Everett tosses the mangled napkin down. He slides out and stands too, blocking Will's path up the aisle and to the front door.

"I *will* tell her," he says. "I'll make it right." He holds out his hand. Will studies it for so long that I think Everett's about to drop it and walk away when Will reaches out too and takes it.

"Please do," he says. He pumps Everett's hand once, quickly, and turns to me.

"Thanks, Noelle," he says.

I hurriedly extricate myself from the booth and hug him. He hugs me back, but it's stiff. He's angry with me; I can tell. It's okay. He should be. I never should have kept everything from either of them. It doesn't matter that my intentions were good. In my effort to keep from hurting them, I just screwed everything up.

"We'll talk later," I promise.

He nods and without another word strides toward the front of the diner, pushes open the door, and disappears into the sun, leaving Everett and me standing there staring at each other without much to say.

23

WHEN I GET home, I'm exhausted. It's only ten o'clock on Sunday morning, and I could literally crawl into bed and sleep for twelve hours straight. I'm so completely drained. Planning a wedding is hard. Planning a wedding in two months is harder. Planning a wedding when three of the main players seem hell-bent on self-destruction is ... well, I guess we'll see if *impossible* ends up being the right word to describe it.

Even though my unmade bed beckons to me through the open bedroom door, I resist all urges to give in to it. I need to be firing on all cylinders when—if—Brooke calls me to tell me the wedding is back on. So instead I pour some water into the kettle and turn on the stove, dig some spiced orange tea out of the cabinet, and throw a couple of slices of bread in the toaster. A few minutes later I sit down with my breakfast and the pile of mail I took out of the mailbox yesterday but haven't had a chance to look at yet. I take a large bite of toast and start to sift through the stack.

As always, eighty percent of it is junk. Credit card offers. Coupons for basement waterproofing, gutter and air duct cleaning, tree trimming, and kitchen remodeling. A few colorfully enveloped cards that get shunted off to the side for when I feel ready to deal with the fact that Christmas is just a week away. A Victoria's Secret catalog that I figure I should keep so I can familiarize myself with the kinds of clothes I might be responsible for selling in a few short weeks. And at the bottom of the pile, almost as if the mailman had known—a letter, addressed to me in the handwriting I now recognize as my father's.

My throat tightens, and the half-chewed mouthful of toasted bread in my mouth suddenly feels like a hunk of gravel. Why? What could he want now? After our phone call he can't still be under the delusion that I want anything to do with him. It's been weeks and he hasn't tried to contact me. Until now. The envelope sits on the table, gleaming whitely, the heavily inked black letters bellowing at me to open it.

"I don't want to," I tell it. And I don't. I want to put it in the pile I've designated as trash, throw it out, take the bag down the hall to the chute, and let the garbage men deal with it on Wednesday when they come to empty the complex's dumpster. Nothing good can come of reading that letter. There's no point in even acknowledging it.

So why, then, do I pick it up and open it?

I don't know. But I do. Before I even realize what I'm doing, I've torn the envelope open, and I'm unfolding a sheaf of papers. It feels like there are three pages. But my dad's handwriting is large and blocky. A three-page letter doesn't necessarily mean that he's written three pages of apology. If that's even what it is.

Dear Noelle, it begins.

> *I know you're angry with me. And believe me, I know why. What I did to you and Kate, and your mom, is one of the worst things a man can do. I left my family. The family I swore to love and protect for as long as I could.*

I have no words that can adequately describe why I did it, nor how sorry I am for doing it at all. But I'm going to try, because I think you deserve to know.

When you and your sister were born, I was the happiest man in the world. I would look at one of you and think "I helped create that." Watching you grow and learn and become your own little people was the most fascinating thing I've seen in my entire life. But somewhere along the way, and I don't know exactly when, or why, I started to feel smothered. One of you, or your mother, always wanted something or needed something, and I felt like I was losing the part of my life that made me who I was. I wasn't me anymore.

I know how selfish that sounds. I'm a selfish man. Much too selfish for a family. Having a family requires sacrifice and the ability to look past a particular moment and see the big picture. I wasn't able to do that. All I saw were three people who relied on me for far more than I was able, or willing, to provide. I loved you both— love you still—but deep down, I knew I wasn't meant to be a dad. Not then and maybe not ever.

I can't imagine how hurt you must have been when I left. How confused. You were just a little girl, and I'm sure you thought you did something to make me leave. But please know that you didn't. The fault was all mine. I should have waited until I was older, until I had a better sense of myself, before getting married and having kids. And once I did have you, I should have dug in my heels and done my job as a father. Or at least tried a little longer, until you were old enough to understand. Or even done the mature thing and asked your mom for a divorce rather than doing what I did. I hate myself for running, but, Noelle, trust me when I say that leaving was the best thing I could have done for both you and Kate. You needed someone who could be there for you, to help you through your problems and answer your questions about the world. That someone wasn't me.

I have no doubt your mom did an excellent job bringing you up. Look at you—you graduated from a fantastic school, you have your own business that appears to be really successful (I admit I spent a lot of time Googling you while I was working up the nerve to contact you—your couples seem to love you), and even though your engagement didn't work out, I'm sure there's someone out there that's dying to find someone like you. I have no doubt that you'll find him, and soon. It looks like you've been doing everything right, honey. Just keep at it. I know I'm not exactly in a position to be asking for any favors, but I love knowing that you're doing something that not only makes you successful but happy, so I'd like to ask that you keep doing it for as long as you can.

I'm sure you and Kate are as close now as you were when you were kids, so I know you're going to tell her about this, and that's okay. I'm writing to her too. I thought about calling, but your reaction when I called you, as much as I deserved it, left me a little gun-shy. I just felt like it was time that the two of you were told that your dad, as terrible a dad as he has always been, still thinks of you and still loves you, and is here if you need him for anything. And in case you do, my number is 574-555-1275. But I won't be contacting you again. I know it's too little, too late, and I'm not asking for nor do I expect or deserve your forgiveness. Anyway, I've bothered you enough, and you have your life to live.

Love always, Dad

My hands tremble so violently the papers clutched in my fingers make a rattling noise. Blood rushes in my ears and burns my cheeks. My heart stutters, and my breath, when I finally manage to catch it, comes short and shallow. I'm a strange mix of furious and elated, disgusted and relieved. He's got one thing right. It's too little, and it's way too late.

But I feel like I've lost fifty pounds. Fifty pounds of anger and resentment and jealousy toward every friend I ever had whose dad didn't go running off in the middle of the night, never to be heard from again. It's just gone—*poof*, like that. I don't think I'll ever remember him again with bitterness seething below the surface, the way I have for twenty years. I can let it go now. Maybe I already have.

I'm not exactly in a position to be asking for any favors, but I love knowing that you're doing something that not only makes you successful but happy, so I'd like to ask that you keep doing it for as long as you can.

How weird is it that my dad, who doesn't know a thing about the woman I've turned out to be, somehow manages to echo the very thought that's been banging around in the back of my head for the last few weeks?

Successful. Happy.

He's right, somehow. Despite the rather large blip that was Drew, planning weddings does make me happy. At least when things are going smoothly, and even when they're not, it makes me happy to set things right. And more than that— I'm good at it. I guess there's a chance that Brooke doesn't forgive Will and they end up not getting married. But I can still be comfortable with the knowledge that the wedding that might have been would have been an awesome one, and that I did everything in my power to make it happen..

I glance toward the lone, half-filled box that's been hanging out in my dining room for the last month.

I guess it's time to stop lying to myself.

Erin doesn't answer the phone when I call, but before I can finish leaving her a message she calls me back.

"Hi," she says. "Sorry—I just got out of a job interview."

Crap. Am I too late? I'd never blame her for getting another position. As far as she knows—and as far as I knew until about ten minutes ago—come the new year, she's unemployed. But I really, really hope I'm not too late.

"What's up?" she says. "How did the meeting go? Is the wedding back on?"

"Not yet," I tell her. "The meeting was okay. Better than okay, I think. Will didn't cheat on Brooke, of course. And Everett admitted everything, and it turns out Will knew the whole time that Everett didn't want him marrying Brooke. Ev promised to tell Brooke everything, and that was how we left it. I haven't heard anything yet but it's only been an hour."

"Wow."

"So. A job interview, huh? Where? How did it go?" *Awful. Terrible. They hated me. They said I wear too much pink.*

"Pretty well, I think!" She sounds happy. Will she be happy when I tell her my decision? "They loved the letter you wrote for me. And they said Silver Bells has a great reputation. It was at Fab Functions, so, you know, it's planning more general parties instead of just weddings. But they said my experience makes me a definite candidate. I should find out sometime next week."

"Oh. Good." Here goes nothing. "Well, I'm actually calling for a reason that doesn't have anything to do with Brooke or Will."

"What is it? Are you okay? Is it Drew?"

"No, no." I take a deep breath. "I'm fine. I just—I decided something. A few minutes ago. I'm, um, not leaving Springhollow. I'm staying. And I'm keeping Silver Bells open."

I hold my breath and wait for her response. It takes so long I'm afraid I might pass out from lack of oxygen.

"Are you serious?" she says after a while.

"Yes. I'm serious. I've kind of been putting off telling my landlord that I'm leaving, and I've only packed half a box, and I got a letter from my dad today and he said something in it that made me realize that I want to keep doing this. I don't know if I ever really wanted to stop. I just wanted to run away." I pause. "And I know you've been looking for a job, and if you're offered something you want to take, please do. I'd never dream of stopping you. But if you don't … you have a place with me. You always will. As an equal partner. Not just my assistant."

"Are you serious?" she says again, but this time it's a little more *omigod omigod omigod* and less *could she be any more flaky?*

"There's no way I could have done any of this without you, Erin. I should have made you my partner a long time ago. Probably the day I hired you."

"Wow." Looks like I've shocked her so much her vocabulary's been reduced to four words.

"But as I said, only if you want to. I'd feel awful if you passed up a great job opportunity to work with me."

"I did that six years ago when you hired me," she says with a laugh. "I was this close to being hired by an event-planning firm in the city when you came along. Something made me want to work for you, though. I don't know what it was. But I still do."

"*With* me," I correct her.

"With you." She sounds happy, which makes me happy. This is the right decision. I know it.

Now to break the news to Kate.

☙

"Hey, Noelle."

It's Jacob, which surprises me. I pull the phone from my ear and look to make sure I dialed Kate's cell number and not her landline. Looks like I did. So why is her husband answering?

"Hi, Jake. Is everything okay? How come Kate didn't answer?"

"She's resting," he says, and it's then I hear the exhaustion in his voice. "It's been a rough morning."

I immediately go cold. "Is she okay? Is it the baby? What happened?"

"She's fine. She woke up at around three o'clock this morning in some pain. We went to the hospital, and they took her in right away. Turns out it was just Braxton-Hicks contractions. Totally normal, and nothing to worry about. But scary, considering."

I close my eyes and take a deep breath. Now I'm doubting my decision. I promised my sister I'd be there for her. What if I'm not, and something goes horribly wrong?

"I bet," I say after a bit. "Is she sleeping? Can she talk? I won't keep her long. I just need to tell her something." Should I risk upsetting her, though? Maybe I should wait.

"Hang on." I hear Jacob's steps on the hardwood stairs I know they refinished over the summer. A creak as I imagine him pushing open the bedroom door and his muffled voice. "It's Noelle. Do you feel up to talking?"

"Sure," she says. She sounds very far away. There's a ruffling noise as I guess the phone changes hands, and there she is. "Hey, Noe." Her voice is tired.

"Hey," I reply. "Jake told me what happened. You okay?"

"We're fine," she says. "Just Braxton-Hicks. Although if that's what the real thing feels like—damn."

"Actually I hear real labor is worse."

"Fantastic. Well, as far as I know there's no law that says the baby *has* to be born."

"You might change your mind when it's time to send it off to kindergarten and its feet are coming out your nose."

Kate's laughing. Good.

"So what's going on?" she asks. "How's the Millionaire Wedding coming along?"

"Eh, we hit a bit of a snag. Not in the planning. Of course I have that perfectly under control. There's just the slight possibility that the bride thinks the groom cheated with a stripper at the bachelor party, and she may have told him the wedding is off. I'm looking into it."

"You're kidding. Right?"

"Wish I was."

"You still get paid, though, don't you?"

I think of the obscenely large check that's been crammed into my desk drawer for the better part of two months. Brooke's never said a word about the fact that I haven't cashed it, nor have I told her when—if—I plan to.

"A percentage, relative to the work I've already done," I say. "But I have a feeling everything's going to work out." Although here it is closing in on noon, and I have yet to hear from Brooke. Is Everett still confessing? Did he bother to confess at all, or were they just words to get Will and me off his back? For all I know he's on his bike right now, headed west with plans to assume a new identity.

"Sounds stressful. Good thing it's your last wedding."

Which brings me crash-landing back on the reason why I called her in the first place.

"Actually, that's why I'm calling," I say. "I need to tell you something."

"Okay."

Just say it. Get the words out.

"I'm staying in Springhollow and keeping Silver Bells open."

"I figured that."

"Really?"

"Of course. You have no idea how well I know you, do you? I knew you weren't going to go through with it the second you said you hadn't told your landlord yet."

"Kate, I'm so sorry."

"For what?"

"For blowing you off. I promised to come and help you."

"You did, and I love you for it. But Noe, I agreed to that because you were in a bad place and I knew you needed a refuge. Not because I can't manage without your help. I'll be fine with Mom and Jake and his mom. I'm sad that you won't be around every second to see the baby grow up, but I'm sad for me, not for you. You have a life there no matter what you think. Drew was only a part of it. He wasn't the whole thing. I'm so glad you see that now."

Tears sting my eyes.

"You're the greatest sister in the world," I wail.

"I happen to agree." We laugh a little before she asks me. "What changed your mind? Is it that guy?"

"What guy?"

"The brother ... what's his name? I can't believe I forgot. You said it enough times."

"Everett?"

"That's it. Has something happened with him?"

"No." I'm kind of shocked. Did I really talk about him that much? What could I have said to make Kate think he has anything to do with my reasons for staying? If I did go on about him, I'm sure it was in the form of complaints. For ninety percent of the two months I've known him he's done little besides piss me off.

And for the other ten percent of the time you've been holding his hand under the dinner table at Thanksgiving, drunkenly kissing him to piss off your ex-fiancé, and almost really kissing him in his living room. Not to mention the fact that he let you stay at his house when you were too drunk to drive home, pretended to be your boyfriend to help you save face in front of Drew, and dropped everything to come pick you up when your car broke down.

"No," I repeat. "He has nothing to do with it."

"Okay." She doesn't believe me, but I won't argue with her. Anyway, I need to tell her what pushed me over the edge.

"I got a letter from Dad."

"Another one?"

"A real letter this time. Not a card. He's going to send you one too. You'll have it any day now, I bet."

"What did it say?" I can tell how hard she's trying to keep the fact that she's interested out of her voice. Kate was hurt even worse than I was when he left. She'd been much more of a daddy's girl. That's probably why he's been trying to contact me instead of her. He knows she'll give it to him way worse than I did. What a coward.

"Lots of apologizing, and even more excuses," I tell her. "A promise to be there if I needed him and a promise not to bother me again."

"Interesting."

"I got mine yesterday," I tell her. "I'm sure you'll have yours tomorrow, if he mailed them the same day. He might be taking more time with yours. You two were so much closer."

"It doesn't matter," she says. "We've gotten along fine for twenty years without him."

"Better than fine."

"Should we mention it to Mom?"

"I don't know." My mom was never very vocal about how she felt about my dad leaving. She was hurt—I know because in those first few months I caught her crying more times than I care to remember—and I know things were rough for a while money-wise, which can't have made her feel kindly toward him. But she never badmouthed him, and she never once told us if she missed him. Even now that we're adults, I can't remember the last time I heard her mention him. "Maybe."

"Let's wait until after the holiday."

"Okay." There's a beeping noise then, and I take the phone from my ear to check. Brooke's name flashes across the screen. "Kate, I'm sorry, but I have to go. It's Brooke. You sure you're okay?"

"I'm fine. And I'm glad you figured out what you need to do. We'll talk later. Good luck."

"Love you," I say before clicking over to the other call. "Hi."

The moment of truth has arrived.

24

"Hi," she replies, and I'm already silently cheering because I can hear the difference in her voice from a mere twenty-four hours ago. It's a good difference. "My brother just left."

"Yeah?"

"Stop playing dumb." There's a hint of laughter in her voice. "I know you know what happened, and I know you were responsible for it."

"Not completely responsible," I say. "It was one-hundred percent his decision to confess everything to you. I didn't have to push him at all or even suggest it. Neither did Will."

"That's good to hear." She pauses. Is she trying to torture me? Or was I wrong about her sounding happier and she's about to tell me some really bad news?"

"Is the wedding…"

"Oh, it's back on." The relief that suffuses me leaves me almost limp enough to slide off my sofa. "I feel like an idiot, Noelle. Why did I ever believe that Will cheated on me? I know him, and that's not him."

"Because of everything that was going wrong," I tell her. "Remember you told me you thought it was all part of some sign that you shouldn't go through with it? You were already waiting for something else to happen. It was just a crappy coincidence that something did."

"Still. I feel awful. I can't believe I thought he'd do that."

"Is he angry with you?"

"He should be. But he's not." A sigh. "He is *way* too good for me."

"He is not. He's just a decent guy. One who loves you and will overlook the occasional mistake."

"Like believing he cheated on me with a *stripper?*" She snorts. "Come on, Noelle. That's more than a little mistake."

"But you got through it, didn't you? And look at it this way. You've already gotten past the worst thing that's probably ever going to happen to you as a couple. And you're not even married yet. There's nowhere else to go but up."

She breaks out laughing. "Okay. I believe you." Her giggles give way to a sniffle. "What would I have done without you?"

The guilt starts to creep. Obviously Everett left out the fact that I pretty much aided and abetted his little crime spree. But I have to tell her. Now. I owe it to her.

"Don't give me too much credit," I say. "I sort of knew what Everett was up to. No. I didn't *sort of* know. I totally knew."

"You did? How?"

"I found out by accident. It was the invitations. They had the wrong date on them when I went to pick them up the first time. Then my car broke down, and he was the only one around to help. I was ranting about Life Made Lovely and how they got the date wrong, and he said something that made me think he already knew about it. When I asked him, he admitted it right away."

"The invitations," she says slowly.

"I didn't tell you because I knew you were stressed out already, and since part of my job is to keep you from getting stressed out in the first place, I figured it wouldn't hurt to keep it to myself." Blood scorches the tips of my ears.

"And the other stuff?"

"I tried to keep one step ahead of him, but I couldn't. I had no idea what he was going to do next. So I just tried to keep you as calm as possible and fix everything as it happened. When you called me to tell me your veil was missing, I knew right away he was behind it. I went to his house and started tearing his couch apart looking for it. The missing deposit check, the marriage license, all of it. Probably even the guest list that disappeared. I knew it was him. I just tried to fix it. I even followed him once, to the florist. But of course that time everything was fine." I hold my breath. Wait for her response.

"Why didn't you tell me?"

Ah, the million-dollar question.

"I should have." The heat in my ears seeps into my cheeks and even down my neck. I'm *such* a jerk. "I had reasons for not telling you, though, and at the time I swore they were good ones. I thought if I said anything, you'd hate your brother and I'd have torn your family apart, and I wouldn't be able to live with myself, because you two are so close. Then I worried that if I stayed out of it, Everett might figure out how to stop your wedding and then you'd know the heartbreak that happens when your whole planned future is ripped out from under you. That's not a pain I'd wish on anyone, but especially not a friend." A lump swells in my throat. "So I decided the best thing I could do was keep it to myself but make sure Everett didn't do anything I couldn't fix. In hindsight, though, that might have been the wrong decision. I'm so sorry, Brooke. I should have told you."

294

My throat's gone dry. Here it comes. Will she fire me? Does she hate me? I'd understand both reactions. Not that I want either one to happen, but it's not like I don't deserve it.

"I guess I understand," she says. And again I almost go tumbling off my couch.

"Really?"

"My brother put you in a tough spot." I open my mouth to argue that while that might be true, I still should have put on my big girl panties and told her what was up, but she goes on. "And I know he regrets that."

"He said that? I thought he didn't say anything about me knowing."

"He didn't. Just trust me on this one."

Okay, sure.

"So I'm not fired?" I ask, only half-joking. She might understand, but first and foremost she's a client, and I broke her trust. That's a pretty big no-no in the business world. Not to mention in the world of friendship, and I'm starting to realize that I do consider Brooke a really good friend.

"Are you crazy? Of course not. You were brave enough to take on Ev when he went into his overprotective-big-brother thing. Not many people would be willing to do that. He can be scary."

Which makes me want to ask a question I know I have no business asking, but maybe I should try it while my luck seems to be holding.

"Why is he like that?" I ask. "I mean, I get that he'd be protective. He told me how young you were when your— when it happened. But trying to break up your engagement? That takes overprotective to a whole other level."

There's silence on the other end, and I have the sinking suspicion that I've finally managed to go too far.

"Don't answer that," I say. "That was really rude of me. It's none of my business."

"No, it's okay. I know it's weird. He's been like that ever since it happened. He had a scholarship to the Los Angeles College of Music that he gave up so I wouldn't have to leave my friends to live with our aunt and uncle in Fresno. But the really overprotective stuff started when I got to high school. He insisted on driving me whenever I was going somewhere with my friends. He interviewed my dates like he was the NSA and they were trying to get some kind of security clearance. It was so embarrassing, but I understood. And now ... well, he took it way too far. And I made sure he knows it. But I guess I wasn't surprised. I've lived with it almost my entire life, and I know the whole story. He's like that because he feels responsible for my parents' deaths."

"He mentioned that. A few times," I say. "He said it was his fault. But he always stopped before he could tell me why."

"It wasn't his fault," she says. "But good luck convincing him of that. I've never been able to."

I won't press her for any more information because for one thing, it really *isn't* my business and for another, I get the feeling it's one of those things he'd want to tell me himself. Not that he'll have much of a chance after Sunday. Once the wedding's over, there won't be much reason to see him.

I won't even attempt to come up with a reason as to why this thought disappoints me.

The next few days pass in a blur of arranging *very* last-minute wedding details, starting the process of making Erin an official, legal partner, unpacking the sad half-box of sundresses, and braving crowds at the Springhollow Mall to get gifts for my mom, Kate, Jacob, and their so-far-genderless baby. I spend Friday putting up Christmas decorations in my apartment. I know it's stupid, since Christmas is just three days away, but I've always gone crazy decorating and now that I'm starting to come around, the bareness of my apartment is depressing. It's true that I hadn't wanted to even look at a snowflake or a candy cane, as anti-Christmas as I'd started the season, but now … I don't know. I feel a little better. Hanging a few wreaths around the place won't kill me.

The rehearsal dinner is Saturday at five o'clock. I get to the fire hall at four-fifteen to make sure everything is as ready as possible.

"The urns are in place. We're just waiting on the flower delivery," Amy says. "The snowflakes came on Monday, and they're safe in the kitchen, along with the linens."

"Perfect," I murmur, and consult my clipboard. There's three things I can check off.

The door opens, letting in a frigid blast of air and Judge McLean. I can check off one more thing. "So I hear this is your last wedding," Amy says. "I'm really sorry to hear that. We love working with you."

"Actually," I say, crossing off *garlands and twinkle lights* since I plainly see them draped around the perimeter of the mahogany-paneled reception room, "I changed my mind. I'm sticking around."

"That's fantastic!" Amy's face lights up, and no doubt she's thinking of the future business Brooke's wedding will bring them. "I'm so glad to hear that."

"Me too." I can't help but smile. I've been weirdly enthusiastic about it myself.

Erin shows up at four-thirty and takes over the checklist for me while I inspect the small room off to the side where Brooke and her attendants will line up prior to the ceremony.

It's tiny, but so is the bridal party. Everyone should fit without being seen by the guests coming in.

I'm in the room where the ceremony will be held, dragging the heavy, garland-wrapped wedding arch a few inches to the left, when I hear Brooke greeting Amy and introducing her to Will. The girlish giggles that ensue make me think Amy is having the same reaction to Will as I did when I first saw him. A quick peek out the door reveals Will, handsome in dark jeans and a black button-down shirt, with his arm wrapped tightly around Brooke's waist as she chats with Amy. He catches me looking and winks. In that moment, I know I'm forgiven.

The rest of the bridal party wanders in over the next fifteen minutes, minus Everett, who manages to sneak in seconds before I pull out my phone to call him and demand to know where he is. He flashes me an apologetic look before he hugs his sister and shakes Will's hand. It still looks like a stiff kind of a truce, but it *is* a truce, so I'll take it.

"Okay," I say, raising my voice so it can be heard over the chatter of voices. "Let's get started." I don't let myself wonder why he was almost late. My mind will only go to bad places if I do.

We run through the ceremony three times, and it goes pretty smoothly. These things are easier with small bridal parties. It's a nondenominational service, too, so the real thing will only last about ten minutes, which means practice takes about three. The whole production lasts no longer than half an hour. Brooke walks alone down the aisle, which I find pretty sad, but she seems okay with it. Everett's gaze never leaves her. I can't help wondering what he's thinking.

"Looks good," I say after the third run. "Everyone seems to know where to be and what to do. So that should do it." I tuck my clipboard under my arm. "Have fun at dinner."

Dinner will be at L'Ecole, the French restaurant in the middle of town that used to be a one-room schoolhouse. It's where I would have had my rehearsal dinner, had I made it that far.

"Are you sure you don't want to come?" Brooke asks. "I bet they'd have no problem adding you on. And Erin, too."

"No, that's okay," I say. I just want to go home. For all of my bravado and thinking I feel better, tonight's been hard. Seeing Will and Brooke up there practicing their vows of eternal love and commitment and all that crap has me feeling gutted. I want nothing more than sweatpants and ice cream. Normally it would be wine, but there's the slightest chance that I'm depressed enough to overindulge, and I know— from experience—that directing a wedding with a wine hangover is not the way I want to spend Christmas Eve. "But thank you. I appreciate the invitation."

"Anytime." She gives me a quick hug and darts over to her bridesmaids, who stand in a chattering group.

Will approaches before I can turn away.

"You've done a great job," he says.

"You ain't seen nothing yet," I reply. "Wait until tomorrow when it actually looks like a wedding."

"Thank you," he says. "I mean that. I owe you big time for what you did yesterday."

I shake my head. "You really don't. *I* owed *you*. I never should have kept quiet. It would have saved so much trouble if I'd spoken up at the very beginning."

"Maybe," Will says. "But we both understand why you didn't. Your heart was in the right place. You're a good person, Noelle. And you've become a good friend to Brooke. I know she's going to miss you."

That's right—I haven't told Brooke yet.

"I'm not leaving," I say. "Guess I forgot to mention that, what with all the excitement."

"That's great," Will says, and a genuine smile creases his handsome face. "I'm glad to hear that. Brooke will be thrilled."

"How's your mom?"

"Resting at Brooke's. The flight was rough on her. She'll be here tomorrow."

"I can't wait to meet her." It's true, too. I'd like to get a load of the lady who produced someone as great as Will.

Brooke appears at his elbow. "Are you ready?" she says. "Our reservation is at six-fifteen."

"I'm ready." He takes her hand. It's so cute—it's like he can't be near her without touching her somehow. "See you tomorrow, Noelle."

"See you tomorrow." I hug my clipboard to my chest as I watch them leave, the rest of the bridal party trickling after them.

"Everything's good to go," Erin says from behind me. "Is there anything else you needed me to do?"

"Nope. I think we're as ready as we can be." Suddenly something occurs to me. "Have you seen Everett?"

"Last I saw he was outside. Jenna was talking to him. Why?"

"No reason." I shrug. "He was almost late. I wanted to ask him why."

"I'm sure he wasn't late because he was planning something nefarious," Erin says.

I wish I could believe her, but the past two months are still fresh in my mind. I try to remember the horrible guilty look on his face at the diner. That wasn't fake guilt. And he did admit everything. Still, what better way to throw us off his trail than to act like he was sorry and then do something that would send the whole thing up in flames?

I shake my head. I'm going crazy. He's sorry. He meant it.

"I'm sure you're right." I scan the vestibule one last time. He's nowhere to be found. "Okay. Let's go."

It's four o'clock, and the sun is just starting to dip beneath the horizon. The stone columns that flank the entrance to the Springhollow Fire Hall are wrapped in swirls of pine garland and twinkling white lights that illuminate the sign that welcomes people to the Hurley/St. John wedding. Occasionally Erin's voice comes through the in-ear headset I'm wearing, but mostly I hear the low hum of excited voices and the soft notes of the string quartet as they play different Christmas songs. They're pretty good.

From the doorway to the ceremony room I can see it looks perfect. On the floor, the scattered confetti snowflakes glitter in the soft golden light cast by the old-fashioned sconces lining the wood-paneled walls. The silver urns on each side of the arch, empty yesterday, are spilling over with bright white roses and waxy camellias set off by silver holly leaves. Will waits by the double-door entrance to the room with his groomsmen, who escort the guests to their seats as they arrive. I try to keep my eyes off them, but wow, can Everett wear a tux. It's a good thing I'm too professional to be distracted by it. I keep my focus on the sixty-something, bald, paunchy Judge McLean who, as sweet as he is, doesn't exactly get my motor running.

"How's it going?" I ask Erin, in the dressing room with Brooke and her bridesmaids. Usually it's me in there, but as a full-fledged partner, I let her take it.

"Fine," her voice crackles in my ear. "The photographer's getting the last shots."

"Perfect. Think you'll be able to get everyone down here in a few minutes?"

"Absolutely."

"Great." I wave at the groomsmen to get their attention. "Get ready," I tell them. "Dave and Stephen, you can go. Phil, you stay."

In a move that almost made me burst into tears when she told me, Brooke had decided that she wanted Will's mom to take the place traditionally taken by the bride's mother. So Mrs. Hurley waits with us at the entrance, Phil on one side holding her arm, an oxygen tank on the other. Susan, the home health aide who came down from Toronto with her, sits with the guests, her eyes on her charge. I've barely had a chance to speak to Mrs. Hurley other than to say hello, but she's an adorable little woman who looks like a cardinal in her bright red pantsuit with matching scarf covering her head. I'm really happy that she was able to make the trip.

"Here we come," says Erin in my ear.

"Okay. Phil, go ahead." We all watch as he inches down the aisle with Will's mom. They're slow, but they make it. Susan helps her get settled on the bench.

"Okay. Now the rest of you." Dave and Stephen go. "Judge McLean, you can go in." He straightens his suit jacket and strides down the aisle, taking his spot beneath the arch and facing the small crowd, which has gone silent at his entrance.

"Your turn, Everett." I keep my tone calm and businesslike.

"Nope."

My heart thumps, stops, then starts up again. No. Please, no. He can't be doing this.

"What do you mean by *nope*?" I'll kill him. I really will.

He grins. "I mean I'm not walking out there. I can't. I'm giving Brooke away."

Oh. Well. Wow.

To my shock and not a little bit of horror, tears seep into my eyes.

"Don't cry," he says. "Think of how happy you are that I'm *not* plotting anything." Beside him Will laughs.

"I'm not crying." I blink furiously.

"Almost there," Erin warns.

"Okay." I pass the back of my hand over my eyes. "Will, get out there. Here they come."

His laughter abruptly disappears, and he actually looks sort of scared.

"Oh, no. Don't even think about it." I put my hand on his back and give him a little shove. "You're going through with this if I have to pick you up by the scruff of your neck like a cat and throw you up there. Now go." He goes, and I turn just in time to see Erin and the bridal party, stunning in ice-blue georgette gowns that sparkle with rhinestones resembling bits of ice.

Erin helps me line them up, with Cassie bringing up the rear as maid of honor. Then there's Brooke.

She's literally the most gorgeous bride I've ever worked with. Clichéd as it sounds, her dress really does fit her like a second skin—a beautiful, snow-white, lacy skin. The silver band around her waist is an unexpected and stunning touch. Lynn worked magic on her hair, twisting it into a thick waterfall of icy blonde curls that fall down her back frosted by her mother's veil. Her makeup's perfect—lightly rosy cheeks, champagne shadow shimmering on her eyelids, and a burgundy lip. A teardrop-shaped diamond the size of my thumbnail hangs on a delicate silver chain around her neck.

The part of me that's her friend is in awe, but the businesswoman side is thinking about how Brooke's photos are *really* going to boost my portfolio.

"You look beautiful," I tell her, and she grins.

"I'd better. It took *forever*." She's clutching her bouquet of white roses. "Is it time?"

"Just about." Erin gently moves her back from view as the door to the ceremony room opens again and Emily steps through. A few seconds later Hannah goes. Then Jenna, followed by Cassie.

The music changes from a delicate version of "Dance of the Sugar Plum Fairy" to the opening strains of "Here Comes the Bride."

"That's our cue," I say. "Are you ready?"

"Yes," both Brooke and Everett reply. They look at each other, and the love I see between them makes me tear up again.

"Congratulations," he says softly, and holds out his arm. She's smiling as she takes it.

"Love you," she says. "You nut."

He chuckles. "Love you too."

"Okay. Here we go." Erin and I each take a door and pull it open, revealing a room full of people who immediately get to their feet.

Hanging onto each other's arms, Brooke and Everett step into the aisle.

25

"Brooke, I take you as my wife, with your faults and your strengths, as I offer myself to you with my faults and my strengths. I will help you when you need help and turn to you when I need help. I choose you as the person with whom I will spend my life."

Will's voice carries confidently over the heads of the people seated in the small room. Brooke's, when it comes, is softer but no less intentional.

"Will, I take you as my husband, with your faults and your strengths, as I offer myself to you with my faults and my strengths. I will help you when you need help and turn to you when I need help. I choose you as the person with whom I will spend my life."

Brooke's face glows as she smiles at him, her hands clutched tightly in his.

"By the power vested in me by the state of Pennsylvania, I now pronounce you husband and wife," Judge McLean says. "You may kiss the bride."

Cheers erupt as Brooke stands on her toes to wrap her arms around Will's neck, and he pulls her close. Tears well up in my eyes for the third time today. I wipe them away as they turn to face their guests and, hand in hand, step away from the altar and head back down the aisle as the string quartet's instruments emit a rather ethereal version of Barry White's "You're the First, the Last, My Everything."

"Where do we go now?" Brooke asks once they've cleared the doors to the ceremony room.

"In there," I say, pointing to the small gathering room off to the side. "You have forty-five minutes for pictures in the park across the street, and then you'll come back here for introductions." They'd decided against a receiving line, since the guest list was so short.

"Okay." They disappear in the general direction of my pointing finger.

Everett's the next one out, Cassie clinging to his elbow. I note with some satisfaction that he detaches himself from her as soon as they're out of sight of the guests.

"In there," I say, pointing again.

"Thanks!" Cassie squeals, digging her talons into Everett's arm again as she starts to drag him away. He throws a look back at me, but I'm too busy to notice. Almost.

We get the rest of the attendants situated while the guests start to stream from the ceremony room and into the vestibule. Erin and Amy direct them into the reception room, where the bar is set up and waiters from Cole Brothers Catering wander around with trays of appetizers. Brady and his assistant take turns running in and out of the kitchen—a fact that evidently doesn't escape Erin's notice, because more than once I catch her straightening her baby-pink dress and tucking her hair behind her ear, all while he's in view.

The photographer whisks the wedding party away, and as the front doors close behind them, I see snowflakes floating down. Weird—the weather people never said anything about snow tonight, and I've been glued to the forecast all week. That's just Brooke's luck, I guess. I have no doubt the pictures will turn out amazing.

I take advantage of cocktail hour to survey the reception area, and even though I've done weddings here before, I'm always amazed at how when the time comes it looks nothing like a fire hall. Tonight it's a glittering, wintry wonderland. White lights strung around the rafters twinkle overhead like stars, and the tall crystal cylinder vases sparkle, thanks to a last minute decision to put a battery-operated LED light in the bottom of each one, making the blue and silver Christmas balls piled inside resemble snowballs rather than ornaments. Crisp white tablecloths are draped over each of the round tables, and as promised, the linen napkins are held in neat bunches by rings made of silver holly leaves and white berries. The deejay's playing instrumental Christmas music from the corner of the room where he's been efficiently hidden away, and the sweetheart table at which Will and Brooke will eat dinner is at the top of the dance floor—a large square of white linoleum that almost glitters, thanks to some creative overhead lighting. Like the ceremony room, the walls in the reception area are paneled in mahogany and lined with wrought-iron sconces holding electric candles that look more real than fake and paint the entire room in a soft, dreamy glow.

"What do you think?" Erin asks, coming up behind me.

"I think we did a pretty awesome job in two months," I say, and we high-five.

Forty-five minutes feel like forty-five seconds, and almost before I know it, the wedding party's back and shivering. Everett's jacket is slung over Cassie's shoulders. I ignore this as best I can while getting them lined up for introductions. I don't know why I even notice, or why I feel bothered by it.

"No goofy entrances!" Brooke calls from the back of the line. "If any of you try it, I'll have you Photoshopped out of the pictures. I'm not kidding."

The deejay calls them out pair by pair, and they must take Brooke seriously because not one of them tries anything. Within minutes everyone's seated but Brooke and Will, who stand in the middle of the dance floor wrapped in each other's arms as the first notes of their song start to play.

It's almost scary how smoothly everything is going. I've planned weddings in two years that were more chaotic than this one. Had it ended up being the last hurrah I'd thought it would be, I would have been ecstatic—there's no better sendoff than a perfect wedding. Instead I decide to take it as a new beginning, an omen of the future. The wedding that sets the precedent for all the weddings I have yet to plan.

After the speeches are done and the dinner plates carried away, Will approaches me.

"Would you like to meet my mom?" he asks with endearing shyness.

"I'd love to."

He leads me to a table where the tiny, frail-looking woman sits tethered to her tank. She didn't have the energy to do a mother-son dance with him, but she's got a spot right by the front, at the edge of the dance floor, where she can see everything.

"Mom," Will says, and she looks up. "This is Noelle. She's the wedding planner, and pretty much the entire reason this wedding happened at all."

"It's so nice to meet you, Mrs. Hurley," I say.

She beckons me closer, and I kneel on the floor beside her.

"I'm sorry," she says. "I can't talk loudly enough to be heard over the music. It's such a pleasure to meet you. Will has so many nice things to say about you." Her voice is thin and papery.

"The pleasure's mine," I tell her. "I've been wanting to meet the woman who's responsible for Will. He's so great. I'm fortunate to have gotten to know him."

"I like him," she wheezes with a smile. "You did a beautiful job."

"Thank you." I pat her small, thin hand. The skin feels like the slightest amount of pressure would tear it. "I'm so glad you could come."

"As long as I've been waiting? I would have walked here!" Her laughter gives way to coughing. The tank beside her jerks a little with every motion. I glance at Will. He looks worried but shakes his head just a little.

"Are you okay, Mom?" Will says when she stops. "If you're ready to go home, just let me know."

"Maybe," she allows.

"Susan?" Will says, and the woman beside Mrs. Hurley jumps from her seat. Susan's been waiting for this. A brief conversation with her, and Mrs. Hurley is safely loaded into the van and on her way back to her hotel. Brooke and Will had wanted her to stay with them, but she refused to inconvenience them, saying they deserved to spend their first night as newlyweds alone.

She's a sweet lady. I'm glad I got to meet her.

As for Erin and me, the hard part is done, so aside from the occasional word to the deejay about the timing of the bouquet toss or to Brady and his team about getting the dessert table ready, we can take off our headsets, step back, and enjoy watching the reception. The deejay, someone I've never worked with before but who came highly recommended by *The Knot*, manages to get nearly all but the oldest guests on the dance floor, and even they pop out of their seats during the standard middle-of-the-reception oldies medley. It's fun to watch Will twirl a laughing Brooke around the floor to *Jailhouse Rock*. Everett takes a few turns with her too, but he seems less concerned with dancing than with watching. He mostly sits at one of the tables with a couple who look to be in their mid-to-late fifties—the aunt and uncle from California, maybe. He catches my eye a few times and smiles. I look away. I know he's just trying to make up for all the trouble he caused, but I'm not sure I'm comfortable with the fact that my heartbeat stumbles every time I look at him. There are so many reasons why that shouldn't happen, mathematicians haven't yet discovered the number I'd need to count them.

Unfortunately, it seems like staying away from him is one of those things that's easier said than done. After the cake cutting I'm helping Brady's assistant Nick put out plates of cake for the guests when there's a tap on my shoulder. In full wedding-planner mode I whirl around, fully expecting to hear that the photographer's camera just broke or a drunk cousin wants to make a speech or something equally horrifying, but instead I find Everett, hands held politely behind his back. A few curls spring loose from the product he applied in an attempt to tame them. My mouth goes just the tiniest bit dry.

"Dance with me?" he says. The song—it's a slow one. I hadn't even noticed. No. No, I won't dance with him.

"I can't. I'm working." I try to make myself look very busy, sliding a plate three inches to the left and rotating it about twelve degrees counterclockwise.

"You're arranging cake." The way he says it makes it sound like the stupidest thing anyone's done, ever, in the history of civilization.

And I have to laugh. It *is* stupid. Still, though…

I shake my head. "I really can't."

"Go ahead," Nick says. "There's only a few left. I can probably get them in one trip."

Traitor. I fix him with a glare he pretends not to see.

I guess I have no choice. "Okay."

As we make our way to the dance floor, I see Erin standing with the photographer. She nudges him with one elbow as she raises her other hand in a thumbs-up. There will be pictures. Fantastic.

When we reach the dance floor, I stand there sort of awkwardly, not entirely sure where to put my arms and hands. Do I put both over his shoulders and around his neck? That feels like it might be a little too intimate; I'm not sixteen and this isn't the junior prom. But I'm also not some spinster aunt—not for another three months, anyway—and the thought of whirling around with our hands up in the air feels a little too formal, considering.

Before I can decide who I am—high-school junior or spinster aunt—he takes me by the waist and pulls me in. With both hands. Okay. I guess he's making the decision for me. Junior-prom style it is.

Anyway, it's not like I haven't been this close to him already. At least this time there are dozens of other people around. We'll be less apt to accidentally kiss.

I hope. Or do I? I don't even know anymore.

"Thank you," he says once we've stumbled into some sort of rhythm.

"For what?"

"For all of this. She's so happy, and everything's perfect."

"Oh." My cheeks burn. I've never been great at accepting compliments. "Well, it's my job. And I'm glad she's happy."

"She is. She wouldn't be, if I'd gotten my way." His cheek is pressed against my temple. As he talks, my hair flutters. I am acutely aware of this. "Thank you for not letting me win."

"As if I would have." His chest is warm against mine. My legs tremble a little. Great. I'm probably going to fall over. Shouldn't have worn these stupid heels.

"I'm serious." He pulls back and looks at me. His expression is serious, indeed. I swallow. "You're good at your job. It's a shame you're not going to do it anymore." He rests his cheek against my temple again.

"I am, actually."

"What do you mean?"

"I'm staying. In town. I'm not going home. And I'm keeping the business."

He doesn't say anything, but his face does something that makes my hair move. Is he smiling?

A flash from the corner of the room nearly blinds me. I guess I'll find out exactly what his face was doing when the pictures come.

We're silent for a few more moments, until I remember something.

"You were almost late last night," I say.

"I know. I saw your face when I came in." He laughs softly into my hair. "You were going to murder me."

"It crossed my mind."

"Did you see the necklace Brooke's wearing today?"

"The teardrop diamond."

"I was picking it up from the jeweler. The diamond was my mom's, and it was in a ring that she kept in a safe deposit box at the bank, so we didn't lose it in the fire. I had it set into a necklace. It was my wedding present to Brooke."

It's so sweet I want to cry, which in turn makes my defenses go up.

"I would have thought your gift was letting the wedding happen at all."

"You're still angry with me." It's not a question.

I don't know. Am I? He definitely seems remorseful. But I don't know. I guess I just have a really hard time anymore knowing when a person's telling the truth and when they're trying to pull an entire hand-knitted afghan's worth of wool over my eyes.

The song ends before I can respond, morphing into an Earth, Wind, and Fire classic that promptly shatters whatever mood might have remained. And there's no chance of it being restored because Cassie, white wine sloshing out of her overfull glass, slithers up to Everett and grabs his arm.

"I love this song!" she gushes. "Come and dance."

"No, thanks," he says. "I'm not much of a dancer."

She pouts. "You just were."

"That's different," he says. "Slow dancing doesn't require much rhythm."

"But—"

"I have to get back to work," I say, grateful I have an excuse to escape. Everett's eyes plead with me, and I know I have the power to rescue him, but I won't. I can't. Weddings are romantic, and I let myself get caught up in the moment, but I need to start being more careful. The wound in my heart's only just begun to scab over. I'd be an idiot to let someone else rip it right back open.

So I turn and hurry away, sparing only one glance over my shoulder that lasts long enough to witness him being dragged into a swirling pit of twenty-somethings in cocktail dresses.

I manage to keep busy enough for the rest of the night that no one approaches me again, except for a reporter from the *Stalker* who somehow managed to get in and skirt the room—after all, Brooke is the kind of bride that would warrant an article about her wedding. I give her a few quotes when she corners me. It might be good for business. But at ten o'clock, when the deejay announces the final song, I hide in the kitchen pretending to wonder if Brady needs help cleaning up. He doesn't. In fact, it looks like he's been ready to go for quite some time.

"Why are you hanging around?" I ask. "I'd be home in bed if I were you."

"A bunch of us are going out for drinks," he says. "Want to come?"

Erin enters the kitchen. The way her cheeks are already blazing tells me that no, I don't want to come. If she has a shot with Brady, there's no way I'll ruin it by tagging along and moping around. That's not at all how I want her to spend outside-of-work time with him when she's been angling for it for months.

"No, but thanks," I say. "I'm beat. I'm just going to head home."

"If you change your mind, we're going to the Library."

"I guess it is the only bar open on Christmas Eve." *Have fun*, I mouth at Erin. Her cheeks turn even pinker, but her eyes sparkle.

When I finally venture from the safety of the kitchen, Brooke and Will are by the doors hugging the guests as they leave. Everett, thankfully, is nowhere to be seen.

Brooke wraps her arms around me in a hug so tight I almost cough.

"Everything was perfect," she says. "I cannot thank you enough."

"It was my pleasure," I grunt. "Thank you for bullying me into doing it. I mean that. I didn't realize how much I needed this project."

She laughs as she lets me go. "Just the fact that you managed to pull it off with my brother trying to sabotage everything is amazing. So will you cash the check now? Please? You earned every penny."

I think of the crumpled check in my drawer and smile noncommittally. Luckily, she turns to another departing guest before I can muster an answer.

"Thank you," Will says when it's his turn to hug me.

"Let's get together for dinner or something soon," I say.

"Absolutely."

A few minutes later, the last guests straggle out the door. The bridesmaids leave together for the hotel they'll be staying in, to give Brooke and Will the night alone. I note with some satisfaction that Cassie looks a bit glum. I imagine she tried as hard as she could to get Everett to accompany her, and as he has yet to make an appearance, I have to conclude that he turned her down. Of course this is all in my head. She could just be tired or drunk, and he could be meeting her somewhere later. I don't know. And I shouldn't care.

"I don't," I say out loud as I head back into the empty reception area.

"Don't what?"

Everett. Is it possible for a heart to sink and leap at the same time? Because I think mine does.

"I don't. Um. Feel like driving to Blackton." Where did *that* idea come from? That's not to say it's a bad one. I should pay my family a visit. They're only a hundred miles away—it's not like I'd have to drive cross-country. I make a mental note to ask about their plans when I call tomorrow to wish them a merry Christmas.

"Ah."

"Just for a Christmas visit," I babble. "I haven't seen my family in ages, and now that I'm not moving back…"

"Of course." He sounds kind of stiff. Formal. "When are you going?"

"Tuesday or Wednesday. Depends on what they have going on."

"Oh." He's winding among the tables, as if searching for a missing object. "Well, have fun."

"Thanks." I don't know what it is—the distant tone he's suddenly using, the way he won't make eye contact with me, his distracted air—but he's making me uncomfortable. "Did you lose something?"

"My phone. There it is." He grabs something off one of the tables and stuffs it into his pocket. "Well, enjoy your trip."

"Thanks."

"Merry Christmas." He gives me a half wave before he turns and practically runs out of the building.

"Merry Christmas," I say, but he's already gone.

When I get home I waste no time stripping off my cobalt blue dress and ditching the heels in the corner of my bedroom. I turn the shower on as hot as I can stand it, then crank it a little higher and stand under it for a good twenty minutes, letting all of the stress and confusion and sadness and everything that's built up over the last two months mix with the suds from my almond shower gel and run down the drain.

By the time I crawl into bed, it's near midnight and I don't think I've ever been so exhausted. But I don't fall asleep right away. Instead I lie in the dark thinking about how quiet things are when it's just me. How big and empty everything seems—not just the bed, of course, but the entire room. The entire apartment. I've been so busy over the last two months that I kind of shoved that to the back of my mind. Sure I knew that Drew was gone, and after seeing the obnoxious rock on Heidi's finger I knew he wasn't coming back no matter how hard I wished he would. But now that I don't have Brooke's wedding looming over me, I have nothing to keep the thoughts from intruding. No barrier against them.

So I let them come.

The funny thing is that I don't feel devastated. I'm sad, but I know tomorrow morning I'll get up and go about my day and I'll be fine. Well, mostly fine. Why is that? Have I already fallen out of love with the guy I planned to marry? It seems soon. It's only been two months. I was with Drew for eight years. Don't they say it takes half the length of the relationship to get over someone? That means I should be sad for another three years and ten months.

I *am* still sad. But even though Drew is gone and I seem to have blown my chance with Everett—that is, if I really *wanted* a chance with him, which I still don't know—there's something underneath the sadness. Something that's keeping me from giving into it, from crumbling under its weight.

It seems obscene to say it, but I think it might be hope.

26

THE DAY AFTER Christmas, I'm still sleeping when my phone goes off. And despite the fact that my eyes are glued shut and I've still got one foot firmly planted in the dream I was having—my first-grade teacher had crashed our high-school reunion and was ranting that a student who'd died of cancer in real life had actually been murdered—I scrabble for the phone, because my other foot is connected to the small part of my brain that is capable of reason and immediately thinks *please, not Kate.* Even though she assured me when I called her yesterday that her doctor cleared her, and the light spotting she was experiencing was completely harmless, a little piece of me can't help expecting the phone call that will come when she inevitably miscarries again.

My fingers make contact with the phone on my bedside table, and I bring it to my eyes as I force them open. One glance at the screen calms my fears. Not a phone call—a text message. If Kate was having more problems, someone would call. Not rely on texting.

Then I scramble to sit up.

Can you meet? it says.

It's Everett.

I push straggly, sleep-tangled hair out of my eyes and stare at the words until they blur. *Can* I meet? Yes. Do I want to? I don't know. Why does *he* want to? He didn't seem super-enamored of me when he left the wedding on Christmas Eve. I still haven't even figured out what I did. Or why I care.

Maybe if I go, I can start sorting it all out.

Okay, I type. *When and where? Just woke up.*

Sorry if I woke you. How's The Daily Grind in an hour?

I shut my eyes. The Daily Grind. What are the chances that walking in there and smelling the aroma of their house blend, the one that two months ago was pretty much solely responsible for getting me out of bed in the morning, won't make me puke right there on the floor? I might think I'm getting over Drew, but maybe that's just because I've been careful to steer clear of anything that might remind me of him. Of us.

Then again, if I'm really *not* getting over him and I've just tricked myself into thinking I am, walking into the very place where he broke my heart will clear up the confusion pretty quick, and then I'll know where I stand and I can start to work on getting past it.

Okay. I can do this, I think.

Sounds good.

I climb out of my bed and into the shower. I put on minimal makeup. I'm not trying to impress anyone, which is a thought that goes right out the door as soon as I realize I've spent five minutes picking out a lip gloss. I dry my hair before pulling it all up and winding it into something that looks better than what I'd typically wear to exercise, but not as good as Brooke's messy bun. I remind myself to ask her the next time I see her to teach me how to do it. She taught me the Dutch braid easily enough. I pull on the new jeans I treated myself to for Christmas—medium-wash, straight-leg, and distressed—an oversized black turtleneck sweater and the black Chelsea boots I bought in hopes of looking like a native Londoner. Instead of a coat I wind a red and black plaid blanket scarf over my neck and shoulders. I stick tiny gold hoops through my earlobes, and before I leave, I allow myself thirty seconds in front of the mirror for a final check. No more than that.

And it's not bad. It doesn't look like I'm trying, either, which is better. Can't have that.

The remains of Christmas Eve's light snow crunch under my boots as I head down the sidewalk. I'd planned to drive, but now I think I want to walk. It's not painfully cold today, and a half-mile in the fresh air might help calm my nerves, since they're suddenly demanding attention. My heartbeat skips a little, and the tips of my fingers tingle.

So I set off. Two months ago when I did this, it was a gorgeously sunny, crisp fall day. The sun painted the sidewalk a burnished copper and everything else, from the walls of buildings to the trees to the cars parked along the street, glittered gold. Now that I'm thinking about it, I almost want to laugh at how ironic it is that my whole world was ripped out from under me on such an otherwise perfect day.

Today's not so pretty. The sky looks like it can't decide if it wants to be blue or gray so it's settled on some kind of murky in-between. The bright leaves of two months ago are long gone, and the bare branches of the trees along Main Street are stark and black. Everything looks like I'm seeing it through a vague gray-white filter. And it's colder than I thought. I should have worn gloves. Or driven my car.

My steps slow as I approach Silver Bells' front door. There's something I should probably do first. Everett's always late, right? I have time.

I unlock the door and go inside, flipping on the light. I drop my bag on Erin's desk and go straight back to the meeting area, which doubles as my own work area. I've got half-finished foam core vision boards on the walls, a bookshelf cluttered with magazines, and my desk, with a locked drawer in which I keep everything of importance.

Like Brooke's check.

I turn the key in the drawer's lock, and it clicks open. There isn't much in there now, and the check is lying right on top. I take it out and look at it. *Pay to the order of Silver Bells Wedding Designs, in the amount of twenty-five thousand dollars.*

I smile. She was so *stubborn.* What if I'd stuck to my guns and turned her away? Where would I be right now? In Blackton, maybe, running Kate to doctor's appointments when I wasn't arranging bras by color or fastening garters around plastic thighs and trying to figure out how to put my degree to good use.

My shredder is next to the desk. I bend down and flick it on, then take the check between two fingers and gently feed it into the top. The shredder makes a high-pitched mechanical whine as it eats the check, spitting the diamond-shaped pieces into the bottom. There's no way that check is ever getting taped back together.

A few minutes later I'm in front of The Daily Grind's familiar glass door. Cheerful Christmas images are painted on the big window that overlooks the sidewalk, and from where I stand I can see the exact table I was sitting at when Drew told me he didn't want me anymore. A gaudy white snowflake dangles over it.

Nausea gathers in the pit of my stomach and threatens to rise. I swallow and wrap my arms around my waist. I can't do this. What was I thinking?

But then a montage of images flashes through my head. Drew and Heidi cuddling in a booth at the Library. Standing together in line at the Holiday Village. The giant sparkly ring on Heidi's finger. The angry flex of the muscle in Drew's jaw when he thought Everett and I were together, and the rigid way he stood after we walked away. And the memory of his voice on the phone, as he begged me to promise to stay away from Everett. Fury floods me. Who is he to think he has any kind of power over me after everything? And why am I letting him?

I grasp the cold metal handle of the door. Pull it open.

The bell chimes a welcome, and the scent of coffee and pastry hits my nose immediately. I take a deep breath.

It's okay. I'm not going to cry or throw up. I'm okay.

A quick glance around the shop lets me know that Everett isn't here yet, so I can choose where we'll sit. My feet seem to want to carry me toward the table by the window, but I won't go. Instead I choose a spot by the back corner. I can keep an eye on the door from here. I don't go to the counter for a black coffee or a plate of croissants. Instead I tuck myself into the chair closest to the wall, hug my purse to my chest, and observe.

The blackboard by the counter, last time I saw it, had chalk drawings of jack o'lanterns and leaves and listed special menu items like pumpkin lattes, s'mores hot chocolate, and glazed maple scones. Now it advertises eggnog lattes, iced gingerbread cake, and something called sugar plum tea. Hmm. That sounds pretty interesting. Also, Surfer Boy appears to have gotten a Christmas haircut. He doesn't have to push his bangs out of his eyes to look at the cash register anymore.

The tinkle of the bell grabs my attention, and I look away from the register and the line of people in front of it to the door. Everett's there, framed by the open door, scanning the shop. When his gaze lands on me, I give him a little wave.

"Hey," he says as he takes off his charcoal peacoat—I was right, it looks good on him; more than good—and drapes it over the back of his chair. "I'm going to grab a coffee. Do you want anything? No coffee, I know."

I can't help a tiny smile.

"I'm intrigued by the sugar plum tea," I say. I reach into my bag for my wallet, but he waves me off.

"Be right back," he says.

I sit back in my chair. This is all eerily familiar. My heart starts to thump.

Until Everett returns, drops into his chair, and slides a mug of steaming tea across the table at me. For one thing, he's not popping back up to fiddle with the sugar packets and stirrers. For another, he looks glad to see me. Not what I was expecting, after our last interaction at the wedding.

"Thank you," I say as I draw the mug to me. Swirls of fragrant steam rise up and I inhale. "This smells good."

"Is a sugar plum even a real thing?" he asks.

"I think it's a candy. I'm not sure. I've never eaten one."

"Interesting." He lifts his cup and takes a sip.

He didn't ask to meet so we could talk about the possible existence of sugar plums. That much I know.

I'm trying to screw up the courage to ask why he *did* want to meet me when he finally does speak.

"I'm glad you could come," he says. "Sorry I woke you up."

"It's okay. I'm glad it was you." He lifts an eyebrow. "I mean, I thought you were my sister. She's pregnant, and she's had some trouble in the past. Whenever I hear my phone go off at a weird time, I panic that someone's calling to tell me she miscarried." My ears burn. I wish I'd left my hair down.

"In that case, I'm extra sorry."

"It's okay," I repeat. I wrap my hands around the mug. "So why *did* you want to meet?"

His expression is serious. "I wanted to apologize."

"For what?" I'm confused. I can't think of anything else he might have done that he'd have to be sorry for.

"For all of the trouble I caused." He shakes his head. "I still can't believe I did that. Any of it."

"You already apologized," I remind him. "Remember? A few times."

"I know. But you're obviously still angry about it. I know why, of course. I put you through hell. And I'm pretty pissed at myself for it."

I refrain from pointing out that it was Brooke he put through hell. He just inconvenienced me. He feels bad enough; I won't make it worse.

"You thought you were doing the right thing," I say instead.

"I thought I was doing what my parents would want. But I took it way too far."

He's right, of course. I seriously doubt his parents would have wanted him to destroy their daughter's happiness. But of course I'm not going to say that. He knows it.

"The important thing is that it all worked out in the end." He nods. "I just wish I'd realized it sooner. I thought I was keeping my promise. They died because of me. Keeping her safe was the least I could do to make it up to them."

There it is again. He thinks his parents died because of him. How? Did he set the fire? Am I sitting across from a pyromaniac?

"What do you mean, they died because of you?" I have to ask, but I make my voice as gentle as possible. I don't want to upset him, but I have a feeling this story is the key to understanding him. To figuring out how—if—I can ever trust him.

I don't stop to ask myself why I feel the need to understand him at all. Or trust him.

He shakes his head again and grips his cup so tight his knuckles blanch.

"You don't have to tell me. It's none of my business. I'm sorry."

"No. Maybe I should. I've never told anyone else." He laughs shortly. "Except the police, and the shrink the court made me see for a while afterward. Although I find it kind of ironic that Drew Emmons' fiancée is the first outsider to hear it."

"Ironic—how?" My heartbeat stumbles a little.

"It's kind of a long story. And I'll need to start at the beginning."

I nod and take a gulp of tea for fortitude. "Go ahead."

Something tells me that everything is about to change.

27

"I was seventeen," he begins. "A few weeks away from turning eighteen. Brooke was nine. It was a Friday night, and I'd been invited to a party. I was grounded, though, and my parents wouldn't let me go." He sips his coffee. "So I waited until everyone was asleep. I disarmed the security system and left. Drew was my ride. He'd parked his car at the end of the street and waited for me."

"You and Drew were friends?" How had I not known that? I'd lived in Springhollow for twelve years. Eight of those as Drew's girlfriend. I'd never even heard of Everett St. John until two months ago when he walked into my shop and threw his wet jacket on my couch.

And the way Everett talked about him, the single interaction I'd seen between them and the desperate phone call I got from Drew hardly suggested any kind of friendly past.

Everett grins wryly. "I'll get to that part."

"Okay."

"The party was supposed to be at another guy's house. Scott DiStefano. But we never got there. Drew just drove in circles around town. I kept asking what was going on, and he was giving me the dumbest excuses. I don't even remember them all now. I just remember we were passing the school for probably the sixth time when I heard the fire trucks."

My hands tremble. I squeeze my own mug tighter.

"Of course I didn't realize they were headed to my house. But then Drew started telling me what was really happening, that it was all a big joke. I guess he figured he'd kept me away long enough. I told him to stop the car, and I got out. I walked back home. But the street was blocked off, and all of the fire trucks were in front of my house. There were..." His Adam's apple moves as he swallows. "Flames. Coming out of the front windows. My parents' bedroom was at the front of the house. They never even managed to get into the hall. They were found a couple of feet from the door."

Tears scorch my eyes. My throat aches. Even if I could get words out, I wouldn't know which ones to use.

"Brooke was wrapped in a blanket and sitting on the back of an ambulance. She was fine. Her bedroom was on the other side of the house, and the fire never even got near it. I remember seeing her sitting there, hair sticking up like she'd been electrocuted, in her SpongeBob nightgown. Barefoot. She had a juice box in her hand and some soot on her face. When they finally let me go near her, she didn't say a word. She just stared at me. I don't know if she was in shock or what. She didn't talk. I felt like she was blaming me. She should have been."

"Why?" The word bursts from me. "Everett, you did nothing. Nothing a normal teenager wouldn't do. So you snuck out. Big deal. Do you have any idea how many times I did that as a kid?"

He's already shaking his head again.

"Did you lie to your parents about going to bed when you were really planning to go to a party that a bunch of classmates made up just so they could break into your house?" he demands. I feel dizzy. "It's my fault on so many levels, Noelle. If I hadn't gone out, I would have been there when they tried to break in, and they probably would've left. If they didn't blow off the plan altogether. If I hadn't been too lazy to re-arm the security system, it would've gone off, and the cops would have been there before they even found my room. And if I hadn't left that damn candle burning so my parents would smell it and think I was in there, there wouldn't have been anything to set a fire with in the first place." He runs his hand through his hair. "It was my fault. There's no other way around it. If I'd listened to them, they'd still be alive. And that's why I promised to spend the rest of my life taking care of Brooke. If I couldn't make it up to them, I'd make it up to her."

I bite my lip, hard. I need to focus on something to keep from crying for him and Brooke, and the sharp pain helps.

"Why did they do that to you? If Drew was your friend—I don't understand."

"He wasn't my friend," Everett says with a short laugh. "I just wanted him to be. I wasn't too popular in school. It was a big jock school, and I was much happier in music class than gym class. I got picked on a lot for that. But it only got really bad when a girl Scott DiStefano was trying to hook up with decided she liked me instead. I never even went out with her. It was just stupid high-school crap."

He pushes his coffee cup away and leans back in his chair. "They decided to get back at me by breaking into my house and stealing my guitar. They thought that would teach me. So at school one day Scott and his friends, including Drew, come up to me and tell me that they're sorry and there's a party that night." He shrugs. "I don't know why I said yes. I knew they didn't like me. But I did. I told them I was grounded because my dad had caught me and one of my friends smoking in the garage. They said they'd wait until my parents were asleep, and I could sneak out. So I did. Drew's job was to keep me away while Scott and two of his friends broke into the house, found my room, and took my guitar. They knocked the candle over while they were trying to get out. From what they said in court they tried to put it out, but it landed on one of my curtains and spread too fast. They were actually lucky to get out. My parents, not so much."

This is the most horrible story I've ever heard. And my ex-fiancé is front and center. Why hadn't Drew ever mentioned any of this to me?

"There were legal repercussions?" He said *court*. I don't know much about the law, but two people ended up dead. They had to have been charged with *something*.

Everett exhales. "Yeah. It was about to go to trial when Scott and his friends took a plea deal. They plead guilty to misdemeanor manslaughter, and the breaking and entering and theft charges were dropped. Not one of them served more than nine months in juvenile prison. Scott's a football coach at Springhollow High School now. Rich dads sure come in handy."

My mind is whirling. This is too much. I didn't know. Why didn't I know?

"What about—"

"Drew?" he asks. "He was charged as an accessory. He got community service. His dad was tight with the judge."

I feel sick. That must be why he called me after the Holiday Village. He knew Everett would tell me.

He's practically a murderer. *I almost married a murderer.*

"God," I whisper. That's proof enough that I'm in shock. Despite my love for Christmas I haven't actually believed in a god since I was ten and my dad left. The fact that I'm calling out for one now is telling indeed. "I'm so sorry. I had no idea that Drew…"

"Don't be. But I wonder why he kept it secret from you. He had to know that you'd hear it from someone if you lived here. I'm sure he thought he could play it off like some big misunderstanding if you found out. Not," he says in a hurry, "that you're that gullible."

"Maybe I am. I almost married him." I feel like I need a shower. Several showers. Scalding hot ones, to rinse the past eight years off me. My skin crawls at the fact that I ever let Drew Emmons touch me.

"But you didn't."

"No. I didn't." Funny how things can change so fast. This morning I was wondering if I'd be able to face the memory of finding out that he'd been cheating on me. Now I'm more than half tempted to call and thank him for doing me the biggest favor anyone's ever done for me. I might do it, too, if I didn't believe the sound of his voice would make me vomit. "That's why you hated me when you met me. You thought I knew. And that I didn't care."

"I didn't hate you," he says. "Well, hate's a strong word. I didn't want anything to do with you. I figured you must have heard about what happened, and that Drew was involved, and I thought you should stay miles away from Brooke's wedding, which I already hoped would never take place."

I shake my head. "I didn't know."

"I know that now. Brooke was sure from the beginning that you didn't. Don't ask me what convinced her. Maybe the universe told her." He laughs. "It's partly why she was willing to offer you so much money, you know. She considered you as much a victim as we were. Maybe insisting you do her wedding wasn't the most sensitive choice, but she meant well.

She wanted to do something nice for you and take your mind off your own problems."

"What?" I gasp. "Okay. That's crazy. First of all, he only cheated on me. That's nothing compared to—to what he did to you." I'm having a hard time meeting his eyes. "And, really. Twenty-five thousand dollars? That's more than nice. That's *amazing*."

"Don't think I didn't make the same points when she told me." He laughs again. "It took me a little longer to come around, but eventually I had to tell myself that you were completely in the dark. It says a lot about Drew's arrogance, that he thought you'd never find out."

"I almost didn't." Something occurs to me. "Is that why you saved me, at the Holiday Village? You wanted to piss him off?"

"Maybe, partly," he admits. "But mostly I wanted to help you. I was watching you. As soon as they turned around, you got the deer-in-headlights look. I wanted to help you escape gracefully."

Warmth crawls from my ears down my jaw, into my cheeks. He was watching me.

"Anyway, so you see why I had trouble accepting Will. I'm naturally suspicious, after that. And when it looked like he might hurt her … I was wrong. I can admit that. And I'm glad I was." He picks up his coffee cup and puts it back down without drinking. "There've been times when I was right. And that sucks."

Immediately I get that he's referring to Amanda and her mysterious disappearance after two years.

That story, though, I'll let him keep for another day. If there is a day after this, that is.

"Did you think the same about me?" I ask instead. "When Brooke offered me so much money. You must have thought that's the only reason I took the job. You even hinted at it once or twice. And if you believed I knew what Drew did and I was with him anyway, you must have thought the money's all that mattered."

"It crossed my mind. When you didn't immediately cash the check, though…"

"I tore it up."

He leans forward. "What?"

"I tore it up. On my way here. I stopped in my office and put it through the shredder."

"Why?"

"It didn't feel right." I shrug.

"But you did the work. You did a lot of work. You still deserve to get paid for it."

"I have been," I say. "Just not in money."

Let him puzzle that one out.

"Brooke won't like it."

I smile. "It's not her decision."

He smiles too.

We're silent for a few minutes. He traces a pattern in the Formica with his finger, while I sip my rapidly cooling tea and wonder what to do now.

"So why did you tell me this?" I finally ask.

"It wasn't my intent when I asked if you could meet me here. I couldn't stand the thought of you still angry with me, or hating me or anything like that. So I meant to apologize one more time, buy you a latte and maybe a muffin, and…" He trails off. And? And what? "But I'm glad I told you. I think—" He shifts in his chair. Leans back, then forward, putting his elbows on the table. His cheeks, beneath the scruff I'd have hated two months ago but that seems to be growing on me, turn slightly pink. "I know I haven't given you much reason to trust me. Or even like me." Are there flames shooting out of the tips of my ears? It feels like it. "And if I had to guess I'd say you're not exactly in a spot where you're looking for a relationship. My last one ended six months ago, and I don't know if I am either."

Did he just say *relationship*?

"But there's something about you. I don't know what it is. Maybe your tenacity?"

"Tenacity." Hey, my voice isn't shaking. Look at that. "Nice. I believe you referred to me as a bulldog."

He grins. "I did. Sorry. I should have used a different animal. How do you feel about donkeys?"

"Lovely." I shake my head. "I suggest you stop at the bookstore on the corner and get a thesaurus."

Now he laughs. "I don't know. I just keep thinking about you storming into my house, ripping my couch apart, and telling me I'm going to need Jesus. I was so pissed off, but as soon as you left I wanted to laugh about it. I should have known then there was no way you were going to let me get away with anything. I liked that. People have always let me get away with stuff. Either because of the money, or because they feel sorry for me. But you?" He stretches his hand halfway across the table, and for one dizzying second I think he wants to hold mine, but then he pulls it back and folds his arms over his stomach. "You're different. I need someone like you around. I think you would be good for me."

"What exactly are you saying?" I ask, after a sip of my sugar plum tea lubricates my throat enough for speech.

"I'm saying that I want to get to know you."

I look down at the round tabletop, at the speckled Formica with its tiny bits of glitter, and smile. He's right—about a few things. I don't trust him. Not entirely. I don't doubt that he'll do whatever he can to change that, but I have to wonder if I'm not already too damaged from Drew, and my dad, to ever completely put my faith in a guy again.

And no, I'm not in a new-relationship kind of place right now. But if it turns out I'm not permanently broken, I might be ready again, someday. Maybe. Maybe even someday soon. Who knows these things? I'm not getting any younger. I'll be thirty-one in a few weeks.

It's also probably time to stop lying to myself about the fact that I've been attracted to him since the beginning. I always have liked an air of mystery.

So let's see. Possible irrevocable damage rendering me incapable of ever trusting, or loving, another person, compared with the facts that I really have no desire to be Kate's kid's spinster aunt and that Everett intrigues me. Is that enough to go on? Am I as crazy as I feel?

"I think I could allow that," I say, and look up at him. Maybe I am.

"Okay." He smiles. "Good."

We sit there grinning like idiots at each other for nearly thirty seconds before I can't take how ridiculous this whole thing is and start laughing. After a few seconds, he joins in.

"Sorry," he says. "It's been a long time since I've been in a situation like this."

"Longer for me," I say. "Eight years to your how many?"

"Two," he confesses. "You win." He glances at his watch. "So about that whole getting to know each other thing. When would you like to start?"

"In a few days? I'm headed out of town today to visit my mom and sister. I'll be back sometime on Friday." I feel strangely disappointed by this.

"Okay. Well, if you don't have any plans on New Year's Eve—and I know how that sounds, and there is no pressure *whatsoever*—I'm having a little party at my house. Nothing fancy. Will and Brooke will be there. You're more than welcome to come. Erin, too, if she's free."

"Well, it's not like it's Valentine's Day," I joke. "Yes. No, I don't have plans. I'd like to come. I'll call you." Ugh. I feel like I'm thirteen years old. What is it about this guy that brings every awkward feeling of my adolescence roaring back?

"Good." He picks up his mug and takes a sip, then grimaces. Must be cold. "There's one more thing, though."

"Oh, God. What?"

"I guess I deserve that," he says with a laugh. "No, I just wanted you to know. I'm serious about trying to let go of things. I'm thirty-two. It's time to put the past in the past. So I made a decision. I'm going to see a therapist. I did it before, but I guess it didn't really take. This whole thing with the wedding, though … I can't let anything like that happen again. I have to get myself sorted out."

"Good," I say. "I'm serious. That's a big step. I'm proud of you."

He smiles. "So I guess you have to go."

"I do," I say, reluctantly.

"Okay." We both stand, and he picks my bag up from the floor, handing it to me before shrugging into his coat.

He lets me walk in front of him as we make our way to the door, then reaches around me to pull it open so I can step outside. It's not until the air hits my face that I realize how warm my cheeks are and how red I must have been inside. I hope the light in the corner I picked was dim enough to hide it.

"Have a good time," he says as we stand in front of the window.

"Thanks."

"Talk to you when you get back?"

"Friday," I confirm.

"Friday."

I switch my bag from one arm to the other for lack of anything better to do. I'm not sure what the next move should be. Do I shake his hand? Hug him?

He decides for me. He kisses my cheek. There's no lingering, no fingertips grazing my jaw or anything even close to as intimate as what happened in his living room or even at the Holiday Village in front of Drew, but it's okay. It's full of promise. It almost feels like he's making a wish.

I close my eyes and make one, too.

Epilogue

DEC 26—THE PERFECT WEDDING IS A BIG PRODUCTION.

Just ask Noelle Silver, owner of Silver Bells Wedding Designs. A few days before Halloween she was approached by Brooke St. John, lifelong Springhollow resident, and hired to coordinate Miss St. John's wedding—on Christmas Eve.

Of this year.

"She kind of bullied me into it," laughs Silver, who has owned the business on Main Street for the last six years. "She wouldn't take no for an answer. For some reason, it had to be me."

That reason was evident to the sixty-eight guests that celebrated Miss St. John's marriage to William Hurley of Philadelphia—formerly of Toronto, Ontario, Canada—on Christmas Eve. The Springhollow Fire Hall was transformed into a holiday wonderland for the event, with columns wrapped in pine garlands, tasteful snowflake decorations, glowing candlelight, and wintry bouquets of white roses, camellias, baby's breath, and silver holly leaves. The menu featured a choice between filet mignon and salmon, accompanied by rainbow carrots and broccolini. The cake was a towering vanilla and Meyer lemon tour de force by

Cuthbert's Confections, and guests sipped on "snowflake cocktails"—martinis made of vodka, peppermint schnapps, and crème de cacao.

Silver specializes in Christmas weddings, and with the St. John/Hurley nuptials in the books, she has another masterpiece to add to her portfolio.

"I'm really amazed that it all came together," Silver confessed. "Brooke is fantastic, but it wasn't the easiest wedding I've ever planned. I'm thrilled with the result."

She refuses to take credit, however, for the unexpected snow that started to fall at the precise moment the photographer began to take pictures.

"That's just Brooke," Silver insists.

The bride was born in Springhollow and graduated from Coventry Preparatory High School. She is the daughter of the late Dr. Michael and Stephanie St. John, both of Springhollow. She owns Art in Motion Studio of Dance on Cambridge Road. The groom is the son of the late Joseph Hurley and his wife, Janet, of Toronto. He graduated from Northview Heights Secondary School and the University of the Arts in Philadelphia. He is employed as a freelance photojournalist. Hurley met St. John when the photography company she hired for her dance studio's Picture Day sent him to do the job.

"He was gorgeous," the bride confesses with a girlish giggle. "I had an immediate crush. I was so flustered I almost ended up putting a group of baby tappers into the teenage ballet group's photo."

For his part, the groom was equally as enchanted.

"I knew as soon as I saw her that I had to get to know her," he said. "And I'm so lucky she let me. There's no one quite like her."

"My sister's been to hell and back," said the bride's brother, Everett St. John—no doubt referencing the tragic fire that killed their parents when he was just seventeen and his sister was nine. "I'm really glad she's found happiness with Will. He's a great guy. They're good together."

"They're the perfect couple," Silver agrees.

The perfect couple will depart after the New Year for a mini-honeymoon in Niagara Falls.

After a week's vacation, Silver Bells Wedding Designs will reopen for business on January 2. They are now accepting clients for the upcoming wedding season.

Acknowledgments

To my family, for everything—I love you guys! (But you knew that.)

To John for knowing when to leave me alone to write, and for knowing when I want to tell the world about it—then doing it for me so I don't look like I'm bragging. I love you, too.

To Heather for demanding a new chapter on a near-daily basis and then liking it when I gave you one. Without you I might not have finished, let alone in less than a year.

To the Hallmark Channel for *Christmas in July*. You made it easy to write about snow when it was 92 degrees outside.

To Gabrielle Mathieu for the invaluable feedback.

And finally to CP and Ariadne. Thank you for the coffee, the treats, the insights, the listening, the laughs, the inspiration, and the last eight years.

PRAISE FOR COURTNEY J. HALL

"*Some Rise by Sin* is a sumptuous tale of romance, religious turmoil, and political intrigue set against the dramatic backdrop of the dying days of Mary Tudor's reign. With the keen eye of an artist Courtney J. Hall paints a vivid picture, rich in historical detail, of this turbulent time of transition at the Tudor court."

—Marie Macpherson, author of
The First Blast of the Trumpet

"Tudor history comes alive in this enthralling tale of a reluctant heir to an earldom and the high-spirited lady who wins his heart. An absorbing and memorable read."

—Pamela Mingle, author of *Kissing Shakespeare* and
The Pursuit of Mary Bennet

Five Directions Press publishes contemporary women's fiction, historical fiction, science fiction, fantasy, and memoirs.

For more information, see

FIVE DIRECTIONS PRESS